Keisha !
Thank you for your
support, & love you with
an agape love

Valee

ALTERED DIRECTIONS

by Vikee

authorHOUSE®

AuthorHouse™
1663 Liberty Drive, Suite 200
Bloomington, IN 47403
www.authorhouse.com
Phone: 1-800-839-8640

First published by AuthorHouse 7/24/2008

ISBN: 978-1-4343-4397-0 (sc)

Printed in the United States of America
Bloomington, Indiana

This book is printed on acid-free paper.

Mark 5:1 they went across the Sea of Galilee to the area of the Geersenes. Jesus got out of the boat. A man with an evil spirit came from the tombs to meet him. The man lived in the tombs. No one could keep him tied up anymore. Not even a chain could hold him. His hands and feet had often been chained. But he tore the chains apart....Night and day he screamed among the tombs and in the hills. He cut himself with stones. When he saw Jesus a long way off, he ran to him. He fell on his knees in front of him. He shouted at the top of his voice, "Jesus, son of the Most High, what do you want with me? Promise before God that you won't hurt me"!! This was because Jesus said, "Come out of the man you evil spirit!'

Jesus asked the demon, what *is* your name?" "My name is Legion", he replied, "There *are* many of *us*".

Walking and driving around in the streets of Baltimore has often times made my spirit weep. There are so many men, women and children hurting. They are walking around, existing but not. Many know God, but do not depend on Him. They are walking about this land, empty, confused, angry and lost.

Most of us are trying to find a way out, we all use different devices; drugs, alcohol, sex, violence, overeating, disattachment trying to escape the emptiness and hurt feelings that live within us every single day of our lives. We walk around this city all dressed up in our Roc A Wear, Sean Jean, DKNY, Baby Phat, FUBU, anything that has a designer tag, it's adorned on the streets of Baltimore, we all are a bunch of dressed up messes, Spending thousands of dollars on fake hair, high powered cars and jewelry trying to cover up and hide behind the mask that we make for ourselves. Trying to impress others with our stories of everything *fine* line. I heard one day at a meeting that fine was an acronym for **F**rustrated, **I**nsecure, **N**eurotic, **and E**motional, yes, we are *fine!* We know deep down that we are fighting some past pains, disappointments, heartaches and loneliness. Our minds are clogged with misdirection, worry, fear, and deep insecurities.

If you know anything about the bible Proverbs 1:1-3 says: **To know wisdom and instruction, to make clear the words of understanding…To fear the Lord is the beginning of knowledge; but fools despise wisdom and instruction.**

Many times, we have been fools. As a child, my aunt took me to church every Sunday. I sat in the pews and listened to the preacher preach fire and brimstone. I feared the Lord. All my young life I have learned or encountered the Lords words, rules and wisdom to have a "good life". I have often felt the spirit of the Lord working on me, convicting my spirit. Although I realized at a young age that God was the Way and the light, I don't think I went to church enough. I loved church, I was on the choir and I was baptized at an early age. I even remember receiving the Holy Spirit. My aunt called everyone she knew to tell them, I felt special, and I felt that God truly had his hand on me at a young age. I loved being in church, I loved trying to read the bible. My aunt gave me a children's bible with the pictures but I knew deep down what those words meant. My aunt Gracie used to tell me that I had a calling on my life but I sure didn't know what that meant. All I knew is when I went to church I felt light and happy. I sang those songs as if they were written for me. Sitting in Sunday school was a joy for me. However, going to church on Sundays, I found out when I was older, was not enough. Going to church on Sundays is like eating only on Mondays. If you only eat on Mondays and not eat the rest of the week, you are going to get weak and your senses will become warped and confused. You have to feed your body every day so that you can remain strong and focused. That is what the word of God is, food, you have to feed your spirit everyday so that you will remain strong and focused, so when adversity comes, you are able to deal with it, strong and focused.

My name is Sabrina, I am 45 years old. I was born and raised in Baltimore Maryland in the year 1956. I came from a family that is known today by psychologists as *dysfunctional.* I am the youngest sibling of eight children. My mother and father are originally from Raleigh, North Carolina. . I am not what you call eye candy, but I have been known to turn a few heads. I am Carmel in complexion with deep brown eyes. In addition, I am about an even 5'8. My build is what society would call overweight but not obese, but what real America would call average booty having, big boobs sista!

I loved the Lord with all my heart and soul. When I sang, I sang for the Lord. Although my family was not the two parent, apple pie, white picket fence family, I felt good most of my young life. However, in life, there are circumstances that will turn your life upside down. Those things will alter your path and get you off course. In my faith, there is a belief that our lives are predestined and our steps are ordered. If you live right and do God has will for your life and be obedient, ultimately you will reach the gates of heaven. Of course, I am paraphrasing.

The Lord says in Matthew 11:28, 29: **Come to me, all of you who are tired and are carrying heavy loads. I will give you rest. Become my servants and learn from me. I am gentle and free of pride. You will find rest for your souls. Serving me is easy and my load is light.**

As I said, I loved the Lord but my problem was I did not feel worthy of the Lord's love. I don't know why I didn't, but I never felt good enough for the Lord, I never felt that he should do anything for me. I didn't' know that I could take everything to the Lord and He would direct my path so not to get off course. I did not know that the Lord could give me rest. That's why you have to read your word and carry it in your heart, so that you will know what to do in the times of wilderness. I didn't realize it then, but that was a part of the evil spirits' job to place doubt in my life, to take away my relationship with my Father. Evil spirits have work to do too and they do it well. The closer you are with the Lord the more the spirits will find a way to destroy you. And because I didn't' know the word like I should and because I only went to church on Sundays, the devil had a foothold to enter into my life. The devil's primary job description is to depress, obsess and possess your mind so that he may ultimately destroy and kill you. Nevertheless, as I said, I did not know that.

As I said, walking down the streets of Baltimore sometimes makes my spirit wept but many times, I weep for my own spirit because I too was hurt, confused, angry and insecure. The beginning of Satan's quest to destroy me. There were times in my life where I feared the Lord but my error was I was not rooted in the word and only fed my spirit on Sundays, I was in church a lot but many times, I didn't pay attention. I knew that God had a blessing for me each Sunday when I walked in those church doors. But I was only able to go to church during the summer months when I visited my aunt Gracie, my mother wasn't able to take me to church when I was at home because she worked all the time, and because I was the baby, all my siblings were older than me and had their own lives. Therefore, I wasn't able to stay close to God as I could. I understand that I was not at the age of accountability *now*, but then I didn't know that. I could not fight the forces of evil on a half tank of the word. Satan comes at us with full force and a full tank! Moreover, he comes with two things, one is temptation and the other is other people, other forces to alter us. If you understand anything about the word or about the enemy, you understand that he is a copycat, the same way God places people in your life to bless you, Satan places people in your life to destroy you. He mimics God in so many ways, except for his is for evil and God's is for good.

Years later I know what caused me so much pain and agony. I know that the devil wanted to destroy me years ago. I know in my very young life at the age of seven the devil sent his demons into my life to destroy me. I didn't know it was the devil back then. There were many incidents in my life in which Satan came into my life and tried to destroy me. Incidents that altered my path in life and sent me spiraling into the depths of self-destruction. Had I known then what I know now, my life would probably be different. However, as my favorite author, Maya Angelou, once said "I wouldn't take nothing' for my journey". I wish I understood when I was a child that "**greater in He that is in me than He that is in the world**". But that kind of wisdom only comes with growth and experience. When I was a child, I thought as a child.….

TABLE OF CONTENTS

Chapter 1
GROWING UP IN TURMOIL

I believe my first encounter with Satan and his demons was when I was around seven years old and it was Christmas time. If you can remember anything about being a child at Christmas, you remember that those memories are with you a lifetime. The decorations, the family gatherings and the toys, gifts and food! The *good times*. My entire family was at our house on Christmas Eve; both my parents were there, all of my sisters and brother, brothers'-in-laws, just everyone. The gifts were under the tree, the food was in the stove and the cookies were being made. My mother and father were not fighting for the first time in a long time. My sisters and I were fighting over which cookies we were making first. The house was full of joy. Smokey Robinson and the Miracles were singing "I'll Be Home for Christmas" and my brother-in-law was singing along, off key, with them. It was a good night and in my little mind, this was heaven. This is what those white folks were talking about on the televisions when the talked about Season's Greetings. This holiday was nothing like Thanksgiving, when my father and brother-in-law started fighting and my father ended up with a busted mouth that was filled with white rice and turkey at the time he was hit. No, this was different, *everybody was happy*". The time approached when it was time for my sister and me to go to bed and wait for Santa Claus. I was excited, I had been a good girl that year and I knew that Santa was going to be nice to me. My mother had told me so. I gave everyone a hug and ran upstairs to my bedroom that I shared with my sister.

I was awakened by noises and unfamiliar voices. I ran over to my sister's bed and shook her, "wake up, wake up!!, he's here!, he's here!" She looked at me kind of crazy, "girl shut up, you gonna scare him away!". We crept down the hallway and down to the top of the stairs. I could see the red, white and blue flashing lights and I could hear muffled voices. I was so happy; it was Santa's sled and his reindeer outside! I knew that I was a good girl; I knew that he would bring me all the things I asked for. We peeped downstairs and it was suddenly cold in the house. I looked down further and could see the front door open and I could hear voices clear now. Then I saw a lot of white men in blue suits. In the sixties, to see a white man in your house, usually met trouble. My heart jumped and I became nervous. It was not until I saw the police badges did I know they were police. I watched the other men bending down on the floor, holding bottles with clear tubes. I could see my mother sitting on the sofa talking softly to one of the police. I could see my sisters in the dining room crying. I looked at the Christmas tree and my eyes immediately went to my Dutch Hutch with matching dishes, just as I asked for, but it was not right, it was stained with red splatters. My dishes were all turned over and some had fallen to the floor. I could hear sounds coming from the waists of the men out of little black boxes. I wanted my mother, my sister, somebody. I started crying. and my sister, who was 2 years old than me, took my hand "stop crying". She whispered and hugged me. When the men stop bending down, I could clearly see my father looking like he was dead. I tried to scream but nothing came out. My sister just held on to me and tried to shield my eyes. Police were taking family members away and never knowing the full details why. My young heart was in fear, constant fear of losing my daddy. Would the people that did this to him come back and get all of us? Would I be able to go back outside and play, how did the mean bad people get into the house to hurt daddy when all of my family was there? Didn't they see who hurt my daddy, was my daddy going to die, on Christmas Day!"

I found out many months later, (quite by accident) that my father was stabbed in the back over an argument that he had with one of my family members, no one ever told me which family member, but he was stabbed after we were sent to bed. I never understood why my family always fought as they did and I didn't understand who would hurt my father like that. I wanted to know what would make someone stab someone on Christmas, the day of Jesus' birth. I couldn't ask those questions, because I was a child and I was told to stay in a child's place, you know, be seen and not heard.

My daddy didn't die, thank God. But that one event caused my life to be altered for many years. I didn't feel like I was ever protected by anyone in my family. I had nightmares and I was always scared. I never talked a lot and was scared to death of yelling and screaming, and whenever I heard it, I would see my father's body lying in blood in front of the Christmas tree. If anyone raised his or her voice or started fighting or arguing, I would become fearful. I stopped being the outgoing little person that I used to be. I was afraid to raise my voice, to look at people in the eyes. I was afraid to hold my head up. I wanted to disappear and not to be seen or heard. I didn't want to cause any friction because I didn't want anyone else to get hurt like my daddy. The only solace I found was in church and when I spent summers at my Aunt Gracie's house, Aunt Gracie was my mother's aunt but we called her our aunt too. She had one son who was grown and living back in North Carolina, when my mother worked during the summer, I stayed with Aunt Gracie. She was a beautiful woman who was so light she could have passed for white but she was proud of her heritage and always told me stories of how my uncle was so brave back in the forties when things were hard for blacks. She always thought that the white people hated Uncle Henry so much, because he was so dark skinned. She would talk with fire in her eyes when she spoke about Uncle Henry; "He was a proud man!" she would say. He never bowed down to no white man!' Then her eyes would glisten with tears as she talked about how they dragged Uncle Henry from the house one night. Her voice would fade as she spoke of how Charles, her son, found him dead by the outhouse just down the road from their home. I would listen to Aunt Gracie until she stopped speaking and nothing more than tears told the rest of her story. She would hum Precious Lord and sit a while. I would leave her in her chair until she was ready to talk some more. I guess that's why she was always in the church, always talking about how the Lord kept her through it all. I loved to hear her talk about the Lord and I wanted to know Him as she did. Therefore, I kept going to church.

The only place I wasn't afraid was in church. I felt so light when I went there, as if I didn't have a care in the world. I felt like a child. However, at home, I felt like I had the weight of the world on my shoulders. I didn't want to be a burden on anyone and I tried to stay out of the way at home because I never knew when my daddy would start a fight or come home drinking, I sat in church and I absorbed every word the preacher preached. I didn't fully understand all of what he said but I did believe in the devil and I believed that my daddy's stabbing on Christmas was something that the devil had planned; it was his first foothold in my life.

I realized that after daddy was stabbed, he wasn't the same either. He was angrier. He would drink a lot more than usual and he never seemed to find any peace in his life. He continued to drink and fight, fight and drink. My nerves were on end all the time. But I stayed in church because that's where I found peace. I tried to understand why my daddy drank but I didn't and no one told me so I stayed quiet and out of the way. I thought that even though my daddy drank and my mother worked a lot, they would always protect me and they would always know what was best for me. After all, they were my parents and they knew these things.

When you are young, you have the belief that people who love you and care about you will always protect you and always love you, no matter what. You take their word when they tell you things, because when you are a child, you think as a child. You really do not know about untruths and being deceived. You are naïve and believe what you are told. After the summer months with my Aunt Gracie, I had to come back home but my mother worked at night so she told me that I would have to stay at my sister's house at times because she had to work, I didn't mind. I loved my sister, she was my big sister but not the oldest sister I had, I had one sister older than her. My sister was a pretty woman; she was caramel brown with deep brown eyes. She was an accountant who worked at a bank. She dressed somewhat plain for a woman of her age and she did not smile a lot but I thought she was happy, she was married and had two children when she was young. Staying there some days while my mother worked was not a problem. I packed my little bag, we were not fortunate enough to have suitcases, I was singing and dancing because I was going to get to play with my little nephew and niece. I could have a chance to be a big sister. My mother took me over the house. My sister had a big house out on Reisterstown Road. It was so pretty and clean. She always kept a clean house. The beds were always made and there were never any dishes in the sink. I really liked her house. I didn't have many friends, so I often amused myself with reading and playing marbles. After I ate my lunch, I went outside to the backyard. I was a tomboy and I loved playing in the dirt and shooting marbles. Besides reading, it was my favorite past time. I made sure to bring my bag of marbles I had won from the boys on my street. They were my prized possessions. I didn't like dolls so my mother brought me a small bag of marbles every chance she could. I had taken my very best ones to my sister's house with me. There were many boys in her neighborhood and I knew they would think I couldn't play because I was a girl. I ran down the steps that led to the dirt patch in the center of the yard, found a stick, and drew my circle for my marbles.

It was a hot day. I was having a good time by myself when Uncle Manny came out into the yard. He was my sister's husband. He was tall, probably about 6 or 7 feet tall. He was what my mother and sisters called "high yellow". He had huge hands and always wore a green uniform. When he came out into the yard, I kept playing marbles. He put his beer down on the steps. Whatcha doing out here in this heat"? "Playing marbles Uncle Manny". I said smiling. "Wanna play a game with me?" If you win, you can stay up an extra ½ hour. If I win you have to take your nap early". This was easy, I thought to myself. I know I can beat him. He is old and I know I he can't shoot that well. We played three games. I won. I was so happy. I was jumping up and down and yelling, "I won! I won"! He smiled. "Ok, time for your nap". "But I won". I said. Making sure not to yell and averting my eyes from his so not to upset him. "But I'm the boss so you have to take a nap". Confusion and anger consumed me. "I won"! I screamed inside. I dare not challenge him. I gathered up my marbles and started back up to the porch. He rubbed my back. "Are you mad?" "No sir, but I won". "Come sit down on the steps". I sat down, eyes glistening with tears, but praying that they did not leave my eyes and venture down my face.

He pulled me on top of his lap and started rubbing my back, "don't cry, I'll make you feel better". His hands moved all over my non- existent breasts and between my thighs. I pushed his hand away. "Don't, I said, making sure not to yell. I'm making you feel better". "No"! I yelled, "I don't like this". I closed my eyes, oops, I am gonna get it now, I raised my voice, I closed my eyes and could see my daddy lying in his own blood, I could see the police leading my family out of the house. Don't scream anymore, I could hear a voice tell me, it will be over in a minute. I didn't know who was speaking but my voice was stuck, I could feel his hot breath all over me. I tried to move and wiggled off his lap but he had a grip on me. After much panting and groping, he stopped and let me go. I ran to the room and shut the door. I slid down in front of it, trying to hold it shut with my little body. I didn't understand. I couldn't understand. However, I knew it was wrong. It felt wrong. Fear gripped me into shock. I know that God does not give us the spirit of fear so it had to be Satan. When Satan starts to enter your life, he deals directly with you, if you are prayed up and have your armor and your sword, he cannot enter in, so he will use other vices and even other people. But I didn't know that then, I was 7 years old, skinny as rails with pig tails all over my head with big eyes. My little body was so afraid and I was visibly shaking.

My mother used to say, "Child the devil is busy". I didn't know what she meant when she said it but in that moment, I knew it was one of those times that he was busy. My life as a child was gone. My innocence was gone. I must have sat by that door for what seemed like hours but I discovered it was only for several minutes. I heard a knock on the door. "Open the door Sabrina, I'm sorry". I promise it won't happen again". My entire body shook with fear. I remembered that I had to see him again, I had to face him again, and I had to sleep in the same house with him. I was so scared that I must have passed out, when I woke up; I had a cold rag on my head. I looked at him. "I want to go home". I said. "You can't go home. Your mother is not there". I'm sorry. I promise it won't happen again". "I want to go home, call my momma and tell her I want to go home". I can't call your momma". Your sister will be home soon.

Please don't say anything". "I'm gonna tell my momma what you did to me" Suddenly, the pleas became threats. He grabbed me by my shirt. "You better not tell, no one would believe you anyway, you hear me, you better not tell, I'll do the same thing to you that they did to your drunken ass father if you open your mouth!. I blinked twice. I could see the vision of my father, the blood the police. "They won't believe you, you are a child, and no one will ever believe you!" He still had a grip on my shirt. I shook my head, "I won't tell, please let me go".

Chapter 2

THE TAKING OF INNOCENCE

If there were ever a chance to visit hell, I think I did. Guilt and shame consumed me. I begged my mother and my sister not to send me back there but they wouldn't listen to me. Each time they asked me why, I would start to shake and cry. I could feel my breath being cut off as if he was gripping my shirt. Many nights when I was force to stay there, I wore several layers of clothes and pretended to be sleep but nothing helped, he always managed to grope me, touch me, and place his private parts on me until it grew limp. I hated him. I wanted to kill him, but fear consumed me. Even when I tried to tell, he was right, no one believed me. "Girl, don't be scared of him, he's just playing with you, stop acting like a baby". I never went outside anymore; I never played with boys again. . I tried very hard not to be 'cute" because I didn't want Uncle Manny to get me again. I stopped going to church. Satan and his demons were succeeding in my life. I was mad at God because he let this happen to me, I was a good girl and I did everything I was suppose to do, but still I was being hurt. Therefore, I gave up on myself. I believed that I deserved what I was getting. I would scrub my body so hard that the skin would come off my arms. My mother would slap me with the towel. "Are you crazy girl, stop scrubbing so hard!". It was killing me, the fear and shame was mentally killing me.

I had several encounters with Uncle Manny, ducking him, and running from him, sleeping with my niece and nephew when I had to stay over there so he wouldn't touch me. I locked bathroom doors and tried to keep him off me. It was draining. I would try my best to look like a little boy; not comb my hair, wear big clothes, not take a bath, anything to keep this monster off me but nothing worked. He always seemed to find a way to find me alone, touch me, pull me on his lap, and stick his fingers deep inside of me until he released himself all over me. I hated him so much. I wanted to kill him. I wanted him to die a death as the coyote did in the Road Runner cartoon, I wanted a big rock to fall out of the sky and crush him. I couldn't eat, sleep or even think straight anymore, I was so consumed in trying to find ways to keep Uncle Manny off me. When I was able to stay at home, I read every single book I could think of. I could read a lot of big books but I started out with The Cat in the Hat and every week I was reading a new book, I tried to take my mind off of my life. I would cry at the drop of a hat and would start to shake anytime I had to think about visiting my sister's house.

I lived this nightmare until I was around 9 ½ years old. I thought that maybe he would leave me alone if I were older, but it only got worse. I had to find a way to stop him, since no one else would believe me. My straight A's were falling into quick C's and still l nobody noticed.

Then I remembered how safe I felt when I was in church. I remembered how the songs made me feel good when I sang. Although, I decided I wanted to go back to church, I was still angry with God. I felt like He let me down. The Saturday before church, I walked by myself to the church and sat down on the steps. I was rocking back and forth. I was so angry with God and I wanted to tell him that I was. I wanted to tell Him that everybody in my life was hurting me or deserting me. I decided that the next day in church I would confront God and tell Him about all of the stuff that was inside of me. I walked home feeling a little better about my decision.

Chapter 3

SAFE AT HOME

I went to church the next day. As soon as I entered the doors of the church, I felt at peace, I felt light inside; I almost forgot how mad I was with God. I sat down way in the front, next to my aunt, I wanted to be close to the alter so God could hear me. The choir marched down the isle of the church singing, What a Friend, We Have in Jesus. I started singing along, "what a friend, we have in Jesus, What a friend, He is to have, what a privilege it is to ca-rr-y, everything to God in prayer!" I could hear the preacher shouting, sing chile, sing! I got up to my feet, singing louder, "The Lord has been so good to me, He's opened doors, I could not see! And times when I am feeling low, Nowhere to run, no place to go! My father is rich in houses and land; He holds the power the world in His hand! I loved that song, and I sang with the choir until we went into prayer. After much shouting and praising God, the church finally calmed down, The preacher started talking about salvation and how it could be anybody's if they gave their life to Christ, how God would protect you from all things, how we should give our burdens to the Lord. The sermon was good. However, my heart was torn; I gave God everything, why was He not helping me with Uncle Manny? How could every body in my family be so blind to what he was doing to me? If God could protect me, then where was He? When the preacher did alter call, I ran up to the altar. "What do you need, child?" I need God to know that I am mad at Him". The preacher smiled. "Well, you come and tell the Lord about all of your troubles child". The church sang out "Amen". I got down on my knees and told the Lord why I was mad. I told Him that He was supposed to love me. I told Him I wasn't a bad girl and that I listened to my mother and to elders, I had respect and I didn't know what I did to be treated like this. The tears were running down my face and I cried. I felt arms around me and they felt good. I was not afraid of these arms, this touch that I felt. I did not feel dirty when these arms held me. I just kept on crying. I begged God to help me. To make the mean man stop hurting me. I told Him it hurt inside. I told him that I didn't act grown like he said I did. I told Him I didn't like it like he said I did. I told Him that I was not a woman like he said I was. I begged Him to make him stop touching me. I begged him to take all the quarters back that Uncle Manny had given me to keep quiet, I told Him I was sorry that I used the quarters to buy penny candy, and that I was sorry! Those arms never left me. Even after I got up off my knees and the usher gave me a napkin, I felt those arms around me. I felt safe.

For weeks, I stayed home. I didn't' have to go back to my sister's house who I know knew as dirty. In spite of its clean look and smell of pine soil. I knew now that this person, Uncle Manny, who professed to care about me only, wanted to touch me everywhere and every time he got a chance. I knew that it was not right and it was not my fault. In addition, I did not provoke him. The next time I had to stay at her house she had moved to another house. I had to go; my mother said it would only be for a few hours. I prayed before I left. When I got there, I even smiled. I was only there a few minutes before he said, "Let's go to Gino's for chicken". The children yelled and jumped up and down. But Uncle Manny stopped them. "I want you to go with me, Sabrina; they have to get ready for their baths". I looked at my sister, wondering in my little mind, you have to know this man is a monster, I can see it so clear, why can't you? But she didn't help me, she just said, "go on, Brina, you'll get to pick out the chicken". I went to the truck, I was afraid but not like, I used to be. I felt those arms around me again. I even smiled as I jumped in the passenger's side of the truck. "I missed you a lot". He said. "I love you; I didn't think I was going to see you again". His hand moved up and down my thigh. I started praying to myself. "Help me please God, you promised". He drove down an alley and cut the lights off in the truck. He got out of his seat and went to the back of the truck. "Come on back here with me". "No". I said. "Come on, it won't take long". He already had his pants down. "NO!" I shouted. "I'm not doing this no more". "I said come here now Sabrina!" I was 9 hears old now and I was not going to do this again, even if I had to die that night, I was going to die tonight free from this nasty disgusting thing he was doing to me. I needed for this to stop, I needed for this stop right now and tonight, I don't know why I felt so strongly about it that particular night but I knew tonight either he was going to kill me or I was going to kill him. He snatched me by my arm. As I was turning towards him, I reached under the seat and I could feel something cold and hard, like a rod of some kind. When I lost my grip to from holding on to the chair, he pulled me to the back; I grabbed it and hit him hard as I turned to look at him. I saw the blood. "You little bitch! Dammit you little bitch!" He shouted, holding his head and looking at the blood that was trickling down his hand. I hit him again. I held the rod in both hand, I realized later it was a crowbar. "Stay away from me, or I swear, I'll hit you again!" I felt those arms holding me again. He grabbed his head and looked at the blood. "Ok, ok, just don't hit me again". I watched him pull his pants up while trying to hold his head and keep the blood from gushing out, he climbed back into the driver's seat, he got the chicken and didn't say another word to me. When we got home, my sister asked him what happened, and he told her that he hit it while getting out the truck. She looked at me, and I just smiled. He never touched me again. I believe my prayers that Sunday before saved me that night. I believe that those arms I felt were the arms of the angels that God commissioned to take care of me, help me and protect me. God is just good like that! Everyday I prayed. I constantly read Psalm 23 and Psalm 25. Those words kept me for many years. Those years changed me; I never really understood why Uncle Manny chose me, except that maybe I wasn't his first victim. Nevertheless, over the years I tried to like myself, I tried to be happy and feel different about myself, but the shame and guilt of what happened to me, haunted me for years to come, I didn't know that it would, but it did. However, the 23rd and 25th Psalms helped me through the tough times. They kept me until I was fourteen years old.

Chapter 4
THE TEENAGED YEARS..

All my sisters had moved out the house except for one, my sister Dionna, Dionna was two years older than me and she was pretty. She was dark skinned like my older sister but she was a beautiful girl. She had so much confidence and she never seemed afraid of anything. She used to protect me from the bullies at my school and beat up anyone that bothered me. She was my idol. She was tall like my father and she had the prettiest almond shaped eyes I have ever seen. She was a tomboy and could fight like a man. She and my brother Brian, in my eyes, were the coolest two people I had ever seen in my life. They liked to fight, smoke reefer, hang out with the riff raff as my mother called them, and they didn't give a damn about nothing or nobody; and they didn't care about what anybody thought about them. Although she was only 2 years older than I was, she seemed much older than that. Maybe it was the beer and alcohol she drank or the reefer she smoked or her big afro; nevertheless, she scared the hell out of me. However, I knew she would never hurt me. Dionna never stayed home, so I had to find out things my own way. Fourteen was a rough age for me. I became rebellious and angry. I had carried all that hatred for Uncle Manny in my heart and head. I had no self-esteem. I never thought I was pretty enough, smart enough, or anything positive about myself. I lost my innocence to a grown man and I couldn't get it back, no matter how hard I tried. Although I was an A student, I would get into fights all the time and get suspended. I lashed out is so many ways, my mother threatened to take me to Girls Village and put me on the steps. She warned me "I will drive you out to Girls Village and leave your ass on the steps and dare you to tell them where you live at! " I believed her so I tried to calm down.

I would read about victims of abuse but it wasn't a lot to read, it was so hush hush that it was hard to read about it without someone questioning me. I would look at the news to see if anyone else had been through what I had been through but it was never anything on television about it so I thought I was the only person that it had happened to, which made me feel even worse. Those teenage years just about killed me.

When my mother finally decided to leave my father years before, I think I was about nine or 10 years old when she finally left him, I didn't see him much. It was hard not having my father in my life. I knew years later that he was an alcoholic. I remembered all the times that he came home drunk and wanted to fight my mother and caused hell in the house. I remember when he was stabbed in the stomach and got over 50 stitches in his stomach and he told my mother to call all the children around the bed because he knew he was going to die, we all stood around that bed all night waiting for him to die because he said he was. But he didn't.

Then were was the time that he disappeared for months and my mother took out a missing person's report on him because she didn't know where he was, and again, we had a vigil waiting for the police to knock on the door to say he was dead, they found him in some alley or flop house dead from alcohol overdose or something, but again, he surfaced and all was well. I really didn't have any one to show me how men were suppose to treat me, he wasn't there and when he was, he was fighting and drinking, or so quiet that we barely knew he was in the house. When my mother left him, I was young and I was so alone and lost without him. Even his arguments were better than the silence of him not being there.

I remember going to school one day when I was in the fourth grade. We were living on Park Heights Avenue. I was walking to school with some of the kids in the neighborhood. My mother in her wisdom never bad-mouthed my father. She would tell us that he was sick and needed help. She also told me that he still loved me and always would. She never told me he was stupid, or a liar or anything cruel like that.

I loved my father and I missed him in my life. As I said I was walking to school with some of the kids in the neighborhood and I saw this man, digging in the trash can outside of the Little Tavern. When I got closer, I realized it was my father. I walked up to him and gave him my lunch money. I went inside the Little Tavern and brought him some hamburgers and hot coffee. My 'friends" teased me and laughed at me the rest of the school year but I didn't care. He was my father, and I loved him. I wanted to help him. I sat in the gutter with him while he ate and drank his coffee. After he finished, he looked at me, "you better get going to school, now". "I love you daddy". I gave him a hug and a kiss on his scratchy cheek. He smiled and walked away with his hamburgers. That was the last time I saw my daddy alive. He died when I was fourteen.

The night before he died, he asked to see my brother, my mother, and me. But my brother was angry with him and wouldn't go. But I was happy to go, I wanted to be with him again, I wanted to see his face, to see how much I looked like him, his pug nose and deep brown eyes. I wanted to remember all the things I had forgotten about my father, the way he would dance and sing when he was drinking, the way he would put my feet on top of his and dance around the living room with me. I wanted to remember the scent of Old Spice when he finished shaving. I wanted him to sing, "Sitting on the Dock of the Bay, or Born to Lose, off key, like he always did when he was drinking. He was my father, he wanted to see me, and I was going, no matter what. He was staying with my oldest sister, he was too sick to stay alone anymore, because of the damage to his liver he needed someone to take care of him. I was glad that he was there. I knew my sister would take care of him the best she could. I went in the bedroom and there he was lying in the bed. I sat down beside the bed. "Hi daddy". He took my hand into his. "I want you to listen to me Sabrina, I want you to be a good girl, I want you to listen to your mother, do well in school, keeping reading and studying your math" He coughed and motioned for me to get him a drink of water and his medicine. He drank a little and took his pills. "Never let men use your body, always hold your head up, and never let a man take your soul away. Always do the best you can in everything you do, even clean floors, or wait tables, always do the best that you can. Never settle for less, your body is a temple keep it sacred, don't drink, smoke or do any type of drugs, they will kill your spirit and steal your dreams. Love your self no matter what and never give a man one hundred percent, leave something for yourself in case he treats you bad or walk out of your life. He looked up at me and his eyes stained with tears and said "never stop going to church Sabrina, God is your strength". He will protect from all hurt, harm and danger, trust Him and believe in His word. Always remember that you have a calling on your life and you must stay focused on God's word if you are to become what He born you to be, do you understand me Sabrina? I nodded yes. I really didn't understand him, because I had never seen my father in church in his life, how would he know what God had for me? However, I listened to him, simply because he was my father. .

I guess he was trying to make up for all the years that he was out of my life. I listened to every single word he said, and I promised him that I would do everything he asked. I promised him that I would do all the right things in my life. I kissed him on the forehead and he was so cold but he was sweating badly. I sat with him for a long time after that. We didn't speak just smiled at each other and tried to remember the lines in our faces that looked alike, the complexion of our skin, everything. I tried to remember the times that I couldn't, the young years when I was too young to remember, he was my daddy and I loved him, he was still a giant in my life and I loved him more than I loved myself. I told him about what Uncle Manny did to me and he apologized for not protecting me but he applauded me for being so strong and keeping myself together. He held on to my hand until he fell off to sleep. I promised him that I would come back the next day and sit with him again.

But that was not to be, my father died the next day, while I was getting dressed for school. I was still thinking about all the lessons I had learned from him the night before and I smiled. The phone rang and it was my brother in law. He told me that my daddy died a few minutes ago. I was so hurt when he died. I was angry because he left me. He was the first man I knew and he was supposed to show me how a man is supposed to treat me. But he was not in my life and I never knew. I saw the way my brother in laws treated my sisters and I knew even then, that was not the right way but that was the only example I had, we had. And that's what I dealt with in my life. My father was a young man when he died, leaving my mother a young widow. He was 47 years old when he died. He lost his battle with alcohol, and I lost my strength to go forward.

It wasn't long after my father died, when we moved to another part of town. The church I was attending was too far for me to attend on the bus. By the time I finished catching three buses, church was done. Therefore, I stopped going. I hated my new neighborhood, I was mad at my mother for moving so far away from my friends. I didn't like my new school. Every chance I got I was back on the West side of town. I rebelled against my mother, my teachers anyone of authority. I was spiraling out of control. They didn't know a damn thing about me. I realized later that as soon as I stopped going to church and stopped being around people that worshipped the Lord my life became unraveled. Satan, so very subtle. Whispering in my ear, "don't listen to your mother, look how she took you away from your friends, after it took so many years to find friends, you don't need to go to school or church you can stay in bed you can go next week. He whispered and I listened.

Soon my mind was consumed in clothes, money, music, dancing and going to shows at the Civic Center. And drinking and drugging every single weekend. Purple Haze, Acid, wine, and Bacardi Rum Dark were my drinks and drugs of choice. I would get so drunk that I couldn't even walk sometimes. Many times, I found myself in more dangerous situations that I cared to think about. However, I would be okay the next day. I would usually wake up at one of my girlfriend's houses. We would laugh and joke about the night before, take a shower and start all over again. One night my girls and me went to a Cabaret on North Avenue. I had a boyfriend, who was too old for me, according to my mother, but Dennis was just the right age for me, and I saw him every single chance I got. He really wasn't very cute and he was light skinned but he was my first love so I really didn't care much about his looks. We had been together since I was fourteen. He treated me good, brought me clothes and showed me how to smoke, drink and take drugs, he never let me get high alone or without him, so no one would take advantage of me, but he was becoming very controlling and our relationship was shaky, I was growing tired of him. He was too jealous and he was dangerous when he drank. Besides that, he had cheated on me. He never knew I saw him and I never let him know it but I paid him back every single chance I got. This was one of those times I paid him back.

He didn't want me to go to the cabaret but I told him I was going anyway. I was fifteen and he was almost nineteen years old. He was my first love and I was sprung on the sex he gave me. But he was messing with the girl down the street from him and I wanted to get even. He didn't know that knew but she did. Me and my friends pulled her out of her house one night and took her to the playground and scared the hell out of her, we didn't beat her up or anything but I told her that I knew she was messing with my man and that I was going to kick her ass, but not that nigh. , I used psychology on her, I wasn't going to hurt her at all, but I put fear in her to make her think that I was going to beat her up. She eventually stopped hanging out all together. She never ventured from her steps for as long as we were together. She was pretty too and that hurt me, I didn't' have long hair and I never thought I was pretty but I had big breasts and body to kill for, so I got a lot of attention from the guys, but I wanted to be beautiful, feel beautiful but I never really felt this inside, when Dennis messed with her it made me believe that I wasn't pretty enough to keep him. So I dogged him every chance I got.

Me and my friends were known all over West Baltimore for our dancing and we wanted to go to this cabaret because they were having a dance contest and the winners would receive new albums and one hundred dollars and a chance to compete in the dance at another cabaret that the club was giving. Of course, we should not have been there but we knew people and we were able to get tickets. Sharon, Niecy, Mieka, and myself all showed up at the cabaret we all had on black Lee jeans with crisp white Jack Purcell's and black and white Tee shirts with our name emblazed on them. Me and Meika's hair was short so we slicked it down. Niecy and Sharon had long hair so they put it in a ponytail, which made it look like it was slicked back like Meika and mine. We got a table and sat down. We were casing the place, trying to see who else would be in the contest but we couldn't tell because the other people competing were not dressed alike, a plus for us. Then they dropped a bomb and said that only one person could compete at a time, so that meant that we would have to dance solo. Sharon was pissed, she wanted to cut the disc jockey but we cooled her off. We drank some wine in the bathroom and decided who would dance. I told Meika to let Niecy dance, but she was not having it. "Hell no, that bitch can't dance, she is just with us because we make her ass look good! ". "Go to hell, Meika, I can get down just as good as you can" "bitch please! ". "look, it don't matter whoever wins, we gonna split the damn money now Niecy you gotta do your thing girl don't make us look stupid, if you win we will dance at the next one okay Meika?". Meika was pissed but she didn't' say anything probably because she knew her ass was too damn high to win. They made us wait for about an hour before they started the contest. The funny thing about it, we didn't even know contest started until we had been dancing for about ten minutes. The disc jockey was tearing it up. The music was all that. We started dancing with the other people that were on the floor with us. It was not until the music stopped that we realized that they were the people we were competing with. It was not one on one, it was group on group but they didn't tell us that, we thought that it was going to be like any other dance contest but this was different and I was glad because we were dancing nice without even trying, that's how we won. Because it was boys that we were dancing against, made us tear it up even more. I was spinning around and dropping down. I tapped my partner on the shoulder and threw my head at him and spun around the crowd went crazy. He did a slick little move he was grinding on my butt, I stuck my butt out for him to take it, and then I stopped when the music did, froze and then shook my butt at his midsection again. The announcer was screaming, Aw shit, it's about to get crazy in here. After a few minutes, there was no one on the floor but Sharon and her partner and me and this fine ass guy that was getting me wet in more ways than one. After the music stopped, the crowd went crazy. "More, more, ". I was sweating badly but I kept dancing, soon my girls and me took the floor over doing the dance that we practiced. Of course, we won without trouble but the guys that we danced with got money and some albums too. We didn't' care. We were in for the next contest and that one was five hundred dollars. We went back to our tables. At least they did. I went to the bathroom to find a paper towel and to take another drink. When I got there, it was pretty full so I just leaned on the wall. "Girl you was tearing it up out there! ". One girl told me. "Thanks". "Where did y'all learn to dance like that? ". "It just comes naturally". "Damn that move you put on Kenny, put his ass to shame! ". "Who? " The guy you were dancing with, he is one of the best dancers on Ellamont Street". "Oh really? " "Yeah, I think this is the first time he lost one". I grinned. I went in the bathroom, took care of business and walked back to my table. When I got there, Kenny and three of his friends were sitting at our table. "Hey y'all'. Sharon looked up at me and winked. "Hey come here, I got something to ask you". She pulled me away from the table, "They got some good reefer and lots of drinks, they said if you want to we can go down their house, ain't nobody home and we already did what we came for so let's go". Now you would think that we had sense enough to find out a little more about these guys but we didn't, we were young and didn't believe that anything could happen to us, so of course we went.

We smoked more reefer and got drunk and Meika and Sharon shared a bedroom with Billy and Mark, Niecy went to the living room and Kenny and me used his older brother's bedroom. His mother came home but we were very quiet until she went in her bedroom and closed the door. Kenny and I talked for a little bit. I think he was as nervous as I was but you would be surprised what a little wine and reefer can do to calm the nerves. I had sexed with this man after knowing him for a few hours. I know it was God that kept me safe from any diseases because I was so foolish. The sex was good to me and I really did it to get revenge on Dennis. However, nobody had to know that. After they cooked us something to eat and we cut up for while teasing Meika because she was making so much noise that Billy had to cover her head with the pillow. We exchanged phone numbers. They called us a cab and we left. I promised Kenny that I would hook back up with him, and I did a few times but it never amounted to anything, I wasn't trying to get a boyfriend, I just wanted it to be about sex. They showed up at the next dance contest but neither of us won because a fight broke out before we could even get started. We were separated after the fight but not before the promoter gave us a few dollars for showing up. He said he didn't have to but most of the people at the cabaret showed up to see us get down.

At any rate, we caught the cab up to Meika's house, which was a few blocks from Dennis house. We got out the cab and was getting ready to walk into Meika's house when we heard Dennis voice. "Where you been Sabrina?" I looked around, lit a cigarette and played it off. "I told you I went to the cabaret". "I just left the cabaret, and no body was there in fact the damn cabaret was over hours ago, now I'ma ask you one more time, where in the hell have you been!" Sharon and Niecy pulled me by the arm, "Come on Sabrina, you don't owe him nothing, he ain't your daddy or nothing". "I'm okay, y'all go on in the house, I can deal with this". I sat down on the step and took a hale off my cigarette. Dennis slapped the cigarette out of my hand. "You think I'm playing wit you or something?" I didn't yell, I just pulled out another cigarette out of my pack. I was still high from the drugs and alcohol that we consumed that night. . I smiled because I was thinking about Kenny and his expression when he reached a climax. Dennis became enraged. He slapped me in the face, "Bitch you think this is funny?" I jumped up and slapped him back. "You betta keep your damn hands offa me, don't be asking me nothing about where the hell I been, where were you last Thursday?" He looked somewhat startled, "what are you talking about?" Yea punk, where were you, wit that freak down the street from you, sucking on her titties on the front porch, kiss my ass!" I turned to walk away but he was not having it. He grabbed me by the back of my shirt and pulled me to the ground, he stood overtop of me and slapped me again. Sharon, Niecy and Meika came from nowhere and jumped on him. "Get offa her, get offa her, you can't be beating on her like that!" His friend grabbed him and pulled him down the street. "Come on man, you drunk, I told you don't go down there any way". I got up off the ground. "You bastard, we are done, go and suck on that freak for now on!" I was wrong because I did sleep with Kenny more than once and would have slept with him that night if not for the fight but Dennis didn't know that and by the time he figured it out it was over between us.

Every time a new group came to the Civic Center, my girlfriends and me. We went to see the Isley Brothers, James Brown, Earth Wind and Fire. We hung out in the nightclubs; we snuck in and paid people at the door to let us in the Cabarets. We went to the Famous Ball Room, the Gatsby. I went to school long enough to collect my Social Security check from my father's death benefits. Soon, I was meeting boys and I would act as if I was going to school, get on the Number 3 bus, go straight to West Baltimore, and hang out with my girlfriends, who never went to school. I would come home, way after school was out, drunk, high or both. I would pass out in my bedroom until late in the evening. I would wake up, take a hot bath, and cook something to eat and put my mother's plate in the oven and go back to bed. My mother would slap me around and tell me she was going to put me away. She was a good mother and I feared her, but I was hardheaded. She warned me several times, "a hard head makes a soft behind". "Yeah, yeah, yeah". She didn't know what she was talking about". I was wrong. It wasn't long before I was doing everything the devil would have me to do. I should have listened to my mother when she said that a hard head makes a soft behind. She even had my Aunt Gracie call me and talk to me and boy was I convicted, but I was having too much fun. She warned me that God knew about everything I was doing and that if I continued to backslide that I was in danger of God giving me up to a reprobate mind. I knew what that meant because I did read the word of God but I didn't care at the time. When I hung up from Aunt Gracie, I felt bad for about ten minutes and I was out the door again.

Chapter 5
SIMPLY OUT OF CONTROL

Living for the Lord is so very easy. We just make it hard. **Proverbs 22:6 train up a child in the way that he should go: and when he is old, he will not depart from it.** When I was small, I was taught the word, lived the word and loved the word. Which in turn allow me to have a happy life. Even when tragedies arose, when I needed the Lord the most, I called on Him and He delivered me from the enemy. As a child, demons came into my life and altered my path. Nonetheless, I believe in my heart that "if it had not been for the Lord on my side" I don't know where I would have ended up. Maybe in a home for killing my molester. Even though that was tragic, the Lord got the victory because I know that His angels saved me that night in the truck. However, times in our lives we become disobedient. I was back allowing Satan have a foothold in my life. Truthfully, I can't put it all on him, it was sometimes my own foolishness that put me in harms way. I was almost sixteen years old and I was wild and irony and hardheaded. I didn't want to listen, I broke every rule my mother set for me. She tried to explain boundaries to me and why I should have them but I was not hearing anything she had to say. I wanted to do what I wanted to do. Satan stood by and watched me give him the foothold once more.

My mother stood in the living room yelling at me. "You better take your ass to school and bring it right home, do not pass go, do not collect two hundred dollars, but home!" I rolled my eyes and before I could open them back up, I was picking myself up off the floor. My mother was a little woman, but she was not one to play with. "You are too damn grown, I don't know what's gotten into you, but you better believe that I will slap your little ass into the middle of next week the next time you roll your eyes at me!" Somehow, I believed that she could actually knock me into next week. I promptly got my butt back up the stairs and got ready for school. My mother's motto was if I got to go to work, every able body in the house got to go to work, if you aren't old enough to work, your job is to go to school and get good grades, not C's or D's because that was failing as far as she was concerned. You had to graduate from high and college if you wanted to stay in my mother's house and she didn't give a doggone how grown you thought you were, you had better get across somebody's stage or she would beat the hell out of you. Even when my sister had a baby at 17 years old, she made her finish school and take care of her baby. She would say, every baby that comes into the world, God has a purpose for it, so don't be walking around my house looking all ashamed! Hold your head up and get your education so you can take care of that baby, I took care of nine of you, you all can damn well take care of 1 damn baby!" Like I said she was little in stature but mean as a snake and believe me, all of my sisters graduated, went to college and got decent jobs. My mother wouldn't have it any other way. Therefore, when she told me to get my butt ready for school, no matter how much I didn't want to go, I got up and got myself out of her house.

I found school to be very nice. It was nothing like the school I had left, the people really cared about if you did your work or not. I didn't know anybody and that was a good thing because at my old school I knew everybody and all I did was cut class. I didn't meet anybody that week in school but at least I did go. However, the weekend was coming and I wanted to be ready. I got my clothes on and stood at the bus stop. My mother told me that I could go in town since I had been to school all week and I hadn't talked back. I even did my homework. After hanging out with my friends on the West Side, they walked me to the busy stop and I started on my long journey home to Northeast Baltimore. It was late and I still had my book bag full of books on my back. While I was waiting on North and Charles Street, I went inside the Little Tavern and had a twenty-five cent hamburger and a soda. It was late and I thought I had missed the last bus, but I didn't' want to leave the bus stop because I didn't know where else to go. I knew if I walked down a few more blocks that I would be able to catch the Number 8 but that was going to take me too far out past my stop so I just sat in the Tavern. I watched the hookers and pimps walk around the street in the their cars. I watched the hustle and bustle of North Avenue, I shouldn't have been down their at that time of night but I wasn't scared. Then he walked in. He was so nice looking, and although I was sexually active this man would have probably would have been a man that I would have chosen for that "special night". I was fifteen years old and I had the body of an eighteen year old easy! I didn't make eye contact with him but he knew right away that he had me where he wanted me. He walked over to my stool. "Hey pretty lady". "Hey". "Watcha doing out here this time of night?" I hunched my shoulders. "Are you waiting for someone?" "Naw, just hanging out". I tried to sound grown. He knew I was lying and started laughing. "Pretty lady, you are sitting here with your book bag from school, grade school probably and you telling' me that you are hanging out". I had forgotten about the book bag. I had to laugh with him. "Okay, I am waiting for the bus to come so I can go home". He sat down beside me, He smelled so good. He pulled out a twenty dollar bill and gave it to the waitress; get Miss Lady another burger and some fries or something". "No, I don't' want anything else thank you". "You watching your weight or something?" "No, I just had a burger and I'm cool". I sat there and pulled out my Newport, still trying to be grown. He pulled out a lighter and lit the cigarette for me. I checked out his wrist and he had on a Citizen's watch with a gold diamond pinkie ring. I swore I felt myself getting warm. I lit my cigarette and blew "O's in the air. "Oh you got skills". He laughed. I smiled. I looked at the clock on the wall and it was close to 1 am in the morning. I got up off the stool and walked towards the door. "Where you going pretty lady?" I am going outside and wait for my bus". "Come on now, you know that bus ain't coming until next shift at two in the morning, let me take you home". "No thank you, I'm cool". "Look pretty lady, I am not going to hurt you or rape you, look I tell you what, I will even take another female with us so that you won't be scared". I shook my head no. "Okay, then I'll see you again some time." He got into a very nice car, I don't remember what kind it was but it was hot! I stood out on that bus stop for another hour and still that damn bus did not come, it was well past two now and I was getting cold and tired and just a little leery being out there with the night life. Then I saw him. His nice car was back. He pulled up beside me. "Hey pretty lady, you ready for that ride now". I shook my head yes. I don't know why I got in the car and I don't know why I wasn't scared, but I got in and lit a cigarette as if we were old friends. "Where do you live pretty lady?" "In Northwood". "Damn, what in the hell you doing downtown?" I was coming from my friend's house". "You got some sorry ass friends if they let you catch the bus home. I hope you ain't giving those "friends" any of that good stuff you got stashed in those tight ass jeans". I just smiled, now I was getting nervous. We drove down North Avenue and pass Greenmount Avenue and through the city, I knew I could have gotten home that way but I was way too nervous to ask where the hell we were going. He must have sensed what I was thinking. "Don't worry pretty lady, I will get you home in one piece, I promise, I just gotta take care of some business". "Cool". "You like that word don't you?" I just smiled. We ended up at the Grand Motel on Monument Street and Pulaski Highway. He had, as he promised, another female in the car. However, what I didn't know was there was another car that was following us all a long. When we piled out of the car, there were about six people with us and he was leading the pack. We went into a room that was already occupied with two more girls. Then it dawned on me that this man was a pimp. What in the hell did I just walk into, I thought to myself but I kept my cool. I was a hell raiser and I had smoked my share of weed, drinks, getting high and hanging out but I was definitely out of my league with this crowd, but I fronted as if I knew what was up. The room was filled with reefer smoke. There was cocaine. And the girls looked young but were dressed like they were older. "Have a seat pretty lady; this will only take a few minutes". "Naw, I'll stand". He nodded and went into the bathroom with one of the girls. I heard this yell and then this moaning. That went on for about twenty minutes. No one said anything when they came out of the bathroom. She went to the table, snorted some cocaine, and started kissing another person. I felt like I was in the damn movies or something. "Hey pretty lady, let's go for a walk". We left the room and went to another room. It was quiet in there but there was someone else in the room, an older woman who was lying in some man's arms. We sat down on the bed. "Look, I am not going to hurt you so you don't have to look so scared. I am going to take you home but I want to know what you wanna do with yourself". 'What do you mean by that?" "Look pretty lady, you should be home studying you work and you are in a low rate hotel with a fool you don't' even know, I could kill you put your body in a dumpster and no one would ever find you". He pushed me down on the bed and kissed me hard on the lips and I responded, I don't' know why but I did. I kissed him back and my body was on fire, here I was lying in a hotel room with a man who was sure to be over 10 years older than I was. He stopped kissing me and looked at me. "Come on pretty lady, He pulled me up on my feet and kissed me again. We kissed for a long time and I felt his manhood swell in his pants. Someone knocked on the door. "We gotta go man". He pushed me on the bed, "Fuck!" In an instant, his demeanor changed. "Bitch, don't leave this room". I didn't even think he was talking to me until I saw the look in his eyes. He pushed me in the bathroom and locked the door. After about ten minutes, he came in the bathroom with me and locked the door behind him. "You tell me that you want me right now!" I want you right now". I was so scared that I said whatever he wanted me to say, I knew I was dead; my body would be found months later in a damn dumpster just like he said. I started talking. "Look baby, we were having such a good time, why are we fighting right now, it was good before he knocked on the door, come on let's do this". All of a sudden, he started crying. I just did what my instincts told me to do, I held him in my arms, until he stopped crying. I don't know what happened that night but by the time I got home, it was about five or six, He dropped me off right in front of my door and made sure that I got inside. He blew his horn and I never saw him again.

That morning changed me, somewhere in my soul, things changed for me, I still don't know why I didn't' die that night, why I was not raped that night, why I was not somehow forced into some prostitution ring. Again, I realized that God was with me. My spirit was telling not to continue down that path, it was telling me that God has a purpose for me and that's why I did not die that night. I didn't want to live like I did, but I was being pulled in all types of directions, I felt like I had a devil on one shoulder and a angel on the other one, each telling me what to do, it was really hard for me. That night in the hotel should have stopped my madness but somehow I kept being pulled into a dangerous lifestyle. The drinking and drugging were almost every weekend; I still hung out all night long, but stopped having sex for a while. Even though I was still talking to guys, the sex had stopped. I didn't feel good about that anymore at least not for a while. I felt dirty, I didn't love any of these guys, I thought they loved me but they didn't it was just easier to say yes than no to them. I didn't have any respect for myself anymore, and I never felt worthy of anyone's love. I was damaged goods; just like my Uncle Manny had told me and I lived up to that title.

I had just ended my relationship with my boyfriend. He was too jealous and he hated my friends, but most of all we broke up because I caught him kissing my best friend or at least I thought she was my best friend, but friends don't kiss on your boyfriends, especially like they were kissing, I was really hurt behind that, she was like a sister to me and we did a whole lotta of stuff together that we promised to take to our graves. We were close and we loved each other. She had a good looking boyfriend and so many times I was tempted to be with him, sometimes I would close my eyes and think of him when I was with my boyfriend but I didn't cross that line because she was my friend, when I caught her and my ex groping all over each other in her living room, I lost it. I walked to the bar and told my man Chip to cop me some Richard's Wild Irish Rose Wine and a pack of Newport's. I sat on the playground and got so drunk. My girlfriend Meika comforted me but it didn't help I was betrayed and I felt hurt, so after much fighting and trying to keep it together, we broke up.

More than not, he tried to come back to me but it was too late, the damage was done. I had slept with another guy down by my brother's house; well let's tell the truth I had slept with two guys down by my brother's house. I used one guy to cover the older one I was seeing on the side. I couldn't tell anyone about Jackson because he was much older than I was. He was nice and I liked him. I didn't intend on sleeping with him it just happened one night. at his apartment. My girlfriend Evie and I smoked some reefer and drank some wine that night I was sixteen and I thought I was grown. Usually when I drank

I thought about my life and how messed up it was, then I would cry because I wanted to be the person I knew I could be deep down, I wanted to be back in church on the choir and sitting in bible study, but my mind was all messed up and confused. I drank more and smoked more to drown out the guilt I felt about not being in church and not fighting Uncle Manny off, and I did not care anymore.

My best friend Evie had snuck off with her married man she was dating on the side and I slipped up to Jackson's apartment without anyone seeing me. We had been seeing each other for months but he made me promise not to say anything since I was sixteen and he was almost thirty. I told him I didn't care about his age but he said that he could go to prison if anyone knew that we were seeing each other. I told him that he wouldn't' because we weren't having sex. However, he made me promise anyway and I did.

I often wondered if I was attracted to Jackson because he was older, did Uncle Manny damage me so much that I couldn't even conceive that what I was doing was wrong. I always hated myself afterwards and I scrubbed my body like I used to when I was a little girl. I slipped over to Jackson's with the full intention of him giving me some of that thirty-year-old manhood. I had already seen it, touched and I wanted to feel it but he wouldn't' let me. Not until this night. When he opened the door, he was surprised to see me. "Hey what are you doing here?" "I came to see you", I said in a slurred manner. "Come on in, you look and smell like you are drunk". I stumbled into the apartment. He had Marvin Gaye's greatest hits on the radio and incense was burning. I could smell the reefer in the air. He motioned me to sit down next to him on the beanbag. I pulled on his shirt and he took it off. I took my shirt off and began to kiss him on his chest. He stopped me. "Let me show you how to make love". I don't know what I was thinking but at that moment I didn't' care. I thought about all the men that hurt me, all the men that fondled me and tried to get me to have sex with them. I hated the fact that my innocence was gone. After that night of passion, we stopped seeing each other, me because the sex was addictive and him because he was getting careless with his feelings for me. He started catching feelings and getting upset when he saw me with other guys. I watched him one night beat a man so badly that they had to put him in the hospital, all the guy did was call me sexy and asked me if he could squeeze my breast. Jackson slammed his head into a tree and beat the hell out of him. Of course, it being North Avenue, the police showed up in minutes. They locked Jackson up for assault. I was yelling and screaming at the police but Jackson kept telling me that he didn't know me and to get me out of there. They told me move across the street or they would arrest me too. Jackson looked at me as if he were saying go away. Therefore, I did. When he was bailed out, he forbade me to come around anymore, and I respected his wishes.

For weeks, I stayed home and went to school. I was sick and tired of my life. I missed my friends, but I was getting tired of going back and forth over there all the time. They wouldn't come to see me because they said my neighborhood was boring.

There were no bars on the corner, and there was no loud music coming out of basement and living room windows. There were no police cars flying up and down the street at all hours of the day and night, so they wouldn't come out to visit me. I decided to go downtown and buy some clothes for school. I wanted to change everything about myself. I dyed my hair jet black and cut it short. I threw away all the clothes that I accumulated from guys and brought my own. I kept my Lee's and my Jack Purcell's but I stop wearing the tight shirts and tops. I got on the bus with my bags and turned on my radio. Not too loud. The bus driver kept looking at me as if he was giving me a sign not to turn it up one notch or he would throw me off the bus. I acknowledged that I understood and turned it down a notch instead. When the bus approached the stop by 33rd street, he got on the bus. Oh my goodness! He was not tall but he was good looking. I couldn't keep my eyes off him. I made sure that he did not see me looking at him. I checked out the Brown Kangol cap, the brown leather coat and the brown and beige shirt with double knit pants. He topped off the outfit with a pair of brown patent leather and suede shoes with the dice in the glass heels. He had a pinky ring on that had a diamond that could put your eye out. I was impressed.

My spirit spoke to me. "**Matthew 7:15 Beware of false prophets which come to you in sheep's clothing but inwardly they are ravenous wolves**". However, I wasn't listening. He looked good to me. Again, Satan subtle, cunning and on his job. It wasn't long before we were talking and laughing and exchanging phone numbers. His name was Trenton, He lived about ten blocks from me and he was not in school. He was in the job corps. He just got home and was staying with his mother. He was a Sagittarius and he didn't have a girlfriend (which I did not believe). When I got off the bus, I was on air. I couldn't wait to get home and call my girlfriend to tell her about his guy I had met. I thought about him all night long. I wrote his name on my notebook and I envisioned his last name with my first name. I went to school all the next week and I even stayed from across town in the hopes of catching him home. However, it took almost two months before we saw each other again. I told him that he could come up to see me but it had to be early because it was a school night. He came up and we talked some more and got to know each other. I liked him a lot and I wanted to be around him. It wasn't long before he was a like a drug to me. His presence made me feel like I was high. Before he left that night, he asked me to be his girlfriend. I said yes.

It wasn't long before we were always together, always on the phone, always spending time together. My mother's warnings were coming at me every day. "You and that boy, you better behave yourself and not get pregnant. I will put you out of here if you get pregnant". I promised her I wasn't having sex and that I was still a virgin. However, she was right; he was pressuring me to have sex and to hook school. I was afraid not of losing him, but the wrath of my mother. I really was scared to have sex with him because I thought he would know how many guys I had been with. Then I was afraid that he wouldn't like me anymore if he found out that he was not the first. She raised my sisters and even though they had babies out of wedlock, they were doing well in their lives, they had finished school, and some were completing college and graduate school. I didn't want my life to go backwards. Having babies first, and then a career. I wanted to do it the right way.

We had been together almost a year and I had seen some changes in him. Worse, I saw changes in me. He was popping pills and I was popping them with him. We did acid and purple haze. We tripped in the basement under the black lights, jamming to heavy rock. He smoked weed, drank wine, and got drunk. I found myself slipping into a lifestyle that I was not accustomed. I liked the high. I was used to the alcohol but I was not used to pill popping. I liked the money he was giving me and I liked the clothes he was buying me. Each time I tried to leave that lifestyle alone, I would find someone else that wanted to give me things, my only problem, I kept forgetting the price I would pay for it. I fell in love with Trenton, one of those kinds of love that even though you knew what you were doing was wrong, it didn't matter because love would make it all better. I felt the pull of evil and good. I had two people on my shoulders constantly. My spirit was telling me not to live this life, it was not good for me and it would destroy me and misdirect my path. The other spirit was telling me that I was young and had my whole life ahead of me. It told me to go on and have fun, let my hair down and live a little...after all what did I have to lose...I didn't know then, but my soul....

Soon after that speech from my mother, I became pregnant. I cried and was so afraid that I couldn't even look my mother in the eye. However, she knew, mothers like my mother always knew she was so angry and disappointed in me. But she never said a word against me. She yelled for about a week, about school, work, life future and money. What was I going to do about school, all of her children had finished school or at the very least received a GED and I was going to be no different. Trenton tried to explain to her that he worked had a good job, in fact and would take care of the baby and me if he had to. "Just give me a chance to prove to you", he would tell her. After he left she came in my room. "you don't' even know anything about him. He drinks, smokes and God know what else". Why do you want to throw your life away?" I didn't say a word. I listened to her. "What about all the things your father told you before he died?" I had let her down and I felt bad. I did go to school and I was doing very well but nonetheless, I let her down.

Chapter 6
MY MOTHER'S WORDS HAUNT ME......

It was not until my seventh month that I discovered exactly what Matthew 7:15 meant. He called me and told me he was on his way up. I could tell by his voice that he had been drinking. I became nervous. For some reason, he reminded me of my father when he drank, always loud, obnoxious and mean. I figured I get some money for the baby's clothes and talk to him a few minutes before I'd tell him to leave. It was a school night and I had to get up early and catch the yellow school bus to Number 1 in the city. He showed up with his friend. He kissed me and smelled of alcohol. It made me sick and I turned my head. "Oh you don't want to kiss me now". "No that's not it. I can't stand the smell". "Fine, I won't kiss you then, you think you're the only girl I can kiss"? I laughed it off but I was scared. That scene played in my head again. It hadn't been shown up in years, why was it resurfacing now?' Nevertheless, I saw my father lying there in blood and I closed me eyes and promised not to yell. He introduced me to his friend. Jerry was fine, I mean F-I-N-E! He was too fine. He was tall, his eyes were a light green, and he had a body that would put an older man to shame. I looked at him but quickly looked away, for some reason I felt ashamed to be in his presence. "This is my wife; she will do anything I tell her". Trenton smirked. "And that's my kid in that belly". I nodded at his friend. He must have seen the fear in my eyes. "Man it's getting late, let's get ready to go. We can come back another day when it's not so late". "Man please, I leave when I say I'm ready to leave". "It's ok; y'all can stay for a few more minutes". We went in in the house and sat in the living room. My mother came downstairs with her coat on. "I'm going to the store, when I come back, they better be gone". "Yes mam". He said. As soon as she left, he started ranting and raving. "Why she don't' want me here?" I shrugged my shoulders. "What the f--- you mean by dat?" "I don't know, I guess it's getting late, that's all". His friend looked at him. "Man come on, lets go, she gotta get up in the morning". I could see the look in Jerry's eyes. He wanted to knock the hell out of him. But he was trying to stay cool for my sake. "Aw ite, I'm going, come 'ere and gimme me a kiss". I tried to kiss him lightly but he pulled me close to him and stuck his tongue down my throat, I immediately got sick because of the taste of the alcohol. I pulled away. "Stop it, you taste like liquor". I wiped my mouth with the back of my hand. The next thing I remember was a flash of light. He had slapped me so hard that I literally saw flashes of light before I hit the floor. "Bitch, you don't wipe my kiss off!'. I was stunned. I could not believe that he hit me. He actually hit me, hard! Jerry grabbed him by his shirt and started shaking him. "Man what the hell is wrong with you, have you lost your damn mind!" you do not hit women, especially a pregnant woman. You must have lost your damn mind!" I didn't see it right then, but it seemed to me that Jerry was a little bit more upset than he should have been since he just met me. I was so embarrassed and I really didn't know what to say or do, so I just lay on the floor. Jerry was yelling and throwing him around like a rag doll, slamming him into the walls. He finally let him go and helped me off the floor. I could taste the blood in my mouth. "Are you alright?" I couldn't speak. I was still in shock. A man had never hit me in my life. Even when I was with my other boyfriend. Except for time I fought with Dennis. "Please get him out of here". I managed to say. He pulled him by his arm. "Come on fool you are disgusting!" "F___ her man! I don't want no damn baby no damn way, I ain't ready for this s___!". "You killin me!' He tried to hit me again but Jerry blocked it and busted him in the mouth. "Man don't make me beat your ass in here tonight, I said let's go!" He pushed him out the front door. "I'm sorry, I will call you later to see how you're feeling okay?" Jerry rubbed my face and wiped my tears away. I nodded okay. I never thought about where he would get the phone number. At any rate, the fear was back, the insecurities were back. Where did this come from?" I couldn't understand what just happened. I ran up to my room and cried until I fell asleep.

It was about two o clock in the morning when my phone rang in my bedroom, that was the time I was grateful to have my own phone line. I picked it up on the first ring. "Hello". "Hey, how ya feelin?" I couldn't quite grasp the voice. "Who is this?" I told you I would call you to see how you were feeling?". "Oh hello". I'm okay". "I should have kicked his ass; I shouldn't have let him hit you like that". "It's okay, I'm okay". I'm glad, if you need me for anything, and I mean anything, let me know". "Where is he?" "Drunk, sleep". I took his dumb ass home and rolled out". I just got in and I wanted to keep my word by calling you. I didn't wake your mother did I?". "No I have my own line, how did you get my number?" I took it from him. He doesn't deserve you, but I didn't call for that, only to make sure you and the baby were fine". "We are, thank you for checking". Aw ite, I'ma go, but you know you can call me anytime". He gave me his number and hung up. Fear would not allow me to keep it, I thought Trenton would find it and hit me again.

I tore it up and threw it in the trashcan. However, my subconscious took the number into my memory.

There is a cycle of abuse. It does not come with a hit or a jab. It comes slowly and without warning. It stars with taking of self-esteem. Why are you wearing that dress? You don't look good in that dress; you should wear this one, etc". Then there is the control. Why do you have to go out with your friends, aren't I enough company for you? Can't you talk to me? Then the constant calls. Where you been, when you get back, how long will you be gone, I want you home at this time. First, you think it's cute, he really loves me, and he wants to spend all his time with me. He cares about how I look. After he has succeeded in the other things, control and jealousy, he starts with the self-esteem....and he breaks you down, talks about your family and uses all the secrets that you told him against you. Then just when you have lost your self, the physical abuse starts. The little pushes and shoves and ultimately the punches. I had never seen any of it coming but now it was rushing like the Jordan River.

Chapter 7

TUNNEL OF TERROR....

As I sat in my bedroom falling apart wondering where in the world I had gone wrong. I thought about those words. I couldn't understand why I was falling back into the same old habits. I thought that I had defeated my demons, but they were back full force. There I was, eighteen years old and about to have a baby and my life was a mess. I thanked God for my mother. She was hanging in there with me. She tried not to lecture me about him, but I knew she wanted to. The last few months of my pregnancy were the worst. The more pregnant I became, the more abusive he became. He would slap me, push me, hit me, whenever he felt like it, I tried to fight back but it was always worse when I did. The bruises were getting harder and harder to hide. I cried almost every day. It was as if Trenton was jealous of the baby. He was never there for me. When he did come around, he was high or drunk or on his way to get high or drunk. I didn't feel pretty anymore and he never told me that I was. He had taken my self-esteem and buried it. I was fat, had a big nose, and I was not desirable as a woman or a girlfriend. I tried not to worry for the baby's sake. He went to jail, got out, went back to jail again, and got bailed out again. His mother had a wonderful attorney and saw to it that he didn't do any time. However, she warned him that she would not bail him out again. The next time he was on his own. He stayed out of jail. However, the drinking did not cease. I tried to talk to him and let him know how I was feeling and what his drinking was doing to our relationship. He promised to change and get himself some help, but it did not last. Each time he tried to stop drinking, something would make him mad and he would start up again. I turned to prayer again. I knew what prayer did for me in the past and I needed prayer to do it for me again. I got on my knees that night and I talked to God. I repented and asked Him to forgive me. I told Him all about my troubles. I told Him how sad and empty I was feeling. I told Him that I did not understand why I was in this abusive relationship. I cried and asked Him to help me. When I got up off my knees, Trenton was asleep on the sofa. I went in the bedroom and got my bible. I read **Ephesians 6:10 finally my brother be strong in the Lord and in power of his might. Put on the whole armor of God that you may be able to stand against the wiles of the devil. For we wrestle not against flesh and blood, but against principalities, against powers, against the rulers of the darkness of this world, against spiritual wickedness in high places. Where take unto you the whole armour of God, that you may be able to withstand in the evil day and having done all that, stand…praying always with all prayer and supplication for all saints.** I understood that scripture so well that I thought it was written just for me. It does not matter if you backslide. Once you have given your life to Christ, you will never be the same again. Once you are saved, you are saved indeed. However, being saved was not my problem, I knew I was saved, but I wasn't set free. In addition, I wanted to be set free. I understood that night that I was still in bondage but I didn't know how to get out of it. I was still holding on to fears and insecurities from my past and I realized that I was allowing myself to be in this relationship, I simply didn't feel worthy of having any other kind. It was true that he was abusive, but I was allowing him to be. I allowed him to take my self-esteem. I wanted to get out of this mess but I didn't trust God to deliver me. So there I stayed, still allowing Satan and his demons to destroy my life.

I did finally call Jerry and we talked a while, we became close friends. I knew he wanted more but I wasn't ready for that and I knew that Trenton would kill us both if he ever found out that we were friends. We managed to meet once at the house when Trenton was out with some other female. Jerry rode over and stayed with me for a while. I was so big that I thought I was going to bust. We sat downstairs in the basement. "Sabrina, you know that you don't have to stay with that dumb ass don't you?" "I can't leave him Jerry, I love him and he is the father of my baby". "So what! He is going to beat you every single chance he gets don't you know that?" "He is going to get better, it's just the pressure of the baby coming and his job and everything you know". "Why are you defending him?" I hunched my shoulders. He turned my face to his and kissed me. I kissed him back, but I quickly pulled away. "I really like you Sabrina". "I like you to Jerry, but we can't do this, it's not right". That's what my mouth was saying, but I was really screaming, "Yes, yes, yes!" Fear is a powerful emotion. I knew it was wrong but I didn't care, I wanted to be kissed like I was desirable again it had been a long time since Trenton had even looked at me, let alone kissed me. I wanted to hold on to him forever. "Do you know how I feel about you Sabrina"? "Yes I do". "Then let me take care of you and the baby, I can handle Trenton, I'll make sure he won't hurt you again". "No we can't do that Jerry, we can't, he will hurt you and then he will kill me". Just then, I could hear my sister yelling at me telling me that my phone was ringing. "Can you get it for me?" After a few minutes, she yelled back down the stairs, "It's Trenton, d you want me to tell him that you have *company*?" "No! I yelled back, I will be there in a minute". I wobbled up the steps and got the phone. "What the hell are you doing?" What took you so long to get the damn phone! I was in the basement washing clothes baby, how are you, where are you?". "I'm at my mother's house I will be there in a few". "Okay, I will see you when you get here". I hung up and wobbled back down the steps. "Jerry you got to go, Trenton is at his mother's house and he is on his way up here". "Good, now I can tell that fool how I feel". "Please don't do that Jerry, please don't". "Okay, but not for him for you". You need to leave that man alone Sabrina, you don't know him like I do, he will hurt you and he won't care when he does". "It's the pressure of the baby coming that's all; I promise I will talk to him". "It won't do you any good Sabrina, but outta respect for you, I will leave". He kissed me again and left out the back door.

I thought about what Jerry said, I wanted to leave but I couldn't. I loved Trenton and I really didn't think anyone else wanted me. Trenton had all but destroyed my self-esteem, although there wasn't much to destroy, when he laughed about Uncle Manny, it truly hurt me, but I acted as if it didn't. I was sitting in the kitchen when he walked in.

That night, I went into labor. I thought I was going to die. I begged my mother to help me. She took me to the hospital, rolled me in the middle of the hospital room, and left me there. She told me that I would be fine and sit there; someone would come out to help me. I realized that she left me not because she didn't love me, but because she could do nothing about my pain. She called my sister to come down to the hospital and sit with me. Trenton was nowhere to be found. My labor was so hard. I honestly thought I was going to die. I must have been out of my mind to think that I was woman enough to bear this pain; I was promising God and ten other folks that I would never have another baby. I just wanted the pain to stop. I was so tired of blowing, panting, and not pushing. My sister was trying so hard to keep me focused on one thing but I was all over the place, I would scream out but the tears were coming down my cheeks and I wanted to scream loud enough for the folks in the other part of the hospital to hear me. After over 20 hours of hard labor, the doctors decided that since the baby was in distress, they would have to perform a C-section. When I woke up, my son was lying next to me asleep in the incubator. I looked over at him to make sure all of his fingers and toes were there, and to make sure he was breathing. He was cute little yellow baby, in fact he looked almost white but I knew he was mine and the love I felt for him was something I never felt. I thanked God that he was healthy.

My life was headed in yet another direction. I wondered if I would ever get back on the right track. First I was trying to be a junior usher in the church, Uncle Manny took that away from me, I always wanted to be more than what I was but my life was going in s so many directions that I couldn't get a hold on it. I wanted to scream out "God, what am I doing so wrong? I could not be happy about anything in my life! Why do I always feel like I am letting someone down? I looked over at my son who I named Darius Trenton Taylor and he was sleeping so peaceful, that's the peace I was yearning for in my life but deep down, I knew I would never have. Trenton, who had finally shown up right before they took me to the operating room, was in the chair beside the incubator asleep. I didn't wake him. I just thanked God that my son was healthy, had all his fingers and toes and could see well.

When I went home, things got a little better for a while. My mother helped me for the first few months. She would come in my bedroom, get the baby, and let me sleep. I would sometimes come go to her room, lie in her bed, and watch television with her and the baby.

A mini-series called Roots was on when I got home from the hospital and I would curl up in my mother's bed and watch it with her. That show really made me mad, I was upset constantly when I watched it but I couldn't turn away from it, because it was about my heritage and of course my mother would run down history to me and try to explain that I should use that anger to better myself to prove the "white man wrong". It was ironic since Trenton was back in jail on a robbery charge. That fool was stupid enough to rob a store right in the neighborhood we lived and shopped. It was such a contrast, I watching a show about people dying for their freedom and this fool is giving his freedom away for a few dollars. I didn't know how much time he would serve, but I was too exhausted to worry about him. I just wanted to take care of my son and help my mother until I was able to move on my own. I wanted to move because I didn't want my mother to think that she was going to be responsible for my son and me. I found an apartment but decided not to move until the baby was older. I was excited about the move. Trenton, who was still in jail, was excited too. I somehow thought that if we had our own apartment, then he would feel better about us and the fighting would stop. When I moved into my apartment, I was alone and afraid, but I was at peace too. For the first time in my life, I felt peace. I didn't feel like I was walking on eggshells. I could sleep at night. I went to visit him every chance I got. He really seemed to get himself together in jail. After eight months, he came home. It wasn't long before he was drinking and drugging and beating me. I had invited Satan into my home to dwell with me. **Romans 8:18 For I know that in me, that is my flesh, dwelleth no good thing.....**Even though he wanted to do right, he couldn't. His spirit was not right. It was not long before the beatings started. I don't quite remember what started the beatings all I know that every time I turned around, I was getting beat. When the check was short, I got beat, when it was too hot outside, too cold outside, the beer was hot and the chicken was cold, I got beat. It didn't matter that I had no control over the weather, or the fact that his check was short because he borrowed money every single day, by the time Friday came, he was broke, it didn't matter that he put his food in the refrigerator and left it there until he was too drunk to even taste it, I got beat. If he was caught in the rain, I got beat. It didn't matter. My son was always afraid. I was always worried about how to talk to him. I didn't know what to say because I didn't know what set him off.

The first time Satan tried to kill me in my house; I was sitting on my bed, talking to my girlfriend on the phone. It had been a long while since I talked to her, since Trenton had isolated every friend I had from me. The ones that came around could not stand him or was trying to sleep with him; it didn't matter to me, to hear her on the phone made me feel so good again. We reminisced about all the fun we used to have, the people we used to hang out with and how we used to party every weekend before the babies came. I felt like myself for a while. Trenton wasn't there and I was relieved. I didn't see him come in. When I turned around to speak to him, he snatched the receiver from me. "Who in the f___ are you talking to?' Before I could speak, he slammed the receiver down on the side of my head. I saw the blood streaming down my face. I tried to get up off the bed and he hit me again. The receiver became dis-attached from the phone. I picked the phone up and threw it at him. He tried to duck but it hit him anyway. I got to my feet and charged him and he fell into the wall. However, it did not last. He pushed me into the floor. I crawled into the hallway and managed to get to my feet and run to the kitchen. I grabbed the knife off the table. I chased him back into the bedroom. I tried to cut him but he grabbed my arm. "Bitch, you tryin to kill me!" He snatched the knife out of my hand and swung it. I put my hand up and felt the sharpness pierce my hand. He swung it again and cut my wrist. I fell. He kicked me across the floor. I screamed and screamed. He must have gotten scared and ran out the house. One of my neighbors must have called the police. They called the ambulance and I was taken to the ER. I got thirteen stitches in my hand, four in my wrist and three in my head. I had a black eye and a bruised rib. But Satan did not succeed in killing me, for that reason alone, I knew he would back for me.

Whatever you so reap also will you sow..if you reap the flesh, you will sow destruction....if you reap the sprit........

Chapter 8

HIGH SCHOOL CRUSH

Did you know that Satan comes in many forms? Did you know that Satan could come to you in whatever from your weakness may be? It sounds strange, but when things are going well and you are a child of God, Satan seems to know just what to place in your life. If you need money, Satan will place something or someone in your life for you to get that money. Never mind the consequences you may have to pay. Take me for instance, I have always wanted a family because my father was not there in my life and I came from a broken home. I wanted to have that dream family, a mother, a father, and children, but my problem was I did not care at what cost. I did not take into consideration that having a man in your life did not mean I had to give up myself. All the men in my life were alcoholics and abusers, so naturally I thought that was the normal way of life. I thought that I was supposed to go through mess all the time. I didn't have a man to show me the right way to be treated. My father was not there because of his alcohol, my brother in law was there but he was sexually abusive and mentally and emotionally destructive to my well-being. He robbed me of my childhood and my innocence. My brother did not know how to show me the right way. Therefore, when I desired a man and a family, there Satan sat, providing me what I desired. He dressed him up in nice clothes, showed him how to reel me in with the lure of money, clothes and all the attention I wanted and yearned for. I could not see that "ravenous wolf in sheep's clothing".

The police found him and locked him up. He was down in his old neighborhood with some little young girl he was sleeping with. It hurt but at least he was gone. I couldn't understand why he would beat me like that and he was the one cheating on me. He got eighteen months, but he only did nine of them. While he was in jail, I started going to school and keeping my grades up, I wanted to graduate and get out of school so that I could spend some time with my son, it was somewhat hard with school and studying and all that but I did it, I was not going to stay on the system. My Social Security checks would run out soon after I graduated from school, so I needed to get out and find me a job to take care of my son and myself. I couldn't depend on Trenton because he was in and out of jail so much I thought that any minute we would be out on the streets if we waited for him to take care of us. I visited him in jail but my heart was not in it anymore, I still loved him but I wasn't in love with him anymore. I wanted a normal life, well as normal as it would get with me having a baby. I knew that my life had more to offer than just being beat up on and hurt the way Trenton had been hurting me over the past few years. I wanted to be free from all of that. When I went to school, I was a different person, although I only had morning because I only needed eight credits to graduate. My last class was Math. I hated that class because I was not good at it but I needed it to graduate and my math teacher knew that and she worked me hard because as she said she saw my potential. She rode me for all it was worth, telling me that she knew I could do better. So as I sat there pulling my hair out he walked in. Ms. Stewart looked up from her wire-rimmed glasses. "How nice of you to join us Mr. Saunders". "I'm sorry Ms. Stewart I lost track of time while I was in gym class". :"Now how in the world did you lose track of time if the bell rings to remind you that class is over Mr. Saunders?" I was in the shower Ms. Stewart, dang! Give me a break". "Sit down Mr. Saunders, just because you believe that this work is so easy, doesn't mean that you can come to my class when you get ready". "I'm sorry that I disrupted your class Ms. Stewart". He sat down in the chair in front of me. I could smell his soap, and he smelled good. Reggie was about 5'11 and dark-skinned. He caught my eye immediately, maybe because I was just lonely or maybe because he had the sexist eyes you ever wanted to see. I adjusted in my seat because just his presence was making me nervous. He turned around and tapped his pencil on my desk. "Excuse me, what page are we working on?" I was startled. I dropped my pencil on the floor and he picked it up for me. Our eyes met, yes page 47" or I-we, I think we are on page 47. "Are you sure?" He said with a smile. "Yes I'm sure, yes page 47, algebra". "Thanks". He turned back around. I looked up and Ms. Stewart was looking right at us. "Is there something you two would like to share with the rest of the class Ms. Thomas?" "No Ms. Stewart, he was just asking me what page we were on dang!" "Well Mr. Saunders, the next time you want to know, just look at the blackboard". The class erupted in laughter; the page number was on the blackboard in large print along with the problems that was on the page. He just smiled and turned back in his seat. The rest of the day was uneventful. When the bell rang, he went his way and I went mine but I could not take my mind off him. He was cute! When I saw my friend Angela at the bus stop, who also got out a half day she was talking to some guy. "Call me okay?" "Aw'ite Angie". She noticed me and smiled. "What up girl?" "Nothing much, glad to get out of that damn math class, Ms. Stewart is going to be the reason I don't graduate". "You'll catch up in time to get a C at least won't you?" That's what you need don't you to graduate?". "Yes but I don't want a C Angela, I want a B or an A". "Well we both know you ain't' gonna git no damn A". The word is isn't and going to". "Well if you needed an A in English that's fine but you need an A in Math smart ass". We both laughed, I loved Angie, she was cool and she was a good person. She was very tall and olive skinned with long hair. She was cool for a white girl. She was an only child and her parents had paper but she was not a spoiled rich kid, she fought with her parents all the time but she was pretty cool. Reggie was popular, fine and he was dark skinned. I didn't want to be with Trenton anymore but I still had not let him go. However, he was in jail and it was my opportunity to try to start my life over again. I was tired of being in a relationship where I didn't find love or respect. I was tired of all the sex I was having and no lovemaking. I needed to be loved, desired and held. So I kinda got involved with Reggie, it was subtle at first but then we started hanging out and he started helping with my math work. Ms. Stewart for one was glad about it because I was failing miserably and I needed that class to graduate. I was glad that we were starting the friendship because I liked his company, soon we were meeting after class and he would sit with me until my bus came, he still went to school the whole day but he would spend part of his lunch break with me, while I waited for the bus. Sometimes it would be all three of us, Angie, him and me but most of the time it would just him and me. I gave him my phone number, I don't know why, I knew when Trenton got out of jail that he would be right back at my house but I didn't care. I told Reggie about Trenton that he was my son's father and that sometimes he would show up unannounced and sometimes answer my phone. I told him that when he called that he would have to use some type of signal to let me know it was him and he was fine with it, I don't think he even cared that Trenton was in my life and that was good for both of us because I didn't care anymore either.

Ms. Stewart allowed Reggie to help with my final exam project, of course, she would not let us be on the same team but she let him help with the math part of it. It was getting harder and harder for me to not jump his bones but I didn't want our relationship to wind up being one of those "bed buddy" things, you know, just sex me and we can still be friends shit, I wanted more out of it than that. Therefore, I didn't push the issue. We kicked it but we were discreet, I didn't want anyone to know that I was seeing Reggie because so many people knew about Trenton and I didn't want anyone going back telling him once he came home from jail. It was almost prom time and I wanted everything to go smoothly at the prom if I took Trenton and Reggie showed up with someone from the school. If it got out that we were seeing each other on the side, then it would make for a disaster at the prom and I didn't want to embarrass myself or cause anything crazy at my prom for my classmates, they didn't' deserve it.

The final exam went well but Ms. Stewart had to push the issue. "Ms. Thomas, that was in excellent project but the next time remember that Mr. Saunders is not the only person in this class". Of course everyone laughed, even Reggie and me. I was so happy that I passed my exam and I was so happy that he was there to share it with me. As I walked to my seat and the other group was setting up for their project, we all heard some noise at the back door of the classroom. "Reggie baby, it was soooo good last night!!!". Everybody eyes went to me. I didn't dare raise my head. "Reggie baby, thanks for last night, I can't wait until we do it again!". Thank God for Ms. Stewart. "Young lady, if you don't' get away from this door this instant I will have you removed from this school so fast that you won't even remember if you went here or not". "I'm going". She peeked her head in the classroom. "Hey Reggie, I hope you enjoyed it as much as I did". "That's it young lady". Ms. Stewart grabbed her arm and called the office. "Can you please send someone down here to detain a student until I can get to the office to file the paperwork"? "For what, because I yelled in a classroom!" "No because I asked you to leave and you didn't". Before long, the other teachers came out of their classes. The bell rang and I gathered my books but not before she got her dig in. "Hey Brina, I had him last night, and I will have him again, you bitch!" Before I could respond, Reggie grabbed my arm. "Sabrina, she ain't worth it, you are getting ready to graduate". "You better control your whore, pimp!!". I snatched my arm away, grabbed my books and left out the side exit, setting off the fire alarms. I didn't care; I needed to get away from there. I sat on the bench and waited for my bus. I could see Angie coming towards me, and then I saw Reggie run up to her. They exchanged words and then I saw Reggie walk back into the building. Angie lit a cigarette and sat down beside me. "What's up?" I just nodded. "Why are you pissed off Sabrina?" I looked at her as if she was crazy. "What?" "Why are you pissed off, let me remind you of something, Reggie is single and has a lot of girlfriends, something you knew at the door, you are *living* with a man and fucking him on a daily basis, how in the hell can you get upset because some freak put him out there, you're not mad that she did it, you're mad because he wasn't fucking you last night, admit it!". She was right, I had no right to be angry with Reggie, he was not my man, he wasn't anybody's man, I on the other hand was living with a man and had a baby by him. "Look, I love you like a junkie like dope, but you were wrong to get all pissed off like that. You didn't want anyone to know that you were seeing Reggie, and now everybody knows so what, what in the hell can happen, so what if somebody tells Trenton, you didn't sleep with Reggie and if you did, so what. As far as the freak is concerned, she ain't coming to the prom; she can't because she just got suspended". She took my hand. "You deserve the best Sabrina and if you think Reggie is it, then so what, but don't get caught up, he is still a single man that can sleep with, hang out with and do whoever he so chooses to. You cannot be mad at that, you chose to have a baby and have responsibility at your age, your choice, don't get mad at him for the choices he made."

She was right and I didn't speak. I got off at my stop. I went home. I was lost in thoughts. I wanted to see Reggie and at least apologize but I couldn't. I had his number but I didn't want to use it. He didn't come to class the last couple of weeks of school. He didn't need to since he passed the math class. I was still doing make up work. Ms. Stewart and I were alone in the class. She walked up to my desk. "How are you Sabrina"? "I'm okay, glad this is almost over". "You know you've come a long way". "Thank you". "Are you sure you are alright?" yes I am fine, just tired, you know I have a little boy that I take care of Ms. Stewart, the nights can be long". "Yes I can imagine". I handed her my paper. "Well this is it, a few weeks and it will be over". She took my paper and I left. I thought she may have wanted to say more but she didn't.

The weeks ahead were hectic. Prom time was crazy, Reggie and I were strained. I had talked to him a few times but things were different between us. Then Trenton came home. He had a party but I wasn't invited, at least not mentally. I was a nervous wreck; he kept drinking and smoking all night long. He kept looking at me crazy as if he knew something that I didn't. I called Angie and talked to her, I told her that I was scared. She told me not to say anything to deny everything like men did when they were caught. I laughed but I was scared.

It was about two in the morning when his friends left. I did get a chance to say hello to Jerry but we didn't say anything else to each other, we never were sure if Trenton knew about us or not and we didn't want him getting suspicious. Trenton kept looking at me and smirking. However, I played it off. After a few minutes, we went to bed. I got in before he did and I prayed that he wouldn't start anything with me. He came in the bedroom he looked different, gained a little weight or something. His hair was freshly braided and that made me realize that I wasn't the first person he came to see when he got out of jail, but I didn't say anything to him, he was drunk and I didn't want to set him off. He stood over top of me naked as the day he was born. "Did you miss me?"" You know I did baby". "Show me!" I took care of him, just like I always did. I thought about Reggie all through the session, as he reached his climax, tears rolled down my cheeks because I was sad it wasn't Reggie. I faked an orgasm and rolled over on my side. I must have dozed off because when opened my eyes. Trenton was standing over me with his member stuck in my face. "Suck it for me". "No, get offa me". He slapped me hard. "You think I don't know you was thinking about that little fool you go to school with?" "What fool?" He slapped me again. "Bitch I got eyes all over the damn city, you think I wouldn't find out about that little fool!" I covered my face. He pulled my hands away from my face and pinned my arms down. "I'ma teach you a lesson about cheating on me". I was crying, "I didn't cheat on you Trenton, I swear!" I was crying, maybe I did cheat on him in my mind but I didn't cheat on him literally. "Shut up!" He turned me on my stomach and forced himself into me. He pressed my head into the pillow so I could muffle my screams. I think I must have passed out. When I woke up, he was gone. Blood was on my pillow and on my sheets. I crawled out the bed, went into the bathroom, and turned on the shower. I tried to wash away the pain I felt. When I looked into the mirror, I covered my mouth to stop the screams. My face was disfigured. I had a black eye and my lip was two sizes bigger than it should have been. I had bite marks all over my neck and breasts. My back was stinging and when I looked at my back, it too had bite marks all over it. I felt like he had shoved something inside of me but I could not be sure. I sat in the bathtub and tried to soak. I cried and cried. I finally got out the tub and dried myself off. I heard my phone rang over and over again but I wouldn't' answer it. After about an hour, I did get back into bed. I didn't go out that next day and I unplugged the phone. I knew my son wouldn't be back until Monday after I got out of school. I did not go to school that Monday and I almost didn't go that Tuesday but I had to pay for my prom tickets. I put makeup on and tried to cover my black eye. My lip was still swollen but went down a lot. I was able to hide it by telling people I got my tooth pulled and my face was swollen. I kept the ice pack over my lip. I only had a few hours in school, I could make and not seeing Reggie was going to be a plus. When I got off the bus, I saw Angie. She knew immediately what Trenton did. She had seen me like this more times than not. She grabbed me and hugged me. "Are you okay baby?" "Yes I am, I will be okay, just bruised and battered. She took my glasses off and saw my black eye. "Sabrina, what did he hit you with?" "His fists". "Oh my God, it looks terrible". "Can you tell me if the makeup helped"? "Not much". "I have to go to class Angie,

I can't miss any time". "You know my daddy knows a few I-talians if you need me to take care of that asshole for you". "No I am okay Angie". "Seriously Brina, I can't stand to see you like this again, damn he is going to kill you!" "No he's not, Trenton just gets mad, that's all". "Stop making excuses for him Brina, that damn man is crazy, and he is going to kill you if you don't get away from him". "Where am I going to go, who is gonna want me Angie, remember I am damaged goods". She stood in front of me and started shaking me. "Stop it, Sabrina, just stop it, stop listening to that crap from your uncle, that bastard was crazy and he didn't know what he was talking about". "Who's gonna want me with a baby, and what good man is gonna want me after they know what happened to me Angie, I can't be with anyone else but Trenton, he still wants me". "No he doesn't Brina, he wants to hurt you every single chance he gets, hell look at you!" I put my head down and she hugged me. "You don't deserve this Brina, I don't care what anyone tells you, you don't deserve this". "I try to not listen to the voices in my head Angie but I can't." "Didn't you say you used to go to church and pray?" "Yes". "Did it work?" I think it did". "Then do it again, pray I mean, go back to church, do whatever you have to Sabrina, please". We sat on the bench and cried like the two best friends in Beaches. "I love you like Bull winkle loves Rocky". I laughed. "And I love you like the Silly Rabbit like Trix". "Go on, it will be over soon". She walked me to my classes, I was fine in my English class as well as my gym class, but when I walked into the math class and saw Reggie, I lost it. I sat at my desk and tried not to lift my head for any reason.

Of course, Ms. Stewart was not having it. "Ms. Thomas do you think in the last few weeks in class that you can possibly dress for the occasion?" "Excuse me?" "I mean take those sunglasses off in my class". "I can't, I have a headache and the lights hurt my eyes". That wasn't a complete lie, I did have a headache. "I'll send you to the nurse but you have to take those glasses off in my class." Reggie and the rest of the class were looking at me. I took the glasses off but kept my head down. "That's better". I went back to looking down. The bell rang and I gathered my books quickly. The class dispersed except for Ms. Stewart, Reggie, and a few other people. I got my book bag but it was caught in the leg of the chair when I pulled it the chair fell over making a thud sound. Ms. Stewart, Reggie and the two other people looked at me,

I instinctively raised my head and that's when they noticed my eye and my lip. I quickly put my head back down but it was too late, Ms. Stewart gasped and so did Reggie. Ms. Stewart dismissed the rest of the people but Reggie wouldn't leave. "Let me talk to her please Ms. Stewart". I was so distraught, I didn't want them to see me like that, but what's worse I didn't want to have to explain to them that I was being beat by my boyfriend. How do you explain that to people? Ms. Stewart sat down beside me. "Sabrina, who did this to you?" "Don't worry about this Ms. Stewart,, I can handle this". "Sabrina, please tell me who did this to you?". "Nobody did anything to me, I fell that's all. I have to leave now, can I go now please?". She moved away from the desk. However, she stopped me. "Get help Sabrina, you don't have to live like this". "I know". The tears were coming down my face I ran right into Reggie who put his arms around me. "Its okay baby, you will be okay". We walked out of the class in silence. We didn't wait for the bus that day. We both got into his brother's car and went to his house. He made me something to eat and we talked for a long time. It was well past 6 p.m. when I called home to tell my babysitter where I was. She told me that Trenton had been there several times looking for me, but I made her promise not to say a word. I asked her to take my son to her house and locked my apartment up. She did. "Are you okay?" "Yes I am fine". Would you like to lie down and get some rest?". "That would be good".

He pulled the covers back and I slipped my shoes and jacket off and slid under the sheets. I could smell his cologne on the pillow as I laid my head down. He sat down beside me and rubbed my face. "I'm sorry about this Sabrina, ". It's not your fault Reggie, Trenton needs help". "You can't stay with him Sabrina, he will kill you". "Please can we talk about this later? ". He got up, walked towards his dresser, and pulled out a tee shirt. "Here put this on so you will be comfortable while you rest". I got undressed, when he saw my back and arms, he became visibly shook. "What did he do to you?" He examined my back. "Oh my God Sabrina". He held me in his arms. "He beat me Reggie, he beat me and raped me and sodomized me". He held me in his arms for a long time. After a while, I reached up and kissed him. He pulled away. "I can't do this with you right now". "Why?" "Because I don't want you to think that I am taking advantage of you". "Please Reggie, I want you so bad".

He kissed me gently. It wasn't long before we were both lying naked on his bed. He kissed each one of my bruises and made love to me, for the first time in 5 years someone made love to me. It was beautiful. We made love for a better part of an hour. I reached depths that I didn't realize existed. I now knew why this man had such a reputation; he was simply good in bed. He knew exactly what to do with what he had. He made me feel special like I was the only woman in his life. We talked some more before I left. He took me home. I made him drop me off around the corner but he was mad about it. "I am not letting you walk a damn block away from your house in this neighborhood; I don't give a damn about Trenton, punk bitch". "I'll be okay, please go home". I will call you when I think you are there to let you know that I am okay. I promise.". "I will let you out here but I am following you in this car until I see you put the key in the door. If you need me I will come back here to get you". I went in the house but Trenton wasn't there. I called the baby sitter who told me that my son was sleeping. I told her that I would pick him up later on in the evening. She said not to bother that she would bring him home the next day.

I thought about what happened that day and the previous one. I had no idea what had just happened between Reggie and me, I mean I realized what happened, but I didn't know where it was going to go from there. I did love Reggie and I finally admitted to myself that I had loved him for a long time. I didn't love Trenton, but I had enough fear for him that I wouldn't leave. I cried some more. I didn't know why I was crying but the tears wouldn't stop. I found myself back on my knees. Praying to God once again. My life was a mess and I remember a pastor preaching one time that if your spiritual life was a mess it was a good chance that your life in general was a mess. I started out by thanking God for protecting my son and me. I thanked Him for allowing me to survive all the beatings that I got from Trenton. I thanked him for my apartment and I thanked Him for Reggie. I must have fallen asleep on the floor because the phone woke me up. Then it stopped, I knew it was Reggie and I called him back to let him know that I was safe in the house.

I went to my prom and I had a beautiful time. I saw Reggie but he was with someone else as I was with Trenton. Surprisingly, Trenton was a perfect gentleman. He was not drunk or even high. He looked good too. We wore brown and white. Angie was with someone other than her boyfriend because he told her that he had to work, that it was mandatory. However, when we got to the prom, there he was with another girl, who Angie hated, I don't think it was because she was a black girl but because he humiliated her in front of all her classmates. She did well though; she didn't embarrass herself or him by acting a fool. She simply went up to him, kissed him on the lips and told him that he was truly going to miss the mind-blowing blowjobs that she used to give him. She looked back at him, winked her eye and strolled off the dance floor with her date. I know she was hurt but the girl was holding her own that night. Besides her date was not a bad looking person and he had money and a nice baby blue Mustang that he would let Angie drive all the time. Angie changed after the prom. She stopped hanging out with me for a while, and she was always fighting with her parents. She started getting high and hanging out with other people who she didn't usually hang out with, I would see her sometimes and she would blow me a kiss and speed off in her new Mazda. She started hanging out in the city where drugs were easy access. Her drug of choice was cocaine. She was hooked in a matter of months and right after graduation when she was supposed to be entering into a prestigious university in Florida, she instead went into rehab. Her parents would not let her die on drugs. She stayed there for 6 months. She came back home briefly but then her family moved away and I didn't see her anymore. I missed my friend. She was a true friend and I was closer to her than I was any of my sisters. Over the months, I received a letter from her.

Hey Girl:

How are you, I am well, I am sorry that I let you down. I want you to know that I do love you like a sister and there is no one that could ever take away our friendship. I was a damn fool for getting hooked on that white girl but you know me, I must take my chances in life. To my credit, I have been clean for about 4 months now and I am going to stay clean…one day at a time of course.

Please if you have not already; pull yourself away from Trenton before he kills you and that precious baby boy of yours. I know I can't tell you what to do but as a friend, I must tell you that your life is going to end if you stay with a man who doesn't respect you but beats you. Well enough about that, did you know that my parents are getting a divorce…well they are, I found out that my mother is a freak, like the young boys, she is now dating a guy who is probably about 5 years older than me, get that!. Daddy is not mad though, he always had a "chick on the side"…you know like that old song…ha ha ha. They are both spending the money and both happy about it. I am set for life either way; I just gotta get out of this rehab and stay out.

Anyway, if you talk to Reggie, tell him he shoulda got wit this white girl, I could have turned him out…sike You know I wouldn't do you like that, I know how you feel about him. I really wrote to tell you that I will be calling you soon, if you need anything, you know money, anything, call me I will give you whatever you need; you are my best friend Sabrina. I miss you a lot. I am sending you this check (they don't know I still have my checkbook) use it to get the hell away from that psycho nig…ooops that boy friend of yours. If you ever need anything from me, just call my pops, he will get in touch with me and let me know, they always thought you were pretty cool people, imagine this, my mother thought you were a bad influence on me because you had a baby, and here I am sitting in a damn rehab, ain't that nothing ha ha, well I gotta go to my one on one with my counselor, I love you Bree,

Angie

I cried and read the letter over and over again. I looked at the check and it was for one thousand dollars. I missed my friend. I put the letter away because I didn't want Trenton to find it.

I went to the graduation party with my other girlfriend Wendy we had became close after Angie left. I took Trenton but he was so drunk I had to leave him in the car. Wendy and I went to the party and had a good time. While in the party, I ran into Reggie. "Congratulations baby". "Same to you". We hugged and I felt his manhood rise. "Do you have a room here?" "No, and I came with somebody so I can't get away but I wanted to show you something". We walked outside and there was this nice burgundy Honda Accord "Is that you?" "Yes that's me". We walked over to the car and he opened the door. "Get in". I did. It smelled so nice. He kissed me. "I've wanted to do that since I saw you walk in the club". "I'm glad you did, I wanted you to". We kissed some more and then we heard a bang on the window. Whoever he was with was standing outside the car. He let the window down. "What?" "What do you mean What Reggie, who is the hell is this?" "This is Sabrina, stop acting like a fool; I just brought her to see the car". "Well I been inside looking for you so we could take a picture together and people telling me you out here hugged up with somebody else". "I said I brought her to see the car, why are you questioning me?" "I'm not". "Look Sabrina I will talk to you later, he gave me another hug and whispered in my ear "I want you tonight". "I'll see what I can do". I whispered back. I looked at the girl. "I really like your outfit". She rolled her eyes at me.

When I told Wendy, she just laughed. "You are crazy, do you know that Trenton could have woke up and saw you getting in Reggie's car?" "Girl please, that man is so drunk he won't even know he is in the car". We both laughed and went back into the hotel. The Hilton Hotel was jumping and we had a ball. Reggie and I did get a chance to kiss some more and take a picture or two together. He left shortly after we took the picture and girlfriend was not letting him out of her sight. From what I had experienced with him, I couldn't' even blame her, the sex was righteous indeed! Wendy took us home and helped me drag Trenton to the third floor apartment. As I said, he didn't even know that he was even at a party.

We took him to upstairs and I put him to bed. I thanked Wendy for driving and told her to be careful. When I looked out the window there was a car behind her. She waved him to get out and they talked. She looked up at the window and said "you ain't the only one who was trying to get some tonight!" we both laughed and the guy followed her home. I wasn't scared for her, because the guy was a classmate.

School was finally over and I didn't' see Reggie as much as I wanted to. Trenton was back into the drinking on the regular, although he went to work and handled most of the bills he was still as vicious as ever.

Chapter 9

I SHOULDA MADE HIM WEAR A CONDOM….

I spent the summer working at the Hecht Company in the picture gallery. I liked my job. I was still stressing with Trenton and his jealously, his drinking, and his womanizing. He was making enemies all over Baltimore and every time I turned around someone was coming to the house looking for him for one thing or another. I was ready to move but I didn't know where. However, God has a way of forcing your hand even if you are unsure. It's His way of telling you that He is with you no matter what. Times like this made me understand more and more that I needed to turn my life around, but my insecurity wouldn't let me. The more I tried to stay focused on the teachings I learned from my aunt, the more I messed up. I didn't see in me what everybody else saw. Even Reggie would tell me how pretty I was and how much potential I had but when I looked in the mirror, I didn't see that, I had become strong enough to know that I could not stay with Trenton much longer. I made up my mind if I wouldn't leave him for my sake that I would leave him for my son's sake. He surely didn't deserve all the mess that was going on with the two of us. The abuse was so prevalent that he didn't try to hide it anymore. He would slap me outside in front of people, flirt with women in my face, and dare me to say anything. I didn't, but I put I my mind that I was going to find me somewhere to move and not take Trenton with me. I had a love hate relationship with him, I hated him for the way he treated us and I loved him because he would make me feel so special at times. He would come in the bathroom, wash my back and tell me how much he needed me, but in the next minute, he would rape me and call me all types of whores and make me say that I enjoyed Uncle Manny, and when I refused he would slap me across the face until I said I liked it, when I admitted I like it, he would beat me for saying that I did. Sometimes I thought I was going insane. Before I left, I had to devise a plan that he would not find me when I did leave. My plans were delayed.

I was sitting on the job one day, my head started hurting, my stomach started churning, and doing flips. I excused myself and raced to the bathroom. I got violently ill and my coworker had to come in the bathroom and help me. "Are you alright Sabrina?" You know what I hate? For someone to ask me if I am okay while I am puking up my stomach contents. I just looked at her and turned my head back to the toilet. She gave me a cold paper towel to put on my head. I finally got myself together and went home.

For weeks I was sick, I had my period and it made things even worse for me. I couldn't get out the bed. Every time I tried to get up, I would get sick again. Trenton was very attentive and concerned but I kept telling him that I was okay; I just had the flu or something. He kept asking me was I pregnant. I kept telling him no, My son was now 3 years old and I was not trying to have another baby by this fool, I had miscarried one child and aborted another one because I couldn't bring myself to bring another child in the world with Trenton. When he found out, he called me a murderer and spit in my face. I was not trying to have more babies by him; I was trying to get away from him. A few days later, I was able to go back to work, I still didn't feel well but I managed to work my full schedule. I still couldn't eat or keep anything down. So I made an appointment with my doctor. 'I'm going to the doctors in a few days". "I'm going with you". I didn't want him to go but I wasn't going to argue with him.

We rode the bus downtown to the clinic the next day. Trenton kept bugging me, kept asking me was I pregnant and if I was, was he the father. I just looked at him as if he was crazy.

When I got to the clinic, they made me fill out paperwork. I did that all the while Trenton was looking over my shoulder. He was truly getting on my last nerves. I was so glad when the doctor told him that he could not come into the exam room with me. I got undressed and answered more questions…"are you sexually active, do you have birth control, how many pregnancies, how many abortions, last menses, I was answering the questions like a robot I've heard them all before… Okay now Ms. Thomas we are going to do a pelvic exam. What type of birth control do you take"? I have the IUD". Okay, now scoot down. I closed my eyes, I hated these exams but I knew they were necessary. He checked my breasts. "Are you breast tender?" "A little". "Okay I will be back shortly. Just relax". I sat there for what seemed like hours. Finally, he and the nurse came back in the office. He sat down. He looked at my chart. You are twenty?". "Yes", and you have one child?". "Yes". Did you know you were pregnant Ms. Thomas?" I almost fell off the table the nurse grabbed my arm. "Pregnant, I can't be pregnant". "You said you were sexually active". "Yes but I have the IUD". "Nothing is 100% Ms. Thomas". "Oh God I can't be pregnant", "Well you are and by the size of your uterus I would say you were about 13 weeks". "Thirteen weeks, I can't be thirteen weeks, I just had a period last month, oh no this is not happening to me doc". "You are very pregnant Ms. Thomas, maybe fourteen; I have to re-exam you". "how in the world did this happen, I have a IUD and I had my period and all that, Oh God, did you say 13 weeks, not 5 or 6 weeks but 13 weeks! Oh my God, this is not happening". I was crying and shaking and the nurse was holding me in her arms. "Is there something you want to tell us?" "You don't' understand, my boyfriend is going to kill me if he finds out that I'm pregnant, especially this far gone, he is going to think I knew and kept it from him and he is going to think I kept it from him because he may not be the father, Oh god, I can't tell me that I'm 13 weeks, Oh God,". I was panicking and I was hyperventilating. They laid me down on the table and instructed me to breathe slowly. "Let's just take this slowly. I will do a blood test to sure. However, I have to tell you that I have to either take the IUD out now or later as you get bigger, but as you get bigger the hold will become larger and you risk losing the baby and/or bleeding profusely. That was not a period you were having, that was the hole becoming larger as your uterus grew. You have to tell me what you want to do Ms. Thomas "can I have a few minutes?" "Sure, would you like the nurse to stay with you?" I shook my head yes. When he left, she gave me another tissue. "Are you okay?" there was that dumb question again. "Is there any way he can be wrong about how pregnant I am?" Not likely sweetie". Oh God, I can't tell him he is going to kill me I tell you he is going to kill me, he is going to think I kept it from him". She rubbed my back.

Then it hit me at once. I remembered back when I was raped by Trenton and slept with Reggie hours afterwards, when I calculated, those dates coincided with the 13 weeks. "Oh Jesus, I am dead, Oh Jesus I am dead!" I got to get out of here; I can't let him find out". I started vomiting all over the place and the room started spinning. I felt the nurse push me back on the bed and try to calm me down but I couldn't. She gave me a basin and placed it under my chin. "Breath Sabrina, just breath baby". I tried to control my breathing and closed my eyes so the room would stop spinning. I started thinking about Reggie, and Trenton, what in the hell was I going to do, Oh God, I should have made him wear a condom, they should have worn a condom, Oh God if this is Reggie's baby, he is going to think I trapped him, Trenton is going to kill me. I felt the room get quiet and it became dark. They turned the lights out and allowed me to rest. After a little while, the doctor came back and sat down beside me. "Ms. Thomas the blood test confirmed that you are 13 weeks pregnant and that we must remove the IUD today, the test also showed that the IUD is piercing your uterus and it may very possibly be poisoning the blood stream. I need you to lie flat on the table and lift your legs up. We are going to take it out right here and it will feel like a pinch. I want you to go home and stay in the bed for a week. Do not do any heavy lifting. If you start to bleed heavy I want you to go to the nearest hospital." He was nice enough to call Trenton into the room to tell him what is going on and why it's taking so long but he did not reveal to him about the pregnancy.

After I got my paperwork, vitamins and iron pills, I went home. I hid the paper showing my expected due date. I told Trenton that I may miscarry anytime between now and a couple of months from now. When we got home, he started on the questions, is this my baby, did you sleep with someone else, are you sure you don't know how many weeks you are, didn't they tell you at the clinic, you don't' look like you are eight weeks, you look bigger than eight weeks, did you sleep with that fool I asked you about? If I find out you sleeping with some other fool I'ma kill you and that damn baby! "Trenton, please, stop talking, please just stop talking! I am feeling bad and sick and I want to go to bed." He looked at me as if I had three heads; He grabbed me by my throat. "If I find out you been sexing some other fool, I'ma kill you with my bare hands". He grabbed my private area, "This belongs to me and if you giving it to somebody else, I will kill both of you!" He stuck his tongue down my throat and pushed me on the bed.

For months, I lived in fear, hoping that Trenton wouldn't find out that I was more pregnant than I said I was. I tried to reach Reggie to talk to him but he was MIA. I finally called my friend Wendy who lived right down the street from his best friend. I made sure that Trenton was not around. "Wendy, I need you to get in touch with Reggie". "I'm glad you said that, he is leaving for the service next month and he asked me to tell you to come to his party". "Service, are you for real?" "Yes, he said that he was going into basic training and then the Reserves". I started crying, "What's wrong?" "I'm pregnant Wendy and I don't' know if it's Reggie's' or Trenton's." "How did that happen?" "A few months back when Trenton came home from jail, he found out about Reggie and he beat me but not before he raped me and sodomized me most of the night". "Oh my God Sabrina, why are you still there with him?" "I had planned on moving away before I found out I was pregnant, he is watching every move I make. He went to work so I was able to call you. I need to see Reggie and at least say good-bye". "Are you going to tell him that you are pregnant?" "No I can't do that; he will think that I am trapping him because he is going in the service. I just need to say good-bye to him, he will never know about this". "Are you showing?" "A little but I can hide it enough that he won't know it". "Sabrina, you can't do that, he has the right to know". : why it may not even be his baby". "Oh my goodness, what are you going to do?" "I don't know". "I will call him and let him know that you said you would be at the party". "And that's all you tell him Wendy,

Promise me you won't say anything about this to him". "Does he know about the rape?" "Yes he knows but I don't think he will put two and two together especially since he won't know that I am pregnant". "Are you sure you don't' want me to tell him? "Yes I am and if you do I will never forgive you". "I promise I won't say a word".

Chapter 10
I STILL LOVE YOU!

I went to the party with Wendy, it was nice, and there were so many people at the party that I didn't think I would get one minute with Reggie. I just wanted to give him a hug and say good-bye to him, I would walk out of his life and take the love I felt for him with me. I couldn't do this to him not now, even if I thought it was his baby, I couldn't tell him that, not now, he would believe that I was trapping him and that's the last thing I wanted him to think of me. I really loved him, and it had been a long time since I loved anybody. Finally, the party thinned out and we had a chance to talk. We went for a ride in his car. "Damn Sabrina, it's good to see you, I was hoping I got a chance to see you before I left". "I'm glad too". "I've thought about you a lot over the months you know. I wanted to call you and come by but you know what happened the last time we tried to do that". "Yes I do". While Reggie was in the house with me, Trenton showed up at the door, I had to take Reggie to my brother's apartment and let him stay in there while I got rid of Trenton. It was such a mess and Reggie was upset about that, I know he thought I chose Trenton over him but I didn't. I didn't tell him that I got beat up that night. I kept that to myself. "Well anyway, it's good to see you again. You look good". "So do you Reggie". We stopped at a McDonalds and had something to eat and talked some more. When it was time to go, Reggie said something that shocked me. "Sabrina, why haven't you called me?" "I did call you Reggie, but I found out that you were with someone that you really cared about and I didn't want to come between that". "Why didn't you ask me about it?" I thought it wasn't my business". "Sabrina, did you know that the girl I was talking to was your boyfriends' ex and he put her up to talking to me to find out information about you?" "What". "Yes her name was Butta, you know the color of butter, and I don't know what the freak's real name is". "I know her". "If you would have called me I would have told you that I cut that short as soon as I caught her talking to him on the phone". I was stunned. "Sabrina, why didn't you leave him like you said you were?" I didn't know how to answer that, because truthfully I didn't have an answer. "I don't know, but I am leaving Reggie". "Before or after he kills you?" That hurt…a lot. "Why did you want to see me?" I was shocked now, I never heard Reggie use this tone of voice with me. "What's wrong?" "Nothing let me take you home". "Did I do something to you Reggie?". "Naw". We drove in silence. When we pulled up to my door, he looked me straight in the eyes. "Is there anything you need to say to me"? "There's a lot I want to say to you Reggie, things I've wanted to say since the first time we made love. I never had any man take his time with me, love me the way you did, that was special to me; I do not think I will ever feel that way again. "I love you Reggie, I've always loved you from the first day I laid eyes on you in Ms. Stewarts's class. I wanted to tell you over and over again but I didn't want you to think that you owed it to me to say the same thing". "Why would you say that Sabrina, you don't know how I feel about you?" "I thought that you loved me but as a friend, not the way I loved you". "You know what; you will never be loved the way you want to be loved until you learn to love yourself. I can't make you feel good about yourself baby, you've got to do that, Don't let this man take everything from you Sabrina, how many times has he beat you, given you stitches, put you in the hospital?". I started crying, I was so ashamed. He turned my face towards his. "I care about you Sabrina, I can even tell you that I love you but I can't be with you if you are going to stay with this man". "But you are going to leave me". "I have to leave, I have so much I want to do with my life but I need money to do it. I will be back soon, stop thinking like you aren't going to see me anymore." Can you promise me that you will be back?". "Yes, but first I need to know something from you". "Anything". "Are you pregnant?" I could not speak, I lost my voice. "Are you pregnant Sabrina?" "Who you been fucking?" That hurt. "What?" "How many men are you sleeping with?" "Are you crazy asking me a stupid question like that?" "I'm sorry". 'You know what, forget you Reggie, Yes I am pregnant and no it's not your baby, are you happy now, now you can go to the service with a damn clean slate, don't worry I won't call child support on your ass!". All I ever wanted was for you to love me, and now I see you are just like the rest of these black ass men out here, I hope you had fun, you bastard!" I got out the car; I didn't want him to see me crying. He jumped out the car. "Wait Sabrina, I'm sorry". It's okay I understand, all the good men leave. That's the story of my life Reggie, every time I find a man that is not like what I attract they get what they want and they leave, why wouldn't you. We had some fun, you got your shit off and I got knocked up all is fair in love in war". "That's not fair Sabrina". "Life ain't fair". This time I didn't care if he saw my tears. "Take care of yourself Reggie, and I do understand, believe me I do". "Please Sabrina; we can't end it like this". "End what, we never had a damn thing Reggie, you got what you wanted from me, put a notch in your damn belt and move on!" "Sabrina, I never thought of you as a notch in my belt, I cared about you, and I loved you, You wouldn't let me be with you Sabrina, you stayed with this damn fool, what was I suppose to do?" "You're right Reggie, it's my fault, and it's always my fault. I don't know why I thought you would want me anyway, I'm not even your type, I'm only bed buddy material, not girlfriend material". "Stop it Sabrina! I never treated you like that and you know it!". 'It don't even matter, go on in the service Reggie, walk away, please!". "If that's what you want". "That's what it is Reggie, I know and you know, you already have someone else, you just wanted to see me to see if you were going to get trapped with a baby". The look of pain appeared on his face. "I'm sorry you feel that way". "No I'm sorry, it's true". He walked back towards the car. I wanted to run to him and hold on to him but my pride wouldn't let me. That was the last time I saw Reggie for a long time. When I got in the house, I called Wendy. "How did it go?", "You are a scandalous bitch and I don't ever want to talk to you again, all I asked you to do was to keep your damn mouth shut and you couldn't do that, damn Wendy, what in the hell is wrong with you!?" "I'm sorry Bree, he deserved to know". "It wasn't your place to tell him Wendy, it was mine". "Then you shouda told him when you found out, Reggie is a decent man and he deserved better than to be surprised his last damn day home! ". "you seem to be getting a little more upset than you need to about all of this, what's up, you sexing him or something?" "Hell no, why do you think everybody is out to get you Sabrina, I'm your damn friend! I wouldn't cut you like that! ". "Maybe not, but you shouda kept your mouth shut Wendy". "What happened"? I told her the story and starting crying all over again. "I'm so sorry Brina, I didn't know, I am so sorry". "I gotta go, if Trenton comes in here and find me like this, I will have to fight". "I'm sorry Brina, honest I am". I hung up the phone

My life was the equivalent of shit. I hated myself, I hated my condition. I was so miserable. I couldn't stop thinking about Reggie and I couldn't' stop crying, Every time I saw one of those "Uncle Sam Wants You" posters I would cry all over again. Trenton thought it was the pregnancy that was causing me to cry all the time so he barely asked me why I was crying anymore and on top of all of that, he was cheating on me again, my stomach was growing but I wasn't able to keep any food down, nothing. I kept losing weight, the doctors were furious with me I was stressed out, and I had to leave my job. I couldn't keep calling in. the only light in my life was my son who was growing so well and spoiled as he could be. I watched him one night sleeping and that's when I realized that I had to get away from Trenton or my son would grow up to be just like him. I checked my stash to see how much money I had. Then I called my sister who was moving to a two bedroom and wanted to give up her apartment. I told her that I would take over her lease if she let me. Now all that was left to do was to get out of there without Trenton knowing it. I had packed up most of my things.

Chapter 11
FOR THE SAKE OF THE CHILDREN

It was a cold February night when he came home drunk and ready to fight. I didn't raise my voice nor did I mention my disgust for his behavior. He had a passion mark on his neck and still had the smell of sex on him, but I didn't say a word. I simply sent him to the store to buy more liquor. And he was happy to go. When he left, I called my brother in law and told him to bring his truck around the back. In a matter of minutes, I had moved everything out of the house that I wanted. All the way to my new house, my brother in law kept saying, "girl you are crazy, what are you going to do when he finds you?" "I don't know. I will cross that bridge when I get to it. All I knew now was that I had to get out of that house and away from him for my sanity and for the sake of my children. I did not want to bring another child into the world with the abuse that I was living in. it wasn't fair to my son and it wasn't fair to the baby I was now carrying in my womb. I wanted my life back. I wanted to live a "normal" life. I sat on the passenger's side of the truck with my son in my arms. I didn't look back once. I didn't think about what he could do to me if he caught me. I knew in my heart of hearts that this life was not what God intended for me. I knew deep down he had better things for my life.

My life was calm for a while. I raised my child, went to my appointments, and stayed prayed up. I didn't go back to church but I listened to the Heaven 600 every single morning. When I got up in the morning, I turned it on and let the songs minister to me. I would sing along while I cleaned the house. My son would sing along with me.

Our favorite song was Jesus Will Work It Out. I would sing that song at the top of my lungs. At those times, I missed my church the most. Singing on the choir and feeling the spirit.

Those were also the time I would talk to the Lord. I would tell him how I was feeling that day, or what I did that day, or what I was going to do. I felt that He was listening to me. I often talked to him about Reggie, asking him to keep a hedge around Reggie, bring him back home safely, and if in fact he was already home to please allow him to forgive me. I wasn't working and the money was tight God always found a way to for me. I felt so happy and at peace. My son was growing and he was a sweetheart. He would come in the room, lie down next to me, and rub my stomach. "Mommy, is my little sister in there?" "Yes Darius". "When is she coming out?" "When she is ready, I guess Darius". "I love you mommy". "I love you too Darius". He lie down beside me and fell off to sleep. I wished that Trenton could see how beautiful his son was and how beautiful life could be if he just stopped drinking all the time, but I knew there was nothing I could do about that. I got down on my knees and thanked God for all the things He had done for me and how He always found a way for me to get the bills paid and I always had food on the table. I kissed my baby goodnight and fell off to sleep.

I was still human and I still missed Trenton in a strange sort of way. I missed the companionship what little we did have. There were some good times. I prayed constantly for him. I wanted him to stop drinking. I prayed that he would. We had been together for a long time and it was hard not to still feel love for him. He was an abusive man and I knew that, but I still forgave him. I just felt that it was the right thing to do. I knew he was fighting something much bigger than he was and I knew he was losing. Still I loved him and I missed him. The night times were the hardest time for me. I couldn't sleep and the pregnancy was not going well. I had more problems than I did with my son. I wasn't gaining weight and the baby was not moving like it should. I was eight months pregnant but I looked like I was six months. However, I pressed on because I knew that the Lord was not going to take my baby away from me. I sat in the doctor' office reading a pamphlet. "Ms. Thomas, are you taking your vitamins and iron pills?" "Yes I am, why?" I looked at the nurse suspiciously. "I don't think you are taking them right, you haven't gained any more weight?" "Well, I don't really care what you think, I am taking my medicine like I was instructed to take them, and I can't help if I don't have an appetite". "It's no need to get upset Ms. Thomas, we just want what's best for the baby". I stood up. "And who is "we". "The doctor and I". "Well, all you are suppose to do is make sure this baby is delivered on the day it is supposed to be, not what's best for her or him, what's best for my baby, is what I say, not what you say!". I grabbed my bag and left. "Please don't leave like that Ms. Thomas, I didn't mean anything about it, I just think you have a lot of stuff going on and you may need to talk to someone about it". "Go to hell, when I'll need somebody to talk to, I find somebody to talk to, and I don't need you to tell me I need somebody to talk to!" I snatched my prescription out of her hand and stormed out of the clinic. I was mad as hell. Who in the hell did she think she was, talking to me like that!" I wobbled my way down to the elevators and down the stairs out to the bus stop. By the time I reached my destination, I was out of breath and still pissed off. However, I calmed down before I got home, I didn't want Darius to think something was wrong with the baby.

John 14:1-3 let not your heart be troubled ye believe in God, believe also in me. In my Father's house are many mansions, if it were not so, I would have told you. I go to prepare a place for you. And if I go to prepare a place for you, I will come again, and receive you unto myself, that where I am, you will be also. Those words kept me sane in "times such as these". I knew that god would take care of me. I knew that his spirit dwelled within me. I knew that He loved me.

I started going out of the house more. I was in that house for months trying not to let anyone see me. I didn't know who he knew and I don't want anyone to tell him if they saw me. However, I was tired of staying in the house. I needed to get out; I took my grocery car and walked to the shopping center. It was a nice day. The sun was shining and it wasn't hot, just nice and warm. I could feel the sun on my back as I stood on the corner waiting for the light to change. It was indeed a beautiful day. I felt like I was being released from prison. I hummed. It wasn't too crowded and I got finished early. I pulled my cart behind me. I was wobbling down the sidewalk when she walked toward me.

My heart jumped. I tried to keep my head down, maybe she wouldn't recognize me if I kept my head down. However, she did. "How are you Sabrina?" I smiled a little. "I'm fine" "Where is the baby?" "With my sister". I kept walking but where was I going to go. I didn't want her to know where I lived so I slowed down. "You know my brothers' been looking for you". "Really?" "Yes, I think it's pretty dirty how you just left him there in that empty house". "I did what I had to do, and I didn't leave the apartment empty, I left things there for him". "It wasn't' right Sabrina". "If you think your brother is so great, then why don't you go and live with him, let him use you for a punching bag Cynthia, let him beat you until you pass out, I cannot take it anymore, you don't know the hell I've lived in with your brother". My brother loves you Sabrina". I pulled my hair back so she could see the stitches on my forehead and then I pulled my shirt up in the back so she could see the marks from his teeth. "You call this love, look at me". This mark here is because his little girlfriend wouldn't give him any head, and this one here on my arm, was when I didn't reach a climax when he wanted me to." Don't tell me about love Cynthia, this is not love!". "You pulled a knife on my brother Sabrina that wasn't right". Your brother hit me in the face with a telephone receiver for no reason other than he thought he could. I grabbed the knife to protect myself and look what I got". I showed her my stitches in my hand. "Look, I know you love your brother, he is your brother and I love him too but at some point in my life I have to stop being a victim, I have to survive. I have a baby and one on the way, your brother has done nothing but stressed me out I can't live like that anymore". I can't live like that anymore Cynthia, I just can't. "I'm sure he didn't mean to hurt you Sabrina, he just gets like that when he is drinking and he hasn't been drinking lately". "Let me say this to you Cynthia, your brother is sick, he needs help serious help. You brother has beat me, stabbed me, broken my ribs, I have me so many black eyes, I can't even count. He has raped me and sodomized me. I don't need that in my life. I want to be in normal, sane relationship". "He really misses you". "Yes I'm sure he does, but I am not ready to be with your brother right now, I need to get me together, I have to stay strong and healthy for these children, I can't be healthy if your brother is constantly beating me". She didn't say anything. "Look, I've got to go". I walked slowly towards my sister's house because I didn't know if she was going to follow me or not. I didn't know if she lived in the complex or not but I knew she must have been close if she was doing laundry. I noticed the laundry bag before I noticed her . I used to really like Cynthia when I first met her but then I found out that Trenton was taking all of his girlfriends to her house when he wanted to have sex with them and she was cool with that.. After that, I stop dealing with her all together. The only reason I was dealing with her at all because she loved Darius.

It was hard to sleep that night but I did. I called a friend of mine and told him that I thought that he may know where I lived at. He assured me that nothing was going to happen to me and just relax.

II Corinthians 2:11 Lest Satan should get an advantage of us; for we are not ignorant to his devices.

But I was ignorant to his devices. It wasn't long before Trenton did find me. I was on the bus one evening. I got off at my stop and there he was. "How are you?". I couldn't speak

"You k know I miss you". I still didn't speak. "I'm sorry for everything I did, please forgive me". I tried to walk past him. "I know you're mad with me, but I am sorry and I promise you I won't hurt you again". I walked away. "Say something". "I'm not mad, I just want to be by myself". "Why?". "Because Trenton, you don't want to act right". "I haven't had a drink in over 3 months". I looked at him. He did look sober and he looked refreshed. "I'm happy for you". I did it for you". "You should have done it for yourself". "I mean I did it for me too, but for the most part, I did it for our family. You know I want our family to be together. We have been together for a long time and I know that we can work this out, that's what families do. Look at all we been through and still we are at least able to talk.". I didn't move from the bus stop. "Why don't you let me walk you home so we can talk?" "I don't think so, not right now". "Okay, I understand". He rubbed my stomach. "I love you". I nodded my head. I didn't want to be with him but I did want our children to have a father, but I wouldn't give in. He walked away. I tried to see where he was going but he walked across the street and got into a car. I knew it would only be a matter of time before he found me. I didn't want to move again. I liked my apartment and I was comfortable. The rent was reasonable and I was able to afford it without his money. After I saw the car turn onto the beltway, I went to my house.

Isaiah 43:1-2 The Lord created you. He formed you. Do not be afraid, I will set you free. I will send for you by name. You belong to me. You will pass through deep waters but I will be with you. You will pass through the rivers but their waters will not sweep over you. You will walk through fire, but you will not be burned. The flames will not harm you. I am the Lord your God. I am the Holy One of Israel. I am the one who saves you. One of the wonderful things about God , is that He never leaves you or forsakes you. We leave him.

Chapter 12
RETURNING TO EGYPT

I left God again. I wanted my family to work. After a few weeks of courting, wining and dining me, we were a family again. My son was happy and I was happy. He was working and coming right home and not drinking. He cooked and cleaned the house and took care of me. **II Corinthians 2:11.....**We got up early that day and decided to go shopping. I had saved some money for the baby and wanted undershirts and sleeps and things like that. After shopping, we went to get his check. We got off the bus in front of his job. I knew that something was wrong the minute he came back. His face was all screwed up in a look that could not be described. I was glad that we left my son at home with my sister. "That bastard he didn't pay me for two days". "Did you ask him why?"?" He said that he forgot about it and that he would pay me on Monday". "Well don't worry about it; you can pick it up then". He didn't say anything. We waited for the bus and headed home. When we got on the bus, he was still pissed off. I didn't say anything I knew that this was not going to be a good day and my heart was beating and I was starting to feel uneasy, it was as if my spirit was warning me of impending danger. I couldn't stop the feeling so I just started praying. I must have been crazy to think that this relationship was going to work.. Trenton was simply not going to stop drinking and he was not going to be the man that I wanted and needed him to be. I should have known that from the beginning, but I was naïve to think that he was strong enough to stop this thing on his own. All these thoughts were running through my head. I was almost

8 months pregnant and I was big and I just wanted somebody to love me for a change, I wasn't going to find anyone with my stomach in my face so I just settled and went back to Trenton. He was familiar to me. I didn't invest enough time in getting myself straight. My thoughts were interrupted by Trenton's yelling. "What you hell are you looking at man!" the young man looked at him. "You talking to me Slim?" "Who you think I'm talkin' to?" "Yo, I don't know you man!" His girlfriend and I both looked at each other. "Y'all stop it". She said. "He talkin' greasy to me, I don't even know that fool man!" Trenton jumped up and pulled the guy out of his seat and the fight was on. It was a mess, I was trying to break it up, the other girl was trying to break it up but it was no use, they were too strong for both of us.

The bus driver called the police and we were all thrown off the bus. I wanted to slap Trenton. All of this was uncalled for and I let him know it. "Why would you pick a fight with that man, he didn't say a damn thing to you Trenton?" "Oh you taking up for that fool, what you sexing' him or sumtin?" "Please boy, you are not making sense, look at me". "Boy! Who the hell you callin a boy?" I just looked at him. "You callin me a boy!" I just walked away, I didn't realize it until then that he was high, but it was not an alcohol high, it was more than that, I kept walking towards home, we weren't that far away from our complex. I wanted to get away from him....**The enemy comes to destroy, steal and kill!**

I could hear him yelling behind me, calling me all kinds of names and cursing. I kept walking, I wasn't moving too fast but fast enough to stay ahead of him. I thought if I could make it home then I could lock him out until he cooled off. I was tired and it was warm out, which made it hot to me. I had to go to the bathroom. I stood on the sidewalk and waited for the light to change. All I heard was "Miss watch out!" When I turned my head, I saw the grocery cart coming straight at me. I moved to late. It crashed into me and forced me into the street. I heard the cars screeching and slamming on brakes and into one another. **Ye though I walk through the valley of the shadow of death, I will fear no evil, for you are with me, your rod and your staff, they comfort me...when the wicked even my enemies and my foes, came up to eat my flesh they stumbled and fell......**the car missed me by a few inches. The ambulance attendant told me later. He came up to me, kicked me in the side, and snatched my purse with my keys and my money. I could feel the water streaming down my leg, I thought my water broke. I laid there because I couldn't move, people were yelling for me not to move. Someone stayed with me and talked to me while I waited for the ambulance. "Did my water break?" "I don't know miss, your pants are wet, though". "I can't have my baby out here on the street like this". "Don't worry miss, the ambulance is coming". "Am I bleeding?" "Your head, leg and elbow are bleeding but not a lot, miss please don't talk anymore, wait for the ambulance to come and help you". He kept rubbing my face and I saw tears form in his eyes. The police and ambulance came at the same time; they were very nice to me and took their time with me. I answered their questions and allowed them to take me to the hospital.

After a few hours in the hospital for observation, I was allowed to go home, but I think I was still in shock. I couldn't believe that this man whose child I was carrying would try to harm me. The nurse at the hospital was nice enough to call my family. I had a lot of cuts and bruises but the baby was not harmed. I had a terrible headache and the doctor said it was from a concussion from banging my head on the pavement. My knees were scraped and my elbows were bruised. Physically, I was fine but mentally I had snapped. I wanted to kill him and that is exactly what I was going to do, the first chance I got. Nothing mattered anymore, he tried to kill my unborn child and me and he was going to pay for it. I could hear voices in my head....*where is your god now....where was he when he threw that cart into your stomach...why would your god let him beat you like that, destroy you like that....when he fractured your ribs...where was he...kill him...kill him....take away the pain...he cannot hurt you if you kill him......*Jesus said "what is your name...my name is Legion...for there are many of us".......

After my girlfriend left, I took my son back to my sister's house. I asked her if he could stay until tomorrow. She said it was fine. I guess she felt sorry for me. I was beat up and bruised and I was so sore that I felt like I did ten rounds with Sugar Ray or Mike Tyson. After dropping my son off, I walked back to my house and went in the kitchen. I knew he would be back he had nowhere else to go. I put on a pot of water and waited for it to boil. After I boiled, I put in a ½ bottle of bleach. After I did that, I let it sit on the stove. I went into the bedroom and unscrewed the light bulb. I went into the bathroom and did the same thing. I took the light out of the hallway. I took the light out of the lamps in the living room and finally unscrewed the one in the kitchen. All the light I had was the one from the refrigerator. I was humming a song, I don't remember which one but I was humming all the while. I believe I was trying to drown out the voices in my head. I sat in the kitchenette with the pan of hot water and bleach and broom. I waited for what seemed like hours. It had become dark outside. I knew he wouldn't come back while it was still light because the police were still looking for him. Soon it was dark....my legs were hurting, my back was bothering me but when I heard the key in the door, I stopped feeling anything. I could hear my heart beat and I hoped that he didn't hear it too. I got up and stood on the side of the refrigerator with the broom. I made sure the pot of bleach and hot water was close to me and it was still hot. I could hear him flicking the light switch. "Damn lights...always blowin' out". He yelled my name out but I didn't breathe...."where the hell is that dumb bitch?" He walked into the hallway and tried after... light...nothing...he yelled my name again. I still did not move. He walked into the bedroom but tried the switch, still no light. I could hear him mumbling as he ran into Darius' big wheel. He stumbled into the bathroom. I could hear him going to the bathroom and clearly missing the toilet. The sound echoed through the apartment. He finally came into the living room. "That dumb ass bitch didn't pay the light bill, dumb ass," his voice slurred. Drunk no doubt. I could hear him laugh..."I guess she can't since I got all the gotdamn money! I had all the gotdamn money, dat shit gone now!" He walked towards the kitchenette. "Kill him! I could hear the voices in my head. He opened the refrigerator door when I saw him; I hit him with the broom. I kept hitting him until the broom broke. He fell into the floor. When he tried to get up, I ran to the stove and grabbed the pot of hot water and bleach. When he reached me, I threw it in his face. He let out a scream that was equivalent to gut wrenching. "I can't see, I can't see!" "Good you bastard, you can't hit what you can't see!" I yelled back. "You will never hurt me again, never!" I hit him again. He was waling his hands. He fell inside the living room table and it broke into pieces along with the broom handle that I was hitting him with. I was now hitting him with my fists. He crawled to the front door and opened the door. I could see from the light at the lamppost. There was blood everywhere. He ran down the hill. I closed the door. I started humming again. I screwed all the lights back in. I cleaned the house and washed the blood off the floor. I was still humming when the police knocked at my door. I went to the door and was facing a female officer. "Mam, can we talk to you?" "Come on in officer". There was a male officer behind her. I could hear voices…you going to jail, you will die in jail, why are you so stupid, now he wins again…I shook my head to try to make the voices stop. "Are you alright?" the female officer asked. "I'm fine, what can I do for you?" Is there anyone else her with you?" "No" "You mind if we look around?" "No". I could smell the bleach. "Miss there is a young man outside who said you tried to kill him". "Are you asking me or telling me?" I asked. "Are you sure you are alright miss?" "I'm fine". "You have blood on your shirt". I looked down and his blood was on my shirt.' It's not mine". "Can you tell us what happened?" I gave them the whole humiliating story. I told them how he had been beating me for years. How he held me in locked in my room for days without letting me go out except to go to the bathroom. How he allowed me out of the room only to feed the baby and make him dinner. How he raped me repeatedly for days when I didn't want it. I told them how he tried to kill me just hours before. They took both of us away. He went to the hospital and I went to the police precinct. They questioned me and sent me home.

Chapter 13
NEW BEGINNINGS

On a beautiful March day, I had my daughter China, I named her China, because she was rare and beautiful and delicate like China. She was so pretty and she had eyes that were black as coal. Her hair was curly and thick… She was healthy and beautiful. I looked at her and immediately thought of Reggie, I really did not want to think about him but I did. I had not seen him in so long, I thought maybe he forgot about the argument and me we had the last time we saw one another. I didn't have many visitors in the hospital, so many of my friends were gone. I thought of calling them but I decided against it, I really didn't want to be bothered with anyone. I was allowed to see my son for a while but I asked my mother to take him home. Trenton was nowhere to be found, I didn't know if he had made bail or was still in jail. It really didn't matter to me. I watched China in her crib, sleeping and looking so beautiful. I dozed off but was awaken when Wendy tapped me on the shoulder. "Hey Sabrina". "Hey yourself". "I hope you don't mind me being here". "It's all good, I was just dozing". "I know you and me had our stuff, but I had to come and see you". "Don't worry about it". "I heard what happened to you and I am so sorry". "Don't worry about it Wendy, I don't want to talk about that anyway". She walked over to the crib. "She is so cute Sabrina". "I think so too". "Who do you think she looks like Sabrina". I just looked at her. "Why would you ask me something like that Wendy?" "I'm just saying she is so pretty and her eyes are so black:" "okay". She just waved her hand at me at picked the baby up. She was pretty but she never had any kind of expression on her face, and never seemed to cry. The nurse came in to take her. I gave her a kiss, hug, and gave her to the nurse. "Will you bring her back?" "Sure honey". After she was gone, Wendy looked at me. "What?" "Nothing, I have something to tell you bur I don't want you to get upset". "Now what, what could possibly go wrong now, I mean I don't know if Trenton is in jail or he is going to come up here and beat the hell outta me again, I have no food in my house, I'm stuck in this damn hospital for another few days and I have a fever, so what else could go wrong?". "Reggie is home from the service". I was stunned. "What, when did he come home?" He's been home for a while now." "How long Wendy, how long has he been home and when in the hell were you going to tell me?'. "He asked me not to tell you". "You talked to him?" "Yes I did, he knows what happened to you, and what Trenton did to you". "How?" "I told him, he came home last month and he came by, we talked for a while and when he asked about you, "Are you sleeping with Reggie, for real, are you giving it up to him?" "No, you know me and Reggie been friends forever". "I know but I think you are sleeping with him, you two are too damn close". "Brina, I like Reggie, that's true, but he is like a brother to me, you know that". "Naw I don't know that". "Look, Reggie was a friend of Scooter's before he was killed and we have been close every since".

I had forgotten that. Wendy was in love with this guy named Scooter and they were inseparable until Scooter was hooked on heroin. Wendy stuck by him no matter what. She didn't care that he was stealing from her, or bringing her back STD's or stealing her car so he could hack for drug money, she loved Scooter from the heart. Reggie and Scooter were tight but Reggie stop hanging with him when he starting getting high. He would give Scooter money from time to time but he wouldn't hang out with him because everybody knew Scooter was always in trouble. The day Scooter was killed; Reggie had just dropped him off at the bar. According to the story, Scooter owed money to a local drug dealer but did not pay up fast enough and he shot Scooter in the face right in front of the bar.

I am sorry Wendy, I forgot. "It okay Sabrina, anyway, I told Reggie. He wanted to know if you had the baby yet and where you were going to have the baby and I told him". "Why would you do that Wendy?" "Because he wants to see her, he wants to know if she is his baby or not". "Well, she's not and I don't appreciate you telling him anything about me or my baby". "Why are you mad Sabrina, you know how you feel about him, you know how you felt about him all this time and you didn't do anything about it, you just let him go without telling him and not even trying to reach him to explain things to him". "I didn't have anything to explain to him Wendy; he treated me like I was a whore or something, asking me how many men I was sleeping with". "He was hurt Sabrina, what did you expect him to do?" "I don't know what I expected but not that, it took me almost 2 years to sleep with him, why in the world would he think I was sleeping around like that?" "I don't know but you need to call him". "I'm not calling him and you bet not tell him that I'm here". "Too late, I already did that, but he promised me he wasn't coming up here". I threw my pillow at her. "How could you do that?" "Don't worry about it, he's not coming up here, he's only here for the weekend and then he has to go back to the base". "You are lying and I know you are". "No for real, he is leaving this weekend". I wouldn't talk to her for the rest of the visit so she left and went to visit the nursery.

My heart was beating and I was so afraid that he would come to the hospital and question me. I didn't realize how much I cared about him until we had that argument outside the apartment, I had cried so much since then that I was not able to really sleep. Knowing that Trenton was out on bail and now Reggie was home, I was a wreck. I didn't get any better in the hospital either. I had a bad infection and I was not able to go home. Then another bomb dropped. It was about two in the morning when my phone rang. I thought it strange that the phone would ring especially since I thought they turned them off at a certain time. "Hello". "Hello, may I speak with Ms. Thomas?" "This is Ms. Thomas" "Mam, this is Mr. Jenkins and I am calling from the pre-release center at Central Booking and Intake and I have Mr. Trenton." Before you finish, I am in the hospital, and I just had a baby and I don't really care that you have him there with you, I don't have anything good to say about him, if you want my opinion, I think he needs some help, Alcoholics Anonymous or something, please do not call me again". "I'm sorry to bother you miss, he didn't tell me you were in the hospital, and congratulations". I hung up the phone. The nurse came in to exam me repeatedly; I had to be put on IV meds because the infection was not clearing up.

The next day I spent most of the day with China and we talked and smiled at each other. She didn't cry at all and I thought something was wrong with her but the nurse said she was fine. Soon after that, another woman came into my room. "Ms. Thomas, my name is Ms. Uckert from the Department of Social Services; I wanted to talk to you about your children". "What about my children?" "We understand that you have had some problems at home with your children's father". "And?" "Now don't get upset Ms. Thomas, I just want to talk to you about options". "What options?" She sat down on the side of my bed. "Well, we were thinking that maybe you want to have someone else take care of your children until you are able to get in a stable environment". "You are out of your damn mind if you or anybody thinks they are going to take my children from me!" My head started hurting and I was panicking. I remembered that nurse at the clinic and now it all came together, why she was saying all that she was saying to me. "Give me my daughter right now". "She is being fed by the nurses right now". "I said bring me my baby or I will start hurting somebody up in here". I started pressing the button for the nurse. "I want my daughter right now!" I started getting out of the bed, the pain was unbearable but when it comes to your children, none of that matter. I made it down to the nursery and there was my baby, being fed by some woman, I didn't know if she was a nurse or not because she didn't' have on a uniform, I ran in the nursery and grabbed my baby out of her hands. "I'll take her now". She just looked at me and looked at the woman who followed me to the nursery. She nodded her head and she handed my baby to me. I would not let her out of my sight; I made them bring me her bottles and everything to my room. I was scared to leave her alone because I thought they were going to steal her and tell me something happened to her. I was a wreck and it didn't' help that I was still sick as a dog. Finally, they gave me something to sleep and promised that they would not let anyone take her away. I finally drifted off to sleep.

It was late when I woke up, sometime in the evening; it wasn't too late because people were still visiting. I looked around and saw the nurse putting a diaper on my daughter. "Well hello sleepy head". "What time is it?" It's just about eight". "How is she?" "She is fine, she has been fed, burped and dried, she is sleeping now". "Can I hold her?" "Of course you can sweetie". She handed her to me. "You know she kind of looks like her father". What did you say?" I said she kind of looks like her father". My heart skipped a beat. "When did you see her father?" "He just left about twenty minutes ago". "What did he look like?" She looked at me as if I had two heads. "Excuse me?" "I said what did he look like?" "He was tall, dark with brown eyes and dark brown hair, with a uniform on". I couldn't breath. "Are you okay Sabrina?" I shook my head yes. I held my baby tighter. It had to be Reggie, it had to be, Trenton was still in jail after the stunt he pulled at the hospital, coming up here drunk after he got out on bail, they hauled his ass right back to jail after he came to the floor drunk. "Can you repeat that for me miss"?

"Sabrina are you alright?""Yes, can you tell me what he said if he said anything"? "He said that he was only in town for the weekend and he didn't want to bother you but he wanted to see the baby before he went back. I asked him if he wanted to see you and he said he didn't want to bother you. I told him that you probably wouldn't mind since you didn't have any visitors today but he declined anyway." I didn't say anything, I couldn't' believe that he came by to see the baby; he said it wasn't his baby and I believed that she was not. I didn't even let it enter my mind after that night. Although I thought that was one of the reasons that Trenton had beaten me the way he did when we first got back together. He was drinking and talking out of his head and told me that he knew I was lying about who the father is and that he would kill me when he found out. I didn't even think about it until just that moment.

I went home with my new baby and my new life. Trenton was in jail and he was not coming back into my life. It was over for good. I tried to make it work for so long but it wasn't meant to be. I needed to get my life back together. I needed to go back to basics. My life was a real mess, but it was my time to pull it back together. I didn't dwell on Reggie either. He didn't come by the house, he didn't call me either, and I chalked it up to him just making sure she wasn't his and I guess I could respect that. He had a need to know. We did sleep together the same time that Trenton raped me. I loved Reggie truly loved him but it hurt because he did not want me, and I hurt because he was the type of man I wanted in my life but simply was not ready for. I had too much baggage and not enough time to heal. It seemed like my life was always filled with something. I couldn't' stand the silence. I needed the noise to drown out all the pain I was feeling deep down. I tried to encourage myself. I read the bible and stayed in prayer. It hurt but this time I was going to go through all the pain I needed to go through to get past it. It seemed that every time the pain became unbearable I would turn back so that I didn't have to deal with it, but I realized that if I truly wanted to get over Trenton and the pain in my life, that I would have to go through it. I was determined to change my life. I was determined to make my life worthwhile, if not for me for my children.

Chapter 14
GETTING BACK TO BASICS

My life did a 360-degree turn. I was living by myself or without a man at least. I started throwing parties for my girls and their men and it was a good time to be had. I was single and I enjoyed it. I needed to get back to basics. I needed to find time for me and to love me again. It had been a long time since I even smiled, and to be around my friends. I loved throwing parties for my friends; everyone always had a good time. I still hadn't gotten back in church and the Lord was tugging at my heart. I continued to pray daily and listen to the radio preachers. I was not having sex and that alone made me feel good inside. I was not worrying about pleasing anyone but me now. It felt good to lie in my bed next to nothing but my pillows. It felt good to look in the mirror and like what I saw. It felt good to live again. It had been a long time since I had really laughed aloud and enjoyed myself. The children were growing and happy. There were no more nightmares and outbursts from my son. I started hanging out with my girlfriends that I had met in my mother's neighborhood. It was good to know that they still cared about me. We always called one another and looked out for one another. We promised each other that we would not let a day go by without touching base with each other to make sure each one of us were alright. I even heard from Angie, who was now living in California with her parents. She sent a letter to my mother's house. It was so good to hear from her. She was doing well; she was pregnant and getting married. She was still sober and her boyfriend was according to her "the finest black ass man you ever wanted to meet". Her parents were happy for her and she was happy they were happy. She was not going to have a big wedding, something small and intimate but she would send me pictures. I sat down and took my time to write her back, I wanted to tell her so much but the words in my head didn't surface, only the words from my heart.

I sent her pictures of the children and told her I was doing fine. I told her that Trenton and I were done for good and that he was in jail. I also told her that Reggie and I were no longer friends and I hadn't heard from him but it was cool. I thanked her for the money that she sent me. It was good to hear from Angie, I missed her a lot, she was a cool white chick and I would never forget her.

I had no idea how much the world had changed while I was in my fog. I had missed so much that I felt like I was in prison and just came home. Gina laughed at me when I asked her what she was listening to. "Girl, where in the hell have you been, that's the Sugar Hill Gang girl, with Rappers' Delight! ". She started singing the hook to the song, I just laughed at her. "I tell you Sabrina, this stuff here girl, is going to change the game, you watch what I tell you". "It's nothing but a bunch of guys talking over music". "No girl, its fine ass men rapping". "Yea, about chicken tasting like wood! ". We both laughed. But she wouldn't turn it off. We listen to music the rest of the day.

Things seemed bigger than they were. I was twenty-one years old and I had made up my mind that I would not talk to any more guys my age. I felt they were immature and unable to deal with a woman with two small children. I never lied about my age or my children. Not because I wanted a man to take care of them but because I wanted him to understand that they may come and go, but my children were forever. They were not going to come before my children. I also decided that I was ready to move to a two-bedroom townhouse. My apartment was getting smaller since the kids were getting bigger. I gave the children my bedroom and I slept in the living room, except when they stayed with their grandmother or my sister. But just when my life was going in the right direction, things from my past came back to haunt me. I was sitting at my table with Lisa and a few more girlfriends. We were all sitting around drinking beer and cutting up. I was getting ready to throw another party. We invited so many guys we knew that it was going to be more men than women but the women we invited were hot to trot and we knew it. The guys asked us to invite them because they knew they were going to wind up taking them home or to some hotel off Pulaski Highway to get down. I invited a few guys that I used to talk to and a few of them that was still trying to get at me, I invited them because I wanted them to know that there was no hard feelings and I could handle the fact that for the most part we were just bed buddies.

The party was going full blast, it was about eleven at night, the music was live, and the food was good. I had invited these two brothers Antoine and Fendi that I had been with, neither one of them knew that. My girlfriend told me I was crazy for inviting them but I needed to face the guys, they were a part of my life that I was leaving for good. No more crazy sex and all that. Antoine arrived first. "Hey baby, how are you? ". "I'm fine Antoine, what's going on with you. "Nothing much, you heard I got a baby on the way?". "No I didn't congratulations". "Thanks but you know you should be my baby momma". "Boy, stop playing". "I'm serious Sabrina; you know how we got down". "Yes, I know, that's why I always wore a condom with your simple ass". We both laughed. He gave me a hug and put some money in my hand. "This is for your seeds baby, I know you doing it by yo self, I just wanna let you know, that I got love for you and those babies". I looked down and it was about four or five twenties in my hand. "Thanks Antoine". He whispered in my ear. "You know I know about you and my brother too". I looked at him as if he was crazy. "Don't trip; I just wanted you to know that I knew no hard feeling or nothing'". "Who told you that Antoine?" "Don't try to deny it baby, it's good, one question, who was better?" "I'm not telling you that boy". "Why not?" "Cause, it would hurt your bother's feelings". I winked at him. He gave me a hug. "Bout time I beat that punk at something'". We both laughed and he walked away. I shook my head and walked in the other direction. Soon after, Fend walked in, gave me hug and pressed some bills into my hand. "I love you baby, you know that don't you?" Fendi was older than Antoine was and I was hooked on him, I wanted more than to be a bed buddy to him but he wasn't into relationships. "Thanks Fendi". "Look, if you need anything, call me, I got you". "Okay". "If you wanna hit one of the hotels, let me know". I hit him playfully. "No thanks you are too damn addictive for me". He winked and walked towards his brother. I don't think Fendi knew about Antoine but I wasn't trying to wait for him to bring it up, so I turned the music up and started passing out cups of spiked punch.

I knew this would be the last party for a while because I wanted no I needed to rededicate my life and my body to Christ and I needed to face my demons and be done with it. I am so glad that "God loves the backslider". My father's stabbing when I was a little girl truly hurt me; it had me bound for years. The molestation from my brother in law left me no self-worth and no self-esteem. He destroyed my childhood and he took away my innocence. I didn't know how to say no to men, I thought sex was love and I paid a great price for that. For years, I tried to escape. I had been with too many men in my young life and it was all because of the molestation and the inability to know what love truly was. At any rate, things were going well and the party was live. A few times, I needed to put some folks out of my bedroom because they thought it was a hotel room. My girlfriend Candi was so drunk that she passed out on the sofa. My girlfriend Lisa left with one of the people that I knew. I told him to be cool with her and not to leave her at the hotel stranded. He promised me that he would not. My other girlfriends had already made up their minds that they were going to leave with. That left me and my girlfriend Gina. The party thinned out and Gina and I were cleaning up and now listening to the oldies station and singing along with Luther Van dross. It was about two-thirty in the morning; my apartment was just about empty. It was a nice turnout and everybody had a good time. Some more of the guys left me money, just because they knew I had the children to take care of. I did not know that they had planned that part of the party but that's how my girlfriends were, they looked out for me. I guess because so many times they used my apartment to "entertain" their men. And it was cool with me as long as they didn't leave any evidence behind. I was emptying the bottles into the trashcan when I heard a knock on my door. Gina and I both looked at each other. "Did you hear that?" "Yes I think it's the door". I looked out the window and almost lost my breath. "Who is it?"

I opened the door. "Hey Sabrina". "Hey yourself". Gina's eyes got wide, "Oh my God, Reggie, baby, how are you!" She ran up to him and hugged him and kissed him all over his face, he tried to pull her off him. "Be cool Gina". "I'm sorry, it's just good to see you, damn you look good!" "Can I let the damn man in the door please hoe?" She backed away from him. That's when I saw his friend Blue behind him. "Hey Blue, how are you?" "I'm good Sabrina, how are you?" "I'm good, come on in, it's good to see y'all". "We heard it was a party here, but looks like we got her too late". "Y'all just missed everyone but we still have some drinks and food if you want something". "Naw, I'm good, how about you Blue?" He was eyeing Gina, who had on a mini skirt with a top on that showed every single curve of her breast. Gina was a cute girl who wore her hair in a bright blond or something close to that. It was cut nice and professionally but at that time it was a mess because she had been dancing and throwing her hair around. She looked very provocative and Blue was about to lose his mind. "Who's your friend Sabrina?" "Oh I'm sorry, Gina, Blue, Blue Gina". She gave him this look and licked her lips. "Hey, how are you?" "I'm cool how about you?" "Fine now'. I looked at Gina and shook my head. "Behave yourself girl". She laughed. "I am". I was still shook that it was Reggie at the door. "You sure I can't offer you something to drink, I really don't need this liquor in my house". "You got any rum and coke?" "Yes I do". Gina and I went into the kitchen area while Reggie and Blue sat down in the living room. "Girl, he is too damn fine and where in the hell did Reggie get that body from?" "I know, he does look good". Gina looked over at Blue. She started singing this old song, "I think I wanna give the drummer some girl". I started laughing. "You are a hoe". "I just want to jump his bones, I don't want any money from him, I will do him for free girl, and he is fine!" Blue was fine, he was about 6'2 but built like a football player that worked out all the time. He had nice eyes and always looked like he was on his way to a modeling session. We started laughing again. I was laughing because I was nervous I didn't know what in the world Reggie was really doing here but I was going to find out".

Gina and Blue hit it off and he offered to take her to his house. He and Reggie went outside and talked for a few before he came back in the house. We were alone. And my heart was beating out of my chest, I was truly afraid to be alone with him, I didn't trust myself. We sat down on the sofa. "How have you been Sabrina?" "I'm doing okay

Reggie, how about you?" "I'm doing okay. But I want to tell you the truth". "The truth about what?" He moved closer to me. "Brina, I came by tonight because I needed to talk to you". "Okay, talk". "I need to know if she is mine Sabrina, it's killing me inside". "Please Reggie, let's not do this". "Please Sabrina, I can't go on another day like this, I've been going back and forth through my mind, trying to add up days and months and it's all mixed up in my head. I've got to know". "It's not important Reggie". "It is important". "You said that you weren't the father and that's what we agreed to". "Sabrina, I know I said some cruel things to you and I shouldn't have. I was hurt and angry with you, I had to find out through people not you that you were pregnant, that wasn't fair to me and you know that". "I didn't want to stop your dreams Reggie, I didn't want you to think I was trying to trap you'. "Trap me!". "Yes, you were going in the service, I didn't want you to think that I was trying to get your money". "Look at me and tell me if she is my baby". "I can't tell you that Reggie". "Why?" "Not now," "Do you know?" Yes I know, but I don't want to talk about it, not tonight". Her name is China?" "Yes, how did you know that?" "I stopped at the hospital one night and the nurse told me her name". "Why didn't you come and see me?" I didn't want to bother you or upset you, besides, I felt bad about how I talked to you the last night I saw you'. "I didn't mean those things I said Reggie". "Yes you did, but it's cool but don't do this to me Sabrina, please don't do this to me, if she is mine, I have the right to know, and do I have my doubts of course I do, you were living with a man and sexing him on a daily basis, what am I suppose to do, walk around the rest of my life wondering?". "No". I will tell you but not right now". "When!'. "Soon". "That's fair. "Do you need any money, diapers, milk anything?". "Children always need, but I can't ask you to do that". "You didn't ask, I offered". He reached in his pocket, pulled out some twenties, and placed them in my hand. Then he kissed me. I kissed him back, I didn't know how much I missed him until he was here in my arms holding me and kissing me. I thought I was over him, but it was clear to us both that I wasn't. We made love in the living room, the hall way and finally in the bedroom. When we opened our eyes again, it was from the sound of the phone ringing. I reached over and answered it. "Sabrina, are y'all cool". "Yes, why?" "Blue is out of it girl, I put it on him and he is out". I laughed. "You are a true hoe

Gina". "Look ask Reggie is it cool if Blue picks him up a little later on this morning, around six maybe". I nudged Reggie who was out of it too and asked him if he needed to leave. He said no and held me by my waist. "He's cool, see you later". I fell asleep in his arms. When we woke up, it was morning. It was dawn but morning nonetheless. Reggie got up and showered while I fixed him some eggs. God he looked so good walking around the apartment with nothing on but his boxers. I wanted to jump him again, but I knew that he had to leave. We made small talk while we waited for Blue to come back with the car. They showed up just as he was finishing his eggs. Gina was still smiling the same way she was when she left. Blue had a smirk on his face. "Hey girls and boys how are we this fine morning!" We all shook our heads and laughed. Blue called Reggie to the door and whispered something in his ear. I didn't want to know, it was probably about some female. I pulled my robe closer and followed him in the bedroom. "Look, I have to be in Virginia in an hour, I should have been there but, you know what happened. So Blue called my commander and told him that I was on my way, you know I would stay if I could, but I will come back, I promise you". "you don't have to Reggie, you don't' owe me anything". He grabbed my face. "Why do you do that to yourself, treat yourself like you're not worth anything. I didn't come here to sex you Sabrina, I came to talk to you and find out some things I need to know. It was not my intention to do this but it happened and I'm glad it did. You are not a whore Sabrina, you are someone that I care about and very possible the mother of my child, so please don't disrespect yourself like that. I'm giving you an explanation because you deserve one. I will come back as soon as I can". He reached down and kissed me again. I didn't want to let him go but I knew I had to. Not just for the moment but forever.

They left. Blue and Gina exchanged numbers. She talked non-stop about Blue, how fine he was, how good he was in bed, how many times they did it. I just shook my head and kept calling her a hoe. She laughed and waved some money in my face. "Yes I do get paid". I laughed harder. I could not believe that she took money from him. "You really took money from him? ". "I didn't take anything, but he wouldn't take it back, he said he wasn't able to get me something nice so he gave me the money to buy something sexy, so he can see me in it later on tonight!!". She was screaming. "Girl, he gonna turn this hooka into a housewife! ". I laughed. You are crazy". "For real, he just wants me to get something nice, he said he really likes me Brina'. "I've known Blue a long time, he is a good guy". "I think so too". "Are you really going to see him again? ". "Yes, I want to spend some with him with my clothes on! ". She laughed again. I knew they would see each other again. Reggie and I were another story.

Chapter *14*
GOTTA LET HIM GO

Over the past few months, I had received so many collect calls from Trenton that I finally got my number changed. I started seriously looking for a two-bedroom townhouse for me and my children. I couldn't stay there anymore. Too many memories and after Reggie, I had to get out of there, I couldn't' stand to sleep in my bed, knowing that he was in it and wasn't anymore. He did come back like he said and we made love again, this went on for several weeks. I couldn't get enough of him. I knew that I said I wasn't going to sleep with anyone else, but Reggie was a drug to me, every time I saw him, I wanted him. As much as I tried to have a civil conversation about the Reserves, the children, life, we would still wind up in bed like dogs in heat. I knew I had to let him go but I couldn't, I tried over and over again, and when I told him not to come back, he would kiss me and beg me to let him see me one more time. I couldn't say no to him. The last time I saw him, I had to put a stop to the madness and beside, I needed to give him some more news. "Reggie, when are you going away? ". "In about a week or two, why? ". "I just wanted to know. I have to tell you something and I don't want you to be upset". "I know you want this to end Sabrina and I am trying to stay away from you, but it's hard". "I know but that's not what I needed to talk to you about". He sat down on the bed. "What's up? '. Please don't be mad with me Reggie". "Brina, I could never be mad with you". "I know about your girlfriend". He looked stunned. "What? ". "I know about your girlfriend and it's cool, I just wanted to let you know that I know about her and I can't see you anymore.

When I didn't know, it was cool, but now that I do, I have to move out of the picture". "What? ". I can't do this knowing what I am doing to another woman, it's not cool Reggie". 'We are friends Brina, that's all". "I heard you tell her that you loved her Reggie". He put his head down. "It's cool, honest, but I have to tell you one more thing". He looked at me with those eyes. "I'm pregnant". 'Huh? ". "I know, I didn't mean for this to happen". "Are you shitting me? ". "No, I wouldn't do that, not after our history". 'When did you find out? ". I knew for a while, ". "How many months? ". 'Two". "What do you want to do? ". 'I don't know, but don't worry, I will handle this, please don't be mad at me". He hugged me. "I'm not mad Brina, I sexed you raw, so I should expect whatever happens". "I still have to stop this with you Reggie, at least until you make up your mind, who you want to be with". "Give me some time? ". I shook my head yes. I was hurt, I wanted him to say I don't need time, but I knew I was fooling myself to think that. I also knew I wouldn't see him anymore after that night.

Two weeks later, I miscarried. I called Reggie from the hospital and told him that I miscarried. He cried with me but I know deep down he was relieved. I told him not to come back. He tried to convince me that he still wanted me, but I held my ground. He was disappointed but I couldn't' do it anymore, I was falling hard in love with him and I knew he didn't feel the same way. I felt like he thought he was obligated to sex me, not because he wanted to. It was hard to say good-bye to him but I knew I had too. I never did tell him if he was the father or not. I didn't plan on ever revealing that to anyone.

Chapter 15
WHAT GOD HAS JOINED TOGETHER…?

It was the early 80's, both China and Darius were in school and I was living in my two-bedroom townhouse and working as a Medicine Tech a nursing home. I had rededicated my life to Christ, just like I said I would. I was going to church and bible study. I was now twenty-four years old and married. I married a man that my girlfriend Tanya introduced me to. His name was Barry. He worked at the warehouse down the street from where Tanya and I worked, but Tanya knew him since he was a teenager. We dated for nine months, and when he asked for sex, I asked for a ring. He happily obliged and we were married three months after that. . I fell in love hard with that man, the kind of love where you lose yourself just to be all you can be to someone else. I was truly in love with him. I believed in him and he believed in me. But I lost myself to be with him. I didn't know that then, but I did. He was a good provider at first but after I became pregnant, I found out what type of man he was. I married a whore, plain and simple. He could never equate his manhood with anything else but his manhood. We weren't married two years before he cheated on me. I was devastated but pregnant so I stayed. He cheated on me with so many women and I kept taking him back, making me believe that he would change. But he didn't. And it really didn't matter to him who he slept with, young, old, older, whatever, if she wore a skirt and smiled at him, he would sex her. He slept with my fifteen-year-old neighbor while I was pregnant with our daughter. It hurt me so badly that I moved out of the bedroom and into the kid's room. I hated him but I didn't want to lose him. I allowed Barry to become my God. And it wasn't until I was married for eight years did I realize that I was going about this marriage all wrong. So instead of watching him, watch everybody else on Sundays, my children and me returned to church. He wouldn't go and it was fine with me, but I became insecure and afraid that Barry would bring another woman into our home, so after a few months, I stopped going.

Time away from the word does something to you. It makes you weak and affords the enemy the opportunity to place doubt into your mind. The word tells us to study to show ourselves approved, but when you do not study the word and surround yourself with unsaved people; it is not long before you are doing ungodly things. God commands us to do certain things when we become Christians. He instructs us not to walk in the counsel of the ungodly. He instructs us to try the spirit by the spirit. There are many things that we should do to continue our relationship with God. But if we do not, our relationship will become stale and the power that we are given because he died for us is quickened. Not to say that it is gone, but quickened. It is like a new relationship. When you meet that man or woman for the first time, you want to spend time with him/her so that your relationship will become strong. You want to maintain a conversation and fellowship with him/her so that your relationship can become stronger. That's how it is with God. He wants you to maintain a fellowship with Him so the relationship can become stronger. But since I had stopped going to church, my relationship weakened. Then things around me became not of God. I accepted people coming in my home drinking, cursing, and fighting one another. I again, welcomed the wrong spirit.

My marriage was falling apart at the seams and my husband was unfaithful at least twice that I knew of for sure. . His best friend had confided me that that he had cheated on me and that killed my spirit for my marriage. "I wasn't going to tell you anything Sabrina, but I don't think its right that Barry slept with that girl". "Why are you snitching on him, he is suppose to be your friend? ". "You are my friend too; I told him that I was going to tell you, if he didn't". "I am gonna kill that bastard! " Sabrina, try and talk to him, see if he will tell you the truth". "No, he is only going to lie, like he always does". I hung up the phone and waited for Barry to come home. But not before I confronted the girl that he slept with and she confirmed it, said that they slept together in my bed.

Barry sat in the car outside the bar with one of his women. "I got to go home; I can't keep living like this". Shelly rubbed his leg. "Why are you still with her, you know you don't love her". "Don't talk to me about my wife okay?" "I'm just saying Barry, if you love her so much, why are you here with me?" "Because I can be, that's why!" "Whachu mean by that?" "Girl, you knew from the door what this was all about; I ain't leaving my wife for somebody like you!" She pushed him. "Whachu mean somebody like me Barry, I know you ain't calling me no hoe". Barry looked at her and laughed. "Git the hell outta my car!" He pushed the door open and pushed her out on the sidewalk. Shelly tried to break her fall but fell right on her butt". She scrambled to her feet, but Barry drove off. "I"ma call yo wife and tell her everything you bastard!"

Barry turned up the sound on the radio and drove towards home. "What in the hell am I doing, why can't I stop this shit?" He stopped at the red light and the tears rolled down his face. For the first time, he felt bad for cheating on Sabrina. He gripped the steering wheel tighter. "God forgive me!" The light turned green but Barry couldn't move. He heard the horns behind him, but he couldn't move. People started driving around him and cursing at him, but Barry stood at the light with tears streaming down his face. He slowly went through the light, anticipating how he was going to apologize to Sabrina. He drove around for hours before he finally ended up in front of the door. All the lights were out, except for the light under the stove. He sat in the car long enough to light a cigarette. He spoke to a few neighbors that were sitting on their porches and put the key in the door. He could still smell the aroma from dinner. He looked in the oven and just like always, there was his plate. He took it out and placed it in the microwave. As he sat down, Sabrina came down the steps. "What are you doing up babe?". "I needed to talk to you". Sabrina looked so beautiful, he thought. She had on a silk robe and slippers and she smelled like fresh vanilla. She sat down across from Barry. She didn't speak and Barry became nervous. He had cheated many times before, but this night seemed different. How many times had he sat across from his wife while she watched him eat and made small talk. How much night more he had with her, he wondered. "Barry is there something you want to tell me? ". "Sabrina, don't start this tonight please". "Just tell me, why? ". "Why what? ". He could see the tears rolling down her soft cheeks and his heart broke for her. "Please don't sit here and act like you don't know what I'm talking about? ". "Sabrina, please, not tonight, I can't have his conversation with you tonight". Sabrina stood up and slapped him across the face. "Do you think I am crazy? Didn't you think I would find out that you brought another woman my home! ". "Barry was stunned. "What, I didn't bring a damn woman in this house? ". "You right about that, she was a damn child Barry! How could you do this to me! I want you out of this house tonight Barry or so help me, I will kill you in your sleep! ". Sabrina threw the glass at him and it broke and cut him across the forehead. He touched the blood and grabbed her by her hands". "Are you crazy woman! ". "I said get the hell out of my house, NOW! ". That woke the kids and the next-door neighbors. Charles banged at the door. Barry tried to let him in but Sabrina grabbed him by his shirt and starting beating on him. "I'ma kill you, you bastard! Barry did not want to hit her so he tried to hold her hands, while opening the door; he knew that he would have to have someone else calm Sabrina down while he got out of there. "Man hold her so I can get out of here". Charles grabbed Sabrina and took her in the living room. "Get offa me, you are dead, do you hear me dead, you bring a whore in my house, in my bed, where we conceived our child, I hate you!!!". Barry grabbed his keys and jacket and left out. He still couldn't figure out how Sabrina found out about Cynthia, but he knew that he would have to leave for a while until she calmed down. He called his father and asked to stay there for a while. Of course, he knew that he would have to lie in order to stay there; he couldn't tell his father that he cheated on his wife again.

Barry stayed way for 3 months, and I was sad an angry all at the same time. I loved this man but I didn't understand why I loved him, especially after he cheated on me, but I did. Here I was now with three children. I allowed him to move back in the house but our marriage was a façade. I told myself that once the children got older I was leaving him and my heart turned to ice. I couldn't love him anymore, not as a wife. I had become depressed and angry all the time. I felt myself becoming physically ill because of his treatment towards me.

Chapter 16

MARRIED BUT LIVING SINGLE

I changed after that. I went back to school, got my drivers' license and brought me a brand new car. I started going out on Ladies Night with my girlfriend Cheryl that lived across the street from me. I didn't really care about my marriage but inside of me was something that wouldn't allow me to be unfaithful to him. I don't know why something in me was convicting me. I wanted to pay him back so badly, I wanted to hurt him as much as he hurt me but my heart wouldn't let me. It wasn't that I cared that much about him, but I didn't want to disappoint God by committing adultery. Therefore, I spent my time at the Club Izod located on Charles Street. I loved the club. I remember when I was younger I couldn't' get in because they were strict about carding people. Now I was over 21 and taking good advantage of it. My girlfriend and I stayed at Ladies night, her because she wanted to get out of the house, me I wanted to dance, dance and dance, I was always an excellent dancer and I was in my element in that club and I always took the floor over when I got there.

I was probably at the club three or four times before, I realized who the owners were. I found out the last Thursday of the month of April. I walked in the club. I went by myself that night; I knew that I would find someone to hang out with because I was a regular. I sat at the bar and ordered a Jack Daniels cooler. I was smoking a cigarette when I heard one of my songs come on. The DJ was jamming and mixing it up, I loved it. I got on the floor by myself and started doing my thing when one of the guy from the bar got on the floor with me; I killed him on that floor. He looked at me and shook his head after the music slowed. "Why you have to beat me up like that baby?" "Nothing against you cutie, that was just my jam". I nodded at Dean the DJ and he gave me a shout out. "Yeah baby, take him to school, show him how it's done here at the Izod". I nodded and grabbed my drink. It was freshened up. I thanked the bartender. "Don't thank me baby, the man of the house brought you one. "What man of the house". He pointed to the end of the bar and there he was standing there looking as fine as hell. He wore a nice 2-piece leisure suit. His hair was in a jheri curl that was perfect, not dripping for looking dry but just neat and shaped up. Those brown eyes were sexier than I remembered them to be and he had the sweetest smile on his face. I wanted to jump behind the bar and kiss him but I knew I couldn't.. He grabbed my hand. "Hey Sabrina, do you still drink Jack Daniel's coolers". "Yes". "Good", He fixed me another drink. I stopped him. ""I'm driving tonight'. "Good for you, when did you get your license? "Almost a year now". "Good". "When did you become an entrepreneur? He laughed. "About a year ago". "To you". I clinked glasses with him and we laughed. It was good to see Reggie, he looked better than he used to. He had gained a few pounds in all the right places. We talked for a good while about our lives, he told me he had a baby, and that he was happy. I told him that I got married had another baby and was doing okay too. I didn't' lie and tell him that I was happy. It started getting busy so he left me and took care of his business. Some of my friends showed up. I got a table with them and spent the rest of my time with them.

Club Izod became my refuge; I lived for those Thursday nights. Barry was really pissed about it but he couldn't stop me. "You going out again? ". "Yup". "Who's gonna watch these kids? ". "You are". "I'm going out too". "No problem". I walked up the street to my girlfriend's house and tapped on the window, as usual, she had a house full of people. "Trina, you got a minute". "Come on in Sabrina". I walked in and spoke to everybody. "Hey girl, where you going all dressed up? ". I had on a red top with black jeans and red heels. My hair was cut like Toni Braxtons'. "Izod". "Damn girl, who you know over there, you over there all the time? ". I looked at Trina's brother Larry. "When you pay my bills and sleep in my bed, then maybe you can question me". Everybody at the table laughed. "You a mean ass woman! ". I gave him a hug. "I'm playing with you man, not getting hyped". "Don't pay his ass no mind girl, whatchu need? ". Trina was a heavyset girl with beautiful eyes and hair. She looked white but she wasn't. She had four children and always talked to them as if they were grown. She would call her girls bitches and her sons "a bunch of little bastards" that were just like their daddy! I would laugh at her because she was so funny, the kids didn't pay her any mind when she talked like that, and it was like they knew she would never do anything to hurt them no matter how bad she talked to them. Charles as the father of the girls but the boys was from a previous relationship. "Can you keep an eye on the children for me? ". "Sure, send them up they can go upstairs and play with the kids until you come back. I'm let them stay up for a while since they don't' have school tomorrow. Do you want me to send them down your house when they get sleepy? ". "If stupid is there you can, if not, I will get them when I come in". "Okay". I gave her a hug and slipped a twenty in her blouse pocket. Charles wasn't working and neither was she; I knew they could use the change, even though she got a check for the kids. "Thanks Trina". "No problem girl, next time, take me wit chu" "You got that! ". I waved good night and headed for Izod. I never went back in the house. The kids were waiting at the door. When I told them to go to Trina's they bolted out the door and up the street. Barry stood in the door fuming, but I turned up the radio and sped off down the street.

I started catching feelings for Reggie again and I knew it was wrong but I didn't' care. I wanted him and I thought about him constantly. He never asked me for sex or anything but we flirted so badly that it was a shame. People started thinking we were doing the do in his office. I would come out of his office grinning and smiling and he would come out afterwards and act like he didn't even know I was there. This went on for a while until one night I went there on a Saturday night. The place was lit up and so many people were there that was a line outside. I saw all of Reggie's homeboys and they noticed me and let me and my girlfriends without waiting for the line. People didn't find it cool but they couldn't' do anything about it. I had never been to the Izod on a Saturday but I was not mad about it since it was jumping. Reggie and all of his boys were dressed up in nice suits and their ties were loose around their necks, they had on Stacy Adams and was looking sharp and smelling good. I looked for Reggie about an hour before he surfaced. By then I was on my third drink. I was feeling good and the music was jumping like crazy. I was dancing and tearing up the floor again. The crowd was cheering and checking me and this guy out on the floor that by the way was pretty much keeping up with me but I knew I could kill him just by the next move I made. I got right in his face grabbed his hips and gyrated my hips with his. Then I turned around so my butt was gyrating against his waist, I looked over my shoulder and he was looking down at my breasts which were wet and bouncing out of my blouse. I grabbed his hands and placed them on my hips so that he would rock with me. The crowd was going mad, yelling and screaming, "work him girl, work him!" I walked away from him, he was just standing there rocking back and forth, and grinning, I stood a little ways from him started dancing by myself and looking him dead in his eyes. He started towards me and I met him halfway spun around about three times before I faced him again and grabbed his shoulders so we could touch. I started grinding him back and forth with me so that we looked like we were one. The DJ was screaming "Sabrina on the floor y'all and the song was beating out "hurt me hurt me!!" and the crowed joined in "hurt me Hurt me!'. We danced that entire dance. When the song was over, the guy came up to me. "Baby I haven't danced liked that since I was a teenager, it was a real pleasure to get my ass beat up on the floor by such a sexy ass woman, thank you". I smiled. He walked over to his boys and slapped them five. "I just smiled and sat down. When I got to my table all of my girls were looking somber. "What's up with y'all damn, get a drink, take a pee, do something to take those looks off of your face". "Sit down Sabrina". I sat down. "What's up, y'all seen my husband or something while I was out on the floor". "No Brina, but we did find someone's husband". "Huh" I was very confused, she and I were the only married women at the table except for Rena and she was separated. Cheryl took a sip of her drink. The music was loud so she had to yell. "We found her husband". We all looked in the direction she was talking about and there was a nice looking young woman sitting at the table with all of these other females who were really dressed nice. "Who is she?" I yelled. "That's Reggie's wife and we are at their damn wedding reception". I almost passed out, in fact, I'm sure I probably did, except for the fact that I didn't fall in the floor. Everybody got quiet and looked at me. I played it off. "Well, I need to go and congratulate the groom." "Sabrina, you can't do that". "I'm playing; I am not going to say anything to that man". I am happy for him after all how can I get upset, I am a married woman remember". But truthfully, I was truly hurt. I didn't know why but I was. I tried to enjoy the rest of the night but it was a bust. I didn't let anyone know how crushed I was.

Right before the night was over I ran into Reggie, or he ran into me. He walked over to our table. "Are you ladies having a good time"? They all nodded yes and smiled. I didn't say anything. He looked at me. "Can I speak to you for a minute?" "Don't you think that would upset your *wife?*" "Please Sabrina, let me talk to you". "Leave me alone please!" I snatched my arm back and walked out of the club. I sat in my car and I cried and cried, I was hurt and drunk.

I don't know how long I sat in my car before Reggie came out to my car. He knocked on the window and I was singing to Gladys's Knight's Midnight Train to Georgia. I looked over at him and rolled my window down. "My world, his world, my world mine and his alone, I got to go, I got to," I was singing at the top of my lungs. "Let me in Sabrina". I opened the door. "Slide over". I slid over in the seat. "What do you want Reggie, isn't your wife going to be looking for you?" "Sabrina, let me just explain". "You don't owe me shit boo, I am okay wit this here, I got a man! I pushed my ring finger in his face. "See, I got a man, I don't need you man!" He just looked at me and said nothing. "That's right, you ain't my man, you don't owe me a got damn thing, ya know!" "Sabrina, you are drunk and you can't drive like this". "Man leave me the hell alone, go back in there to your reception before your WIFE come out here looking for you and get her butt kicked". He grabbed my arms, I didn't realize that I was crying, I was so drunk I didn't know half the stuff I called him. He grabbed my hands and kissed me so hard that I couldn't breath. I tried to resist him but I couldn't. I fell into his arms and we kissed and caressed each other for several minutes before we heard another knock on the window.

Looking for Love.......

When we looked up, it was Blue. He was still fine as hell. He had a real look of concern on his face. Reggie rolled down the window. "Give me a minute man, I will be right there". "Man, you need to come now, somebody's looking for you and they were told that you were out in the parking lot". "Go on". "We need to talk". "No you need to be a husband to your wife". "Please meet me, let me explain". "Nothing to explain, you got married, I got married, I'm drunk and you gonna go home and sex ya wife and think about me the whole time". I know it was a cruel thing to say but I was hurting. Blue grabbed him by his arm. "Come on man, lets go, all this is gonna get you is in a world of trouble". "Go to hell Blue!" "Sabrina, it ain't even like that, you know this man can't be seen with you out here on his wedding night now, be for real". I lit a cigarette. "Yeah, yeah, I know, take his ass on in the club".

I never went back in the club that night; I sat outside with some others while I waited

For my friends. I did not think it was fair for them not to have a good time because of me. By the time they got outside, I was sobering up a little and was talking to a guy that was waiting for his girl to get out.

After a few minutes, my friends came out. Cheryl was the first one to speak. "Brina, are you okay girl?" "I'm fine, are y'all ready to go?" They all nodded yes. We piled in cars and started out the parking lot. I heard someone calling my name. I looked around and it was Blue. I walked back towards him. "What's up?" "Let me talk to you for a minute". We walked away from the crowd. "Brina, I love you like a sister, but you can't keep coming around here, you are seriously messing with my man's head". "I didn't come here on purpose Blue, how in the hell was I suppose to know he was getting married today, tonight or whenever?" "I know Brina, I know but he still wants to be with you". "I can't mess with him like that Blue, he is married now". "And you've been married and it was cool with you, how many times did y'all get busy in the office?" "We didn't". "Yeah right". "I'm serious Blue, Reggie and I haven't been together, for a while and if I knew he was getting married, I would have never messed with him like that". "I know". "What did you want, if you want me to stop coming here, okay, I won't and tell your friend I said, I started singing the Vesta's song "Congratulations!" I was trying to be smart but I cried. Blue grabbed me and held me. "Let it out Brina, it's going to be okay". I guess my friends saw me crying and they all came over. "What happened?"

"Take her home man, can one of you drive her, she is in no condition to drive". "I'll take her". Rena said. "Check it out, I want you to take this, and use it, work this out". He gave me a pager number. I wanted to ask whose it was but I was just too damn distraught. We got in the car. "Do you want to go home; you look like you have been crying". "I have been crying,

Yes take me home, I don't give a damn about Barry or his shit, hell he probably somewhere F-ing the next door neighbor". I laughed but I was crushed inside. I laid in the backseat of my car and went to sleep.

When I got home, I had pretty much sobered up. I was still upset about Reggie and his marriage, but what could I do? I was married as Cheryl kept reminding me in the trip home. "why did you react like that, you are married Brina and you act like you and him were some kind of couple or something, so what he is married!". Before I could answer, Rena jumped in. "why you cutting her up like that Cheryl? Damn the woman is hurt and you just talking like her heart ain't involved. Mind you damn business and worry about your man!". "At least I got a man!". "Don't get it wrong girl, I am single by choice!". "Sure you are". "You know just what you can for me Cheryl, and if you don't, I don't have a problem telling you hoe". I sat up in the back seat. "Ladies, please, don't do this, it's not worth it. I am fine, honest, it hurts but it will pass". We drove the rest of the way in silence. I thanked Rena for driving Mieka and me home for driving my car. I didn't want to hear Barry's mouth so when I went in the house I slept on the sofa. I decided then, no more Izod for me. It was time to move on with my life. I knew I would miss Reggie but being there knowing that he was married would tear me up inside. Besides, I knew his wife was not going to let him alone in that club. I resolved in my mind that that part of my life was over. I didn't' know if I would stop going out, I just knew that was no longer a regular at Izod.

Your body is here with me…but..

Matthew 5:27- you have heard that it was said in the old time, you shall not commit adultery, but I say unto you that who ever look at a woman to lust after her has committed adultery already in his heart.

My marriage was in shambles, I was ignoring all the signs. It was not that I didn't care, but it hurt too much to deal with it. We moved to a beautiful three bedroom home. But it was just a house to me. I was happy that my children didn't have to all be in one bedroom and my son was able to have his own room, but it was still a house. I graduated from college, and thought I was happy, but I wasn't. Barry and I were always at odds. We didn't do anything as a couple anymore. He went about his business, as did I. I found good job was making good money. Barry had become a supervisor on his job, but our beautiful house was just a house, it was not a home. I found solace in my job. I loved my job, it was challenging and rewarding for me. I landed it a month before I graduated from college and was so happy finally be getting some real benefits and a paycheck that I could do something with. I had many friends on my job and most of them were men. Of course, Barry thought I was fooling around on him. I told him he had a lot of nerve since he had cheated on me God knows how many times over the course of our relationship. That always shut him up. However, he was almost right. In the five years I had been employed on that job, I had met a lot of people. But there was one man I was very fond of. I knew deep down that what I was thinking and eventually doing was wrong, but I couldn't stop myself. I was so starved for love and attention that I ventured beyond my marriage to find it. And find it I did. His name as Roy. He was a young man, younger than I was. He was 28 years old and I was 31. He was tall and fine. He was very soft spoken but I knew he had some freak in him just by the way he looked at me. I never acted on any advances that he made because of my marriage. I was always faithful to Barry, I don't know why but I didn't want to cross the line with anyone, at least not at first. I had no desire to sleep with Barry anymore, especially since he was coming home three and four in the morning with no explanation.

I went to work and Roy was always there. Although he was not mean or evil or caused me any pain, Roy was someone I didn't need in my life. Instead of turning to God for strength, guidance and comfort, I turned to a man. There are times in your life that you do things that you know will cause you grief later on down the road but at the time, all you want is peace and to stop the pain. That's what I wanted and Roy provided that for me. We would meet for lunch and go for walks around the campus. He would tell me to pray and to hang in there. He would say not to give up the fight. "I don't know how to fight anymore Roy; I don't even know if I want to fight anymore Barry makes me feel like I am not woman enough for him. He makes me feel that I am less than a woman, I can't even keep him out of other women's beds". He turned and looked at me. "Sabrina, it's not your fault that your husband is cheating or has cheated on you. You don't have anything to do with why he does what he does. He has a problem, not you Sabrina. If you weren't married to him, he would be cheating on the woman he was with, why, because that's who he is. Until he surrenders and turns his sickness or illness or selfishness over to God, he will always be the way he is". "I still can't help it, I feel like it's my fault". "Sabrina, it's not you, look you may not want to admit this, but from what you've told me about him, your husband is a whore, he was a whore when you met him and he is still a whore and he will be whore until he decides that he needs to change". I could feel the tears forming and before I could stop them, they traveled down my face. He wiped my tears and held me in his arms.

For months and months, this went on. Roy and I became so close and I found myself looking forward to seeing him, and the days that we was not working, I found myself anxious and wondering what he was doing. I tried to stop what I was doing, I knew it was wrong and even though there was no physical act, I knew I was cheating on my husband, but at the same time, Barry was making it so easy for me. We rarely talked about anything but bills. He would come home, eat, take a shower, hang out with the kids for a while and then leave out. I would sit at the table, mail the bills off and ignore the fact that we had nothing to talk about anymore. We were going through the motions. We never went to bed at the same time, and we never ate dinner at the same time. The money was great and we were living well. However, emotionally, our lives were a mess.

I confided in Roy that I felt like I was losing my mind sometimes. "I can't sleep anymore Roy, I feel anxious all the time". "Why don't you get some help Sabrina, everybody needs help every now and again". "You mean psychiatric help?" "Counseling or something, you need someone to talk to". "I can talk to you". "I know that, but I mean someone professional that can maybe help you get over the anxiety that you're feeling". "I might". "It may do you some good, you never know".

"Do you think I'm crazy?" "No, I think you are overworked, and stressed out, anybody that has children, a husband and a challenging job have to be stressed at some point". "True". "Look, at least think about it". I gave him a hug. "Thanks Roy". "Anytime". So many times after talking to him, I wanted more from him but I wasn't sure if he wanted anything more from me. I didn't want to be rejected again so I tried to stay neutral.

I followed Roy's suggestion and I started going to therapy. I didn't feel good at first talking about my problems with a stranger but I needed something to keep my sanity. Mike was wonderful at his job and he made me feel at ease the first time I went to see him. He even asked me if I preferred a female. "You know Sabrina, we have female therapist you can talk to". "Why would you think I want a female? ". "Because women relate better to other women at times". "I'm fine with you Mike, unless you have some objections". "No, not at all". Mike was older, maybe fifitish and salt and pepper hair. He wasn't a tall man at all but he was nice. He wore wire-framed glasses and always rubbed his goatee when he was thinking. We talked a lot about my life now and then. It was hard for me to talk about my father or my family period. We weren't as close as we could have been. I told him about my sisters and my brother. It was very hard to talk about my molestation and my marriage; those two things hurt me the most in my life. I talked about my friends, Angie, Reggie, Gina, Wendy and so many others whom I had thought I forgotten over the years but once I talked about them it was as if it was yesterday. After a few sessions, Mike suggested that I meet with the psychiatrist because he felt that I needed something for anxiety and to help me sleep. I didn't object, truthfully, I was exhausted. He also suggested that I bring Barry to at least one of my sessions. "Sabrina, it may do you some good if you are able to tell Barry how you feel about things". "He's not going to listen to me Mike, hell we don't even speak to each other and we live in the same damn house". "That's why you need to talk about this". "Maybe soon". "How does he feel about you taking medication?" "I don't know, I didn't ask him, and he probably doesn't even notice". "Has he seen the bottle?" "I don't know, when he comes in, I am asleep". Try over the next few days to talk to him about meeting, you all should talk about your problems as a couple". "Whatever!"

To my surprise when I asked Barry, he agreed to go with me. But of course, when he got there, he acted like I expected him to. He told the therapist that he didn't know what was wrong with me, and that he tried to talk to me but I wasn't trying to hear what he had to say. I tried to explain to him how hurt I was feeling because of his infidelities and constant staying out late, but he said I was overreacting. After and hour of back and forth and playing the blame game, Mike stopped the meeting. Of course, Barry and I drove home in silence and that was pretty much how the rest of the night went.

When I went to work the next day, I told Roy how my counseling session went. "I'm sorry that things didn't go as you expected". "Oh they went just as I expected, he ass lying and making me look like I was crazy, and he playing the victim! ". "He doesn't know what to do Sabrina, if you were him, would you be happy about being there? ". "He agreed to go Roy". "Only because he thought that he would be able to make you look bad in someone else's eyesight, hell, he already looks bad in everybody's eyesight, every body knows about his cheating". "I guess you're right". Suddenly, he got quiet. I looked at him and he did not seem quite right to me, so I asked him. "What's wrong Roy?" "I need to talk to you about something; do you have a few minutes?" "Sure". I have to go to the archives over in the other building, do you want to meet me over there?". "Okay, I'll see you in a few?". "Yes, I just have to go back and get the keys and the paperwork". I gave him a hug and walked away. I answered a few phone calls, and slipped my lab coat on, I had on a two hundred dollar suit and I did not want to get it messed up in that dusty archive room. I buttoned the coat up, slipped on my low heel shoes and told my supervisor where I was going. "Can you bring me something back from the cafeteria on your way back"? "Sure".

My supervisor and I had a shaky relationship. I knew she did not like me but she had to tolerate me, as I had to tolerate her. She knew that I was going through some problems at home so she tried to be civil towards me. She was actually a very fair person, but she had this thing about favoritism with the other women in the office. I do not know if it was because I was the only black in the office or the fact that she was jealous of me because of my clothes. I could not figure it out but I made up my mind to deal with her as professional as possible. The words of

God rang in my head *"to have friends, you have to show yourself friendly".*
I walked over to the shuttle and got on. I saw Roy sitting on the back
of the shuttle but I did not acknowledge him. We worked in a hospital
and everybody knew everybody, it was difficult to be discreet but we
tried. I got off at the front door and he rode around back. When I got
to the archive room, he was already standing there as if he was working
on the door. I unlocked the door, walked in, and turned the light on.
He did not come in right away. I pulled a few films before he came in.
I grabbed the files I needed and started back out the door. "Are you
leaving so soon?" "I was trying to move slowly to give you a chance
to come in". He grabbed me by my waist and kissed me. I kissed him
back. We stumbled into the boxes, and we almost fell to the floor. He
held me tight so I would not fall down. He pinned me against the wall
and kissed me hard. I was so hot that I felt he beads forming on my
head. "Umm, Sabrina, I've wanted to do that for so long". I bit his lip.
"I've wanted you to do that for so long". We kissed and fondled each
other some more. I felt his manhood through his uniform. "Umm, that
feels good". "It would feel better if I were inside you". "I want that".
I forgot that we were at work, and I forgot that I was married. After
several minutes, we both sat on the boxes not looking at each other.
The guilt I felt was so heavy on me I thought I was not able to breathe.
Roy wouldn't look at me. He gave me his bandana out of his back
pocket. I tried to fix my skirt and blouse. I was happy that I had that
lab coat. I wrapped it around me and buttoned a few of the buttons.
He looked over at me and smiled. "Don't worry, that suit is still looking
fly". I smiled. "You might want to do something about your *look*". We
both looked down at his pants and laughed. "I'll be okay in a few". I
gathered the films again. "What did you want to talk to me about?"
He walked over to me and pulled me close. "I wanted to tell you that I
am falling in love with you. Sabrina, I do not expect you to love me. I
know you are married and I know you are older than I am. But I can't
stop what my heart feels for you". I kissed him again. It was hard for
me to hear those words. I had heard them too many times before, only
to find tremendous hurt behind them. "Don't tell me that Roy". "Why
not?'. "It's hard for me to hear those words". "I know you've been hurt
Sabrina, but I love you and I can't hide it. I tried to tell myself it was
not what I felt, I tried to tell myself over and over again that you were

a married woman an older woman, but when I hold you and listen to you, my heart does things that I can't control. Even when I pray, you consume my thoughts. For months I fought these feelings but I can't do it anymore Sabrina and I can't lie to you or myself anymore".

I was so ashamed because deep down, I felt the same way he did. I tried for months to deny any feelings I was feeling for Roy. I fought with myself and felt guilty because I realized that I didn't want my marriage to work because I wanted to be with Roy. I wanted to leave Barry right there in that beautiful four bedroom house with all the bells and whistles and move over to Roy's two bedroom condo in Ellicott City. I didn't want to feel the pain of separation, I just want to leave and live my life with Roy, be happy for once in my damn life!" Roy looked concerned. "I'm sorry; I didn't mean to make things more complicated for you". He kissed me again and walked away. I stopped him. "I'm not upset with you, don't apologize for your feelings, I am not apologizing for mine". "I don't follow you". "I'm trying to tell you that I feel the same way about you. I do not know when my feelings changed Roy and I do not even care anymore. I don't want to be married anymore, I don't want to fight for my marriage, and I don't want to feel guilty or ashamed for what I feel for you anymore". He hugged me. "We better get out of here". "You go first". "We will finish talking at lunch. He kissed me again and left. I grabbed the films and turned the lights back out.

When I got back to my office, I was relieved. I needed to get away from him for a minute. My body was still throbbing and I needed to get myself together. It was hard to do. I sat at my desk and wrote him a note. On the way to the gift shop, I stopped at his mailbox and slipped it in there. An hour later, he called me and thanked me.

After work, I went home. I thought about Barry and asked myself if I loved him anymore. I knew I did, but I didn't trust him. He didn't give me any reason to anymore. We hardly ever talked anymore. I kept thinking about Roy. I knew that what happened between us shouldn't have but I couldn't stop thinking about it. His touch had me hot inside and I wanted to be with him. After I cooked and got the children straight for the evening, I called my friend Trina. She was still living in the old neighborhood but we still hung out and talked. "Hello?" "Hey Trina, you got a minute?" "Hey girl, how the hell are you?" "I'm doing okay". "What's wrong Sabrina?" Trina always knew when something was wrong with me. "I just need to talk to somebody". "Hold on, let me make sure these little bastards are out of the tub and in the bed". I just laughed, after I heard her fussing and cussing at the children for a few minutes, it got quiet and she picked the phone back up. "Let me light a fog and go somewhere these nosy ass people in this house won't eavesdrop". I heard her cussing at her brother and turn the television down in the room. "Okay, what's up?" "Is Barry over there with Charles?" "Naw, I ain't seen Barry in a while". "Okay, I just didn't want to talk and he was there'. "Naw, he ain't here, what's wrong, you caught that limp dick bastard again?" Trina just didn't care what she said out of her mouth and that's probably why I loved her so much, she was so real. "No, girl". "Oh, cause you know I'm from the Island, I will put a root on that bastard". She stopped herself. "I'm sorry Sabrina; I know you don't go for that kind of talk". 'I don't think I should judge anybody at all Trina". "What did you do girl?" "I kind of cheated on Barry". "What!" "Shh" "I can't believe it, it's about time dammit!" "Trina stop it". "I'm serious, forget him, tell me, was it Roy?" "Yes".

I told her what happened and then I just hung up the phone. I realized that I shouldn't be telling her about my infidelity, I should be on my knees talking to God about it. I was so conflicted, and I felt so far away from God, but I tried to pray anyway, but I couldn't stay focused, so I called Roy. "Hey". "Hey yourself, are you busy?" "No, just waiting for my brother to come past and bring me the money he owes me". "How are you feeling?" "Good, I'm good, I needed to come home and work this thing off". "Huh?" "Well since you didn't finish your job today, I had to when I got in the privacy of my home". I laughed. "I'm sorry; I didn't mean to do that to you". "Yes you did and it's good, I wanted it as much as you did, but I couldn't disrespect you by sexing you in an archive room. It should be romantic not crazy". We both laughed. We talked for a few more minutes and then he asked what I knew he would. "Where is your husband?" "I don't know, he didn't come home from work yet". "It's after nine". "I don't care anymore Roy, this is not the first time and it won't be the last". "Are you okay?" "No but I will be, I know he's got somebody else, he always does". He was silent. "Look, if you want me to come over I can". "Boy you live all the way in Ellicott City, I will be fine, don't worry about me, I'm going to bed". "Okay, call me if you want to talk some more". "Okay".

About four a.m., Barry came in the bedroom. I could smell the alcohol and the perfume on him. He was drunk and his clothes were wrinkled. I looked up from the bed. "You could have least taken your whore to a motel room instead of screwing her in the back seat of my damn car!" "Don't start with me, go and take your medication or something, I told that damn doctor that you were crazy!" "I'm crazy, you come in four o clock in the damn morning, smelling like you been screwing and I'm crazy, let me tell you what crazy is you bastard, go to sleep! I dare your ass to close your eyes in this bitch! I dare you!" He looked at me as if to see if I was serious. "You think I'm playing Barry?" I jumped out the bed and picked up the ashtray that was on his nightstand. He ran out the bedroom and slammed the door, but not before, I threw the ashtray at his head. I did not care if he was hit or not. I locked the bedroom door. "Go back and sleep with that whore you hanging out with till four in the morning, you trifling son of a bitch!'. I heard him walk downstairs. I looked out at the parking pad to see if he was going to get back in the car, but he didn't. I heard the TV in the living room turn on.

I lay down and cried. I don't know why, was I crying because I was hurt, or because I wished that, I had slept with Roy? I looked at the clock it was four-thirty. I dialed Roy's number. It rang twice. "Yeah?" "Roy, is that you?" "Naw, this is Kenny, hold on". I heard him call Roy's name and then I heard the extension pick up. "Yeah". God they sounded just alike. "I'm sorry, I know you have to get up, but I needed to talk". "Sabrina?" "Yes". "Oh hold on baby, let me get a cigarette". "What happened?" Roy asked me. I told him about how Barry had just gotten in and was drunk and smelling like perfume. I didn't want to cry but I did. I just couldn't seem to get this relationship thing right. It seemed that every single relationship was riddled with lies and betrayals. Where was I going wrong, why did I keep choosing these type of men. I cried and Roy listened. This went on until five-thirty. "Look baby, I need to get ready for work and so do you, get yourself together and I will see you at work later on today. It's going to be okay. Don't stress about it". I agreed and hung up.

I called my office and left a message that I would be late. I slept for about two hours before I got up and got ready for work. When I went downstairs, Barry was already gone. I was glad; I didn't have the strength to fight with him again. I got the children ready for school and then left for work. On the way, I thought about Roy. He was young but he was sweet. I made a mental note to ask him if he had a girlfriend. That was the last thing in needed. Some young girl all up in my face.

The day was uneventful. I did see Roy a few times but we were both so busy we didn't have a chance to talk. Barry called me several times but I didn't' take any of his calls. I was tired of him. I didn't have anything to say to him at all. I worked so hard that my supervisor asked me was I trying to get a raise. I laughed and told her that working hard for five years never got me a raise so why should it do it now. I could tell by the way her face turned red that I had pissed her off but I didn't care. I was tired of everyone in the office getting merit raises and I was not getting anything. She stayed in her office the rest of the day and that was fine with me. I typed about fifteen reports, pulled some films and made some phone calls. Before I knew it, the day was over and I had only seen Roy in passing. But I wasn't upset about it. I walked past the loading dock on the way home and saw him and some of the other guys sitting there smoking a
cigarette. "Hey good people."

The guys turned around and spoke to me. I caught Roy's eye immediately. He plucked his cigarette off the dock and walked towards me. Jesse spoke up. "Hey man, where you going, she spoke to everybody, not just you". "Man go on, she came to see me". He walked to me and gave me a hug. "I missed you today". "Me too". Everybody laughed. "Oh it's like that?" Jesse smiled. "Young blood got the finest thing in the hospital, damn!" We all laughed. He walked with me to the end of the hall. "How are you feeling?" "I'm sleepy, I can't wait to get home and fall out". "I know what you mean, me too". "I'm sorry I kept you up so late". "I told you to call me if you wanted to talk". "Thank you". He kissed me. "I missed you today". "Me too". "Oh I wanted to tell you that I was buying a car this weekend". "For real?" "Yes, I was thinking about a Sentra". "Can you drive?" "Yes I can drive; I've had my license for a while". "When are you going to make up your mind?" "Basically, I have, I just need to know how much I want to spend and everything". "That's a big step buying a car". "Yes but I can handle it baby, I promise, I will be careful and I won't drive too fast okay"? "Okay but you know how you young folks are". He laughed. "I am not that much younger than you." "I know, I just like to tease you". He walked me to my car, gave me a hug and I pulled off.

Roy was really a nice looking young man. His body was all that. I told myself that I didn't want him sexually but I was lying to myself. Just looking at him in that uniform turned me on, He was strong and built. When he hugged me, I could feel him rising and I wanted to drag him in one of the locker rooms and give myself to him. We had spent a lot of time in the archive rooms, the elevators and empty hallways. I could feel God tugging at my spirit but I couldn't seem to turn myself around. Mike knew that I was hiding something but I wouldn't tell him, I didn't know how to tell him that I was cheating on my husband although I didn't really complete the act of sex, just being with Roy in a compromising way was cheating. Not to mention the times I thought about him while lying in the bed with Barry. So many times, I thought about Roy being next to me and my thoughts would take over my body.

Barry hadn't stayed out since that morning but he was still hanging out at the bar around the corner from the house and a few people had told me that he was there with another woman but I hadn't checked it out yet. I knew in my heart there was someone else but I wasn't ready to face it and beside, I had Roy to occupy my mind. Mike figured out that I was seeing another man and he suggested that I talk to Barry about it and try to find a way to work things out if in fact that's what I wanted. I told him I didn't know what I wanted. In addition, I didn't, but God would intervene and all my decisions were about to be made for me.

The struggle of two natures....

I spent a lot of time reflecting on a lot of things in my life since I had been going to the therapist. He delved into my life so deeply that it hurt just to breathe some days. I spent hours, days and weeks, talking about all the pain I had endured over the years. I found out through my therapy that my need to be with men were a reflection of not having my father in my life. I also learned that my promiscuity, alcohol and drug abuse was all a part of being sexually abused. I never felt worthy of real love and I acted out in different ways to deal with it. Mike told me that subconsciously I knew the man that took me to the motel was dangerous but I didn't love myself enough to care. He felt that I placed myself in danger because I felt I deserved to get hurt. I couldn't understand all the psychobabble but I was drained after that session and my head hurt. I did believe him when he said that I allowed men to treat me any way they chose because the fear of them leaving paralyzed me. I needed them to love me no matter what the circumstances was. Trenton beating me over the years, Dennis' betrayals, Reggie marrying someone else, even the fling I had with Trenton's best friend, even though no sex was involved. All of those relationships were from men who were unavailable to me. Trenton didn't respect me, Reggie had other females the whole time we were together, Dennis slept with the girl down the street from his house. Even the one nightstand I had the night that Dennis beat me up was someone who was not available to me, but yet, I gave myself to him. I didn't even care that all he wanted was sex, because that's what I wanted, it was attention, albeit negative, it was still attention. Mike made me remember things that I had buried deep inside of me. I kept piling things and people on top of things and people. He warned me that if I didn't deal with each of my issues that my issues were going to deal with me. I was struggling between getting healthy and giving up. My flesh was giving up and my spirit was fighting for me.

So many nights I left therapy with a headache and tears streaming down my face. I felt dirty, empty and used. Over the months, I had found out so many things about my life, my marriage and my infidelities. I knew this was not the person I wanted to be but I couldn't stop myself. Mike tried other medications with me. He felt that drug I was prescribed was not working. I changed medications so many times; I thought I was losing my mind. I kept going back though. The need for me to feel better and to get better was stronger than the need to stay in the bed and pull the covers over my head. My job was stressing me out. Roy was worried about me and he expressed it one Friday before we left work. "Sabrina, what is going on with you?'? You don't seem like you feel good". "I'm fine baby, I just need some rest". "No Sabrina, you need something more than that". "Like what?" "I don't know, I am worried about you. You seemed to be preoccupied and you seem sad all the time. Is your husband still messing around?". "I'm sure he is, I don't talk to him and I don't sleep with him so I don't know and I don't care". "Sabrina, you have to get yourself together, you can't keep going on like this". "I'm fine Roy, honest". "Look, I can't tell you what to do but let me suggest that you get your therapist to get you some time off, you need a break baby, you're losing weight, you look stress, the medications makes you look like you're high all the time". "I am fine Roy, please let it go". "Okay, if you say so". I gave him a hug. "What are you doing for the weekend?'. "I don't know, I will probably hang out with my brother". "What about your girlfriend?" He frowned his face up. "Why do you do that Sabrina, I don't have no girlfriend, I have associates but I am not in no relationship with anybody, if I was, do you think I would be with you like this?" "Why not, you ain't my man". "Why do you do that Sabrina?" "Do what?" I knew what I was doing but I didn't know why I was doing it. I was sabotaging my friendship with him but I didn't know why. "Why are you trying to start a fight with me, I care about you and I want you to get better, don't push me out of your life". I started crying I don't know why I started crying but I did. My emotions were on a roller coaster, I couldn't keep things together. I fell into his arms and cried. He was patient and let me cry, while telling me that everything was going to be okay. We walked back from the garage. "Are you going to be okay?" "Yes I will be fine". "Why don't you come with me?" "Where?" "Home". "Home?" "Yes, Sabrina, home". Now?". "Yes, follow me in my car and we can go to my house, I can ask my brother to stay at his girl's house and you can come with me for at least a little while". "I'll have to see if I can find someone to keep an eye on the children". "Okay, I'll wait". I called Trina and she was happy to get the kids for me. I followed Roy to his beautiful condo. It was simply beautiful. It did not look like a man's home, it was so well decorated and spotless. He didn't even have dishes in the sink. It was immaculate in there. His furniture was not black or gray as I expected from a bachelor, but it was a burgundy and stark white, I couldn't stop staring. "Are you okay". "I just didn't expect your house to look like this". "I know, I'm not into dark colors, I like nice colors it makes the house feel cozier" You must entertain a lot". "Naw, I just have a mom with wonderful taste". He burst out laughing, "I didn't decorate this Sabrina, my mom's did, it was a house warming gift for me and my brother". I hit him on the arm. We laughed as he showed me the rest of the condo. It was beautiful. We ordered Chinese food and listened to music and talked, a lot. We kissed and made love and talked a made love some more, I didn't want to leave and he didn't want me too, but I was not quite ready to stay out all night, I knew Barry wasn't there, he was probably at the bar with his girlfriend and that made me want to stay, but I couldn't explain to my children where I was all night. After I showered and put my clothes on, I walked into the bedroom. "Are you feeling better?" "Much better". He kissed me again and I wanted to make love to him again, but I pulled away. "I will call you this weekend and check on you. You know how I feel about you right?' "Yes I do and you know how I feel about you". He gave me a hug and walked me to my car.

I told him how much I liked his little black car, it looked just like him. He laughed. "Any time you want to give up that baby Beamer, let me know". I looked at him and laughed, "Naw, can't do that". I got in he bent over and kissed me again. "I'll call you later". I pulled out, tapped the horn and rode home.

I made it home without Barry ever finding out I was even gone. I got the kids from Trina's and went home. I was still thinking of Roy and our time together when Barry came in. I didn't speak to him and he didn't speak to me. I lay in bed and thought about Roy. I wondered if Barry knew I had been with another man, like I knew when he was with another woman. I shook the thought out of my mind. I prayed for forgiveness but I wasn't ready to be forgiven, because I knew I was going to be with this man again.

Roy did call and I told him I was fine and that Barry was there so I needed to get off the phone He understood.

The following Monday I had another turbulent session with Mike that, again, left me in tears. I I was still teary eyed when I went home. I was thinking about Roy and how he made me feel deep inside. I was going to visit his home on Tuesday and I was going to call in sick. I wanted to make love to him; the times we spent were too short and rushed because the places we went. All we had was our lunch breaks and it was not enough time for the way, he made love, he was patient and romantic. I couldn't believe that this young man was handling things the way he was. I shook the last time we were together out of my mind. The children were eating when I got home. Barry was sitting at the kitchen table with them. I walked in. "Hey babies, how are you all?" They all waved but didn't speak because they were stuffing their faces with spaghetti and meatballs. Barry always could cook. "Sit down baby and let me make you a plate". "I'm not hungry". "Try to eat a little bit; you look like you're losing weight". I started to say something nasty but it was caught in my throat. I coughed a little and sat down. "Thanks". He kissed me on my forehead. "Sure". There wasn't much conversation at the table. After dinner, the kids went outside for a while and I went up, got a shower, and fell asleep almost immediately.

Unexpected pain....

Monday came too soon for me. It was an uneventful weekend. Barry and I tried to act like husband and wife but there was too much tension. There were so many lies between us and so much distrust that it was a wonder we could even look at each other. Twice on Sunday, I caught him in the bathroom on the phone, and once he caught me on the phone but neither one of us said a word. It was sad how far we had come materially but so far emotionally. Our home was beautiful, we had all the latest equipment and appliances, and all the nice clothes but other parts of our lives were pitiful. I showered and got ready for work. I kissed Barry and left.

The day went slowly and I was not focused on anything. I hadn't heard from Roy since I left on Friday. I had been caught on the phone but it was with someone else, of course Barry didn't know he caught me because I played it off like I was talking to a female. I tried hard not to think about Roy but I was starting to get worried about him. I was so boggled down with work that I didn't even get a chance to walk around to the dock to see if he had come in but the day ended and I still didn't hear from him. I tried to reach him at his condo but I didn't get an answer, I left him a message on the answering machine. After I showered, I laid down on the sofa. When I got up again, it was night. I looked in the kitchen and the dishes had been washed and put away. The kids were in their rooms watching television. I went to my bedroom and opened the door. Barry was sitting on the bed naked. "I missed you today". "Oh really?" "I don't want us to fight anymore". "Oh really?" I couldn't understand why he thought I would sleep with him after he stayed out all night long, well at least until four in the morning. "Come and sit down with me". I didn't look at him. He was still sexy but I had no desire for him anymore.. "I'll pass on the sex but I do want to talk to you". "What do you mean, you'll pass on the sex, what the hell is wrong with you are you a dyke or something, you

haven't slept with me in two months". "Why are you worried, I'm sure you getting sexed on the regular with that whore you hanging out with at the bar every damn weekend and now during the week". "Don't start that shit again Sabrina!" "Why not, the truth hurts, do you think I am that stupid to think that you are just going to the bar to shoot pool, do you realize how stupid you think I am, you really think I believe that you are not having sex with her, I know you Barry, you are a whore, and you have always been a whore and you will be a whore until your black ass go away from here!!. If I have sex with you, something as big as me will jump outta your ass!" "What's wrong with you, you are my wife and you are supposed to provide me with what I need!" "Need, need are you kidding me with that shit, need, let me tell you what I need Barry, I needed you to be faithful to me, I needed you to love me unconditionally, I needed you to be supportive and understand me, that's what I needed. You told me that you would never hurt me like the others did; you told me that you cared about my feelings and my heart but you lied, just like everyone in my life. The tears were streaming down my face but I didn't care, I wanted him to know how much he hurt me. "Why are you so damn hateful Sabrina, you act like you are the only person in this relationship that's hurting, you act like you hold the market on pain, and you are not the only person with feelings Sabrina!" "What do you know about feelings Barry? I did everything you wanted me to do, I loved you, married you, gave you whatever your heart desired, made sure your dinner was in the oven, your bath was drawn and the whole nine yards and how do you repay me, by sleeping with the next door neighbor in our bed, the same bed that our child was conceived on Barry!!". "When are you going to forgive me for that Sabrina, that was eight years ago!" "How can I forgive you when you are still doing the same thing, it's just with some other trick!" He pushed me on the bed. "Now you listen to me, I have been faithful to you. I know I messed up but I have been faithful". "When Barry, when you're sleeping?" "Why won't you believe me?" "I will when you tell me where you were until four in the morning Barry,

on a work night and when the bars close at two!" Didn't you momma
ever tell you that the only thing open after two in the morning was
some whore's legs!? Of course you would know all about that now
wouldn't you Barry!" "You wouldn't believe me if I told you". "Sure
I would, if you tell me you were with that trick you been meeting up
with at the bar". He let me go. "There is no sense in talking to you, you
mind is already made up". "I didn't think your sorry ass could come up
with a story that quickly, you haven't told the truth in years Barry". He
didn't respond. He just put his clothes on and walked out. I didn't care
where he was going, I knew in my heart that he was sleeping around.
It hurt so badly. I loved him but I couldn't let go of the betrayal, it was
like a voice in my head constantly reminding me of it, I would dream
of snakes and blood and then the image of him and that girl would
pop in my head with both of them laughing at me. I would try to wake
up but it was as if someone was holding my eyes shut. I struggled to
breathe and fight the images but they were too real to me. I hated him.
I couldn't forgive him, I knew it was wrong but my heart was hard. I
didn't even matter that I cheated on him, in my mind it's was justified,
self-defense! He hurt me first! My mind was screaming, self-defense,
adultery! You are no better Sabrina!' My mental status was diminishing,
I wouldn't admit to anyone, not even Mike or the psychiatrist but in
my heart, I was losing my mind. I was starting to hear voices, I could
hear voices laughing at me, and prodding me to kill myself over and
over again in my head. Every time I tried to read the bible, and get a
handle on my life, the voices became louder and louder until I couldn't
hear myself think. I kept taking the pills, pills to wake up, pills to go
to sleep, pills to function on a daily basis. I cried out to God because
He was always the one who made my life seem manageable but I didn't
feel worthy enough to call on Him now because of Roy and because
of all the men and dirt, I had done over the years. I felt like I was
being punished because of Roy, and Jackson and having babies out of
wedlock, my abortion, my miscarriages, and even being molested, it
was all my fault and I couldn't stand it anymore. But each time I would
try to give it to God, the voices in my head would alter my direction,
the voices would take me away from what I knew could help me and
that was God and his loving kindness. I tried to hold on to His hand
but each time I reached out for it, it would disappear and I couldn't

grasp it. I was dying and I couldn't save myself and the only Man that could, in my mind, could not hear me crying out to Him, so my direction continue to be deterred.

I cooked the children a pizza for later. They came home late, took their baths and headed for bed. Barry called and told me that he was at his sister's house and would see me later. I didn't respond. I hung up. I was hoping it was Roy. I still hadn't heard anything from him. I went to bed early. I kept thinking about Roy, why hadn't he called me, why hadn't he come by my office and visit like he usually did. I was exhausted. I took my medication and slept. I was awakened yet again, I had a nightmare. I couldn't remember what the nightmare was about but it scared me. I looked at the clock and it was two a.m. I looked over and Barry was snoring. I jabbed him in the arm and he stopped. I lay on my side of the bed, afraid to go to sleep.

Six a.m. came too soon. I got up and showered. I stayed longer than usual, trying to wake myself up and besides I didn't' want to be in the same room with Barry. I got the children ready for school and then I was off to work. I drove slowly because I was early. I left early to avoid Barry. He really looked pitiful but it was too late. My heart hurt. It was getting harder and harder to be angry. It's true when people say its takes too much energy to stay angry. I stopped at a phone booth and called him. :"Hello". "I'm sorry, I talked to you like I did, I didn't mean to hurt you like that, I'm going through something Barry and I can't get a handle on it, I just want you to know that I do love you but right now I have to get myself together, I am going through some things that you wouldn't understand, hell I can't even understand it. "Baby, I love you, I've always loved you, I'm sorry I hurt you, I'm sorry about everything, please I am trying to love you, I am trying so hard to be there for you". "I know". "Sabrina, you still turn me on and I still want you, just like I did the first time I ever made love to you, but you got to let me in". "Look, I got to get to work, I just wanted to apologize". "Apology accepted, I love you". I hung up the phone and continued to work. I felt a little better. I went to work trying to convince myself that I was not going to worry about Roy. I figured that I would talk to him mid-morning after he was settled. I went to my office. It was busy as usual. I had about six tapes on my desk with notes attached. "Damn, they can work a sista for sure". I said to myself. I gathered the tapes and looked for messages from my two doctors. Please send film over to Hopkins, please send film to GBMB, "yeah yeah". I said to myself. The doctors were in their offices talking on the phone; my supervisor was talking to one of the other secretaries. I turned my system on., turned on my radio and started to relax. It was not long before I saw one of my friends, Jesse coming down the hallway. "Hey baby". "Hey Jesse, what's going on?" "You got a minute?" "Sure come follow me to the film room, I have to pull some tapes to send downtown". He was unusually quiet but I didn't say anything. We talked out to the adjoining room. "Sit down". Sabrina, I need to say something to you". "Sure" I kept pulling the films. "I need you to sit down with me baby". I sat down. I saw the tears in his eyes. "What's wrong Jesse?" He held my hand. "Sabrina, Roy is dead". I blinked maybe five or six times. "What did you say?" "Roy is dead baby, he's dead". He was crying freely now. He held tightly on to my hand, as if he needed strength to hold him together. "What in the hell are you talking about Jesse, don't play like that, Roy is not dead, I just talked to him on Friday, how in the hell is he dead!, what happened, did he get shot, what happened to him Jesse?". My makeup was smeared and my eyes were red. He was in a car accident; he lost control of the car and slammed into the wall. He died instantly". "Why didn't somebody call me yesterday?" "Nobody knew until this morning. His body was at the morgue. The police tried to reach the next of kin, but his brother wasn't home and the only phone number he had on him was his brother's. The police went to the house three or four times but his brother wasn't there. They finally reached him about five o clock this morning, He just went down to identify the body". "I'm sorry babe, I know how you felt about him, he cared about you too". I cried for what seemed like an hour. He sat with me until I got myself together. "I've got to get back to my desk". "I'm sorry Sabrina, I'm so sorry. Roy told me that you and he were really getting along good and he was serious about you, I know you know that. He didn't really care about these other young girls around here, he really did care about the friendship you two had, remember that, we were tight and he told me things he didn't share with a lot of other guys around here". "Thanks Jesse". I gave him a hug. "Come on around to the docks when you get a free moment". The news spread fast about Roy. I couldn't' make myself go to the main building. I couldn't walk past the area. I took one of my pills and tried to keep calm but I couldn't. I was so angry with him. I told him not to buy that car, I told him he was inexperienced, damn it why wouldn't he listen to me. A few of his friends came to the office and tried to take me to lunch but I couldn't' eat. I worked through lunch and my break. I was finished with those tapes before the day was done. I drowned myself in work. I didn't want to be there but I had to hang on until quitting time. The pills were talking affect. I was sleepy and I felt like I was high. I kept sipping on the soda that I asked one of the girls to get me while she was on break, but it wasn't helping. My supervisor asked me if I needed to go home. I told her no. I didn't' realize how many people knew about Roy and me. I was a little ashamed because they also knew I was married and older than he was. I cried every time I thought about his smile and his laugh. He was a good person. He really was a good man and now he was gone. He had his car all of two months and now he was dead. It didn't seem real to me. I believed that I would go around the corner and there he would be, leaning up against the wall with his gray uniform on, smiling like the cat that ate the canary. He was quiet but he had a smile that lit up the whole hallway. He had so many friends, male and female and you knew it because it seemed like everyone was sad that day. Some of my friends that I confided in came to my office or called to make sure I was all right.

Finally, the day was over and I could get out of there. I forced myself to walk towards his area. When I did, all the people were sitting on the deck smoking and talking about Roy. They spotted me and motioned me to come in a sit with them. Jesse gave me his jacket and I sat down on the dock with them. "How are you doing?" "Not so good". "It's going to be okay babe; it's just going to take some time". The tears were back. "Did anybody else hear any news?" "Naw". "Is it true that he didn't have on his seatbelt"? "Yeah, at least that's what the police told Kenny". "I heard he was going close to thirty-five or forty miles". James said. "I couldn't stop crying". One of the other guys held me. "It's all right Sabrina, you go on and cry, we all know how you felt about him, and we know how he felt about you".

Chapter 16

TIME TO SAY GOOD-BYE TO MY FRIEND…

Now I didn't know at the time that Satan was setting me up. I was so engrossed in my own pain and my own mess that I hadn't even realized that Satan was setting me up to destroy me once again. Over the years, I could see some things in my life that had to be nothing but enemy sent. When my dad was stabbed Christmas Eve, was I really supposed to see that? On the other hand, was it something that was set up for me to see? Something to make me so afraid that my mind couldn't consume it? Then my brother in law, his perverted ways, the things he did to me as a child, the way he took my innocence away. The way he made me have oral sex with him. The shame I felt when I sometimes gave in. How I stopped going to church and left the children's choir. Was it all Satan? Why was my direction in life being altered, why did Satan want me dead, what did I possess that he didn't want people to know? Why did God allow so much pain in my young life? In addition, why did I bring so much pain to myself? All things were sent through Satan, some mess I created for myself. Why didn't I leave Trenton, even after he raped me and sodomized me, held me in the bedroom for three days without feeding me, why did I let that happen? What was wrong with me? Did it all come from something deep inside of me? Why did I leave God, was it something I did on my own, or was it something that was planned from birth for me…The word of God says **I knew you before you were formed in your mother's womb"** God knew me, he knew every hair on my head..so He knew all about my life and what it would be like, but why did He allow all of this to happen to me? Alternatively, was it just me doing all this to myself? Did I hate myself that much, or was everything just set up for me to fall? Here I was again, in pain, so much pain because I have to say good-bye to my friend. My friend who cared about me, who possibly loved me as much as I loved him, or did I really love Roy, or was it lust? Did I allow myself to care about yet another man that was unavailable to me? Or was he the man that would have taken me away from all of this madness in my life, I would never know because he was gone.

When I think about it, I can see how God was with me all the time, fighting my battles for me, I didn't think he was but He was. He knew what Satan was doing all the time. With my husband's infidelities, with placing another man in my life to take my mind off Him. Satan is clever and sly. As I said, he will not come like the beast that he is, but will coming looking like someone you desire and looks good. Roy was a good friend and a good man but we were wrong. I was married and we were lusting after one another. Satan was also using Barry he didn't know it…but I did.

My mind should have been focusing on my marriage and how to salvage it, but instead my heart was broken because of my feeling for another man. It hurt because I didn't want to be in this situation, but it was too late. Roy made an impact on my life and I missed him badly. I was almost glad when my husband left out and didn't come home, then I could grieve for my friend. I could think about him without interruption I asked God to forgive me for my feelings. Mike just about begged me to open up but I couldn't. I was ashamed to tell him that I was grieving over a man instead of my marriage falling a part at the seams.

The funeral was so hard for me. There were so many people there. He had no children and no significant other. He was well liked and loved by many. I was surprised how many people knew who I was. I tried to stay out of the loop. I wore a navy blue suit and sat in the back of the chapel but people were coming up to me, asking me to sit in the front. I declined. What we had was private and I wanted it to stay that way.

After the funeral, I took his mother a fruit basket and a card. We talked for a while. I started to leave and she gave me a hug. "Thank you for the basket and your kind words". I hugged her back and left. It hurt but I had to get over it. It was not easy to grieve for a man who was not my husband.

I went home and Barry was there. He had been drinking. I saw the bottle in the trashcan. I went to the bedrooms and checked on my children. They were fine. I went to my room and to my shock, Barry was reading my journal. "Who in the hell are you talking about in this book?" At Mike's suggestion, I had gotten a journal to express my feeling and to get things out. I didn't think that Barry would read my journal but there he was reading all about my pain and agony I was feeling about Roy and his infidelities, and everything, even the voices in my head, which were almost second nature to me now, "None of your damn business!" I shouted. "You better tell me or I'm gonna beat your ass black and blue". "You put one damn hand on me and I promise you, you ass will draw back a nub!, I've been getting beat up all my damn life and you think I am just gonna let you beat the hell outta me too, not today, not ever again!". "Sabrina, don't think for a minute, I won't kick your ass all over this damn house!" "You do, and I will kill you where you stand Barry, I swear to you, I will kill you!" I was tired of running and defending myself… He threw the book across the room. "Just tell me Sabrina, tell me who you are talking about in this book, did you sleep with him, did you sex him like you should have been sexing me!" He woke the kids up. Darius, who was now fourteen years old, came running in the room. "Stop screaming at my mother you punk!" "Go to bed!" "No, you stop screaming at my mother right now!" I tried to come between them. "Darius, go back to bed, I am fine, honest". My two girls were crying in the hallway. "I am fine babies, go back to bed, promise, mommy is fine". Darius looked at Barry. "You touch her and I will kill you! No body is gonna ever hit my mother again, not as long as I'm living!". "Darius, please take your sisters to bed, I promise you I am fine, tell them I am fine Barry". "Yes, every thing is fine, go back to bed." They looked at me one last time and went back to bed. I closed the bedroom door. "What the hell is wrong with you? What did you think, did you think I didn't know about you and Shirley around the corner, you think I didn't know you slept with that girl in the park, and when you stayed out until four, you were at Shirley's house eating breakfast after y'all left the bar and finished screwing.", You think I'm stupid Barry, you think I don't know all about all the other women, Yes I knew all about it, I knew about all of it. You wanna know who I'm talking about in that book?" I'm talking about my friend, who I cared a lot about, why, because he cared about me , he wiped my tears when you should have been, he held me when you were holding that tramp that you met in a bar, When you wouldn't come home, he was telling me to hold on, pray for our marriage. He was respecting me when you didn't have the balls to. That's who I'm talking about, someone who cared about me and my feelings Barry, the way you should have, the way you couldn't because you were too busy worrying about how many women you could sleep with because that's how you equate your manhood, by your damn manhood! You don't' love me Barry, hell I don't think you ever did. "I tried to love you Sabrina, I tried to make it up to you, the things I did to you". "And how did you think you would make up for it Barry, how, by sleeping with yet another woman, how many is it Barry, how many dammit!" "You know what, you are crazy, I used to think it but now I know you are crazy Sabrina, you've always been crazy, I thought maybe it was because of the surgery, or the pain of your childhood, but you know what, you need help, you need to be in the damn hospital something is really wrong with you". "Go to hell Barry". "I'm leaving you; I should have left a long time ago". "Go on, do what you want to do, you always did, and now I am suppose to think that you haven't been waiting for a reason". "I wasn't going to leave you Sabrina, I tried to make it work, I wouldn't sleep with…" He stopped. I slapped him in his face. "You wouldn't sleep with whom, those bum bitches around the corner, huh, well guess what, you go ahead, it's not like you haven't done it before!" He grabbed a few of his things and left out. "I'll come back for the rest of my stuff". "Go to hell, if you don't get it now, I will burn it up!"

Barry left a few weeks later. He moved in with the woman he met at the bar, just as if I knew he would. I went to the bar one night, just to prove to him that I knew what he was doing. My girlfriend went with me and made me promise that I wouldn't do anything if I in fact found him with that Shirley person. I put my clothes on and went to the bar and there he was sitting at the bar with her sharing a drink. I tapped him on the shoulder and scared the hell out of him. "You can come and get the rest of your things before I burn them up." "Don't start nothing in this bar Sabrina". "Start something, I haven't started it, you have but guess what, you can have this bar whore if you want her, the way I hear it, every guy in here had her too, so please don't feel left out". She turned and looked at me. I looked at her and smiled. "You really think you got somebody special, well keep your little girls away from him, he likes sexing the young ones, don't you Barry?". Everybody in the bar started laughing. Before he could respond, I took the drink and threw it in his face. I walked out of the bar, I was so hurt that I thought I would die but I didn't. I kept my head up until I got home. Then I broke down and cried like a baby. My girlfriend and her husband stayed with me until I felt better.

The next day, I called my girlfriend Nicole, someone I met while I was in college and asked her to drive with me. Nicole was a pretty woman that was married and had three children. She was also a Christian. She seemed a little standoffish when I met her but every day when I saw her; I would speak to her even though she didn't look like she wanted to be bothered. We became friends and I had a lot of respect for her because she was holding her own. She was married but she kept her individuality about her. She allowed her husband to be a husband without losing herself and I had great respect for her because of that. I had lost myself own identity with Barry and in the end he left me for another woman. However, Nicole was still doing Nicole and that was so cool to me. She didn't want to go with me but she did just because she was my friend. "Now Sabrina, promise me that you are not going to go up here fighting or anything." "I promise Nicole, all I want to do is take him his clothes". We drove up to his new home with his girlfriend, who I found, lived with her mother and four children and God knows who else was living there, I shook my head. "That bastard left his kingdom to live in the basement of a trick's house, that's a damn shame". I parked right out in front of the house and blew the horn. "Hey Barry, bring your sorry butt out here and get your stinkin drawers out of my car you no good, stinking dog!" I was blowing the horn like a fool. Nicole was shaking her head. "Sabrina, you are going to get us killed ". Just then, Barry showed up on the steps of the house and she was standing behind him. I popped the trunk of my car and got out. By then everyone in the neighborhood was standing outside.

I grabbed the trash bag and it ripped, all of his underwear fell out into the street. I picked them up and threw them all over the street. "If she is going to sleep with you and take you away from your family, then she can wash your dirty skid marked drawers!" I threw them all over the street and in the bushes and the lawn. He looked like he was going to die right here. I looked at him and spit on the ground. "You low down filthy dog; I can't wait to see when you get what's coming to you". I got in the car and drove off. Nicole shook her head. "Girl you are something else, I don't know if I could do that". "You'd be surprised what you would do when your heart is broken". I said, with tears coming down my cheeks. I was hurt beyond belief. I know I had done some things, but I didn't' expect him to leave me like this, not for someone right around the corner from us. It hurt, all our friends went to that bar and I was so humiliated. My children went to school with her children and he didn't even care. That broke me, something inside of me died. I had given up my life for that man; he was my god for so long that I knew it was only a matter of time before I would die inside from the break-up. The voices were stronger than me now and they were starting to take over my life.

Chapter 17
GOING INSANE...

In my mind, I thought I was all right with my marriage ending, but I wasn't. My mind was gone and my heart was broken. Satan and his demons were gaining control quickly. I became distraught and my mind was filled with anger and homicidal thoughts. All the hurt and betrayals that ever happened to me were now at the surface. For years, I had stuffed things repeatedly. Man after man after man, not allowing myself to heal from one relationship to another. I went from Dennis to Jackson, Jackson, to Trenton, Trenton to Reggie, Reggie back to Trenton, Trenton to Barry, in between that, there was Reggie again, then Roy. Never did I give myself time to grieve over the relationships ending. It was like piling dirty laundry into a basket until the clothes started overflowing onto the floor. My life was flowing onto the floor. I tried to stop the pain. My girlfriend Nicole was so good. She would listen to me all night long on the phone crying, arguing, and crying again. I hated my husband, I couldn't understand why he left he way he did, the hurt he caused not just me but the children. Nicole would tell me that God is what I needed. "Sabrina, you have to let this go and allow God to handle Barry, you have to take your hands off the situation. God will handle him I promise you that". "No he won't Nicole, God doesn't love me anymore, all the things I did in my marriage, the babies I had out of wedlock, I lied to Reggie and I lied to Trenton, I've done things in my life that I can't be forgiven for". "Sabrina you can be forgiven for anything, God will forgive you; He will not remember anything once you have confessed it and asked for forgiveness". "You don't understand Nicole I did things that I hate myself for". "It doesn't matter, God will still forgive you. Look, I love you but God loves you more than anything in the world. He died for you and for me Sabrina". I started crying. "Nicole, my mind is going, I can't remember anything, I can't think straight, I can't sleep, I can't' eat, I feel like I am dying inside". Come on and pray with me Sabrina". "I don't know how anymore". "Yes you can, I will start okay". "Heavenly Father we come to you tonight thanking you for all things God, thank you for loving us and caring about us and your healthy children and all things that are great and small, thank you for our homes and our jobs. Thank you God. Now God I come to you today, standing in the gap for my friend and your child Sabrina, God she needs you right now, she needs you to breathe on her Father, she needs you to forgive her for the hatred that she feels towards Barry, she needs you to forgive her for the secrets she thinks she is hiding from you, but you know all about it Father, touch her Father from the top of her head to the soles of her feet, keep a hedge around her God, please help her Father, give her strength to do what she needs to do to get well". I was crying so hard that my head was hurting. Nicole prayed some more and before I knew it, I was praying too. We prayed for a while. Afterwards we didn't say goodnight or anything we both just hung up the phone.

The voices in my head were speaking loudly and clearly. I couldn't hear anything but those voices. I tried to fight it by myself but there was no fighting anymore. Remember **the enemy comes to kill steal and destroy** and that's exactly what he came to do to me. I could no longer function at work and took a leave of absence.

Not shortly after taking the leave of absence, I had a break down. Mike called Barry and told him that I was going in the hospital and I needed someone to stay with the children. He was happy to do it, I think it was just guilt but I soon found out why he was so happy to do it for me. While I was being admitted to the hospital, he stayed with me until they told him he had to leave. I did not speak while I was being admitted, I could not, and in fact, I did not speak for fourteen days straight. All I did was cry. I couldn't form a word nor could I even put a single thought together, the voices were all I could here now and they were telling me every thing. I tried to tell the doctors and the nurses that I could hear them but I couldn't form a word. So I cried.

The voices were laughing at me and telling me that I was going to die very soon and that I should just give up and allow myself to die. After fourteen days, I was finally able to speak and the first thing I did was call my children. My baby girl was so upset that she was crying when I called. "What's wrong baby?" "Mommy, I want you to come home with me, I'm scared". "You don't have to be scared baby, nothing it going to happen to you". "I don't like it here mommy, daddy got that ugly woman in your bedroom and I don't like her. I lost it all over again. I was screaming and yelling at him like he was crazy, I told him if he came to this hospital that he was going to die, that was the second time he brought some woman to my bed,. I was fed up with him, and he was going to die the first chance I got. I had to be medicated. They called my sister and told her to get the children. I didn't see Barry for a long time after that. The police were notified that I was homicidal and that Barry should stay away from me. I guess he knew they were serious because he didn't come around for a year.

Daniel 3:23- And these three men, Shadrach, Meshach, and Abendego, fell down bound into the midst of a burning fiery furnace....

Yes, there I was in the fiery furnace, unlike Shadrach, Meshach and Abedengo, I was unable to feel the power of the Lord. I was unable to reach out towards the heavens and receive my strength. My footing was like that of the feet in the miry clay. "All other ground is sinking sand". It was true; I had lost my footing and was falling. However, I know the prayers of my family, friends and one attendant in the hospital saved my life. I was so hurt and so broken hearted the first few days I got there and they put me in the "buck naked room". That's what the patients called it because they put you in the room with nothing on but a gown and a mattress. I was crying and carrying on so badly, my heart was breaking into and it felt like it was breaking physically, I couldn't stop the pain or the tears. Barry was no help. He came to the hospital and told me that he couldn't stay to visit because his girlfriend was downstairs waiting for him. I spit in his face, and threw a puzzle at him that hit him square in the head, when I saw the blood dripping from his forehead, I wanted to laugh and I did. That's when they put me in the room. Sara came in the room and sat down on the floor with me. 'Sabrina, get it out and don't stop until you get it all out. That man is not going to help you, let him go, he is no good for you and he never will be, I cried and cried, she held me in her arms and kept talking, I know a man named Jesus and He will love you unconditionally. That man is just a man, he cannot give you peace to sustain all understanding, and I am telling you that God is all you need. Let Him move that man out of your life and watch God bless you, just watch Him. I cried the rest of the night and well into the morning. I know the prayers of that stranger and the way God used her to minister to me, probably saved my life. I didn't' know it then, but years later, I realized that she and my friend Nicole planted those seeds about the Lord in my heart and those seeds would grow to make me all that He wanted me to be.

I was in the hospital for about a month; it was an experience that could not be described. The people in there were sick indeed but they were very good people with problems. There were people that were rich financially but were so empty inside. Their families were gone or didn't understand them. We were a group of people that needed help, Mental health was always taboo to most people, especially to black America, but I needed help, I didn't think I did in the beginning and I had fought admissions to the hospital for five months but finally I realized that I needed help I could not do heal alone anymore. The voices were all there and there was nothing I could do about them. The medication was not working anymore. Therefore, I conceded and went into the hospital. They had a regimen for us. We had levels that we had to earn before we could go off the floor or eat in the cafeteria. The first thing I had to do was take an AIDS test. It was hard for me to imagine getting AIDS and I cried when I took the test. Not because I thought I had AIDS but because the lifestyle I used to live and the lifestyle Barry had lived our entire marriage. I thought about all the men that I allowed in my spirit. Ninety-nine percent of the time, I used protection, but the one percent that I didn't is what allowed me to take that test without hesitation. It didn't matter to me anymore that the men I was went were my "friends", Friends betray one another every day, What hurt me the most was I knew in my heart I really wanted that test because of the women Barry laid with. I knew he never used a condom. He thought they were too restrictive. AIDS was spreading like wildfire and no one was immune to it, although society tried to think that it only applied to gay people, I was smart enough to know that no disease discriminated.

Barry was a whore, plain and simple and that reason alone had me running to the nurse's station. I cried for two days because it hurt, it hurt to know that my husband had slept with so many women and I allowed it.

I had to face so many things in my life the time I was in that hospital. I had different classes that I had to attend. I had Art class, Swimming, group therapy and individual therapy, on my down time, I would fix puzzles and write in my journal and talk to my children on the phone. The medicine was working and I was not hearing the voices as often anymore. I was still working my way back to God. I would sometimes still cry at night because I was simply just sad about my life all together. I was in my thirties and I was in the hospital and on a leave of absence at my job. I was not even sure if was going to be able to go back to work once I was released.

Although I was in the hospital for people with mental health and emotional issues, I felt good. They put me in the room with three other women. They were the three most wonderful people I had ever met. It is a true that God places people in your life and that is what He did with these women. They kept me focused on what I needed to do to get better, they encouraged me to always write in my journal and get my feelings out. We shared our lives, our pains and our good times with one another. In addition, even though we were all from different faiths we knew that there was only one God that could deliver us from our demons of depression, schizophrenia, and suicidal tendencies and anything that we were battling. We comforted one another and always tried to make ourselves scare when we new one another needed time alone. My experience there made me stronger. It was not long that I was able to speak, talk, and even laugh again. I was able to come home on the weekend and then ultimately for good.

It was good to see my children. It was good to be home again. I was not able to go back to work right away, just as I thought. The doctors suggested that I go to a day hospital. I did not mind it, I knew I was not ready to go back to the stresses of my job or face my colleagues. So there I sat in the day hospital. It was a good experience for me. Not on the first few visits but eventually, I learned what was expected of me and the staff learned to respect me. I guess they were used to dealing with unruly people at some time of their stay, and their defenses were already up when they approached me, but I had to let them know that it was not my illness that made me who I was, It was me. After that, they had no problems out of me and I had none from them. Mike was still able to be my therapist and he helped me a lot.

Chapter 18
HATE IS SUCH AN EVIL WORD!

Although my health was improving, my personal life was still a mess. Barry had done everything in the power to try to ruin me. He would break into my house when I was at work and leave messages on my mirror, or leave messages late at night on the windshield of my car. He came into my home one morning about two a.m. in the morning and was standing over me when I woke. I was scared but I didn't' let him know it. "What do you want and how did you get in here?" "This is still my house and you are still my wife". "I am nothing to you anymore Barry, please leave my home". "I said this was my house". "Why don't you go home to your girlfriend?" "She's at work". I got up out of the bed. "If you don't leave right now, I will have the police escort you out, you do not belong here and I have told you that over and over again, this is what you wanted and you got what you wanted so please leave now". He pushed me on the bed. "You are my wife and I need for you to be my wife tonight". He started unbuckling his belt. "What In the hell do you think you are doing, I know you don't' think I am going to sleep with you after you had that tramp in my bed, in my house". "That's exactly what you are going to do". I pushed him out the way and went downstairs, I knew that if we stayed upstairs that he would wake the children and I did not want that to happen. I walked in the kitchen and grabbed the phone in there. He knocked the phone out of my hand. "Look don't make this hard on you". He grabbed my breasts and tried to kiss me but I pushed him away. He kept trying and I kept fighting. Finally, I kicked him in the family jewels; he buckled over in pain, and ran out the door. I called the police as soon as he left. They came out and told me to get a restraining order against him. Barry's mental abuse went on for several weeks. There was no way of me stopping him from doing any of his dirt.

Hate is such an evil word, but I was bordering on hating this man. I just could not believe the things he did just to hurt our family and me. Shirley worked at night so she did not have any idea of all the things he was doing while she was at work. I tried to talk to her but she was so ignorant. I called the house and asked for her specifically. "Can you please put Shirley on the phone?'? Who ever answered the phone told her that I was on the phone. "What in the hell are you doing calling my house?" "You should be asking me how I got your number. Look I didn't' call to fight with you, I just want you to keep your dog on a damn leash and keep him from my damn house". "What the hell are you talking about?" I am talking about that raggedly ass man you got up there with you, keep a damn leash on him because he is not well trained. He keeps coming to my door, pissing all over my house and I can't take it anymore. The next time he comes to my house, I guarantee you that he will do time in jail". "Don't call my house threatening me". I'm not threatening you Shirley, I'm simply telling you to watch your boy". I hung up the phone and I didn't' wait for a response. Apparently, she did not tell him anything because he continued to harass me. Things finally came to a head a few weeks later.

It was a nice crisp day. I had our daughter in the car. I was coming from the grocery store. The person I had in the car with me was a friend that I meant while I was in the hospital. His name was Jamie, he was Italian and very funny. He kept me laughing all the time. We were good friends. He would come around and visit me and we would hang out. We were coming from the market on this nice crisp day. Nia and I were laughing at some stupid joke that Jamie had just told us. I parked on the street that day because of all the groceries that I had. Jamie took a few bags and I was getting some more out the truck when Barry showed up out of nowhere. "I'm taking my daughter with me today". I looked up and there he was. "No you aren't taking her anywhere, there is a court order against you and you just can't show up at my house and take my child". "She is my daughter too". "Apparently, you didn't give a damn; if you did you wouldn't have left her and this family for some tramp and her four damn kids". At that moment, Jamie came out of the house. "Are you okay, Sabrina?" Barry looked at him as if he was crazy. Jamie was a nice looking man. He was about six feet tall, and he was Italian. His hair was black and curly and he wore it wild. He had five o clock shadow and these piercing dark brown eyes. He was not a big person, but he had a nice six-pack and his legs and arms showed how he worked out before working out was popular. He used to tell me that he had to do something positive to balance all the negative BS that he was doing in his life. He wore a diamond stud in his ear; he said it came from his first girlfriend that he lost in a car accident on I-695. I guess that was the starting point of his addiction. I didn't push him about it; I would listen while he talked about it. I knew just how he talked about her that he truly loved her. He had a daughter that he did not see because the parents did not approve of him; they thought he was not good enough for their daughter.

He looked at Barry as if to say, Negro please. "Oh you got Jungle Fever now!" Jamie came towards the car. "Man look, I know this is your wife and I am not going to get involved, but let me just say this, I ain't your typical white *boy!*" "And what that mean?" "That mean that you ain't gonna talk to me no any kind of way and you sure as hell ain't gonna talk to her like that, you made your choice". "Man look, this ain't even about you!" Jamie ignored him. "Are you okay Sabrina?" "I'm fine, I grabbed Nia and started up the hill towards the house, just then Barry snatched her out of my hand. "I said she was going with me!" I felt my daughter starting to fall so I let her go. "You are not going to take my child away from here today Barry, You have no right to be here and acting like this". Before I could react, he pushed me; he pushed me so hard I fell on the ground. When I fell, he kicked me in my side. "Bitch". I grabbed my side. I heard Jamie. "Man you gonna die for that move! However, before he could reach Barry, he jumped into his van and drove off. Jamie ran after the van but we both knew that he wasn't going to catch a moving van. He ran back towards me and helped me up. Before I could get to my house, the police were there. "Mam, we have a description of the van that drove off. Do you need to go to the hospital?". "No officer, I am fine". "Well we will catch him". The police picked him up in a matter of hours. They locked him up and that's where he stayed for five days before she bailed Barry out of jail.

Chapter 19
I'LL SEE YOU IN COURT!

The months before the court date were hectic and trying. I kept getting threatening phone calls, hang-ups and God knows what else. I called Mike and he suggested that I go to The House of Ruth a refuge for battered women. It was so hard for me to go there; I could not believe that my husband beat me as he did. I really thought those days were over. I don't think I had been hit since Trenton but here I was at the House of Ruth with all these beautiful but battered women who have given their lives and souls to men who torn them apart slowly but surely. Going to the House of Ruth, enlightened me a lot and it made me stronger. When I first went there, I could not even hold my head up, my self-esteem had plummeted all over again and I was back in a hole of darkness. Mike was so upset that I had such a relapse but that beating he gave me out there on the sidewalk in front of my child and my neighbors and my friend took me lower than I thought I could ever go. I stopped thinking well about myself. The phone calls that came with the humiliation did not help me at all. The first few meetings I just sat, cried, and listened. I didn't feel like I had anything to offer anyone but as time went on, I met so many good women and good friends, that were really good people in general but we all had something in common, we allowed men to take our self-respect and our pride and we didn't realize it until way after the first hit ever came. There was one woman that I remembered and will always remember. She came into the meeting and she kept her head down, that was not unusual but something about her stood out. We all sat and listened to the counselors and other women. As we sat and listened, slowly and gradually this young woman put her head up. We didn't look at her right away; we all knew what she was feeling. We all knew how embarrassed we felt when we first came to there so it was not unusual for us. At one point in the conversation, it got quiet and we heard someone crying. When we looked around, it was this young woman. She was crying, low at first, but then she started crying as if her life depended on it. We all consoled while the counselors gave her tissue.

I'm sorry". We all told her that it was okay. "No I am really sorry. I came here to apologize to each and every one of you". Mary, the counselor asked. "Why do you think that you need to apologize to us, there is no need to do that we are all here for the same thing". "No you all don't remember me". We all looked at her. She cleared her throat. "I came here about two months ago with my best friend. She was being beat by her boyfriend of two years. He had burned her with cigarettes, beat her and threw her out in the street with nothing on but her bra and panties. She kept taking him back,

I couldn't' understand why she kept doing it. I called her stupid, crazy, and dumb. But she kept taking him back. She never raised her voice at me and she never stopped loving me as a friend even though I was treating her like dirt. Last month, my best friend was locked up. They locked her up because she decided to fight back. She beat that man within an inch of his life with a baseball bat. Now she is waiting to go to trial. She never hurt anyone in her life and the only reason she fought back this time is that she was fighting for her life. I may never get my friend back. I thought I knew all the answers, I thought I would never be stupid or dumb enough to be caught slipping. I thought I would never be like my best friend". She lifted her head up and we could see the bruise on her face. She took her jacket off and we could see the bruises on her arms and around her neck. She turned around and lifted her shirt, she had huge bite marks that were blue, black and purple, and they looked painful. "See, now I am my best friend, I thought it wouldn't happen to me, no man would ever hurt me like this". She sat back down. "I'm sorry". She started crying again. "Do you need somewhere to stay tonight?" "I can't leave; he will kill me if I leave". "Is there anything you would like us to do?" She shook her head no. "He will kill me, you all don't understand". "Can you go to your family and then call the police?" She laughed a laugh that scared me and probably a few others too. "My man is the police; in fact he is a lieutenant". Well my mouth fell open. There was not much else that we could say. The rest of the meeting was eerily quiet. After it was over, the counselors took her in the office.

I felt bad for her, I went to my car and I prayed for her. I prayed for God to intervene in her life as well as her best friends. I was not surprised by her story though, none of us were, we heard a thousand times how women were put in prison, had court dates coming up, lost their children, lost their vouchers for their Section 8 houses all because of the men that beat them. It was so hard for battered women because no one understood why we stayed. It's not easy to explain that to people who have never been where we were. Everyone thought that abuse started with a hit. But it didn't, it started way before the hit. First, it takes away your self-esteem; always calling you fat, ugly, tell you that you smell bad, that you need to do something with your hair. Then they call you up constantly trying to control your every move, they isolate you from your family and friends and when they have you where they want you, the beating start, oh not immediately, first it's a push, or a shove, then it's a slap and before long, it's a punch that never stops. But it couldn't be explained.

I went home that night with a newfound strength. I was going to testify at that trial and Barry was going to be found guilty. Jamie had to leave to go to Ohio to help his grandmother so he was not able to be there. "Brina baby, I want you to go in that court room and hold your head up high. Do not let that fool intimidate you, humiliate you, or even see you upset. You are a beautiful woman and you are very smart and you deserve the very best that this life has to offer you. I am going to miss you but I know one day I am going to see your name in lights or your face on the television, telling people your story. I know that you are going to be someone very important to this world one day". "I am tired Jamie, really tired". "I know you are baby, but you know what, you have strength that you don't even realize you have. I've watched you over the past few months, and I shake my head and ask myself how in the hell does she do it, but then I realize that you are special Brina baby, God has something special for you one day, you just got to believe and trust". He gave me a kiss on the cheek. "I'm going to miss you Jamie and I know the kids are too". "I really like your kids and I appreciate all you have done for me Brina". "I didn't do anything special". "You believed in me Brina. You trusted me and that's something I lost a long time ago because of my addiction, but you trusted you and me believed in me. You gave me the strength to fight for visitation for my baby girl and it's working out, thank you for being a friend". I gave him a hug and drove him to the bus station. I was going to miss him.

Trial day:

I went to court with my sister, my sister in law and my niece and nephew. I ran right into Barry, his girlfriend and his sister. I didn't acknowledge them but they started talking junk as soon as they saw me. "She got the nerve to get somebody locked up on sexual assault charges that hoe". My attorney and my sister both took my hand. "Don't feed into them Sabrina, he's not worth it and she sure as hell ain't worth it". I didn't know until I got in the actual courtroom how many of his friends were in the courtroom. However, I had a few of my own friends there too. I went up to the table with my attorney to meet the State's Attorney. "Good morning, my name is Peter Taborinna. You just need to answer my questions honestly. When you answer, look directly at the judge. He likes that sort of thing. You know you don't' have to testify because he is your husband". "No I want to testify, after what he did to me, no one will stop me from testifying". "Good, that's what I wanted to hear". I went back to my seat. The people on his side of the courtroom were laughing and pointing at me but I wouldn't let the intimidate me. I looked over at him, he had is arm around her shoulder and laughing as if he had this trial beat hands down. I prayed silently and tried very hard not to let it bother me. When the judge came out, we all stood up and waited for the bailiff to tell us to be seated. Barry's attorney was a white woman who wore a sharp Ann Klein suit that was fitting her nicely. She stood up. "Good morning your Honor, I am Amy Sands and I am the attorney for my client. I will prove this morning, that my client did not hit his wife, kick his wife, or sexually assault her. I will also show that plaintif is suffering from depression, hallucinations from the psychiatric drugs that she has been ordered to take, and made up this whole insane façade simply because Mr. Taylor has moved on with his life with his fiancée who he is sitting with this morning". The courtroom did ooohs and ahhas and "no he didn't come in here with another woman". I didn't blink. I was pissed about all the things she was saying about me but my attorney told me that they would do that so I didn't feel mad enough to cuss her out. As the trial got started, his attorney went on and on assassinating my character, but I didn't let it bother me, I knew that my attorney was going to tear him to shreds. When it was finally my time to testify, his attorney objected. "Your honor, this is still the plaintif's wife and she cannot testify against him". My attorney intervened "your honor, the plaintif has agreed to testify against her husband in this case". The judge looked at me, is that right?". "Yes sir". My attorney was so good at what he did, that the whole courtroom had turned against Barry before we even recessed. And when we did, I was asked to step out in the hallway. However, my sister Dionna was there in the courtroom. She made sure no one started anything with me while I was in the hallway. She looked over at Barry's girlfriend and let her have it. "

You got some nerve coming in this courtroom trying to make my sister look bad, trying to make her seem like she is wrong for bringing charges against this dog that beat her and raped her in front of her children, what kind of woman are you? How in the world do you sleep at night? You had the nerve to come in my sister's house and sleep In her bed while she was in the hospital recovering from a breakdown, what kind of woman does something like that, a whore, plain and simple. You broke my sister's family up over a sorry ass man like that, he is a bum and he will always be a bum, the only reason he has anything is because my sister paid his way through school and took care of his sorry ass while he was calling himself bettering himself, but what did he do, go out of town and sleep with the class tramp, just like you, a tramp, my sister doesn't need his ass, she is much better than that and when his sorry ass is found guilty, yes guilty for every single charge he is being charged with today you are going to look like a damn fool. You sitting there all hugged up like you got something special, all you got is a damn rapist and an abuser that will cheat on you just like if he cheated on my sister. I cannot believe you bailed this dumb fool out of jail; you should have left him there because as soon as he came home, while you are working at night, he was on the phone begging my sister to forgive him and all that crap. You are a damn fool if you think this fool is going to treat you right, he doesn't know how to treat a woman right, because he isn't a man, he is a little boy playing a grown up game, but you better keep that dog on a leash, you know what they say, when you lay down with dogs you get up with fleas! The courtroom went crazy, even her friends were shaking their heads at her. By the time I came back into the courtroom the tables had turned.

His attorney was red and mad, she tried to tear me apart on the stand but I told the truth plain and simple.

"Mrs. Thomas can you tell the court what happened on the day in question?

"I was asleep when I heard a knock on my door"

"Which door?"

"Excuse me?"

"Which door, the front door or the back door?"

"The front door"

"What time was it?"

"Around one or one-thirty"

"Which?"

"Which what?"

"Which time, one or one-thirty?"

"I'm not sure".

"Are you sure about anything you are testifying to today?"

"Objection, she is badgering my witness".

"Sustained, watch yourself counselor".

"Let's just say, it was late".

"What happened after you heard the knock on the door?"

"I looked out the bedroom window and saw the van that he usually drives".

The courtroom ooh and ah'd . I guess because it was his girlfriend's van.

"And then what?"

"I opened the window and asked him what he wanted"

"And what did he say?"

"He said that he was sorry he showed up so late but he just got off of work and had the money for our daughter's field trip and wanted to give it to me".

"I told him to put it in the mailbox but he said that it was cash and he didn't want to leave it out there"

"So you let him in?"

"After I put my clothes on, I did"

"Why?"

"Because I didn't think he would do anything to me, he never did anything physical to me before".

Go on"

"I let him in and he tried to kiss me"

"As soon as you opened the door?"

"Yes as soon as I opened the door", she was getting on my nerves I kept my cool.

"Did you resist?"

"Yes I did, I didn't want him kissing me"

"Did he stop?'

"Yes".

""Is it true that you were admitted to Shepherd Pratt Hospital twice last year?"

"Yes"

"Is it true that you were unable to return to work after you were discharged from the hospital?"

"Yes"

Isn't it also true that you couldn't remember a lot of things on your job and you were told to leave your job?"

"No that's not true, I was asked to take a leave of absence".

"Did you In fact get suspended from your job?"

"No I did not; I took a leave of absence under the recommendation of my counselor and therapist"

"Are you psychotic medication?"

"No"

"No, do I have to remind you that you are under oath?"

No, you do not".

"Then I will ask you again, are you on psychotic medication?"

"No I am not; however, I am on anti-depressants".

The courtroom laughed aloud. Even the judge smirked.

"Are you on medication today?"

"No I am not".

"Didn't you say that you take medication for depression?"

"Yes"

:"And you are not on drugs today?"

"No I am not".

"How can we be sure that you are not on drugs Ms. Thomas?"

"I don't do drugs counselor, I take medication for a mental health condition that I am prescribed prescription medication for, no I am not on it today because if I were, I would not be able to testify because the medication is prescribed for me to take at night only"

"And you are not on any drugs this morning?"

"Objection asked and answered"

"Sustained".

"On the night in question, did your husband beat and kick you?"

"No not on the night in question".

"I'm confused Ms. Thomas, we are here today because you said your husband beat kicked you in the street in front of your daughter"

"Don't be confused, the day that he beat me was not the same day that he tried to rape me".

"And what day was that?"

"What day was what?"

Which day did he try to rape me or when he beat and kicked me"? "Don't be confused".

I looked at her; I wanted to slap her because she was being smart,

"Objection your honor, counselor is badgering the witness".

"Sustained. Counselor, watch your step".

We went back and forth like that for about twenty more minutes before she said she had no further questions, It was good to see my attorney standing in front me.

"Would you like a break?"

"No sir".

"Can you please explain what happened on the night in question?"

"I heard a knock on my door about two am in the morning. I looked out my bedroom window and saw my husband's van. I opened the window and asked he wanted. He said that he had our daughter's money for her field trip. I asked him to put it in the mailbox and I would get it in the morning, he said that he did not' want to leave it in there because he didn't' want anyone to steal It. In addition, that he had an outfit for her. Therefore, I went down and opened the door.

He gave me the money and when I tried to get the bag from him, he pushed his way past me. I asked him to leave but he said he needed to talk to me, I told him that I did not want to have a conversation and that I had to get up early. He asked for a drink of water, and I said no, he told me that it was his house and that he would do what he wanted to do. I tried to ask him to leave again and he pushed me on the sofa and pulled my nightshirt up. I pushed his hand away and he said that I was his wife and that he could come and sleep with me any time he wanted to. I pushed him again and he pinned my hands down. Right before he got my panties off, my son came down stairs and yelled at him. He jumped up and left"

The courtroom was quiet, so quiet all you heard was the recorder going on.

"When did you see your husband again?"

"A week later when he saw me bringing groceries in the house with a friend of mine".

"Did he speak to you?"

"No but he said that he was here for his daughter, and I told him that it was Thursday and that she had to go to school and he could pick her up on the next day. He yelled something and grabbed my daughter">

"Was anyone else there?"

"A friend of mine and a few neighbors were out there along with my daughter".

"What happened after that?"

He got into an argument with my friend. He walked over to the car, snatched my daughter by the arm, I tried to pull her back to me and he pushed me on the ground and kicked me".

"Did you require hospitalization?"

"No".

"Were the police called?"

"Yes"

"Ms. Thomas, I know this is hard but have you heard from your husband since the incident"

"Yes, I've heard from him over twenty five times since the charges".

"How can you be so sure that it was more than twenty five times?"

"I wrote it down in my journal".

"Do you have that journal with you today?"

"Yes I do"

"Objection your honor, there was no talk of a journal for evidence you just can't bring a book in here and let her read it!"

"Counselor, watch your tone and I can do whatever I want, this is my court room. We will take a fifteen minute recess and the journal will be put into evidence."

"All rise!"

I was a wreck; my attorney told me that I could go out in the hall to get some air but not to talk to anyone. I did what I was told, a few of my friends walked out with me because he had so many of his friends out in the hallway,

After a few minutes, the court reconvened.

"Ms. Thomas, do you have the journal?"

"Yes I do"

"Can you read the pages where you heard from the defendant?"

I flipped a few pages. I was praying that they did not ask me to read anything else.

I gave him so many dates; the judge said that it was enough. He looked over at Barry and shook his head.

"I have no further questions".

Ms. Cutie pie attorney stepped back to me.

"May I see that journal?"

I handed it to her and she flipped through the pages, thankfully, she did not read the pages, she would have found where I cried for Barry at nights, and that I was so hurt by what he had done to me. She passed the book back to me.

"Ms. Thomas, do you think your husband wanted to hurt you that night in question?"

"I really don't' know what my husband's intentions were. All I know is that he has yet again taken something from me".

"Excuse me?"

"He took my peace of mind counselor"

The courtroom became quiet, and this time I did cry. Not loud, just the tears.

Finally they put Barry on the stand, he made a complete fool of himself, first of all he looked like he never wore a suit and tie in his life, secondly, we went from not seeing since he walked out to all he did was push me. When my attorney read the notes from my journal aloud for the court to hear it was disaster.

After testifying and being cross-examined for an about twenty more minutes the case rested. The judge looked at him.

"Mr. Taylor, I find you guilty of sexual assault in the 3rd degree, assault and battery, I want to put you back in jail because quite frankly, you make me sick. I have never heard so terrible and horrific testimony all my days on this bench, how dare you come in here with your girlfriend and flaunt her in front of your wife, how you can sit there rub it in her face. You assaulted her, beat her, and kicked her like a dog in the street in front of your own child. I find you guilty and I sentence you to 5 years in prison, all suspended and before you get happy about that, let me say that you will continue to stay away from your wife, you will pay a fine of $5000.00 and you will see that your wife gets all of her child support every single week. And for all of you who came in here to make this victim look bad or to humiliate her let me say that she is one of the bravest women I know to seek help and to work at getting better you are to be commended Ms. Thomas and I wish I could lock him up today but it wouldn't benefit you or your daughter to have your child support stopped".

"Thank you sir."

"Court dismissed".

People were hugging me and crying and telling that I did an excellent job on the stand that they were praying for me and prayed that I would get better soon, they thought that I was brave for standing up against him. They thought that his girlfriend was a whore and they patted my sister on the back and told her that she made her feel two feet tall.

It was over, I won, and I finally won something. I was happy about it. I looked over at Barry and he looked defeated. He did not speak of course his sister and his girlfriend were pissed talking a bunch of crap about they are going to catch a charge if they did not get out of the courtroom. I ignored them. I walked home and I cried, for so many things, but most of all because I was able to stand up and say something that would mean something to someone. I had to let people know what he did to me, no matter how painful it was for me.

Chapter *19*
THE CALM BEFORE THE STORM

The days and nights of my life seemed to mesh. I was not happy nor was I sad about my circumstance. I guess I became numb. I had been through so much over the past 3 years, but my divorce was not yet final. Barry didn't stop his foolishness and my life became like a big target on my back, it seemed that every where I turned, he was doing something to me, my car or my children, it was like he had a vendetta against me, but I never let him know how much he was hurting me. I kept working but the money was short. He wouldn't pay the child support that he was ordered and Trenton was always a no show in my other children's lives, he never gave a dime towards my children but in his defense he was an addict and homeless so I didn't' expect to get anything from him, but struggle and survival was not new to me, it was like second nature. However, it was getting harder and harder to manage. I had given up my last relationship; John was a very sweet man and he would do anything for my children or me but he wouldn't work. I tried to understand a man that wouldn't work but it was very hard for me to do that. I was raised that "if a man shall not work, he shall not eat". To come home each day and find him playing Nintendo with my son or hanging out on the steps with Darius' friends when I worked all day, got under my skin. It hurt me to tell him that it was over but I had no choice in the matter. I sat him down one night after dinner. "John I appreciate everything you have done for me, you know helping me with the kids and making sure they are okay until I get home, but I can't do this with you anymore". "Sabrina, I am going to

find a job, I promise". "I can't live on a promise John; I need someone
to help me with these bills. Barry will not pay his child support and
I am so far in debt that I cannot see my way clear. I need help baby
and you can't provide it for me". "I will get a job soon, I told you that
I been looking". "Well you can stop looking on my account, because
it's over John". "Why you gotta be so cold Sabrina? ". "I'm not being
cold John, I am being realistic, you don't have anything to offer me,
and I can't keep doing this. I will give you to the end of the month to
leave". I knew he was hurt but I could not do it anymore. Living with
someone for the sake of having a man in the house was overrated. I
know he truly cared about me but it was not enough. He was 8 years
younger than I was and he was the sweetest man I have ever known I
was not ready to love anyone the way John wanted me to anyway. I was
not even sure if I loved myself. Maybe if it were another time, another
season, but not in 1993.

It was hard day at work and I just wanted to get home, take a
shower and go to bed but when I got to my front door, I had about 15
court notices on my door.

I pulled them down and walked in the house. I tried to read all of
them but it was so confusing, I made a note to call the management in
the morning. Barry kept coming

around in the van with his girlfriend laughing and staring at me
and riding off. I thought he was truly losing his mind but I found out
the next morning exactly why he was laughing.

I sat down at my desk and called the management. "Good morning,
can I speak to Carol please?" May I ask who is calling?" Yes this is Ms.
Thomas".

She placed me on hold for a few minutes and then Carol came to
the phone.

"How are you Sabrina?" "I'm fine what's going on with all the court
notices?"

"Well, I tried to call you yesterday at your job but the line was
busy, we have to evict you Sabrina". "What, why, because my rent's late
you know I always pay my rent Carol, I know it's been a little tough
these past few months with Barry not sending the child support but
I've made it". "It's not that Sabrina, we got a call stating that your son

was selling drugs and that he was arrested for a sexual assault against a neighbor".

"What?" I was in shock and I could not believe it. "Carol, my son is fifteen years old and he does not sell drugs, if that was the case do you think I would allow that in my home after the way drugs have affected my life?" "I'm sorry Sabrina I have written proof and a petition to get you out of the neighborhood and I have to abide by it":" But you don't even have any proof". "But we do have proof that you haven't paid your rent on time in the last six months and by law that enough to evict you, you have 30 days to leave the premises". "Thirty days, where in the hell am I going to find somewhere to move in 30 days Carol?" "I'm sorry Sabrina, it's not my call, you know if it was my call you would not be moving". My head was swimming, where in the hell was I going to take my children in thirty days. I could not breath, I could even see in front of me, I was so shocked that I just sat there and finished working like it was nothing going on crazy in my life. When I got home, I told John that I was being evicted.

"What the hell happened?" "They said that my son sells drugs".

"Get the hell outta here, D-Man don't sell no damn drugs'.

"I know that but they want me out of here and I have to go, I just don't know where I am going". "You'll find something Sabrina". "With my credit and my income, there is no way I will be able to find somewhere to go, especially in thirty days. I know it's that damn Barry, I just know it John, he kept coming around here like he knew something that I didn't".

The phone rang. John answered it for me.

"Man don't call this damn number no damn more, you punk ass".

He slammed the phone down.

"Your husband is gonna get his ass kicked if he keeps pulling these dumb ass games".

"What did he say?" "He said how you gonna live now, with your homeless ass"

"I got up and dialed his girlfriend's number. She answered the phone.

"Look, I told you to keep that bastard on a damn lease, if he calls my house again, I am going to come up there and personally beat his punk ass!"

"He ain't here and you ain't gonna do nothing!" "Shut up ho, the only reason you want his sorry ass, is because you think he's coming back here, dumb ass, that's why you sleeping with a damn rapist"

I sat at my kitchen table and just cried, I had no idea where I was going and how I was going to tell my children that we were going to have to leave their friends and the comfort of their home, but I knew they would be okay, my children were true soldiers and they were strong beyond their years.

The day that we were evicted, it seemed that everyone was outside in the neighborhood. They did not know we were being evicted I just told them that I was moving out of town to get away from my husband. In truth, I had no idea where I was going. My girls were going to my sister's house and my son was going to my nieces' house. I however, had no idea where I was going. Just when I thought I couldn't take anymore, Barry came driving down the street. All of my stuff was on the sidewalk waiting for the truck to come.

"Hey do you need somewhere to stay?" Kiss my ass Barry!"

"You could always sleep in your car, oh I forgot you can't drive your car can you, you don't' have any tags". John walked up the truck.

"Man get the hell away from here before I pull yo ass out that van and beat the hell outta you, you are a sorry bastard to have your children on the damn street, you call yourself a man, you a sorry ass excuse for a man, to sit here while your family is trying is trying to find a place to lay their head. How in the hell do you sleep at night man, first you rape your wife, beat her in front of her own child and then you get her evicted from her house because you are mad at her, you had your girlfriend and all those hoes at the bar to sign a petition to get her evicted and have her daughter lie and say your own son sexually assaulted her, just to hurt her, it's a damn shame, I'ma pray for you man, you need it".

All of a sudden, Barry looked funny, he looked embarrassed, the people that heard what John said just looked at him and shook their heads. He waved his hand at John and pulled off.

I tried very hard to understand why he would do something so despicable to me and the kids but nothing could surprise me any more. I was tired of fighting him and everything anymore; I just wanted some peace in my life.   I put my things in storage and took some things to my sister's house. I stayed with her sometimes and sometimes with my mother, it was rough but I made it through. John would come by and see me but it was not the same with me anymore, I was not the same person any more. I wanted so many different things but things were jumbled up in my life and I could not decipher what I wanted to do first, except to find a home for my babies and me.

I stayed homeless for several months. Nevertheless, I made it my business to go and get the children and take them out to the movies and store for clothes and shoes and just to treat them, I owed everybody and I was in fifty two thousand dollars worth of debt. My car was gone, and there was a garnishment on my check for the house I just lost, but I was still making it through. I was so much in debt, that I couldn't afford stockings so in the winter time I would try and wear my pants, I didn't have a lot of clothes because I lost a lot of things when I moved. Most of my furniture was gone, what I had kept was in my sister's basement, and it was ruined because of the dampness. It was hard to live with my sister, not because she was awful or anything or treated me badly, she had her own stuff to deal with and it was hard for us to communicate. Still I appreciated what she did for me. I paid her rent but it never seemed enough and I felt bad because I had nothing else to give her.   Mike made sure I had my medication, but my sister would use it to and I would run out sooner than I needed to. I didn't say much about it, it was her house and I had no say so. I didn't even stay home most of the time, I would go to work, come home and walk to my mother's house and stay down there, some nights, it was just to hard to deal with. I had been on my own since I was nineteen years old and here I was thirty-one and homeless.

Finally after three months a woman on my job told me about a townhouse where she lived at, I didn't care where it was, it was going to be my home and the lady didn't' care about my credit or anything else. She just wanted me to come out and look at it. A month and I said three hundred and forty dollars yes before I could even get out the damn front door. It was a very old townhouse and it was brown walls and floors but it had a roof and three bedrooms, so I took it, the kids were excited that we were going to be back together, but we hated where it was but we had to count our blessings, we would be together again and we didn't' have to take any thing off of anybody if we didn't want to. We moved in one day.

Chapter 20
LIVING IN EGYPT

I moved and was for the most part happy. I was happy that my children had a home to come home to. I was glad that we didn't have to take any thing else from people who really didn't want to help us anyway. I thought that things would work out for us for a change. Again, I was wrong. I became ill again. I stopped taking my medicine and fell into a deep depression. I didn't tell my family what I was going through. Even though they didn't want me to live with them, they really did care about me. It hurt them to see me like this, they wanted me to be strong and get over it but I couldn't I tried to be strong, I tried to fight it, I tried to be what every body else wanted me to be but I didn't have in inside of me anymore. In reality, I gave up and didn't know it. The voices were back and they were laughing at me, telling me to kill myself, get over the pain and kill myself. They were louder than usual I could hear them all the time instead of when I was alone or the house was quiet , the voices were constantly laughing and speaking to me, I tried to keep it together but finally it was too much for me to handle so I went into the hospital.

Sometimes it is hard for people to understand the demographics of depression. It is a disease and it is an illness that thousands of people suffer from every day but no one likes to talk about it because mental illness is taboo, especially to African American people. Therefore, I didn't tell anyone. I just doubled on my medication and tried to drown out the voices. I went about my usual day, working, riding the bus home going in the house cooking for the children cleaning and playing with my grand son. I was finally able to buy a car, it wasn't much but it got me back and forth to work and going to the mall and taking the kids to their old neighborhood to visit their friends. I didn't have any real friends. My only friend Robbie moved to South Carolina. I missed her a lot but I knew she was trying to make her marriage work so I respected why she did what she did. My mother tried to comfort me but I believe that it hurt her too much to see me like that, so she called more than she visited.

John 14:1 Let not your heart be troubled, you believe in God, believes also in me.

When we keep our minds on God, God gives us peace of mind. I read that one day in the Daily Bread, but I didn't keep my mind on God. Therefore, I had no peace. II was still going back and forth to counseling but I was still not getting any better, the medicine wasn't working for me but I kept taking it. I went off to counseling and I was agitated. I don't know why, my spirit was really bothering me. I was not able to sleep and I couldn't' eat. I had lost so much weight that the doctor put me back in the hospital and threatened to put me on IV fluids. He made me take all of clothes off in front of the nurse and made me look in the mirror. When I looked at myself, I was so scared. I was so tiny that I could see my bones. My face was sunken in, and my breasts were non-existent. I didn't realize that I hadn't eaten in months, and when I did eat, it wasn't much. For the first three months in the townhouse, there was no stove or refrigerator and I didn't have anywhere to keep food. I would buy chicken boxes every night and bring food home from the hospital so the kids could eat. I would lie and tell them that I ate already because I didn't want them to worry. I really didn't have enough food to feed all of us so I sacrificed and wouldn't eat. My children and grandchild came first at all costs. When the doctor put me on the scale at the hospital, I weighted 107 pounds; I don't ever remember weighting that much in my life. I cried and cried. He made me promise that I would eat and he would let me go home the following day. My father in law brought me a refrigerator after I told him what Barry did. Trenton's brother brought me a stove, took us to the market, and filled our cabinets and house with foods and goodies for the children. I was blessed, God was still with me but

I didn't' recognize it, I was so far gone that I didn't' realize anything anymore, I was existing but I wasn't living.

I didn't want to participate in group and I didn't' want to deal with anyone else that day; I just wanted to go home. However, Mike kept telling me to finish the group session and I could leave.

"Sabrina, what is wrong with you today, you seem so angry". "Nothing is wrong with me; I just want to go home". "Are you still upset about your one on one yesterday?"

"I know I didn't take all those damn pills and I don't appreciate no body telling me that I did, I am not addicted to those damn pills and I sure as hell ain't selling them".

"No one said that Sabrina, she said that you were overmedicating yourself you take those pills and you won't eat or drink anything, you just take the pills and go to bed"

"You ain't in my damn house you don't know what I do!"

"Lower your voice Sabrina,"

"I ain't doing nothing; I said I am ready to go!"

I don't' remember anything else after that.

"Ye though I walk to the valley of the shadow of death, I will fear no evil, for thou art with me, thy rod and thy staff they comfort me....Psalm 23

Chapter 21

HE LOVES ME..AND HE TOLD ME

I heard a voice…*that is enough, it is done. It is time to let go of the anger that you are feeling for your husband. It is time to forgive him and all the others that have hurt you. It is time to let it go and start living the life that I intended for you. There is a will for your life and it will be done. My grace is sufficient.*

Then there was silence. When I awoke, I was strapped to the bed.

"How are you feeling?" I heard the nurse but I couldn't speak. The tears were coming down my face and I was afraid. I didn't know where I was or how I got there. I couldn't' remember anything except for the voice; it was a calm voice but a strong voice. I could see myself asleep with a sheet draped over my body and my head, feet and hands exposed but I couldn't feel anything under me. It was not dark where I was, it was not cold and it had no smell. I couldn't see where the voice was coming from but I heard it loud and clear, in fact it was crystal clear. Now I was somewhere else. I could feel the bed; I could feel the straps confining my movement. I could feel the rubber tip on my forefinger. In addition, I could see the nurse speaking to me. I wanted to tell her what I heard but nothing came out. She patted my head. "It's okay, you're going to be fine, you just need some rest". I kept looking at her and she must have known that I was scared. "Don't be scared, sometimes our brains do things to us when we are upset. Your brain just shut down, but you are all right now. We gave you some medicine and you're going to be fine". "You had a seizure, but you are going to be just fine I promise. The medicine seems to be working fine now. "She wiped my tears away. "Honest, you will be fine. I'll bet you don't' even know where you are" I shook my head no. "You are in the ICU; we didn't want to take any chances with you". Just then the doctor walked in. "Well, it's good to see you awake". He took the chart from the nurse and sat down beside my bed. "How are you feeling?" I shook my head. "Right now, don't try and speak, you have a tube down your throat, we had to do that to help you breath. I guess you want to know what happened." I shook my head yes. He proceeded to tell me that I had a seizure while I was in conference with my therapist. I started screaming and shouting and foaming at the mouth and then I passed out. My brain shut down for about thirty seconds, I was given some medicine and taken to ICU because my heart rate and blood pressure were off the map. I was given medication for seizures and heart palpitations. I had been strapped down because I fought and kept pulling the IV out of my arm and the tube out of my mouth. I had been asleep for at least sixteen hours. It's the scariest feeling I have ever encountered. I did not remember anything the doctor said to me. I wanted to ask him a question but I could not speak, I gestured for him to give me a piece of paper and pen, he realized what I was saying, I wrote down my question. He smiled and said, "No, we didn't move you, you have been here alone in this room except for that guard over there to watch over you in case you woke up suddenly". "Why do you think you were somewhere else?" "I wrote down that I didn't remember being here but I remember seeing myself lying in the bed. He looked at me somewhat strange. "Do you mean that you were somewhere watching yourself?" I shook my head yes. "Tell me about it". I wrote down what I could, the medicine had me groggy but he got the gist of what I was trying to say. "Sometimes things happen to us that we don't understand. I am a scientist and I judge things like a scientist, but sometimes I must confess that spirituality has come to play a lot in my judgment of unexplained things". I started crying again. He patted my hand. "Get some rest". He said a few words to the nurse and walked out. She gave me some more medication and I drifted off to sleep.

I was afraid, and I don't know why. But I wanted to know what happened in those sixteen hours. I knew that I was probably unconscious but still not knowing was frightening. I do know one thing; I was not frightened of the voice that I heard. It was soothing voice and firm.

I know I would never forget those words and that voice that spoke to me that day. However, although I didn't forget the words, I didn't take heed to them. I should have stopped right there and turned my life around but sadly I didn't. I should have run towards Christ, but I didn't.

Stifled....

Months went by. I was better and back at work and feeling good about myself. I had no side affects from the seizures and I did thank God for that. I was finally getting my debt down to a manageable number but I still was not able to move to another area but I didn't care. At least I wasn't homeless and for the most part, I was happy.

When the phone rang and China told me it was John, I was happy, I had not heard from him in a long while. "Hey stranger". "Hey baby, how are doing?" I'm fine and yourself?' "I'm doing okay, I was thinking about you and I wanted to stop by and see you if you want some company". "Sure John, come on out, you know you are always welcome in my house."

The children were happy that he was coming out. When he showed up it was so good to see him. He has lost some weight but that didn't surprise me because he was small anyway.

"It's good to see you Sabrina, how are you?"

"I'm doing fine, you lost some weight?"

"Yeah and you found it".

We sat down on the steps and talked for a while. We ate dinner with the kids and cut up for a while. After that, we watched television. It was getting late so I told him he had to leave. I"I don't want you to miss the last bus John, so I am going to walk you to the bus stop, okay?". "Sure, let me go to the bathroom and we can go". The bus didn't take long. "Take care and I will call you when I get in town, but you could have taken a man home". "I would have John, but I don't have gas like that". "I know baby, I'm just joking with you". He gave me a hug and hopped on the bus.

It wasn't until two days later that did I discover what his real motive was for visiting. I went into my bible, my hiding place for my bill money. When I looked for the money for the car note, it was gone. I kept shaking the bible out. The ten dollars fell out but not my bill money. I started searching around the bedroom and the closet, under the mattress and everywhere else, I would hide my money. I tried not to panic I still had a few more days before the note was due. I went to work as usual and tried not to think about the money. As I prepared my tea and turned on my computer, my girlfriend Valerie that worked in the building in housekeeping came in my office and sat down. We were not talking about much when the phone rang; it was the University of Maryland's Emergency room. "Good morning, my name is Ms. Gibson; I am calling for Ms. Thomas. "This is she". "I am calling to tell you that your friend John Simmons is here in our emergency department, he has been beaten severely" "Where did you all find him?" "He was in an alley off of Maryland Avenue". I called his mother and she told me that he was beaten and robbed. "What was he doing on Maryland Avenue Faye? ". "He said that you asked him to pay your car note for you". "I never asked him anything such thing, I didn't even know he had my money until you just said something". "I'm sorry Sabrina; somebody should have told you that John has been getting high". I was so shocked, I couldn't say anything. "He was fighting to get your money back Sabrina, he knew that he was wrong, he just wanted to try and get some of your money back". I hug up the phone. The sad part is he didn't' even get to spend the money. I was sick about him stealing from me. I trusted him. And he betrayed me.

It took me weeks to get the money for my car note. I didn't want to pay my note late, I had just established my credit and here I was paying late already. My big sister Francine called me and told me that she would lend me the money. "Thanks so much Fran, I am so grateful, I will give it back as soon as I can". "Don't worry about it Sabrina, you can give me to me when you get on your feet". I loved my big sister, she was so intelligent and had so much wisdom, I could listen to her talk for hours because she never raised her voice and she never judged me, no matter what kind of fool I made of myself she loved me unconditionally. My girls and I rode out to her house. Darius and my grandson didn't want to ride with us. They preferred to stay home and watch music videos. I was driving and talking to my children. They were laughing at the way I was trying to sing Dr. Dre's song "Keep Yo Head Bangin". As I turned the corner, I heard my daughter yell. I felt the car move beyond my control and I felt it turn around in a circle and slam into the sidewalk. My head slammed into the windshield and by body was yanked so hard, the seatbelt cut across my chest and started to burn.

I was flown to Shock Trauma and my baby girl was flown to Johns Hopkins Pediatric Shock Trauma. I had at least four seizures by the time I reached Shock Trauma. I could hear the voices again, telling me that I was going to die this time, for sure, that my children were going to die with me, the laughter was so loud that I couldn't hear myself breath. I was banged up pretty bad. I couldn't walk because I tore a ligament in my hip. The seat belt burned my skin right off my breast, my daughter was in a coma and they were not sure she was going to wake up. I kept asking for her but they wouldn't tell me anything, no one would, my family or the doctors, I cried and prayed and prayed and cried asking God to take my life and allow my baby to live. I couldn't' see her or talk to her because I was really in no condition to talk or even try to stay strong in lieu of bad news, so they drugged me and I fell asleep not knowing if my baby was going to live or die.

Tracy did finally wake up, she got a few stitches and lost her short-term memory but she as alive! Barry was there and he prayed for her and begged her to wake up, I heard he cried and cried until she finally woke up. I found out that he brought his girlfriend but they wouldn't let her see my baby, my family saw to that, they made her feel uncomfortable and I knew they did that for both of us.

We both recovered and were able to leave the hospital. I was told that I would always suffer from seizures, but I knew one thing for sure, that the devil was a liar.

I was out of work for a while, and I took that time to try to find out why evil was always in my life; I tried to find out why I heard voices and why they always wanted me to hurt myself or others. I spent hours researching all types of mental illness. I didn't know where the voices came from but I was believed in my heart that Satan was trying to kill me, I didn't know why he was trying to kill me, why he wanted me to perish so I turned to the bible as well and read and researched the book of Mark, I found Legion fascinating and I wanted to learn more about that book. I prayed for understanding and guidance while I read. I prayed and talked to God about Legion and more and more stories in the bible. I took the time to look back over my life as well.

Altered directions, was what my life was about. For years and years, my life never went in the direction that I intended it to go. I tried to understand, I cried so many tears, so many tears, why Satan, why were you doing this to me. What did he see in me that I did not see in myself? When I think of all the ways my life was altered, it scared me, it made me realize that I had a target on my back, and Satan and his demons were the ones holding all the weapons of warfare to take me out. I wondered often, where would I have been if I were in a "normal" family, one that didn't have an alcoholic father, I wondered what direction I would have taken if my father were not stabbed and the fear of losing him engulfed my life, I wondered what direction I would have taken if I were not molested by a sick individual who had no soul, who only took souls, I wondered what direction I would have taken if I were not in an abusive relationship from age sixteen until I was twenty one years old, what direction would I have taken if I had be true to my heart and stayed with Roy, if I would have listened to my heart on my wedding day and not married Barry, what direction would my life had taken, If I would have stayed in church, continue to sing, continue to believe and have the faith, where would I be. Somehow, I was turned around going in a completely different direction. The word of God says **"the enemy comes to steal, kill and destroy"** and I knew that. How many times in my life had he tried to kill and destroy me and steal my joy? This thing I was going through frightened me. It worried me. It made me stop in my tracks so many times in my life. Why couldn't I see what God saw in me? Why couldn't I want what God wanted for me? Where was God and I missing it, He was not missing it, but I was. Fear consumed me, fear was my life, fear took me places were I did not need to go, and I allowed it, I ALLOWED IT! And that's what bothered me, why was fear so strong and dominate in my life, all the men, the shame, the guilt, that's what consumed my life, that's what allowed me to keep putting up with all the stuff that I did. How many times was I going to allow pain, abuse, rape, molestation, lies, deceits, emptiness looking at myself in the mirror, how much more was I going to take? What was so sad is I did not know, I truthfully did not know. It is said that **F**alse **E**vidence **A**ppearing **R**eal, is what fear is, false evidence there is nothing real about fear but what you allow it to do to you, and I let it consume me, take me over and control my life I wanted to cry out, something about that accident made me think differently I guess not being able to walk, not be able to care for myself completely, the loss of my fierce independence, made me think a lot.

Fear the Lord and depart from evil. It will be health to your flesh and strength to your bones. Proverbs 3:7-8.

I wanted to depart from evil, an evil that had control of my life for so many years. That scripture was talking to me, about my sin and uprooting it while it was still manageable. However, I had no understanding of what God was trying to tell me. I knew I was saved but I also knew I was not delivered, not was not set free, I needed to be delivered, and still I didn't know what God was trying to tell me, still. After all of the things that happened to me, the promiscuity, the drinking, the drugging, the raising hell, the pain, the fights the abuse all of it, after all of it, I was still here but still I was lost, I didn't know where I belonged on this stage of my life, when was my scene going to play out, when was the director going to say "cut, it's a wrap!".

Chapter 21

NEW LIFE, NEW START, NEW DEMONS….

While we were both recovering, Nia and I stayed with my sister, Dionna, but I was soon able to go home. My mother would come out, bring me food, and cook for me. She would take me to the doctors and stay with me. I got better but I knew I had a long way to go. While I was waiting for recovery, the townhouse that I had applied for two years before finally came through and I was able to move. When I told the children we were moving, it was probably the best news they had in a long time. Before, all the news had been bad, but finally something was going our way. We did not have a car and the townhouse was not on a bus stop but that did not stop us from being excited. We just wanted to get out of that neighborhood and start our new lives.

It did not take us long to pack, we gathered boxes from the corner store and stored them in the house until the rental manager told us our townhouse was ready. We were so excited, when we moved I didn't' take many things with me. I took the bare necessities. My mother and sister helped me move. Darius and his friend pitched in. It was a good day. The children were so happy to be getting out of there and going to a school where they knew people. I was in my new house in one day. I did go back to Turners one last time to clean the old townhouse. The only person I really would miss was my new grandson and his mother but I was not upset, I knew I would see them.

We walked around the townhouse more than a dozen times

just smiling and laughing. It is strange the little things you take for granted. Like garbage disposals and a washing machine hook-ups and a stove. Being able to plug things up without having to use one and two extension cords. Our wall-to-wall carpeting and windows to bring in a breeze. Our capacity to sit out on our porches without being afraid. The ability to speak to our neighbors without being treated nasty. Having grass on our lawns. The little things in our lives that we never thought about. . I cherished these things. It was a hard two years at our old townhouse, not all the people were bad, I met wonderful Christian people who loved the Lord. However, I called it Egypt, because there we things I went through that allowed me to be humble. Now I had a new townhouse and a new lease on life. I was still out of work on sick leave because of my accident. In addition, I was still on my crutches but I was getting better each day. I had gotten a lot of my strength back but the seizures were not going anywhere. I stayed on my medication and didn't let things upset me. The manager was so surprised when she came out to make sure everything was in working order. She was amazed at how fast the children and I had gotten pictures on the wall and the beds up and the shower curtains hung. She was in awe when she saw all the boxes broken down and sitting out waiting of the trash collectors. But She didn't know was I forever grateful to God and to her for accepting me and my children into that house. I thanked God every day for that woman and His blessings.

A few months had passed and I was back to work, it was hard because I had to walk a ¼ mile to the bus stop. Nevertheless, I did it gladly every day. It was so nice just to come home to the house and know that the children had not been in a fight or no one had threatened them. I was back in church and happy. I even met a new man.

He was two years older than I was and he lived in the city. My girlfriend Valerie, who used to work at the hospital, introduced us.

"Sabrina, I want you to meet this guy on my job:" "Valerie, I don't' want to meet anyone right now, I am just trying to keep my head straight". 'But he is so nice and he is just what you like, tall, dark, and cute, and he is sexy as hell". "Then you go out with him"

"I can't he is A-cee's buddy, and girl I don't like dark skinned men". "There is a first time for everything". "Come on Sabrina, you will like him, I know you will".

"Val, I haven't been in a relationship in two years, girl I don't' know what the hell I am going to talk about with him".

"He is nice Sabrina, honest, you need to meet somebody else, all those fools you used to mess with wasn't shit".

"Thank you very much"

"I love you Sabrina and I am so tired of seeing you alone, you are so pretty and you have such a big heart".

"Girl I can't be with no body right now, I have to get myself together, I just moved and I am back in the word and going to church and I am happy".

I'm not asking you to marry the damn man; I just want you to go out on a date, damn!"

"I understand what you are saying but please understand what I am trying to say, I need this time to regroup, I need this time to do me for a minute".

"Why are you so afraid to step out again? You need someone just like everybody needs somebody"

"Valerie, you have no idea where I've been or what I've come from, it's hard for me to trust men anymore and I don't' want to meet someone with all my baggage, I have to have a chance to get rid of some of it or at least try to handle it so that I don't' bring it with me".

"I know what you're saying but he is so nice and he is just what you need. He is tall and he looks like Aaron Hall you know with he bald head, and you know the bald head is in girl". We both laughed. "How well do you know this man?"

"He is cool I promise you, I will tell you that he just got out of jail a few months ago"

"For what?'

"I don't' know, I didn't pry into his business, but he is he really nice Sabrina".

"Well I tell you what, give him my phone number and we will see what happens".

"Okay, when I go to work I will make sure that he gets it, y'all gonna hit it off I know, I already told him that my sister is very pretty"

"Look I gotta go, I love you"

"Me too sweetie"

I wasn't to sure about this person, and I forgot to ask her for his name so I had to call her back.

"Valerie, you didn't tell me the man's name".

She laughed.

"I'm sorry, it's Chris"

"Okay".

We hung up. I still wasn't sure about meeting or talking to this Chris person, I had been celibate for two years and it cleared my mind a lot. I wasn't pressed for a man in my life. God knows I had enough men in my life over the years to last me a lifetime. I was still thinking about what God wanted from me, what was my purpose in this crazy life, why was I even born. I was back in church, the pastor was more of a teacher than a preacher, and I loved him and his family. I learned so much from going to that church. The word of God really does enlighten you to things of this world. We talked about Gods love, patience, and favor. How much he truly did for us by giving His only Son for our sins. How much He loved the broken, disheartened, confused, and everyone in between. I related to so much of the word. Mary Madelglene and so many others, but God gave them favor. I realized that God never left me, He had always been there over all those years in my life, even in the rough times, and hard times, the painful times, the times when I was being promiscuous and worldly and He still loved me. He was still there when I was sick and tired of being sick and tired. I wanted to be what He wanted me to me, but I was still fearful and still unable to let go of that fear, and still I couldn't understand it. I spent hours and hours writing in my journals and realized that over the years I had so many journals, I vowed that one day I would be able read each one of them to see how I had grown but I had not gotten there yet. I lie across my bed and read a few scriptures, we were learning about forgiveness in bible study. Pastor had given us the question, who is the hardest person to forgive in our lives? I thought that it was a trick question at first because my first thought was the person who molested me, then I thought maybe it was my father for leaving me at an age when I needed him most. I thought about Barry and all the pain he caused me, then I thought about Trenton, with all the abuse, then the person that tried to rape me at a party, or was it Dennis who beat me in the street the day I came from the cabaret. Who was the hardest person in my life to forgive, it was a hard question and I couldn't figure it out. I finally fell asleep. Or I thought I fell asleep but I wasn't sure. I wasn't sure once my eyes opened again.

Daughter, I need to you listen to me and hear. I have forgiven you for all your sins because you have asked in My name. I have forgiven your sins and they have been thrown into the sea of forgetfulness. You must move forward in your life and allow Me to carry you through this journey, turn it over to me, fear is not of me, and anger is not of me. Of all my commandments the greatest is that, you love one another. Trust me. Hold on to my hand and allow me to lead you and guide you to your destiny...

When I woke up, my heart was beating hard and fast. I looked around my room and no one was there. It was just me. Was I dreaming? Or was God speaking directly to me? It was the same voice I heard when I was in the hospital, calm but firm.

The weekend came and went and Monday was here before I knew it. Valerie called me and asked me if Chris had called. "Did he call you?"

"No he didn't call me yet". "I told him to call you and that he better not hurt you either!"

"It's okay Valerie; he'll call when he is ready". "No he promised me that he was going to call you, I am going to cuss him out when I get to work tomorrow". "It's all good, don't worry about it" "No Sabrina, he lied, he said he was going to call you". "Maybe he doesn't have a phone" "So, there is the phone booth". "Valerie it's cool, he will call when he is ready". We talked a little while longer, her fussing about Chris not calling and me about her fussing about Chris not calling.

The next day was a busy day in the office and I worked straight through. When I got home the kids were all outside and doing their thing. It was still good to come home and see them so happy and content and around their friends again. I was looking out the front door when I heard my phone ring. "Hello".

"Hello can I speak to Sabrina?" "This is Sabrina". "Hey how are you, this is Chris".

"Oh how are you?" "I'm fine, I'm sorry I didn't call you the weekend, it got real busy".

"It's okay I understand". "Well your little sister cussed me out royally this morning at work all through the warehouse she was screaming ".

We both laughed. "You would have thought I did something illegal". "Yup, that sounds like Val".

"I said damn baby, I'ma call her, she must be ugly if you want me to call her that bad".

"Excuse me?" "No I mean the way she was pressing me to call you made me think you must be pressed". "Naw, I'm not pressed at all". "I didn't think you were and she said you and her favored so I know you're not ugly". "Good save Mr." We both laughed. We talked for a long time. He kept putting quarters in the phone booth so that we could stay on the phone longer. We talked on the phone for two weeks before we saw one another. When he told me that he was coming out to visit, I told him where I lived and that the bus did not come to my area. "I was thinking of coming after work Friday, how does that sound to you?" "I'm fine with that but let me tell you that my house is not on a bus stop". "Oh that's cool; I will catch a cab to your house after I get off the bus".

"Are you sure?" "Yes, just tell me where I am going and I will take care of it".

I gave him the directions to my house and we made plans to hook up that Friday. I called Val to let her know that he was coming. "I know, he told me that he was going to come out and see you because talking to you on the phone was making him more curious every day. I told him that you were fine girl and that he was going to like what he saw, I told him that you had big boobs and a big butt and he laughed like Oh my goodness!"

"Girl don't' be telling that man I got no big butt"

"Girl please, you are fine and he will be glad to have you on his arm."

"Was he talking about me?" "Was he, hell we were talking about how he don't eat lunch no more because he is always on the phone at lunch time calling yo ass!"

"He's seems to be pretty cool". "He is. Did he tell you he just got out of jail a few months back?" "Yes he did and so did you, but, I'm not worried about that".

"He is your type, he is tall very tall, dark skinned and skinny, but he got big hands!"

We both laughed at that.

"How about big feet, not that I am even thinking about sleeping with that man"

"Trust me, when you see him you will want to".

"Stop playing". "I mean he is not fine, but it's something about him that turns women on, these bitches out here be all over his ass, Hey Chris, Hi Chris, slipping him phone numbers on the side like no body know what they doing, damn hoe's I told them that he was seeing you and they need to back up". "Girl your ass is crazy; you can't be blocking that man's flow". "Yes I can!"

We talked some more and then I got dinner fixed. The kids came in and were doing their own thing. My children had grown so much. Darius. was eighteen years old, China was sixteen and about to graduate from high school with a perfect attendance and a 3.9 grade point average. That was especially good for her since she had the baby and had to take care of him. My baby girl Nia was ten and growing up nicely. They made fun of me and how I stayed on the phone with Chris. I tried to describe him to them as much as I could, hell I didn't see him either so I didn't know what he looked like exactly. But we would find out soon enough.

Friday came and I had my hair in micro braids. I put on a nice pair of jeans and a tee shirt; I told him that he did not need to take anywhere. I told him we could hang out and just talk some more and go for a walk and get to know each other. He said that was okay with him.

Chapter 22
MAYBE I'LL GET THIS LOVE THANG RIGHT!

I sat out on the steps playing with my grandson while I waited for Chris. He had called and told me that he just got off the bus and was waiting for the cab to bring him there. I told him exactly where to come. After about twenty minutes, I saw a cab emerging from the distance. I stood up so I he could see me. When the cab pulled up and he got out, he had balloons, flowers and a box of candy. I walked to the cab with my grandbaby.

"Sabrina?" "Hello Chris". He looked exactly like I thought he would, He was very tall, and dark, just like Val said. I was wondering what he was thinking about me.

I embraced him and gave him a hug. "How are you, did you make it okay?"

"Yes the cab driver knew exactly where you lived, and let me say you live a long way from the hood". I smiled.

"I know that's what everybody tells me". "It's cool though I don't' have a problem with that. These are for you" He handed me the flowers, candy and balloons.

"Oh they are so pretty, thank you". I hugged him again.

We walked in the house and I introduced him to my children who were all very respectful. Of course, my son looked at him crazy, but he caught it.

"Don't worry man; I'm not here to start no trouble".

Darius looked at him. "Make sure about that man, my moms is a beautiful person".

They slapped each other five and Darius. went back outside.

My girls giggled and walked upstairs.

We sat down on the sofa.

"So how are you?"

"I'm fine, you are very pretty Sabrina, I know Val told me you looked like her but I don't think so, you are fine as hell".

Thank you, you ain't so bad yourself. Can I get you something to drink?"

"Sure".

"I don't drink so the strongest I can offer you is a Pepsi"

"That's fine, I don't drink either".

I said a silent thank you to God.

We talked, walked, talked, and walked for hours. He was street smart and well read. He seemed to have himself to together. When we went for our walk, he laughed and said he felt like a white boy in a love story because he had never, ever went for a walk with a girl.

"You are funny, it's not that corny"

"Naw, I'm not saying that, I'm just saying if my people knew I was walking around some quiet white neighborhood holding a woman's hand they would ask for proof."

He stopped and kissed me. I responded.

"I have wanted to do that since I laid eyes on you baby, your lips look so good!"

He kissed me again, and again I responded.

We walked for a few more minutes. It was really getting late.

"Are you ready to go?" "Not yet."

We walked towards the house and sat down in the living room. The kids were upstairs in their rooms. As we sat on the sofa things were probably running through his mind just as they were running through mine. "Do you have any children Chris?"

"Naw, God never blessed me with kids; I guess he had other plans for me" "Do you want any?" "Not now, I'm too old for kids now, I love them and all but I am too old to be raising kids". "You act like you're sixty or something"

"He laughed, naw, but I'm almost forty, it's my time to shine now Shorty".

"Have you ever been married?" "Yes, as a matter of fact, I am married now, but I've been separated for about five years". "Do you think you will get a divorce?"

"Why you wanna marry me?" I laughed. "I don't' know you like that".

"I'ma good catch baby". "Says who?" "Says me". "You should know".

"Naw I'm not trying to be smart or arrogant or anything, it's just that I'm single, I don't have no baby momma drama, I don't drink or get high and I got my shit straight".

"I hear you".

We talked a little over an hour and finally we fell asleep on the sofa. When we woke, it was six thirty in the morning. "Hey" "Hey, what time is it?" "It's six-thirty"

"Do you want something to eat?" "Naw but you can call me a cab"

"Okay". I gave him a washcloth and a toothbrush and let him freshen up in the spare bathroom. I was standing in the doorway waiting for the cab. He came up behind me and kissed me on the back of my neck.

"You're even pretty early in the morning"

"Thank you." Look, I'm gonna call you as soon as I get home".

Okay". The cab blew the horn and I kissed him bye.

I went upstairs and fell across my bed and went back to sleep. But not before I put the phone in the bed with me so I wouldn't' miss his phone call.

Valerie was right, he was cool, he was very nice and smart, and everything she said he was. I prayed silently that this would work out for us. Weeks and months went by and Chris and I became very close. He visited me every weekend and we went to church together often. We talked about every thing. He shared things with me and I shared things with him but I I didn't tell him everything. I was still holding on to a lot of the shame I felt for some of the things I did in my life and how I lived my life. I kept having that recurring dream of that voice talking to me telling me to let go and remember that love was the greatest commandment.

"Chris, do you believe that God can talk to you one on one?"

"Of course, you are His child and He does speak to us, chastise us, embrace us and loves us"

"I know that but what I mean is, does He come down and sit next to us and speak to us?" "I know that I could feel His presence if that's what you mean". "I don't know, this dream is so real that I feel like He is right there when I wake up, like he is sitting on my bed, making sure I am okay". "He probably is". "I mean this dream, it doesn't feel like a dream, you know, it's like I am asleep but not really asleep". "I think I know what you're saying but you have to pray Sabrina, you have to drop your guards and stop hiding behind your pain". "Huh?" "You think I don't know that you are still holding back on me?"

"What are you talking about Chris?"

"I mean, when we get together, you make sure that we are around the children all the time and when we are alone you make sure that we are either coming from bible study or going to church". "I don't do that". "Yes you do. I am not going to do anything that you don't' want me to do Sabrina, I care about you, a lot".

I looked at him. "Don't look at me like that, do you think we are kids and I can't tell you how I feel, I am damn near forty years old, I don't have time for games baby, I love you and I am falling in love with you and you are my baby and I am not going to hurt you".

I didn't respond there was that word again, the word that always come before the hurt.

"What's wrong, you thinking about all those others that hurt you in the past?"

"No". "If you want this relationship to work, I suggest you don't lie to me about anything". "Chris, I'm sorry". "Don't be sorry baby, I understand, but don't push me out of your life okay?" He held me in his arms and kissed me on my forehead.

"Can I ask you a question?" "Sure". "How long have you been celibate?"

"Two years". "Is it hard?" "It wasn't until you came into my life".

"Why?" "Because I didn't have to think about sex because I didn't have a man in my life". "And now?" "And now, you come over and we sit and talk and cuddle and kiss and caress one another and I am about tore to pieces when you leave because I want you so bad". He sat down on the sofa. "Do you want me to stop coming over?"

"No". He excused himself and went into the bathroom. I really was not ready for sex with Chris, we had been together about 3 months but still I was not ready. I didn't want to get hurt again. While he was gone I reached into my file box and pulled out my HIV test, I wanted him to know my status because I didn't want him to think that I was positive and that's the reason I was celibate. We he came back from the bathroom, I motioned him to sit down beside me. "I want you to see this". I handed him the paper.

He looked down. HIV and AIDS and killed so many people and destroyed so many lives throughout the eighties that some people were taking the test every three months. I had to take mine twice only because Barry had cheated on me so many times, I wanted to be sure. But before I stopped having sex, I had my test done. I told my doctor that I was becoming celibate and that I wanted to make sure that I was negative, because when I was ready to give myself to another man, I wanted to be sure that he knew I was negative. I watched him read the paperwork.

"You didn't have to show me that"

"Yes I did, you know yourself that every single man that I laid down with, you will too, just as every woman you laid down with, I will. I just wanted you to know that I am negative to ease your mind. Even with a condom I wanted you to be sure".

He smiled at me, reached in his wallet, and pulled out a piece of paper. I looked at it and smiled, it was his HIV test results. "How long have you been carrying this?"

"Every since I realized that I was in love with you. I couldn't push you Sabrina, and I couldn't ask you to make love to me, I had to respect what you were doing for yourself. I will admit that it was hard for me, pun intended".

We laughed.

"So where do we go from here?"

"I am going to wait for you Sabrina, I don't want you to think that all I want is your body, it's more than that with me. When I make love to you, I want to make love to your mind, body and soul. I want you to remember when I leave you, while you are working, driving, walking, cooking."

"I already do that"

"I love you Sabrina, God I love you so much"

When he kissed me, I felt something inside of me explode. I tried to fight it but I couldn't. He let me go.

"Not like this baby, I will make it special for you, I promise".

He pulled himself away from and tried to regroup, but I was a mess, I couldn't stop thinking about what I was feeling. I walked outside and tried to get some air.

He came behind me.

"Are you okay Sabrina?'

"Yes I'm fine".

He turned me towards him.

"I won't hurt you, I promise you".

He held me for a long time. I had gotten another car and I drove him home.

We were quiet on the way to his house. We were both in deep thought.

For some reason, Chris and I did not make love for a while. I thought that it would be soon since we both knew what we wanted, but he didn't even attempt to make love to me after that night. I talked to Valerie about it. "What's wrong with me?'

"Nothing girl, ask him what's wrong with him". 'I can't do that"

"Why not, you need to jump his damn bones, I know you want to"

"Do you think that he got somebody else?' "Naw, Chris don't never talk to no women out there no more, all he does is call you and spend all his weekends with you, ask him what's wrong" "I can't". "Have you two talked about it since that night you showed each other the papers?"

"No"

"Is he treating you differently?" "Not really but he has been very quiet"

"Look it's almost Christmas, why don't you invite him out on Christmas Eve, make mad, passionate love to him and get it over with".

"He is not going to do that"

"We are going to church, have dinner with the children and then open the gifts at midnight".

"I don't know what to tell you". My phone beeped. "I'll call you back, I think it's Chris".

"Okay". "Hello?"

"Hey"

"Hey yourself". "Look I need to say something to you".

"Okay". "No, I want to wait until I see you on Christmas".

"Okay".

"I gotta go; I need some time to think".

"What's wrong?"

"Nothing, I just got a lot of things on my mind and I need to do a few things before I come out there".

"Okay then, I'll talk to you later".

I didn't push him, he sounded like something was bothering him and I didn't want to push him away by acting all silly about it. I cared about him a lot but I was still afraid of giving my heart to him. Again, that dream came to me, but the words were different.

Daughter I have a promise for you. If you want to be free of all your pain, you must be delivered. I have what you need to be what you want, get out of your own way and allow me to guide and lead you to where your destiny. You are going in the right direction, if you just put your trust in Me.

I woke up again, in a cold sweat. I was sure that He was right in the room with me. I turned the lights on and opened the windows. I couldn't breath. I tried to go back to sleep but then I dreamt about Roy. He was sitting on his black car, with his uniform on from work. He was smiling that Cheshire cat smile. *Sabrina, I miss you so much, you know that I loved you more than you will ever know. I want you to know that you have to forgive , forgive for everything Sabrina, not just what you can feel but the things you have deep down inside of you. I know about what happened to you when you were a little girl, it was not your fault Sabrina, you were a child, he hurt you, and you did not allow him to hurt you. It was not your fault that your father was stabbed, it was not your fault that he left the house, it was not your fault that he died, let it go Sabrina. I know you are afraid to love again but you will in time...*

I tossed and turned but the dream did not end.

Sabrina do you remember when we first laid eyes on one another? I do, you were smiling and you were laughing, you were happy. I need to you let go of your fear. It is time you laughed again. I have to go now, my work is done here. I watched him walk away and then I woke up.

I cried the rest of the night. I had not thought about Roy in a long time but he knew everything that was going on in my heart, He knew about my fear and my guilt, did one voice have anything to do with the other? I did not know but I needed to work this through. I read my bible and drifted back off to sleep.

When Chris came over the next week, it was near Christmas. We had been talking over the phone but for some reason, he did not seem like himself. I tried to ask him but he kept saying that he did not want to talk about it. When he came out, we had a long talk. "Chris are you okay?" "Yes, but we need to talk"

"Do you want me to make you something to eat?" "No, I just want to go somewhere so we can talk". "Oh, okay." We went upstairs and sat in the bedroom.

"Sabrina I need to say some things to you before we can go any further".

"Sure baby". He lit a cigarette.

"Sabrina, I know I told you a lot of things about myself but I kept one thing from you and I would like to tell you that now". "Okay".

"Sabrina, I went to prison".

"You told me that Chris".

""I killed a man".

I didn't say anything; I didn't know what to say.

"I killed him but I was defending myself. He was trying to rob me and I shot him".

"I ran, and I shouldn't have run because that made it harder on me when they caught me. But the judge believed me and gave me five years for manslaughter and five years for using a gun in the commission of a felony".

"Did you do all the time"? "To the door".

"It's okay Chris, I've done some things in my life that I am not proud of". (Boy was that an understatement)

"I need to know if you are okay with this for real Sabrina".

"I am okay with this Chris, honest".

Good now let me drawn you a bath and take care of you".

I smiled and gave him a kiss.

The bathroom was lit with candles. He had made my bath a bubble bath. It was so romantic. I got in the tub and soaked for a while before he came in. When he did, he had strawberries covered with chocolate and sparkling cider. He fed me the strawberries first.

"You know I love you don't you?"

"Yes".

"I mean it Sabrina, I love you so much".

He kissed me and caressed me and I wanted to pull him in the tub with me. I knew this would be the night that I would no longer be celibate.

"Not yet baby, not yet"

He pulled out a piece of paper and starting singing to me, I cried, I couldn't believe that he was actually singing to me and telling me how much he loved me and how much I meant to him. He reached under the towel, pulled out a small blue box, and opened it. Inside it was a beautiful diamond ring.

"Sabrina, will you marry me?"

I put my hand over my mouth, I could not believe it.

"I know you are still married and I know your husband is giving you grief about the divorce but I will wait for as long as I have to, to marry you. I know that I have to so do some things with my marriage too but I love you Sabrina and I don't want to lose you ever".

I didn't know what to say.

"Say something Sabrina, yes, no, get the hell out of my house!"

We both started laughing.

"Yes"

He kissed me. The children were clapping outside the door.

"They knew?"

"Yes, I had to ask your son for your hand in marriage, he is the man of this house".

"That's right!" I heard Darius screaming on the other side of the door.

I got out the tub put my clothes on and went in the bedroom.

Chris called his mother to tell her that I said yes. I was happy but most of all, I felt safe with Chris. I didn't feel threatened or like I was walking on eggshells.

We talked about him moving in with me but we were both leery about it because we knew it was not of God and we tried hard to do the right things by His word. We decided that we would talk to the pastor. I knew already what the answer would be but I just wanted him to confirm it for me. And he did. He said that he would not be right for us to live together and we decided that we would continue to do what we were doing,

Chris gave the children money and cab fare and sent them to the movies so that we could spend time together. I wanted to be with him and he wanted to be with me but we felt so guilty about it that we decided to find other ways to please one another other than making love. It was magical and sweet. I know that he had never done anything like this in his life but he went along with it to please me. The rest of the weekend was just as special as the night Chris purposed to me. We had dinner, cut up with the kids, and had a good time. When Chris left that Sunday, I came home and got down on my knees. My mother always told me when you want to know a man for what he really is and what he is made of to ask God in sincerity and to place him in a crisis. Of course, I prayed about this diligently, I had made up my mind that I would take my time to get married.

Now to say that I was very surprised by the next series of events would be an under statement. I didn't know if what happened was from God or the devil. It is said when a crisis come, if you head for your knees, it's of God, but if you turn to the world, it is the devil.

Two weeks after Chris purposed, I lost my job, I knew it was coming I just didn't know how it was coming. I was the only black in my office and I had an office of my own and a nice little title to go with it. I knew it was more than what they told me, but I could not prove it. They said that the grant was up and there was no more money to keep me there, however, everyone else was able to stay. I was upset at first, but then I realized, I have been here before, so I would be fine. Chris was outside waiting for me in the car. He was very compassionate and told me not to worry about anything.

"Baby, it's going to be okay".

"I don't know why people are so dirty; I never did anything to those ladies".

"You don't' have to" "I have to find another job".

"You are a very intelligent woman baby and you will find another job"

"Thank you baby, I just worked so hard to do a good job and it didn't mean anything"

"Don't worry about it, there are other jobs out here and you will find one".

We drove the rest of the way home in silence, I was in thought and I am sure he was too.

About two weeks after that, Chris and I got in a terrible fight. It started with the bills. "Chris, I need to ask you something". "Sure baby".

"Do you have any money?' "For what?"

I was startled, not that he asked but the way he asked, as if I offended him.

"I need help with the food". "Look baby, you had these bills when I got here so don't try to make me take care of yo ass now".

I almost fell off the bed. "Huh"?

"You heard me; I am not paying no bills".

"Chris I didn't ask you to pay my bills, all I asked was a couple of dollars for some food, what is wrong with you?" "Look, don't' question me about nothing, I said I wasn't paying no damn bills". I put my notepad down. 'Is something wrong?"

"I got a lot on my mind Sabrina" "Do you want to talk about it?"

"No". "If you need to talk I'm here".

He looked at me again with a crazy look. I didn't say anything more. I tried to understand where this was coming from, but I didn't question him anymore that evening. I lay across the bed with my clothes on. In truth, I wanted to cuss him out but I was really trying to change my ways and my mouth, so I just lay on the bed saying nothing. "Oh because I don't wanna give you no money, you don't' wanna sleep with me?" I looked at him as if he was crazy. "What is wrong with you Chris, this is not like you?" "Look, forget it, just move over!"

I scooted over in the bed and didn't' say another word. That night, I prayed again, and I even read the bible for a while, I needed to know what was going on with Chris and why he was showing me such a terrible side of himself. After that day, the silent treatment came, Chris wouldn't come out to see me or take my calls. I was a wreck and I was slipping back into depression, those wonderful days of not walking on eggshells was back. I tried not to bother him or even call him. I wanted him to be able to come to me when he was ready to talk about his problem whatever it was.

Finally, things came to a head and it was over. Chris came out one night to say he wanted to talk. When he got there, he was mad again. "Would you like something to eat?" "Do I have to pay for it?" "Why are you being so mean Chris?"

"I'm sorry"." Tell me what's going on?"

"Nothing". "Then why the change?"

"What changed, this is who I am baby"

"You never acted like this before, now you are angry and mean"

"I'm from the street, what did you expect?"

"I expected you to be a little nicer than you are being right now".

"Please" I shook my head, I was totally confused. He was pushing my buttons and I wasn't quite sure I wanted to walk in the Christian way anymore that night.

"Look, let's just go to bed and end this conversation".

"You go on; I need to do a few things first".

"What?" "Personal things"

"Oh, fine"

I went down to the living room and took my bible. I read for a while. I needed answers that only God could provide. I read James and Romans. Those books usually said it all for me. I read Psalms and Proverbs. I must have fallen asleep because when I woke up it was quiet and all the lights were off. I went to bed and Chris was asleep. I lay at the bottom of the bed.

"Are you okay?" "I thought you were sleep"

"No I was waiting for you to come upstairs. I'm sorry baby, I didn't mean to hurt your feelings but I have a lot going on in my life and I can't do this with you right now".

"Do what?" "I mean we should just be friend's baby, we need to put this thing on pause".

I almost fell out the bed. "What?"

"Look, pastor said we shouldn't be living together and we shouldn't' be doing this so I think I am going to stay at my mother's house".

"Why do we have to put this on pause Chris?"

"Look, don't question me".

"That's it; I am tired of this bullshit!"

"Whoa, who in the hell are you cussing at, I will hurt you in here!"

Now this was the era of O.J. Simpson and murdering your spouse and domestic violence. In my mind, I was not going to allow another anybody to threaten me. Therefore, I asked him to leave. "You want me to leave now!"

"Yes, I want you to leave now!" "I'll leave tomorrow"

"No you will leave now!" "I'm not going any damn where, you better lay your ass down!"

"Look you will get your ass out of here tonight! If you think I am going to sit here and let you talk to me like that allow you to lay your sorry ass up in my bed, you are sadly mistaken!" "Sabrina, it's one in the damn morning and its cold out there! " "You shoulda thought of that shit when you opened your mouth talking to me like that, now I said get the hell out!". "I said I'm not going, call the damn police! " I got up and called the police, who told him that he had to leave.

The next time I heard about Chris was through his sister, who told me that he was married. He was gone all of two months and he was married. I couldn't believe it, since he told me he was still married to his first wife. I was shocked and hurt. It was obvious to me that he made this story up so that he could be with this other woman. To say I was hurt was an understatement I didn't understand it at all, we were doing well or at least I thought we were. My family and friends were in shock for me. I returned the ring to his sister and asked her to give it to him. He was so angry with me I didn't want him to have any reason to come back to my home. The children were hurt and disappointed but they didn't say anything. I told them that we would be okay that we always bounced back and we would from this ordeal as well. I was thankful for one thing, I had God for real this time and He truly walked me through that painful experience. I never really found out why Chris walked away from what we shared. I never knew if it was something I said, or did, or was it just that he wasn't the man for me.

Of course Val thought, "That sorry bastard realized that was going to have to pay some damn bills, so he got the hell outta dodge!"

I remembered something that I heard the voice tell me one night. **Ecclesiastes 3:1-9 To every thing there is a season. And a time to every purpose under the heaven. A time to be born and a time to die; a time to plant and a time to pluck up that which is planted a time to kill and a time to heal; a time to break down and a time to build up, a time to weep and a time to laugh and a time to mourn. And a time to dance a time to cast away stones and a time to gather stones together a time to embrace and a time to refrain from embracing, and a time to get and a time to lose a time to keep and a time to cast away....***daughter withdraw from intimacy and not always take in absolute sense....sometimes, what I have for you will not come in your time, but in my time....trust Me..*

After that night, I realized that Chris was want *I* wanted in my life but not what God intended for me to have, at least not at this time.

Chapter 23

HOW DID I GET HERE?

After several months of being alone and content, I found myself in another relationship. I was not looking for anyone in my life nor did I want anyone in my life. I was really starting to love my life for what it was. I didn't have a man but nor did I need one to validate myself as a woman. I was working and maintaining. My children were almost grown, although I still had two in school, my son had graduated and was working. And was now living with the mother of his child. I was happy for him but I could see the affects of Trenton's abuse and alcohol manifesting in his life. I try hard not to interfere in his life but it wasn't easy for me. He was my first-born and I loved him with all that I had within me. I didn't want him to wind up homeless like Trenton and out of touch with his child because of alcohol and drugs. Unfortunately, we fought so much that I had to ask him to leave my home. He understood but I think he thought I didn't' love him. I did love him with all of heart and soul but he needed to be on his own because he didn't care to follow any boundaries or rules that I set for him. Once he had his son, he felt like he was a man and he was the man of my house. He tried me every time he thought he could and he must have thought that I would not handle him but I did and promptly gave him thirty days to vacate my home. They were happy together but not as happy as I was.

Trenton had finally gotten himself together after many years of drinking and drugging and trying to make amends to his children and I didn't stand in his way. I never thought of keeping them away from him. I was proud of him. He had managed to get his own apartment, secured a nice job and dedicated his life to Christ and I was so happy for him. He also had a beautiful new friend in his life who was a good person. He had been drug and alcohol free for about 3 years and was staying clean and sober. I was proud of him and was glad that he was able to have a relationship with his children that didn't involve me.

I was celibate yet again, after the past that I had, the last thing I needed in my life was sex. God knew that I had enough sex to last me a lifetime. I wasn't stressing it at all. I still loved men and I still desired to have one in my life but I wanted it to be right this time, I wanted someone who wanted me for me, not for my body or anything, just love me for me. I was a good person, although I still struggled with guilt and shame I was a good person. However, I had to admit to myself that I was lonely and at times, I missed the companionship, not enough to be in a relationship but enough to recognize that I was lonely. I would drive down to the lake and sit by the water and feed the ducks when I was feeling that way, I felt closer to God when I did that. I would always drive down to a beach that was near my home, sit there, and watch the ocean waves going back and forth, wishing that one day I could go out and come back refreshed like the ocean waves looked.

On the day that I met him, I was sitting on my car looking out at the ocean. The beach was closed because of some disease in the water. However, I could still see the water from where I was parked so I didn't mind. I saw him from my peripheral vision. My hair was in micro-braids and they were hanging free. I had on a red top with a pair of black jeans with red Champion tennis shoes. My car was freshly washed and was gleaming red. I bit down on my Kentucky Fried Chicken and just listened to the quiet.

"Do you know why the beach is closed?' I didn't' bother to turn around and face him. "The signs says because of something in the water".

"How are you?" "I'm fine". I thought it was kind of rude not to face him when I talked so I turned around. There he was tall, dark and dirty as hell. I looked him up and down. He was nice looking, even cute, but I really couldn't' tell because he was so dirty that I didn't' really know what complexion he was.

"How are you?"

"I am fine and you?"

"I'm just getting off of work so I'm tired, I just brought a co-worker down here because he is from out of town, I thought I would show him some sights".

"That was nice of you". "What's your name?"

"Sabrina"

"Hi, Sabrina my name is Eugene "

"Hello Eugene"

"What you doing out here all by yourself?"

"Just relaxing, I had a hard day at work"

"Oh, where do you work?"

"Towson"

"Doing what?"

"I work for Department of Corrections"

"Oh really?"

"Yes, why, are you a fugitive?"

"Naw, nothing like that, I work for the Baltimore County Public Works, thus all the dirt that you see. We build sub stations"

"Sounds interesting"

"Money's good"

I jumped down off the hood of the car. "Well Eugene it was nice meeting you, I have to get going now, it's getting late"

"Do you have a number where I can call you?"

"Now why would you want to do that?"

"I would like to take you out to dinner or something"

"I don't give my number to strangers, you could be a killer or something"

"Fair enough, then take mine and call me".

He wrote it down and handed it to me. I looked at it. I noticed it was a city number but I didn't' say anything.

"Okay I will do that Eugene"

"I like the way you say my name"

I looked at him, under all that dirt and grime, he was a cutie.

I put the car in reverse and pulled out.

He waved at me. I pulled out and watched him in my rear view mirror. If he looked that sexy that dirty I wondered what he looked like clean. I turn my radio and listened to the music as I passed the fire department, I saw him standing out there with the rest of the workers. He waved me over but I kept driving, I didn't know him that well to be stopping around a bunch of men. I didn't call him that day, in fact I didn't call him for about three or four days. On the fourth day I decided to call him.

"Hello"

"Hello, can I speak to Eugene".

"He's not here"

"Can you tell him that Sabrina called?'

"I sure will baby"

"Thank you"

That must have been his mother, I thought to myself. She sounded like a mother.

I took a hot bath, cooked me something to eat and laid across the bed and read my Essence Magazine. They had an article in there about domestic violence. I was interested in that one since I was going to back to the House of Ruth, just for support. Chris had hurt me mentally and I didn't' want to fall back into that pattern of thinking again. They also had a article on that sexy LL Cool J, I remembered L when he was a little skinny boy with a radio up to his ear in Krush Groovin and now here he was on the cover of Essence with those kissable lips and that body that made a woman want to cheat on her man.

My phone rang, it was my girlfriend Robbie, I hadn't heard from her in a while but she had moved out of state but was back.

"Hey whatch doin' girl?"

"Laying across the bed reading Essence"

"You are always reading something"

"You know me girl, I've got to keep this brain tight, it's been through a lot"

"So what you been doing?"

"Nothing, working, maintaining"

"Have you found yourself a boyfriend yet?"

"Naw girl, I ain't looking, after Chris, sista need a break, after all those fools sista need a break"

"I know Sabrina but you have to get back out there, that was a long time ago"

"Not long enough"

"Have you heard from Chris?"

"No, not since we last talked, there is nothing more to say Robbie, he is with his new wife and I have let that go".

"That was so cold though"

"I'm not surprised, do you know me to ever have a man be faithful to me?"

"Sabrina, that's not your fault"

"Yeah it is, I keep choosing these men and they aren't faithful Robbie"

"You will find someone"

"Not in this life. I don't know what I am doing with men Robbie, I choose them to be a part of my life, thinking that they want what I want and then they flip on me and they are something that I never knew, they were probably that in the beginning but I didn't see it or didn't want to see it. My biggest problem all my life was holding on to dead weight, you know, holding on to a relationship all after it was over"

"But that's not what happened with Chris"

"Girl, I don't know what happened with Chris, one minute I was engaged and the next minute he was gone and married to somebody else"

"I am so sorry Sabrina, you are a good person and you deserve to be happy"

"I will one day, don't know when, not worried about when but one day"

My phone beeped. This new caller ID stuff was truly nice.

"Hold on Robbie"

"Hello"

Hello, can I speak to Sabrina?"

"This is Sabrina"

"Hey this is Eugene"

"Oh, hey, how are you?"

"I'm fine"

"Can you call me right back?"

"How long?"

"About ten minutes, I have a call on my other line"

"Okay"

I clicked back over to Robbie. "Sorry about that, that was that guy I was telling you about last night"

"Who the dirty looking one?"

"Yes, the one that with the sexy brown eyes"

"Oh boy"

"Oh boy what?"

"You said the man got sexy eyes, I didn't know you looked at him that hard"

"I didn't but I couldn't help but see his eyes, he was staring right at me"

"Well I'll let you go so you can wait for your phone call"

"Please, I'm not standing by no phone waiting for no man to call me now"

"But you know you want to talk to him"

"Yes, I'd like to see where his head is."

"Do you have any crabs left from the fourth?"

"Girl please, the way I love seafood, you know ain't nothing left in this house but the claws"

We both laughed. "I'll call you later"

"Okay"

I jumped in the shower and was putting some lotion on my legs when my phone rang.

"Hello"

"Are you still on the phone?"

"No" I looked at the number. "This is a number out here".

"I know I live around the corner from where we met"

"Then why did you give me a city phone number?"

"I don't give my numbers to strangers, they could be killers or something"

We both laughed ."touche"

"Were you busy?'

"No I just got out the shower"

'That a nice visual"

I smiled.

"What are you doing later?'

"Nothing"

"Well I am going to bed soon"

"Bed!?"

"Yeah, I get up at 4:30 in the morning so I get to bed early, but I wanted to call you back so you didn't' think I was that type of person who doesn't return calls, you know the old saying when a woman says they are going to call you back, they mean sometime that week, if a man does it, it means sometimes that year"

I laughed. "you are too funny"

'You mean to tell me that you never heard that one before?"

"Oh yes, I heard it, it just sounds funny coming from a man"

"Thanks for giving me your phone number or giving it to my mother"

"That was your mother's number?"

"Yes who did you think it was?"

"I thought it was your mothers"

"Yes she is my heart, I call her every day to make sure she is okay""

"That's good you love your mom like that"

"Look what time do you get off of work?"

"Five"

"Okay, I get home before you so I will call you when you get home, if that's okay"

"That's fine"

"Well I need to get some rest, I will talk to you tomorrow"

We hung up.

The next day when I got home, I had a dozen of roses and a plate of food waiting for me, home made food.

"Where did this come from?"

"Mr. Eugene said that he hope you enjoy the dinner and the roses"

"Aw that's sweet"

He called me about twenty minutes after I got home.

"How did you know where I lived?'

"The guy I work with was riding around the neighborhood earlier today since we got off due to rain. I rode down your main street and could see your car. You didn't drive today did you?"

"No I didn't I caught a ride with somebody because I someone was coming out to give me an oil change"

"Your boyfriend?"

"Please, I don't have a boyfriend"

"That's good to know"

"I know you must have a girlfriend if you cook like this all the time"

"No, I don't have a girlfriend"

"Thanks for the roses and the food I really appreciate it"

"You can make it up to me"

"How"

"Come and go for a walk with me"

"Okay, where?"

"To the lake, I like to go there when I have things on my mind"

"The lake around the corner?"

"Yeah that's the one"

'I go there all the time"

"I'll meet you halfway"

I changed my clothes and walked towards the lake. When I got there, he was walking towards the lake, he looked so good, he was not dressed up or anything, he just looked good.

From that day forward, Eugene and I became close. We were friends and we had a good time. We talked on the phone until he fell asleep and we walked around the lake and took trips to Rock Creek Park just to spend time together. Our first date was at The Friendly Ice Cream store and we shared a Chocolate Sundae, it was so romantic and fun. We had a good time.

I still loved God and still wanted to be what He wanted me to be. I did not stop worshipping Him or listening for his voice, I still did not know what I was missing that He wanted me to do. I had forgiven all the people in my life and I was becoming frustrated because I could not figure out who else He wanted me to forgive. I had confided in Eugene that I was going through something and he was supportive.

"Baby you will be fine, you have to trust that God will reveal to you what He needs you to do"

I gave him a hug and he pulled me close and kissed me. I had even attempted to kiss this man in two months but when he touched me, it was electric. I kissed him back and I held on to him as if he was my lifeline. I needed that kiss. After Chris, I had closed my heart and my mind to any type of romance.

"Damn that felt good!"

"We both laughed and held hands as we walked back towards my house.

"I'm going to get ready to go but can I call you when I get in?"

"Sure"

"Better yet, call me when you get settled"

"Okay"

I went home, took a shower, settled down, and dialed his number. A female answered the phone.

"Hello"

"Hello, can I speak to Eugene?"

"Hold on"

I heard her tell him the phone was for him.

"Hello"

"Hey do you have company?"

"No"

"Is that you daughter?"

"No, that's my roommate, we are just friends, we don't have anything going on or anything like that, she is just renting a room from me, I have one room and she has another"

All kinds of red flags went up in the air for me, but I ignored them. I rationalized that she answered the phone, she didn't' say that they were a couple or anything so I let it go. It was not until we had been going out about 3 months before I knew what the deal with those two.

Chapter 24
BABY MOMMA DRAMA AND MORE!

Eugene was at my house and we were sitting in the bedroom talking about nothing and everything. I was catching feelings for him and he was catching feelings for me. We were talking about that. And the fact that his daughter was going to live with him because she was having a baby. He was upset about it but I assured him that she would be all right if he did not make her feel bad about herself or her error in judgment. I told him that I had a daughter that was a teenage mother and she was doing well and so would his daughter. I did not hear the phone ring but my daughter knocked on the door and told me that the phone was for Eugene.

He tried to take the phone but I snatched.

"I don't know how you work in your world, but in my world, no woman calls my house asking for a man that I am spending time with okay?"

He put his hands up.

"Hello"

"Hello, I need to speak to Eugene"

"Well you will need to talk to him when he comes home, don't call my house"

"You call this house all the time"

"I was invited to call there you were not invited to call here"

"I need to speak to Eugene; he needs to make up his mind where he wants to be"

"And what is that suppose to mean?"

"You need to ask him"

"No I need to be asking you. Are you and Eugene a couple?"

"No"

"Are you two sleeping together?"

"Hell no!"

"Do you have a relationship other than landlord tenant?"

"No"

"Then I don't see the logic in you calling my house asking for him, you crossed the line, make sure you don't' do it again"

"Just tell him he better make up his mind"

"I'll be sure to do that, you be sure not to call this number again, unless you want to talk to me"

She hung the phone up.

"What the hell is going on Eugene, if you have a relationship with this woman then you need to be there with her and not involve me in your mess. I don't have time for this"

"I don't have a relationship with her"

"Then why is she calling around here for you. You know what, go home, get out of here I don't need this"

"Sabrina, it's not like that, why would I tell you where I live at, give you my phone number and spend all my time with you if I was having a relationship with someone else?"

"I don't' know but I am not going to be used Eugene"

"Look, I will go home and take care of this just calm down and get some rest and I will call you later"

"No, don't' call me later, deal with that"

He tried to kiss me, but I turned my head.

The next few days were tense between us and I felt bad about everything. I didn't want to stop seeing Eugene but I didn't want to be hurt by him either.

Our relationship was strained. I wanted it to be more than what it was but knowing that he was living with another stopped me dead in my tracks. Soon I found out that she was pregnant with his baby, and she admitted that she didn't tell him about the baby until she found out he was in a relationship with me, but that was no consolation to me That one little incident was only indicative to the many months and years we spent as a couple.

After several months of back and forth and finding out that he had more drama than a soap opera, It was so crazy. The back and forth, the good, the bad and the insanity was driving me insane, He was running and I was chasing, he would get caught and I would catch him, and we would fight, make up, fight, make up again. I couldn't do it anymore. The drugs, alcohol lies, betrayal was more than I could take He was so charming and so addictive, It was hard for me to turn away from him, but I knew deep down, I needed to be detoxed from him. The more I tried to stay away from him, the more the pull of his charm and intense love pulled me back towards him.

We fought, made up, broke up, fought more, loved more made up more. It was so hard not be with him. I tried repeatedly to leave him but I was so hard. He was so persuasive and charming. I loved him more than I loved myself. We were even going to get married and we spent money on my wedding gown, but we both knew deep down that we were not ready to be man and wife, there were too many lies and not enough trust and not enough God to make it work. My father's words rang in my ears "never give a man your soul, for that's where your spirit lies". I had given Eugene my soul,

The final straw for me was the intense fight we had over his baby's mother, I couldn't stand him to be with her, but I knew as a woman I was not going to stand between him and his child, I knew the games she was playing but Eugene was not keen enough to know the games she as playing, so I just walked away and allowed him to find out on his own that he could not have me and her too. We tried a few times to make it work but deep down, I knew that he never knew what it was to say no to her or to anyone for that matter, and that alone put a wedge between us. I know in my heart that we truly did love each other but we were damaged, and we were trying to fix each other but what he and I did not realize that we did not have the tools to do that. We needed much more.

Eugene and I parted ways but we remained friends. I would see him walking his baby around but I would go the other way, just so we wouldn't bump into one another. I was proud that he was trying. I missed him and I know he missed me but it was not to be for us.

I missed Eugene and I loved him, even with all the things we did to one another, I loved him. I couldn't understand why I loved him the way I did. Maybe it was the things that he gave me, the attention that he gave me when we was not drugging or drinking. The way he made love to me, I don't know what it was, but it was not healthy. I tried so hard not to fall that hard for him because truthfully, I always knew that he would never really be free of his love that he felt for his baby mother. She was not what he wanted per se, but she allowed him to be with who he wanted to be with, and come back whenever he needed to come back. I didn't hate her or even dislike her but I had no respect for her. Not because of him but because she didn't care enough about herself to put her foot down. However, it didn't matter after every thing we went through and all the baby momma drama, he went back to her. I felt like a failure, I wasted so much time on another damn man that did not deserve it. How many times would I do this before I stopped and just took the time to spend with me? I did not want to be alone but I knew that I could handle being alone. Barry had taught me never to depend on a man again for anything because they will always leave you at some point. I had to ask myself how did I get here, I was minding my business and not bothering a soul and then came Eugene, all fine and chocolate with the sweetest love I had seen in a long time. He showered me with gifts and gave me anything and everything I ever wanted except for one thing…..RESPECT! Now he was gone.

I sat at my dining room table watching my grandson fix a puzzle and I heard this voice again.

When daughter, when? How long will it take you to heed my words and surrender? When will you return to me?

2 Chronicles 7:14 If my people which are called by my name, shall humble themselves, and pray and seek my face, and turn from their wicked way, then will I hear from heaven and will forgive their sin and will heal their land.

Chapter 25
SATAN'S FINAL FURY…..

Here I was again, alone. However, this time I was happy. A few months had passed and I started a new job working at a private investment company. It was a fun job but it didn't pay much. However, the people were nice people, I was paid every week, and there were always bonus for one thing or another. The people that worked the floor and on the different truck were so nice to me, they treated me like their little sister. I felt good about myself and I was not stressing about Eugene at all. The guys couldn't believe I was single but I assured them that I was. I told them that I was taking a reprieve from men for a minute, of course a few of them asked me was I going strictly licky I told them no that I was all woman and I wanted nothing but men in my life when I was ready.

A Conversation between Satan and God:
Job 1:7-9.. Now there was a day when the sons of God came to present themselves before the Lord and Satan came with them. And the Lord said unto Satan, Whence comest thou? Then Satan answered the Lord, and said, "from going to and fro in the earth and from walking up and down in it and the Lord said unto Satan have you considered my servant Job….there is none like him…in the earth…one that feareth God and despises evil…then Satan answered the Lord and said Does he fear you for nothing? Hast not thou made a hedge about him? And about his house and about all that he hast on every side? Thou have blessed the work of his hands and his substance increased in the land

but put forth and touch all that he has and he will curse thee to thy face And the Lord said unto Satan, power only upon himself put not forth thine hand so Satan went forth from the presence of the Lord.

Why have you continued to protect her?

She is my child, there is a will, and purpose for her life as it is with all my children…

She does not recognize her power

She will in My time

I will slain her if she continues to be disobedient

You can do nothing, unless I allow it! She will come to Me in her time of need, as she has all her life, it will not be long before she will be what I destined her to be, and I cannot elevate her until she surrenders all to Me

You are the Lord God make her come to you!

To walk in My will is a choice she must come to me

How long?

How long indeed?

I have a special demon assigned to her and she will die!

She will call on Me and I will answer in her time of need. Remember you can only do what I allow you to do!

She will die and your word will never be manifested in her life

I am the Alpha and the Omega, I know all things

Then know that she will die!

When the appointed time is destined, My will for her life will be done now depart from me you worker of iniquity!

It was now October and it was just starting to get cold. My car was in the shop and I was home. I was sitting on the bed watching some talk show when my beeper went off. I looked at the number it was one I didn't know. I thought maybe since a friend had given me the pager, it was one of his friends, so I called it back. "Hello". "Hello, did someone page me?" He was bewildered. "I'm sorry I thought I paged someone else". "No problem". I said. "Please don't hang up" "Excuse me?" "I mean you sound so sweet on the phone". "Thank you". "My name is Sincere". "What a strange name". "I know" "Is it a nickname or something?" "No but people call me *Sin* for short". "I don't think I would want to be called that for short, that's not a popular name". "I know, only a few select people call me that, people who know me really well, my father had the same name". "Oh", was the only answer I had. "Uh, I know this is awkward, but I am really sorry that I beeped you, my friend and you have the same last digits on your beeper, I think I may have transposed them or something". "It's okay; you didn't disturb me or anything". "Look you are talking but you never told me your name". "Oh I'm sorry, it's Sabrina". "Like Sabrina the Teenaged Witch?" "I guess you could say that". "That's nice, are you white?" "No, why would you ask me that?" "You sound like a white person, on the phone". I had heard that a lot so I was not surprised. "Yes, a lot of people tell me that". "Did you ever consider working on one of those 900 numbers?" "Doing what?"

"A sex operator". "Not hardly". "I'm sorry if I offended you". "No offense, I just don't get down like that".

We talked for a few more minutes and I ended the call. It was funny talking to someone that I never saw, it reminded me of Chris. A few days later, he called me back. "Hello Sabrina, this is Sincere". "Hello Sincere, how are you"? "I'm fine, I just wanted to call to say hello, and I hope it's not a problem". "No, it's okay.

"Do you drive?" "Yes I do, why?"

"I would like to meet you and have lunch or something with you, I'm not a stalker or anything, I just thought we have talked a few times on the phone and I would like to meet you face to face". "I'll think about it and let you know". "Okay, let me know when".

My phone beeped so I told Sincere that I would call him later.

I did not hear from Sincere for a while but it did not bother me because he was not anyone important to me. I continued to go to bible study and worship with my church family, who I adored. I felt at peace finally and I was learning so much from Pastor Hinkle. He just seemed like the word of God rolled off his tongue with ease. He taught the word of God that even a backslider like me could understand. I had notebooks of notes and scripture passages that I studied all the time.

Tuesdays were my day of bible study and I waited with anticipation for six o'clock. I jumped in my car and told China and Nia where I was going and left.

The church was small but it was warm and friendly. There were not many members but the word was powerful. Pastor Hinkle started the praise and worship with a John P. Kee song, "Sweeter". I loved that song so much, I would sing it all the time and when I saw the words on the screen, I was already worshiping before the music started. *"He's sweeter than any friend I knowwww, he's sweeter than any friend I knowww, The Lord is, the Lord is, Sweeter than any friend I knowww"*. I sang as if I was the only person in the church. Praise and worship went on for about forty-five minutes and then we went into the teachings. Pastor Hinkle taught on Romans 7: 13 The Struggle of Two Natures. .

"Sister Sabrina, why don't you read for us tonight?" "Okay Pastor". I smiled. I loved to read. **Was then which is good made death unto me? God forbid, but sin, that it might appear sin, working death in me by that which is good; that sin by the commandments might become exceeding sinful. For we know that the law is spiritual but I am carnal, sold under sin. For that which I do I allow not, for what I would, that do I not, but what I hate, that do I. If then I do that which I would not, I consent unto the law that is good. Now then is no more I that do it, but sin that dwelleth in me. For I know that in me (that is in my flesh) dwelleth no good thing; for to will is present with me; but how to perform that which is good I find not. For the good that I would, I do not, but the evil which I would not, that I do"** it, but sin that dwelleth in me. **I find then a law that when I would do good, evil is present with me"**. **Amen.** The church said Amen. I was confused I didn't know what all that meant but I was sure that Pastor was going to break it down for us. "Now church". The Pastor started. "I know you are wondering what all that may mean so I am going to explain it to you". "The word of God is telling us in this text, "The law is holy, just and good. The law is an expression of god's righteousness. Sin, not the law, produced death, the law shows us that we are helpless under the control of sin and points us to Christ, the only One who can help us. The law is spiritual; the law has the characteristics of the Spirit and is consistent with the character of God. I am carnal: What follows is autobiographical and designed to reveal the real struggle the apostle experienced in the flesh. His experience is also exemplary for it shows the problems that all believers experience in their battle with sin". He went on like that for another hour and I was in awe of how wonderful God truly was and what He did for a backslider like me. Tears flowed freely down my face when I thought about all the things He protected me from and brought me through.

I don't think I remember much more of the teachings. I was in my own special place with God. Church ended and I left feeling so much lighter than I was when I got there.

When I got home, there were several messages from Sincere. All of them were about how he missed me and wanted to see me. I just shook my head, took a hot shower and fell off to sleep right after I ate.

I slept peaceful and when I got up the next morning, I felt refreshed and rested. My phone rang right after I jumped out of the shower. "Hello". "Hey Sabrina, you didn't call me back last night". "I got in late Sincere, how are you this morning?" "I don't know why you have to go to church all the time Sabrina". "Because I want to Sincere, I am grown and I do whatever I please". He got quiet. "So what's going on this early in the morning, it must be important that you are calling me so early". "I just wanted to know when we were going to meet up". "Well how about this evening when I get off of work?" His attitude instantly changed. "Really?" I looked at the phone. "Sure, why don't you call me at my job around four-thirty"? "Okay, I can't wait to meet you". "Okay

Sincere, I have to go now". I didn't wait for a response. I went off to work.

The day was uneventful and it went by slowly. Sincere called me several times throughout the day to make sure we were still going to hang out and I assured him that we were. When he called the last time, I told him where to meet me. When I got off work, my car would not start. Johnny, one of the guys on the job, worked on that car for about 30 minutes and then he told me that the battery was dead because it wouldn't hold a hot shot. I went back in the office and called Sincere to let him know that I couldn't meet him. When I got off, the next day I met him near the library. I made sure that we met in the daytime because as I said I did not know this man like that.

We were to meet on Wednesday but I received a call from the shop to tell me that my car would be in the shop another day. I called him and he was disappointed. I reschedule with sincere after we talked a few.

"You just don't want to meet, do you"?

"What are you talking about, I can give you a rain check, if you want one, if you're that upset then we don't have to meet at all".

"I don't believe you"

"Well guess what, believe what you want, the battery is dead and there is nothing I can do about it today".

"I'm sorry Sabrina; it's just that I was looking forward to meeting you".

'It will happen, just chill".

We arranged to meet that Thursday and disconnected the call; I did not take much thought of his attitude. I did gather from our conversation that he was the type the usually got what he wanted if he pouted long enough.

I worked that Thursday, took a shower and changed my clothes. He called probably six times to see if I was still coming. The last time he called, I told him to cut out the calls. Again, I didn't' give anything for his attitude. I drove downtown found a parking space and met him at the restaurant. He described to me what he looked like and what he was wearing. When I saw him, I knew who he was immediately. He was tall, brown skinned and slim. He had a boyish look about him. He greeted me with a smile and a wave. I got out of my car and walked towards him. "How are you?" I shook his hand. He shook mine. "You're beautiful". "Thank you". "I didn't know you were this beautiful". Again, I thanked him. "Where would you like to go?" "It doesn't matter to me". "The wait in the restaurant more than an hour". "How about Phillips?" "That's fine with me".

We got in the car and he immediately started talking about how his mother was angry with him for playing his music too loud. I didn't respond because I didn't listen to rap music that much. My children did and I expected them to play it loud, according to Darius the music sounded better if it were loud. He reminded me of how I used to play Patti Labelle and Gladys Knight loud.

"What type of music do you listen to?"

I"I like all types of music, but most of all I listen to gospel music".

"I like rap music and R&B". The conversation went like that throughout dinner. I was getting tired because I had to go to work the next day. "I think we better get going, I have an early day tomorrow".

"Okay, thanks for having dinner with me".

"Sure I enjoyed it."

"Are your children old or babies?"

I smiled. "They will always be my babies but no, they are teenagers, except for my baby girl "

"I don't have any children but I have a niece and a nephew".

"Little or teenagers?"

"Oh they are little. I love them a lot. I don't get along with my brother and sister though"

"I'm sorry to hear that".

"Don't worry, I don't care if they hate me or not, I have my own life to live anyway".

I didn't respond to that.

"My father was killed before I was born, he was killed in a bar fight".

"Oh that's too bad". He put a smirk on his face. "Its okay, the people that did it paid for it".

I thought it was strange but I didn't say anything about it. I wondered if they murdered the people but I was not going to ask that question by no means.

We continued to talk until we arrived at his house. "Thanks for bringing me home".

"No problem".

"I have to tell you that I just broke up with my girlfriend and I hate her right now".

"Hate is a pretty strong word Sincere, you shouldn't say that, just say you have a strong dislike for her".

"No because I do hate her, don't you ever hate people?"

"I try not to".

"Well I have to get going so that you can get up in the morning, I will call you". He gave me a hug. "I like you a lot Sabrina". "I like you too Sincere". "You are so beautiful", "I love you". I was taken aback. I didn't respond, I just walked to the car and drove off. I drove home wondering what kind of person he was. There was something about him, but I could not put my finger on it. I put my gospel tape in and listened to some music. It was soothing for me. I was still in church and learning more about the Father each day. It is a true statement when you are getting closer to the Lord you are placed on Satan's hit list.

Sincere and I were hanging out for about 3 months when he finally came out to my house. The children were gone and I just wanted some company, and I didn't feel like driving him all the way back across town. I made it clear that we were friends and we were by no means going to sleep together. "I don't mind that Sabrina, you know I can wait for you as long as you need me to, that's not why I love you". "Please stop telling me that Sincere, we haven't known each other long enough to be talking about love. We are friends and I like you but I am not ready for anything more than that right now". He smirked again. "Do you want to go for a walk?" "Sure, where will be walk?"

"How about around the block?" "Okay". We put our coats on and walked around the block. As we approached the top of the street, he asked me a strange question. "Sabrina, what is that?" "What?"

"Right there" "The woods, don't you know what the woods look like?"

"Yea but where does it lead?" "I don't know". "Let's take a walk in the woods".

"Hell no, I'm not going in the woods, what is wrong with you?"

"What's the matter, you scared?"

"No, I'm not scared; I just don't see any reason to walk in the woods, especially this time of night Sincere".

He laughed; I got a chill down my back. "Let's go, it's getting cold out here".

"Sure". We walked back to the house; I took my coat off and sat down.

"You seem like it's something on your mind Sabrina". "No I'm fine". He did not say anything the rest of the night. He kept complaining that his head hurt and that he was not feeling well. A few times, I heard him talking to himself in the bathroom but I thought it normal because I talked to myself on occasion. I left him alone. He slept on the sofa in the living room and I slept in my room. I read my bible that night. I asked the Holy Spirit to give me a scripture to read an immediately I went to Mark 5. I read intently about Legions and how he was filled with many demons. As I read this scripture, I could feel my body shaking and the room became cold. I shook it off and continued to read. I must have fallen asleep because when I woke up it was daylight. I went downstairs and Sincere was sitting on the sofa reading the bible. "Good morning". I hope you don't mind that I read your bible. I didn't bring mine". "It's all right". "I really like reading the bible but sometimes I find that a lot of the things in the bible are not true". "Why would you say that?" "Because it's true. How do the writers know that God said all that stuff, how do they know it was His spirit speaking and not someone else?" "Because the writers were being led by the Holy Spirit, God breathed on them". "I don't believe that". I started to respond but he abruptly changed the subject. "I thought I would make you some breakfast". He got up, went in the kitchen, and got the eggs ad sausage out. "I love cooking for you". "I love you". "You don't' love me, you don't even know me that well to love me". "I do love you and I will never let you go, you are my woman and I will never let you go". His eyes were big now and I noticed the grip he had on the frying pan. "Don't get upset about it dear," I laughed it off. He smiled. "I can't help it". I'm sorry". "I get nervous when I am around you". "Don't I'm just a woman". "A woman who loves the Lord. My mother always told me to get a woman in in my life who loved the Lord, and she will always be true to you, is that true?" "Is it true that I love the Lord, or if I will always be true to you?'. "Both". "Well I do love the Lord, but the jury is still out on being true to *you*. I mean I won't disrespect you or use you or anything like that but were just friends right now". "Well I want more than that". "Maybe later on down the road, but right now lets just take our time". He didn't seem to like my answer but I didn't' feed into it. I learned over the years that when people have problems, it is their problem. I cannot solve them or bend my beliefs to make them feel good. I had lost my voice before in many relationships. I wasn't going to lose my voice with him.

I took him home later on in the day. As soon as I got home, the phone rang. It was him "I miss you". "I just left you". I know but I miss you already". We talked for a few minutes and his phone beeped, I was glad when he told me that he had to go. I didn't hear from him for a few days. I didn't worry about it because we were not in a real relationship. Then I thought that he was probably with the young woman that he said he broke up with. He told me that he still had feeling for her and that he didn't' think it was right he way they had broken up. That was one of the reasons I didn't try to get into a relationship with him. He was not over the woman he had been seeing. I had guessed that he was still involved with her. That did not bother me one bit.

He called me later in the week and asked me to pick him up in Towson after work. I did not mind because I worked in Towson. However, when I picked him up he was clearly drunk. Before I could pull off, he spotted me. He got in the car and tried to kiss me. I pulled away from him. "You are drunk". "I know, I was having some problems with my mother, she makes me so sick!' I hate her you know, I really hate her, and I hate the other girl too. You know she told me that she loved me and now she doesn't want anything to do with me and I hate her for that" "Don't say thet Sincere, that's not nice, you are probably just upset right now but don't say you hate them, especially your mother, you only get one mother". "Why do you always say that to me?" "Because it's wrong Sincere". "Don't' you hate your husband and the men that walked out on you"? "No I don't hate them". "You should." "No I shouldn't". I should do just what I do". "And what's that, be stupid!" I looked at him as if he was crazy. "What did you say?" "I said you were stupid, stupid for letting them use you and hurt you the way they did. You have to get people before they get you and that way you won't get hurt!" I don't think that way; I give people the benefit of the doubt". "Do you give me the benefit of the doubt?' "Yes I do". "Good because I am what you need in your life. You don't need anybody but me. I am your man and I will take care of you". "I don't need you to take care of me". He got quiet and didn't say anything else almost the time we got to Eastern Avenue; he was so quiet I thought he was sick. "Are you alright?" All of a sudden, he grabbed the steering wheel and tried to control the car. I was fighting to keep control. He was laughing the whole time. "Come on and die with me!" It was only the grace of God that we did not crash. I made a U-turn and drove right back to the bus line. "Get the hell outta of my car, and don't call me again until you get some damn sense!" He got out. "I'm sorry, it wasn't me. You don't understand, it wasn't me. "Yeah right!" I slammed the door and drove away. He called me so much that I unplugged my phone and told my children not to answer my line. He left me so many messages on my voicemail that he filled it up. It was not until I took my bath and was alone when I started to shake. I could not stop shaking. I cried and cried. I finally fell off to sleep. It was a long night. I kept waking up and seeing him. I thought about the last time we had spent together and all the strange things that he said and did. How he would page me so often that I would have to turn my pager off. How he told me that he spent ten years in jail for assault on a female.

I thought about how his mother would never look me in the eye when I went over there. How he hated her one minute and loved her the next. The jealously he felt for his brother and his contempt for his sister. Then there were the times when he was so sweet and funny. He was caring and gentle one minute and the next minute when he would be angry because I spent time with my children and my church family. I tried to go back to sleep, it was draining me just thinking about his behavior. I made a mental note to ask pastor about some of those mood swings I saw in him.

I saw Sincere one more time before I told him that he was no longer welcome in my home. He wanted to come out and talk to me and apologize for "his actions". I told him he could come but he had to leave as soon as he finished what he had to say. He promised me that he would. When he arrived, I was sitting in the living room watching television.

"Sabrina, is it alright if we went upstairs to talk?"

"Why can't we talk right here?"

"I just need to say some things to you and I don't want the kids to hear me".

"I will go upstairs with you but the bedroom door stays open".

"Fair enough".

We walked up to the bedroom. He sat on the bed and I sat in my chair.

"Sabrina, I am so sorry for all the ugly things I said to you, I didn't mean to hurt your feelings, I was just angry that you didn't want to be with me anymore."

"Sincere, I don't' have any problem with you but I am not ready for what you are ready for. I tried to explain that to you. I didn't' get mad when you were talking to your girlfriend while I was standing right there, yes I thought it to be disrespectful to me and to her, but since I was not your woman, I couldn't' stress but so much."

"Why do you keep saying that, you are my woman?"

"No, because I don't share my man, knowingly and I don't play seconds to anyone but God"

"Why does God always got to be in everything you say out of your mouth?"

"What?"

"You heard me, you always throwing God up in my face, like you think I don't know who he is or something".

"I never questioned your faith Sincere, you know that".

"Well I am sick and tired of hearing about God and I am sick and tired of you always thinking you know everything about him, you don't' know nothing about him, you don't' even know if he exist".

"Oh He does exist and I know that, I don't have to see him, I can trust and have faith that He is who He says He is".

"Bullshit!"

"Look Sincere, you are getting upset and it's time for you to go".

"I'll go but give me my shirt and my pictures out of the closet".

"Fine"

I walked to the closet and was reaching up on the shelf, when I felt a sharp pain in the back of my neck. When I tried to turn around, he pushed me against the wall into the clothes and hangers. He took the hangers off the rack and started beating me with them. I tried to get out of the closet but he was standing between the door and my head was pressed against the back wall of the closet, I was trying to fight him but he had my arms pinned behind my back with one hand and he was beating me with all of these hangers with the other. They were getting caught in my micro braids and I was trying to fight.

"Bitch, Bitch, I hate you bitch, always God, God God, I hate you!"

I felt myself blacking out and I could feel the blood coming down my back and face. I started to slide down the wall and he caught me with his hand.

"Don't you run from me!"

I crouched over and tried to cover myself with the clothes that had fallen off the hangers from the beating. As quickly as it started, was as quickly as it stopped.

When I got my baring, he was gone. I called the police and they took a report.

A few days went by and they the police officers told me that that they transferred his paperwork to detectives in the city. I tried to explain that his brother was in law enforcement but they didn't' want to hear it.

I did not hear from Sincere for a while and I was glad about it, I was spending a lot of my time getting closer to God and trying to be what he wanted me to be. I had lost a lot over the years, wasting a lot of my time and effort loving people that did not love me; I made some huge mistakes in my life. I did not dwell on those things because I knew that they were all a part of whom I was and who I was to become. There was no more shame and guilt but I still had a long way to go. The word of God was working in my life. I had come through as pure gold. I have been in the fire with Shadrach, Meschac and Abendego and I had survived it. I had come thorough with my Father holding me upright.

I loved my church and I loved my church family. I learned so much from pastor, he was strong in the word and he made sure that we understood the word of God. He showed me how to receive the gift of speaking in tongues. I thought was amazing but I also knew what God was capable of doing in my life. There were so many wonderful things happening to me that I was finally at last, happy with my life and myself.

Gone were the anti-depressants. I was still weaning myself off the medicine for my seizures because I had prayed to God to take them away from me. I trusted Him to do it and I knew just as He delivered me from cigarettes, alcohol, drugs, anti-depressants and fear that He would deliver me from seizures too. I stayed in prayer and I stayed in the word. Those things along gave me a strength that I did not know I possessed. I wasn't not angry with anyone anymore. I tolerated things without blowing up or losing my temper. I had resolved in my heart and mind that my family loved although they never came to visit.

I read scripture that told me that we must be weary in well doing, we must journey on to see what the end will be. Times in my life changed, for the better. I had grown so much. I used to sit and remember all the things that had evolved in my life. All the pain, broken friendships and relationships. All the things that could have killed me. Then I would break down and cry, because I knew in my heart, I was only alive because of God's wonderful and unmerited faith and love that He had for me. I wanted to thank Him every chance I got and I did. I loved the word of God, it made me feel like I was in another relationship, only this time, I was being loved right back. The more time I spent with

Him, the more He loved me. The more I praised Him, the more He loved me. Even when I cried, acted out, backslid, He still loved me.

I sat in bible study Wednesday listening to the pastor teach about forgiveness.

"I know sometimes forgiveness is hard, especially the pain has come from someone you loved with all your heart and soul and they betrayed you or lied to you or hurt you. But we must forgive, for the Father has forgiven us for our sins". We read scripture after scripture about forgiveness.

I had a question that I had to ask. I was wrestling with one particular person that I knew in my heart I should forgive but I was finding it so hard to do, but I wanted to cleanse myself and I wanted to be free of all things that kept me bound. I raised my hand. "Pastor, can I ask a question?"

"Sure sister".

"I thought I had forgiven all the people that hurt me and betrayed me but I have to confess that I really haven't"

"Are you ready to forgive them tonight sister?"

"I think I am". I started to cry, I could feel the pain rising up inside of me, but I knew I had to do it.

"Come on church, let's gather around our sister and give her strength"

The small congregation stood up and encircled me and Sister Lewis started praying. "*Oh heavenly Father, we come to you tonight giving thanks for your presence in this place, we come giving you thanks for your unmerited favor and love that you have bestowed upon us even though we don't' deserve, it, Father, if we had a thousand tongues we couldn't' thank you enough, we come right Father asking you to touch our sister tonight, God she wants to forgive some people in her life who have hurt her Father give her strength to do so, help her Lord Jesus, touch from the top of her head to the souls of her feet, Oh Jesus we love you tonight Father!, In Jesus name, Amen*".

"*Okay sister; tell the Lord who you need to forgive.*"

I bowed my head and started to speak "God, I help me, help me to forgive, help me". The tears starting flowing down my face, and I did not stop them, I needed them to come out, because those tears cleansed me. "I need to forgive him, I need to forgive him for taking my childhood,

I need to forgive him for taking my innocence, I need to forgive him for hurting me and touching me, I need to forgive him, help me Lord", the congregation was speaking in tongues and screaming amen, amen. Amen, "God I forgive him, I forgive him I forgive him! I forgive you, you can't hold me anymore, you can't keep me bound anymore, you can't use it against me anymore, you are forgiven, you are forgiven!" I heard God speak to me *"the only thing the enemy has is your past, if you forgive and let it go, he can't use it against you anymore, free yourself daughter, free yourself, face it and I will fix it for you"* I opened my eyes to see if anyone else heard the voice but everyone seemed to be slain in the spirit. I kept crying and I kept saying I forgive you. The voice came back. *There is one more daughter, one more you must forgive".* And has quickly as the voice came, it was gone. I think we were praying for about an hour before we calmed down.

"I feel the spirit of God in this place tonight church! He's here, He's here!" Praise God and Amens were being screamed all over the church. I just sat down and rocked back and forth I was drained. After the benediction, we all left. I still didn't know whom the voice was telling me to forgive but I would remember that for the rest of my life. In addition, I prayed that the voice would tell me whom that person was that I needed to forgive. I tried to remember in my mind if there was someone I forgot. But I couldn't' think of anyone.

As we got to the parking lot, Sincere was standing there; it was obvious that he had been drinking. Pastor walked to my car and stood beside me. "How are you young man?"

"I need to know why you are filling Sabrina's head with all of this pagan stuff, why are you brainwashing her, telling that Jesus is still alive".

"Son, Jesus *is* alive, I know it in my heart and with all my being and so does everyone standing out here tonight".

"You're all a bunch of liars and you will burn in hell for it! Sabrina you used to love me before you started coming to this church all the time! You used to love me, why did stop loving me Sabrina, I said I was sorry!"

Pastor gently pulled me by my arm and led me towards his car. "Sister, I want you to drive with my wife and children, give me your keys"

"Pastor, I can't leave you out here with him".

He smiled. "I'll be fine; you all go on home now and have a blessed evening in the Lord".

The congregation was hesitant to leave him but he assured us that he would be okay that God would take care of him whatever happened. We drove slowly away from the small little storefront church, praying all the way. We all sat at the pastor's house waiting for him to come home, we stayed in prayer until we heard the car door slam. We all ran to the door and saw pastor parking my car.

"Where did he go?"

"He had a ride waiting for him".

"What did he say to you?"

"He went on and on about different things, strange things. Sister I am glad that you decided that he was not a person you wanted to spend time with".

"I've only known him about six months, he wasn't trying to do the right things pastor and he didn't respect me. I cared about him but I wasn't in love or anything, but after the mood swings, I decided that it was best"

"Well good for you, are you going to be okay?'

"Yes pastor, thank you for driving".

He gave me a hug and I went in the house.

I thought about Sincere that night, He was a very nice person at times but most of the time he had issues that I was not able to deal with. After that beating he gave me, I was more afraid of him than anything. I felt the fear creeping back into my mind but I kept praying. I was honest enough to tell myself that I was feeling a little depressed about our friendship, he had made me feel so bad, telling me that I was ugly and that I was skinny and that he didn't want to sleep with me because he didn't think I was desirable and that I should find something to do with my hair, I didn't think anything was wrong with me and I tried not to pay him any mind but I was sad about how he talked about me and always compared me to his ex girlfriend and his new white girlfriend how she had a three bedroom condominium and she had a better job, car, and clothes than me, Little things like that were really bothering me and I couldn't understand why, except that I had tried so hard to be good at everything I did. I was proud of my accomplishments and how God had blessed me but this man was playing on my psyche.

Sincere would not leave me alone, after that stunt me pulled at the church I thought I would not hear from him again but he showed up at my job.

It was a cool but beautiful Saturday morning. We had just opened up and we were not quite ready for customers but the door had been unlocked. My supervisor and all the employees knew who Sincere was. The police suggested that we keep his picture available so that everyone would know who he was. Martha had just picked his picture up off her desk. "You know Sabrina, I'm not into jungle fever or anything, but he is a cutie pie". "Yes he is but he is a can short of a six-pack".

"I can't believe that he is that dangerous Sabrina".

"That's why he can get away with so much Martha. The man has issues and that is all it is to it. If you think he is so cute and adorable and all that, then hook up with him so that that he can leave me alone".

"Do you think he will do anything else to you?"

"I pray that he won't but I don't know. The police told that he does have a record and he has assaulted women before so it's his MO to hurt me".

"Are you scared?" "Yes, I have to be, to stay on guard".

"What happens if he does come up here Sabrina, what do we do?"

Victor overheard what she said. "You call the damn police woman are you crazy, this man is a damn nut. How much proof do you need? No disrespect Sabrina, but the man has beat her with hangers, stalked her for the past 3 months, harassed her on the phone, burnt out her damn pager! I don't know why in the hell he is still walking around, his ass should be right up the street at the damn detention center".

I laughed but I was afraid of Sincere. He had stalked me and called me just to tell me what clothes I wore to work. He would yell and tell me that I looked like a whore in one outfit or another. He would tell me whom I went to lunch with, what I brought for lunch. He would tell me which way I took home from work. He had me so paranoid that I couldn't sleep and I wouldn't' go back out once I got home safe. I kept the doors locked at all times and would not' answer my phone. I was spooked. I prayed and prayed for God to protect me.

Just as I came out of thought. There Sincere stood. Smiling with a black leather jacket, blue jeans, a fresh pair of Nikes and a dark blue button down.

"Hey Sabrina".

"Hey Sincere, what are you doing here?"

"I came to see you Sabrina". "You need to leave Sincere".

I walked towards my desk but he blocked my path.

"Aren't you glad to see me?" "Please Sincere, please leave".

"Are you *afraid* of me Sabrina?" I tried to act as if I was not but I was terrified.

"Afraid of you for what?" I love you Sabrina, you know that we belong together".

"Sincere, let's not start that again".

"Are you going to call the police on me Sabrina?"

"No, but somebody else might".

"If they do, then you will pay for it!"

I purposely knocked something off my desk to bring attention to the front of the office. Martha and Vincent came from the back.

"Are you okay Sabrina?"

Before I could answer, they saw Sincere, who was now standing there with his hands in his pockets. His face was grimaced and twisted.

"I'm not going to hurt her!"

Vincent stood toe to toe with him.

"Man we already called the police; you need to get the hell outta here right now, before I catch a case".

"Man I don't want any trouble with you; I just came to see my woman".

"I am not your woman Sincere".

"You will always be my woman Sabrina, always!"

Vincent stood between us.

"Let me walk you to the door brother".

"Sabrina can I at least have a hug before I go, I promise I won't bother you again".

I was scared out of my mind but I still acted as if I was not.

"Sure Sincere, for old time sake".

He put his hand around my waist and pulled me to him. I could smell the liquor on his breath. He took my hand into his and rubbed in down to the middle of his back and placed it on a gun. He whispered in my ear, "You feel that Sabrina". I tried to pull away but he held me tighter. "You feel that, I can kill you anytime I want to!" He kissed on the cheek and walked out. My whole body began to shake and I lost control. When I woke up, I was at GBMC hospital in the emergency room. A few of my co-workers were there beside me.

"How are you feeling baby?"

"I have a headache".

"You hit your head on the side of the desk".

"What happened?"

"You had a seizure baby"

"What?"

"You had a seizure and you went out, we couldn't wake you so we called 911 and they brought you here. I called your mother and sister, they are on the way"

Then it all came back to me. I remembered Sincere placing my hand over the gun.

"He came to kill me".

"What?" I could see the rage in Victor's eyes.

"He put my hand over a gun that he had in his waistband and told me that he could kill me anytime he wanted to".

I started crying again. At that moment, I realized that Sincere *was* going to kill me. He was not going to stop stalking me and calling me and harassing me until he killed me.

"I'ma kill that bastard".

"Please Victor, don't talk like that".

"Sabrina, you don't deserve to be treated like this".

"I'm going to be fine".

"Sabrina, are you going to be alright"

"I'm gonna be fine, God has my back,

I believed that. However, as a woman, and a human being, I was afraid. I did not know where he was and how he was getting around finding out everything about me. I tried so hard to walk away from Sincere with no drama and no pain, but I did not know what or whom I was dealing with. I did not realize that this man was obsessed with me and he would kill me if given the chance I knew that. In my heart I felt like I was dying inside, I felt like I was drowning. I could not breathe, not physically, but mentally, I could not breathe. Every time I tried to breathe normally, he would call me or I would see him in my thoughts. I kept rubbing my hands together because I could still feel the cold steel of the gun.

My mother and sister came and took me back to the job after I was released. I got my car and they followed me home. They stayed with me until I fell off to sleep. They made my kids lock the doors and windows. They parked my car around the corner and turned off all the lights. The kids stayed in my bedroom with me and watched television. The house was dark as if no one was home.

My neighbor and her husband watched my house as I slept. Martin had a .357 and he was ready to use it, he said. "if I see that crazy son of a bitch, I will shoot and ask questions later!" And I believed him.

My week was uneventful. I had not heard a peep out of Sincere, but that frightened me even more. I was so used to him stalking me, or lurking somewhere around close that I almost expected him each day and night. But I had not heard from him in at least a week. He had called my mother begging her to talk to me, asking her to tell me to take him back, she tried to explain to him that she did not meddle in her children's lives but he kept calling and crying until she had to unplug her phone. After that, we did not hear from him. It was quiet, almost too quiet.

I knew that something major was going to happen in my life. I didn't' know what, but God had come to me in several different dreams telling me to trust Him no matter what things seemed like or looked like in my eyes, to continue to trust Him and so I did. He specifically told me in a dream once that **2 Chronicles 14: if my people, who are called by my name, shall humble themselves, and pray and seek my face and turn from their wicked ways; then will I hear from heaven, and will forgive their sin, and will heal their land. My ways are not your ways; my thoughts are not your thoughts.**

His words became more profound every dream I had. I knew they had meaning in my life but I was not quite sure what, but I knew in time that He would reveal it to me, for the word of God never returns void.

Hell on Earth…Satan is Unleashed!

I worked the entire week without as much as a phone call from

Sincere. I was starting to relax. Easter was coming and I was so excited. I had been in church all week listening and reading John, although I knew that Jesus would rise again, it was still sad to know that they crucified Him. The betrayal and the arrest of Jesus were profound to me. I was so immersed in this scripture, I couldn't' get enough of the word of God. It felt like I had never opened up my bible, I was thirsty and the more I read, the better it felt. I was so filled when I went home that I just wanted to relax. We got out of church early.

I took a hot shower and went to bed. The next day at work was just as uneventful. Everyone kept asking me was I okay, had I heard from Sincere, and I told them no, it had been quiet and that maybe God had finally shown him that we were not going to be anymore than we were. I walked to my car and drove home without a second thought. All of a sudden, my pager went off. I looked down at it and it was my house number. I pulled over and called home. "Hello Sabrina".

I couldn't speak, when I heard Sincere' voice on my phone line I lost my voice.

"Sabrina, are you there?" "What are you doing in my house Sincere, how did you get in my house!" "Stop screaming, I just want to talk to you for a minute"

"Get out of my house Sincere; I am calling the police right now!"

"Calm down". "Where are my children, where are my children Sincere!"

"They aren't here, nobody's here but me Sabrina, come home, come home to me".

The phone went dead. I called the police and told them that someone was at my house, someone who they were looking for. By the time I got home, he was gone and my door was broken. They could not find him anywhere. They went to his mother's house but she had not seen him.

Martin fixed my door for me and made sure that no one could get in. He fixed my screen door too, so that once you shut it, it locked from the inside. I did not sleep well that night. I broke down and started crying. When I looked in my bedroom, I looked on my mirror and he had written a message on my mirror. "YOU WILL DIE WITH ME SABRINA; YOU WILL DIE WITH ME SOON!" I started screaming. My son ran in the room and tried to calm me down; when he saw the writing, he grabbed the sheet off the bed and tried to wipe it off. "NO" I yelled, "I need the police to see this". The first part of the writing was smeared but it was enough left for the police to take a picture of.

For the life of me, I couldn't understand why they wouldn't' take a warrant out on this man. I thought after all the harassing and coming on my job, that would at least put a warrant on him for violation of a restraining order, but nothing happened and Sincere kept at me.

The phone calls started up again, the hang-ups, the heavy breathing, and the notes on my car all of it started all over again. I was a wreck. I tried to keep my wits about me and I stayed prayed up in the word of God, I was so close to God that I could not only hear him, I could feel Him walking with me, I mean right in my footsteps with me. I drove my car to work, and tried to function as normally as I could. When I got home that evening, I was exhausted.

I got out of my car and walked up my driveway. I could hear Tupac song "Dear Mama" coming from my house. I smiled. My son sang that song to me all the time. When I stepped in the house, I could smell food cooking and all the lights were on. I yelled in the dining room, "Darius turn that down a little, I can't hear myself think, and what are you cooking?" No answer. "I know you can't hear me, with all that noise boy, turn that music down".

I walked towards the dining room and my heart dropped. "Hey baby, I cooked you dinner?" I dropped my handbag in the floor. "Baby, I will call you back, my baby is home now and I want to spend some time with her, you better be ready when I get there, you hear me!!!?" He put his hand on the button and dialed another number. I was frozen where I stood. "Hey Mom, I just wanted to see how you were doing, I am at Francine's house and I will be home in a little while".

His mother must have said something that he did not like.

"Shut up, I said I am at Francine's house, I hate Sabrina, I am not at her house mom!"

He slammed the phone down.

He looked at me and sipped on a beer and a clear substance in a glass.

"Why do you make me drink Sabrina, you know what happens to me when I drink"

"Sincere, it's nice of you to cook for me sweetie" I had to stay calm because I knew if I didn't I would die. I could see in his eyes that he was not all there.

"Do you know where my children are Sincere?"

"Of course I do, they are all outside, they don't' care about you, they didn't' even cook you anything to eat after a hard days work but I did Sabrina because I love you, I love you more than your own children, but you treat them like queens and kings, they get anything from you, your time, your money, your love and you don't' give me nothing Sabrina, as much as I love you, you don't care about me!!".

"Sincere, that's not true, I care about you" "LIAR!"

He opened up two beers at the same time and drank Vodka straight out the bottle. I looked under the table and saw a case of beer or what was left of a case of beer, he had consumed at least ten beers thus far and he was on his second pint of vodka but he was still standing.

He walked over to the stove. "You know I fixed your favorite, hamburgers, rice, gravy and green beans".

"Thank you sweetie" I was thinking of how I could get out of the house, I was going to die if I didn't. I knew that in my heart. I didn't want my children to come home and find my body so I figured I would run and allow him to get me outside so that maybe someone could see what he was doing and identify him so the police could finally arrest him. I started praying silently in my mind. He walked towards me with the fork in his hand with green beans on it. "Taste this and tell me if it's seasoned right".

I took a bite of the green beans. He shoved the fork in my mouth and held my jaws. "I hate what you make me do to you Sabrina, why do you make me hurt you!"

I pulled away from him and tried to run but he caught me by the back of my neck. "Don't fight me Sabrina, you will lose!"

Just as he was pulling me closer to him, I heard a knock on the front door. He ran for the door before I could and my baby girl was on the other side. "Mommy open the door, I have to go to the bathroom".

He opened the door and pushed my daughter so hard that she fell backwards onto the sidewalk. I screamed "Run Nia, Run!" He slammed the door. I forgot that I was afraid of him. I leaped on his back. "Don't put your hands on my baby; don't put your hands on my baby!" I was banging him on back and head and scratching him. He tossed me off his back like a rag doll. He grabbed me by my blouse and threw me on the steps. He tried to charge me but I ran backwards on my hands and butt. I turned around in the middle of the steps and ran up the steps but he grabbed my foot and tried to drag me back down the stairs. All of sudden, the house became cold, so cold I could see my breath. His voice was so deep that I did not even recognize it. "I am going to kill you Sabrina, tonight you will die!" I turned to look at him and his face was distorted. I kicked him and he let my foot go. I ran in the bedroom and tried to lock the door. He kicked it halfway off the hinges. I tried to run but there was no where to go in the bedroom, I tried to get back to the door, but it shut, like a wind had pulled it shut, I tried to get to the window, but he grabbed me and pulled me off my feet by my skin. His nails felt like steel and his strength was something I had never ever imagined. I was not touching the floor at all. His breath was so foul that I gagged. "TONIGHT YOU DIE, DIE! He threw me against the wall and I fell down. He tried to hit me but I moved and he punched a huge hole in the wall, I could see clear to the other side. His strength was not of his own. He picked me up and threw me on the bed; he threw me so hard that I rolled off on to the floor. He turned the bed including the mattress and box spring upside down. "KILL HER NOW, KILL HER NOW!, please, I don't want to kill her, I love her, I love Sabrina, "I SAID KILL HER" I tried to crawl away but he grabbed me and threw me on the floor on my back and started to choke me. He was foaming at the mouth and his eyes were bulging out of his head. "Please don't make me kill her; I don't want to kill her". Tears were coming from his eyes but suddenly the tears stopped. "I SENT YOU TO KILL HER DO IT, DO IT NOW!" His grip tightened around my neck and I was starting to pass out. *Daughter, Whatsoever ye shall ask the Father in my name, he will give it to you...*I felt myself losing consciousness, I could still hear the battle between Sincere and whatever possessed him. "SIN, YOU ARE MINE, OBEY MY COMMAND! FINISH HER! I could hear a soothing voice.....*whatsoever ye shall ask the Father in my name, he will give it to you....* I whispered "Father, Jesus, help me, help me please, in Jesus' name Father, help me". Suddenly, Sincere' hands released me and he started to scream "UGGH!!! My hands my hands! I kept whispering

"Jesus, Jesus, Jesus, there is no other name I know, Jesus …**at the name of Jesus, Satan you have to flee!!!** I watched as Sincere struggled and thrashed around the room. He started ripping curtains down from the window, and cleared the dresser with one swipe of his hands, he tore at his clothes and tried again and again to grab me but it was like a force between us. I lay on the bed unable to move it was so cold in the room that I started shivering I could hear him gritting his teeth and speaking in two different voices :"I don't want to kill her, help me, YOU WILL DIE FOR THIS SIN, YOU WILL DIE FOR THIS!' the bedroom door opened and Sincere ran downstairs. I could hear things being thrown about the house but I still couldn't move. I lay there with tears streaming down my eyes; I thanked God repeatedly. I heard the sirens in the distance. I tried to get up but my body was so sore that I felt like I had been in a fight with Mike Tyson. I looked around my bedroom and it was a disaster, I did not think I would ever be able to put it back together.

I walked downstairs when I heard the police banging on the door. "Mam, are you alright, Mam, are you in the house alone?"

"I'm up here officer".

They all ran up the stairs. They stopped dead in their tracks when the saw the bedroom and the marks around my neck.

"Do you need an ambulance?"

"I think I will be okay"

"Do you know who did this to you?"

"Yes and so do you, I have been calling you all at least twice a week about this man".

"Mam let me call an ambulance for you, to at least look you over".

"I'm fine officer, have you seen my children?"

"I have them outside, I didn't know what we would find when we came in here so I asked them to stay outside until we checked things out".

"Thank you, I would like to see them".

I walked downstairs, police were everywhere. The ambulance showed up and the paramedics checked me out. I assured them that I was okay.

I walked in the kitchen and I couldn't believe what I saw. My entire kitchen was covered with gravy, rice, hamburgers, all over the floor and walls. My dining room chairs were turned over and broken and there were empty cans of beer all over the floor.

"Mam, do you have somewhere else you can stay?"

"I can't let this man run me away from my home; he has done enough to me".

They took more notes made sure that I was okay, left a police car outside the rest of the night and told me that they were going to find him.

My neighbors came over and stayed with me. Martin refused to leave my sofa that night. He helped put my bed back together, put my rods back up enough to place a sheet at the window. He gave me some type of cleaner to clean the floors and walls. I couldn't' sleep so I stayed up and cleaned. My pager kept going off and my phone kept ringing but Martin kept answering it, telling Sincere that he was a dead man.

This went on for most of the night until I finally passed out on the love seat.

As bad as I felt, I knew God truly loved me, all the time he was speaking to me, and he was strengthening me to trust Him in my time of need. Do not cry out to man or anyone, to cry out to Him and He would deliver me from the evil one and that is what he did. When I thought about that night in my bedroom, I shivered. I could not believe that I actually witness Satan and God battling for my life. God held me in His loving arms and His angels were encamped around me and protected me from Sin and his demons. It was so scary at first, to hear Sincere' voice back and forth like it did, to see the darkness in his eyes and face, and I couldn't the cold, my goodness the cold was almost unbearable. There were no windows open and it was not that cold outside but it was freezing in that room. I knew what took place that night was not of flesh and blood but principalities. I knew that night that God had something special for me to do with my life. I didn't know what but I was going to spend the rest of my life trying to find out.

I had spent the first half living a destructive lifestyle, God had given me a second chance, He saved me that night…He loved me enough to save me…I knew then my life was destined for greatness, for His glory and His glory alone. For the first time, I heard His voice but I was not asleep....*Let not your heart be troubled; ye believe in God, believe also in me. In my Father's house are many mansions, if it were not so, I would have told you, I go to prepare a place for you. And if I go and prepare a place for you I will come again, and receive you unto myself that where I am there ye may be also. And wither I go ye know, and the way ye know...I am the truth and the life no man cometh unto the Father but by me....*I couldn't believe it, I could actually hear the voice and I was sitting up and wide awake...I started talking to Him..Father I love you, I want you to come back into my life, please forgive me for my sins Father, please help me to know you and live my life through your will and not mine...your will is what I want Father, your will is what I want.....*daughter, there is still something that you must do...you must do it so that you can finish this journey*...what Father, what is it that I need to do, please help me, please!...*forgive...daughter..forgive*..I have forgiven Father, I have! I forgave my abusers, my children's father, my husband, all the people who betrayed me....*you have forgotten one daughter....* who Father, please tell me...*you must find out on your own daughter, only then can I enter in.* and the voice was gone....I fell asleep, I couldn't keep my eyes open. I think I slept for hours because when I woke up it was morning.

I decided to go to church. I called Wayne. I had long forgiven him for the money and we were civil. He had paid me all my money back and was clean from cocaine. I was proud of him and I didn't want to hold a grudge so we became friends again. He was staying at his brother's house a few miles from where I lived so I told him that I would pick him up so that we could go to church. I drove down the road listening to Heaven 600 and humming to the music. My pager went off but I didn't answer it. The children were home and safe. Martin was still patrolling my house like a man on a mission. He walked around with that .357 in his waistband covered by a tee shirt and a lumberjack shirt to hide the bulge. His wife and I both tried to get him to put it away but he said, the next time Sincere came back, he was sending him to hell where he came from. There was no reasoning with him so I just let him continue to watch my house for me. I didn't like taking the kids with me because I didn't trust where I would run into Sincere. The police still had not picked him up.

It was early so when I got to Wayne's house we sat and talked for a few.

"It's really good to see you Sabrina"

"You too Wayne, how have you been since I last talked to you?"

"I doing good, one day at a time".

That made me think of Angie, always ending her letters with one day at a time Bee

"How are you, have they found that fool yet?"

"Not yet". "I'm sorry he hurt you" "It's cool; you know I've been beat much worse than that in my life".

"Don't talk like that Sabrina, I don't care what they did it doesn't make it right when somebody else does it".

"I know. I was just trying to make light of the situation".

"Sabrina, there is no light of the situation; this man is trying to kill you".

"I know but I can't think like that Wayne, I've been a victim all my life, it's time I become a survivor, you know what I'm saying?"

"Yes I do, I was a victim remember?"

"Yes, how are you really?"

"It gets hard sometimes, you know what they say, "that stuff be calling me" he tried it imitate Chris Rock in "New Jack City".

"Don't answer"

"One day at a time. Just for today, I am sober".

I gave him a hug. I was happy that he was clean.

I started getting dizzy. "Wayne, I don't feel good"

"What's the matter?"

I don't know". That's all I remember, when I looked again, I was in the emergency room at Franklin Square Hospital. "She's seizing again people, lets get that Dilantin in people," I felt the warmness trickling down my leg. "We got urine let's move, she's going, Sabrina, Sabrina, stay with me sweetie, hold on!"

I kept seizing, I felt the blood in mouth, "she bit her tongue". "Come on people, let's move!" I could hear Wayne's voice. "Please don't die Sabrina, please don't die".

Then I heard nothing. I must have fallen asleep or the medicine took affect because I felt sleepy but not before I heard. "Man I didn't hurt her, I brought her here because she was having a seizure, I never laid a hand on her, Sabrina, tell them it wasn't me!" I blinked and could see the police handcuffing Wayne. I shook my head no, but they mistook it for me fighting. "Stop fighting sweetie, it will be okay".

I grabbed the nurse's hand and whispered. "He didn't do this to me, please, don't take him away". "Now sweetie, I know you may be afraid to tell the truth but you will be okay".

"No, he didn't do this; ask the officer, he knows me". I pointed to the police officer. She pulled the police aside and whispered something to him. He came over towards my bed. "Mam, is this the man that hurt you?"

"Don't you remember me officer Swank, you came to my house the other night. I'm the woman whose house was torn apart". "Oh, yes, I do remember you". "That's not the man?" After a few hours, they let me go home. I felt so sorry for Wayne but he was a trooper. He told me not to worry about it. He took me home and stayed as long as he could before he left. It had started to rain terrible and his brother had to come and pick him up. I gave him a hug and thanked him for helping me out. I apologized again for almost getting him locked up.

It rained so hard that night that they a flash flood warning until the wee hours of the morning. After I said my prayers and read a few chapters of Hebrews, I fell off to sleep.

About one o'clock in the morning I heard some banging on my door. I looked out the window and there stood Sincere soaking wet with no coat on.

"Sabrina, please open the door, I just want to talk to you".

I acted as if I did not hear him. I tried to ignore him.

"Sabrina, please, I love you, I love you, please open the door, I'm sorry!"

"I pulled the window up. "Sincere, I called the police, they're looking for you"

"I'm not leaving until you come down and talk to me!"

"Please Sincere; please go home, I'm not mad I just want you to go home"

"Sabrina, please, I'm sorry" His face was wet but I couldn't' tell if it were tears or rain.

"He made me do it Sabrina, my father made me do it!"

I felt that cold again. I slammed the window shut.

I crept down the stairs and tried to see if he was gone but he was not. He was shaking the screen door. I tried to reason with him. "Sincere, please, go home I promise I will call you later, I promise".

"No you wont' you don't' love me anymore"

"Sincere, please go".

I cracked the door open so that I could see his face. When I did, He was standing there looking truly pitiful. "I'm sorry Sabrina and I want make it up to you".

"Sincere, it's okay please go, I'm sure the police will be here soon"

He shook the door so hard but it still didn't come open. My baby girl came downstairs. "Mommy are you okay?"

"Yes baby, go back to bed, it's alright"

She peeked at the door. She ran back up the steps.

He shook the door again. I tried pulling it but he got a hold on it.

He reached in his pants and pulled out a 9 mm. He grabbed the door and it came open. I tired to move but he had me pinned between the screen door and the front door. He placed the gun to my head. "I told you, if I can't have you, no-one will have you, you will go with me tonight!" He was not loud but his face was demonic. He tried to put the clip in but it would not work and it dropped when he looked down, I slammed the door behind me and fell to the floor. I was so scared that he would shoot through the door. I realized that it was God that jammed that gun; I also realized that it was God who did not allow him to know that there was a bullet in the chamber, there is always a bullet in the chamber of a 9 mm. I would not get up off the floor. I heard the police screaming outside the door. "Mam, please open the door, Baltimore County Police, open the door!!". "No!" he's going to shoot me". "Mam please open the door, I promise you there is no one here but us". I reached up and grabbed the doorknob. The same officer that was at the hospital, kneeled down and helped me off the floor. "It's going to be alright Ms. Thomas, I promise you, we will find him". "He tried to kill me". I broke down and cried. My children were all awake and mad. They kept telling me that I would be okay. "Can you tell us what happened?" "He came by and said something about pictures and that he needed to talk, I told him I didn't' have any pictures and that I didn't want to talk he forced his way through the screen door and that's when he pulled the gun on me. "Can you tell me what kind of gun it was?" "It looks just like the one you have". "Do you have a picture of him?" "I have one; I gave the rest of them back to him months ago". I went upstairs and grabbed the picture that I had of him. I looked at it and could not believe that the man I was staring back at was capable of murder. I gave the officer the picture and they told me that they were getting a warrant that night and going to find him. They had searched the woods, the back and front yards of every single house but could not' find him. I figured he must have gotten a ride by that girl he was seeing. I could not believe that she brought him here to kill me, or maybe she did not know. At any rate, I was in shock by all of it.

The police stayed in the neighborhood the rest of the night and when I woke up the next morning, they were still there. I tried to rest but I could not. I kept seeing the gun in my face; I kept dreaming that he pulled the trigger and the blood splatter all over my children while he laughed. I kept waking up crying. It was a long night.

Wayne came over and kept me company. He would not leave me no matter what I said. "Sabrina, I am not going anywhere so you might as well get some sleep."

"Are you sure?" "Yes I'm sure. It's okay to be scared Sabrina, its okay to cry, you don't have to be strong all the time, allow yourself to cry". "If I do, then he wins Wayne".

"He'll never win Sabrina". I lay on the sofa and drifted off the sleep. I knew that Wayne would not leave my children or me. I was finally allowed to sleep.

The next morning we all went out to breakfast. It was good to get out. Wayne watched over me like a bodyguard. We walked around the mall and tried to forget about the past events. However, it was always in the back of my mind. I kept looking around to see if saw Sincere. I had talked to pastor about him and what I experienced. He said that he was sure it was a battle between good an evil. He showed me how to understand that Sincere was not himself that he was being controlled by something other than himself. I couldn't' explain the coldness and the way Sincere kept talking in different voices. Pastor stopped talking and just started praying for me.

I went to work that Monday and everybody was concerned for me, but I reassured them that I would be fine. My supervisor allowed me to work in the back office. I felt better about that. I had a slow but steady and soon it was over. James walked me to my car, checked it out and made sure that it was safe for me drive it and I went home. I called Wayne and told him that I got home safe. After a hot shower and reading for a while, I went to bed.

I went to work the next day same as usual. I thought that would go back to my desk this morning. My supervisor was nice enough to make sure that someone was always around. The day was busy and it was warm out. The sun was shining. The phones were ringing and I was transferring calls, answering calls, and writing messages quickly. Then my phone line rang.

"Sabrina".

I froze. "Sabrina, please talk to me"

I hung up the phone. He called back four or five times before I spoke to him.

"Sincere, stop calling me"

"I want you to meet me Sabrina, meet me at Gunpowder Park, we need to talk".

"We have nothing to talk about"

"I love you Sabrina, please meet me, we can go together, you and me"

"Sincere, I'm not going anywhere with you".

"Please Sabrina, I love you"

I looked out the door and saw all of these undercover cop cars flying down York Road. Then I was about ten police cars and an ambulance, flying by. I thought where in the world all those police are going; somebody must have robbed a bank.

"Sabrina, we can go together, you know, no one will ever love you the way I do".

That is when I heard the bulletin come over the radio station. "We have a hostage situation in Fullerton, Maryland, children are being told to kept at the schools, if you have to travel that way, towards White Marsh or Belair Road, don't"

"They're coming for me Sabrina; they want to kill me you know"

"Sincere, where are you?"

"I'm in the house Sabrina, and if they kill me, my blood will be on your hands!"

"Sincere, don't talk like that; it's going to be okay".

"No it's not Sabrina, I can't go back to jail, you don't know how it is in there"

"Sincere, please if they come, just let them in and go with them, they won't hurt you"

"Sabrina, I have a .308 rifle, a 9 mm and a few hunting rifles, they are going to have to kill me. If I kill myself Sabrina, then God won't forgive me".

I was crying now. "Sincere, please don't do anything that will make them shoot you"

I heard several "pops" Sincere, Sincere!"

"Did you hear that Sabrina, that's what they will get if they try to come in here?"

"Sincere, listen to me, if you leave with them, I will tell them that you didn't do anything, I won't show up at court, please Sincere, please put the guns down".

"I wasn't going to hurt you Sabrina, I just wanted you to love me, I just wanted you to feel the way I felt about you Sabrina. I wouldn't have hurt you, I love you. I am going to die Sabrina, but I wanted you to know that I love you and I tried to save you honest I did, they wanted me to kill you, the voices in my head wanted me to kill you, but I loved you, I wouldn't let them kill you"

"Please Sincere; listen to me, it going to be okay, I promise you it will be okay"

"The only way I will leave this house is feet first Sabrina, I have nothing to live for anymore, you don't love me, my mother doesn't love me, and there is nothing left for me to live for. You don't love me anymore Sabrina, why don't you love me anymore?"

I was crying but I tried not to let him hear it in my voice.

"Sincere, I do love you; I don't want you to get hurt, please"

"Sabrina, I wanted to tell you that God is angry with me, he knows that I killed a man once, right in front of his wife. I didn't want to kill him Sabrina but they made me do it, they said if I didn't' have the money I owed them then I would pay them another way, so they took me to this house and made me kill him, in front of his wife Sabrina, so you see, I have to do this". Before I could question him, the phone went dead. That's when I knew that the hostage negotiators were on the scene. The first thing they do is cut the phone wires so that they are the only ones that can speak to the suspect. I was shaking and crying. I was so scared for Sincere. He was a troubled man and he was lost, he didn't even know Satan was controlling him and now he was in a situation that I feared he would not come out of alive. I sat at the desk and listened to the radio, every ten minutes was an update. I called my mother and told her that it was Sincere they were talking about all over the news and radios, she was in shock, she kept asking me was I okay. I told her that I had to get out there; I needed to know he was going to be okay. I told my supervisor that I had to leave. By then they knew what was going on. I drove out towards Fullerton but you couldn't get through. I knew where he was, but I couldn't' get past the roadblocks. I sat in my car and prayed and prayed. Finally, after about 4 hours the road started opening up to traffic. I jumped out my car and ran towards the officers. "Is he alright?" "Who are you?" "I'm the person he assaulted". "No he's not alright". I looked past the officer and saw Sincere' feet hanging out the front door. "the only way I am coming out of there is feet first Sabrina" I could hear Sincere' words in my head. When I woke up, I was at Franklin Square's psychiatric ward. I could not believe that they shot him dead. I kept thinking that I was dreaming. The tears would not stop. One of the officers came in the room. "Mam, are you going to be alright?"

I shook my head yes. "I didn't want him to die, you know, I just wanted him to leave me alone". "Mr. Simmons would not put his weapon down. When he came to the door, he was told 5 times to put the weapon down, he placed the gun on his shoulder and peered through the scope, our officers had no choice"

"Did he say anything?"

"He wanted us to kill him, we tried everything to talk him out, we had no choice in the matter". We called his brother, and his mother and no one could talk him out. He kept asking to talk to you, but we couldn't allow that". I cried some more.

He placed a card in my hand,

"Here is a place that you can go to or call when you feel up to it. It will help you deal with this". I thanked him. "I know he would have killed me if given the chance". "Yes mam, I believe that he would have".

I stayed in the psych ward for about 2 more hours before the psychiatrist let me go home. My sister was in the waiting room waiting for me. She ran up to me and hugged me. "It's okay Sabrina, it wasn't your fault"

"I didn't want him to die Dionna, I didn't want him to die!"

She just held me. "It's okay, he wanted to die baby" "But he didn't have to die, he could have walked away". "He did what he needed to do to die Sabrina, you know you can't come to the door with a rifle in your hand, and then cock it, he wanted them to shoot him". Police assisted suicide is what the papers were calling it.

It was all over the news and newspapers. I was interviewed by all the major news stations. That was my 15 minutes of infamy but I had to talk about it. I did not humiliate his memory by telling them how he beat me just days before. I tried to spare his mother and his family that embarrassment but she blamed me anyway. She said it was my fault that her son was dead. That really hurt me. However, I held my own. The story stayed in the news for weeks. My son sat next to me and rubbed my back, "its not your fault mommy, you didn't do anything, all you tried to do was stay alive, it was you or him mommy, you know he would have killed you if he got the chance. It was not your fault". I laid my head on his shoulder and cried. "I didn't want him to die". "I know mommy, but it was not your fault, he came to the door with the gun, you know a black man can't do no stuff like that, especially not in Baltimore County, the man had a death wish". They interviewed his cousin who stated that he told him that he was tired and ready to die. "I told him to hold on, things would get better, but he didn't' want to hear it, he kept saying, man I'm tired, I'm really tired". I knew something had happened the night I saw him but I didn't ask him, he was looking real crazy and he was soaking wet, I asked him what happened but he wouldn't talk to me". I knew something was going to happen, I could feel it". They showed how the police went to his house and his mother who was fussing saying her son didn't own a gun. It was hard for me those weeks. I was able to view his body but I didn't go to the funeral knowing what his mother felt about me. I went in with my niece. But she let me go to him by myself. "Go on and say good bye Sabrina, you need to do this". I walked towards him. He looked really handsome and peaceful. The demons that possessed him were now gone.

"Sincere, I don't know what to say to you. I can't even believe that you are gone. I want you to know that I didn't' want you to die; I didn't want you to go like this. I just wanted to be left alone. I did care about you. I am so sorry if I ever hurt you. I didn't mean to. It was not my intention to bring you any pain." I reached over and kissed him on his cheek. I stood there for several minutes before I left. I didn't want anyone else to come in while I was there, I'm sure they would have recognized me from the news so I put my sunglasses on and went to the car. My niece was waiting for me. "Are you okay auntie"?

"Yes". He really looked good". I went home in silence. For weeks, I mourned for my friend. I sat at my desk the day of his funeral and cried for my friend. It was hard for me to believe that I no longer had to watch my back. He was gone. I had seen it for myself.

That forgiveness thing that God was talking about came to me immediately. I forgave him immediately because it was what I needed to do to heal inside. Although I was still not sure who else God wanted me to forgive, I wanted to forgive Sincere, I wanted God to forgive Sincere. I found a few pictures of him that I didn't know I had. When I looked at him, I could remember all the laughs and tears that we shared because of his pain. I did not realize how much pain Sincere was until I received some mail a few weeks later.

I was getting out of my car. My neighbors were still talking about the incident, how WBAL was at my home but I didn't say anything, I guess that was something to talk about, after all it didn't' happen to them so they did not know the pain I was in. I grabbed the mail and sifted through it. I saw the envelope. It was addressed to me but it did not have a return address. It was thick. I waved to a few of my neighbors and went in the house. I went up to my bedroom, I was curious to find out what this envelope contained. I kicked off my shoes and lay across the bed. I pulled the line paper first. It read:

To Whom It May Concern:
I cannot tell you who I am or where I am, but I must send you this to let you know that you were not responsible for Sincere' death. You didn't know Sincere like I did; I don't think anyone knew him like I did. Nonetheless, enclosed you will find some documents and paperwork that will put you at ease and know that God forgive me, death may have been his only way out of his pain. He was a very sick man with a lot of unresolved pain. He had

a love, hate relationship for women. I am however glad to know that you made it out alive. Sincere, truly loved you and he was being controlled by sources that you may never understand unless you believe that there is a hell and demons do exist. I'm sorry that he hurt you.

I pulled the rest of the paperwork out. There were letters from Medical Services from courts, psychiatrists and therapists. He had been deemed mentally incompetent and anti-social and hosts of other labels. However, the one thing that stood out for me was the fact that he had been involved in murder, rape, satanic worshipping and deep hatred for women. The paperwork went on for hours and I had a headache when I finished.

It allowed me understand him a lot more, but it also made me realize that God was with me that night in my bedroom. He and Jesus alone saved me from my death. It was only then did I realize that God wanted me for something greater and more important than what I was doing with my life. I lay down on my bed and I looked up at the ceiling and my life starting playing out like a movie. I saw myself at seven years old, watching my father's body lying in a pool of blood, that's were it all began, I could see myself crouched up in the corner with demons all around me, but in the midst of it all was Jesus and his angles protecting me and drawing closer to me. My little mind could not comprehend the pain that was being shown to me. A small light flashed and I saw myself standing in the choir loft with my robe on singing Jesus Loves Me, I sang that song from my "belly" like my teacher showed me, and the church was being slain in the spirit. I loved the Lord then; I truly loved him and knew that He loved me too. I saw myself crouched in fetal position in my niece's bed, while my brother in law violated me I could now see the demons that were in the room with us. The tears I felt coming from my eyes were real they were not in the movie but real. I cried but I couldn't' stop looking at the ceiling, I couldn't' stop seeing my life, over and over again, I saw the many men I slept with, in my desperate attempt to find love, Flashes of many faces came to view, Mike, Dennis, Jackson, Reggie, Eugene, even the pimp that I met on North Avenue face flashed through, probably a reminder for me that God was always there even in my foolishness, Then there was Trenton, many, many his different phases showed up, cunning, sly,, vicious, deadly, Then there was Roy, sweet Roy, Chris,

Barry, they were all there looking down at me. So many men, so many spirits I allowed in my soul, I felt ashamed, guilty and dirty, I cried and cried but my eyes would not allow me to wipe the faces away. I started crying out to God: why God, why are you showing me all of this? How long do I have to suffer for all my bad choices, I am sorry God, please forgive me! I do not want to feel this way anymore. I crawled out the bed and fell on my knees. God please, if you hear me, please show me what to do, show him how to stop the pain I feel deep down, oh, it hurts so bad God, it hurts!" I heard music, faint, distant but music, I could hear my father's favorite song playing "Try a Little Tenderness", I heard Jesus Loves Me, I heard It's Over Now, then I heard soft music peaceful, soothing music. I looked around my room but no one was there, I started to wonder if the voices were coming back. "Jesus, help me, show me, please, I don't know what to do!" *Forgive Sabrina, Forgive!* I have Father, I have, I've forgiven Manny, Trenton, Barry, I've forgiven all of them, It wasn't my fault about my daddy, it wasn't my fault about Manny! I have forgiven, please stop it, please stop this pain! *You must forgive Sabrina, you must!* My tears were so free flowing that I could not wipe them away if I wanted to. Then it came to me, I finally understood what my heavenly Father was trying to tell me all those many years. **FORGIVE MYSELF!!!!!** I fell out on the floor and stared at the ceiling, all faces were looking down at me, and I stared at them all! I forgive you Sabrina, I forgive you! I am letting it go now, I am loosing it all, I am taking my hands off it! I am moving forward, no more guilt, no more shame, no more self-destructive thinking, it's over, I forgive you Sabrina, you are a good person, you are a beautiful person, there is more to you than what's under your skirt, I forgive you Sabrina, you have wisdom, strength, and the power to be whatever you want to be, if you just Trust God and allow Him to carry you through it all! I forgive you Sabrina for your promiscuous behavior, your drug and alcohol consumption that allowed you to sin, the fights, the pain you may have caused others, I forgive you Sabrina. As I prayed for myself and to myself, the faces gradually disappeared all but one…my own. I was finally able to look at myself and not be ashamed of what I saw. Sabrina was smiling back at me confirming what God knew all the time.….when you forgive yourself, you can move forward in your life.

2 Corinthians 2: 9 and he said unto me..My grace is sufficient for thee; for my

strength is made perfect in weakness.......

I will bet you all are wondering what happened to some of the characters in the book Well let me see if I can help you out:

Angie- Married and living in LA with her husband. She has no children but works actively as a drug and alcohol counselor. I received a letter a few weeks ago that she still loved her "fine, black, beautiful man" and he loved her back.

Manny- Died of a massive heart attack at the age of 50. I don't know if anyone ever went to the authorities on him. I heard that he died alone.

Neicy and Sharon- Both ladies are married with children. Neicy has one son and Sharon has twin girls. Ironically, Neicy married Mark, yes the same Mark she had the one night stand with. Sharon married a guy she met on her job.

Meika- Killed in a car accident in D.C. coming from a club. She was 24 years old.

Trenton- After getting clean and sober for 6 years, Trenton was caught up in the drug game and is now serving a 25 to life term in prison for drug trafficking

Evie- Serving time for cutting a woman across the face. She is scheduled to be released in 2009. She has two children who are now living with her mother.

Jackson- Convicted of killing his son, serving time on death row at Super Max

Reggie- Reggie died at the age of 41 of a pancreatic cancer. He left to mourn a wife and three children.

Wendy- Ms. Big mouth used her mouth to seal a successful position in the United States Senate office. She is married with two sons.

Gina- Gina married a baller and is now living in Hot-Lanta she writes and tells me "yo Bree, this fool tryin' turn this hooka into a housewifey, Neva! But the jewels and money is lovely!"

Blue- Baltimore City Detective in the Narcotics Unit, single and still fine!

Barry- is single and living with a woman *again!*

Chris- Married but separated from his wife, living a quiet life alone

Eugene- Eugene is doing well, he has moved to the Eastern Shore

Finally Sabrina: I am continuing to seek God will for my life and to find true love with a man who is deserving of it.

I never did tell you all who was my baby's daddy...well, I will let you ponder that question Was it Reggie or Trenton? You decide....

Peace and blessings.

Many thanks to: **My Lord and Savior Jesus Christ**. Father I will always be grateful for your unconditionally love and mercy you bestowed and are still bestowing upon my life. Without you I am nought, with you I can do all things. **My mother and my sisters, Claudia, Celestine, Vernice, Carolyn, Adrienne and my brother Claude** I love you all no matter what, I love you all. **Mommy** thanks for the slaps upside the head and the rule of getting an education, thank you for loving me and respecting me even when I was being a knucklehead, thank you for teaching me the 23rd Psalm! **Claudia,** you always encouraged me to write and be whatever I needed to be, thanks for giving me my first book to read. I wanna be like you when I grow up! **Tina** thanks for all the good meals that you cooked, **Vernice** hold on to God's hand, only then will you find the happiness you seek **Carolyn** keep preaching and word girl!!! **Adrienne** I remember the Harbor and Sakura's thanks for the laughs Claude you are my brother and I love you nuff said. All of my nieces and nephews, God there are so many of you, lets see if I can remember all of you **David** I will always remember your words of wisdom, the pain of staying, is worse than the pain of leaving, luv ya!, **Jeffrey, Steven, Gregory, Michael, Keely, Toni, Tammy, Lynair, Russell, Kevin, Christopher, Duane (RIP) Claude Jr., Aisha, Gregory, Lil Greg** and my brothers and sister in laws **Gregory I, Stanley, Larry, Erline, Gregory II,** I love you all more than you will ever know, keep doing your thing and don't let the things of this world deter you. To all my great nieces and nephews, Auntie loves you, stay focused. My children **Percy,** continue to be sucka free and below the radar in the concrete jungle baby, God has a blessing with your name on it **Natasha,** Mommy is forever praying for you, I love you more than life itself **Keisha** (kee-mee) my baby girl, stay strong and hold on, you're gonna make it, your latter will be greater than your past! and their loved ones **Jerome and Ty,** brothers' life is too short to live it twice in negativity, show some love! **Alicia** you are like a daughter to me, and I love you. My grandchildren **Raheem, Daiquan, Aliyah, India, Asia** the blessings that I feel each time I look at each one of you makes my heart swell with pride. Grand ma loves you dearly. Reach for your dreams and aim for the moon, if you miss, you will still be amongst the stars! Special thanks to **Pastor Doris Gaskins and Gee Gaskins** who showed me so much love in my time of need, Pastor, you will never know the pearls of wisdom you gave me and how much they mean to me today. I will always love and respect you as not only a woman of God but also a woman! There is no doubt that God strategically placed us in similar paths so that I could receive the wisdom I needed to become the woman I am today. **Gee**, thanks for your encouragement and your love. My other "children" who carry a special place in my heart. **Brandon, Derrick Jr., Quiana, Kathy, Trae, Carey, Ebonee** I watched you grow into fine young men and women and I pray that we will always have love and respect for each other. **Robin** thanks for showing the love girl, thanks for the late night support, thanks for always keeping it real with me, you know that God has His hand on you, keep holding on to it, trust and know that He will bring you out I love you! **Joyce,** I cannot even put into words all the love you have shown me, t thank you so much, I love you dearly. **Tyrone, TJ, Zaiah,** I love you all with an agape love, **Momma, Betty,** thanks for all the prayers at those Sunday evening prayer meetings, I love you both! **Pandora and Boone,** peace and blessing to you both **Warren and Anna Watties** what do I say to two people who treated me like family and loved and prayed for me from the day they met me. I love you all so much and I miss you more than you will ever know, call a sista! **The Greater Harvest Baptist Church** family and my pastor **Errol Gilliard Sr.** Pastor, I am so grateful that you were called to preach, I have grown so much under your guidance. **Aunt Chris** thank you for praying for me and with me on all those painful days and nights. I love you. **Sharon** I am gonna need you to take those high heels off and walk a sista to the cafeteria ha ha. **Kristin,** stay cool baby girl! **Gloria,** can you teach a sista some Spanish, lol, **Marquita** baby girl, turn the cell phone off! Thanks for the proof reading. **India, Charlene, LeeTice , Monica, Lil,** what can I say? I love you women each one of you carries a special place in my heart. I am sending a special thank you to my sweetheart **Derrick,** I love you and I appreciate you, and I thank you for allowing God to lead and guide and order your steps, I want to thank you for showing me that I deserve the very best, last but not least **Jamie Markus, Charles Henderson and Authorhouse.**

There are not enough words to thank someone for allowing your dream to come true.

If I have missed anyone, charge it to my head and not my heart.

Special thanks to these groups and staff:

The Alpha Program, Ronald Wright, and staff

Celebrate Recovery

House of Ruth

Thank you all for your loving support........Vikee

About the Author

Valerie is a native of Baltimore, Maryland, who currently resides in White Marsh, Maryland. She has been writing poetry since she was eight years old. Her love for writing came when her oldest sister gave her a book written by Dr. Maya Angelou. After reading the book, she starting penning her own writings, short stories, and poems.

It wasn't until several years later that she started writing poetry for her friends and family. Whatever occassion, holiday or birthday came, Valerie wrote a personal poem centered around the person's character. In 2002 she met Author, Johnathan Luckett, at the mall in White Marsh and they started talking about the craft of writing. It was then she decided to finish a novel she started a few years before. She is mother of three grown children and the grandmother of five grandchildren.

Printed in the United States
204200BV00001B/445-486/P